CREEPING IVY

CREEPING IVY

NATASHA COOPER

St. Martin's Press  New York

acc 08/99

CREEPING IVY. Copyright © 1998 by Daphne Wright. All rights reserved.
Printed in the United States of America. No part of this book may be
used or reproduced in any manner whatsoever without written permission except in the case of brief quotations embodied in critical articles or reviews. For information, address St. Martin's Press, 175 Fifth
Avenue, New York, N.Y. 10010.

Library of Congress Cataloging-in-Publication Data

Cooper, Natasha.
     Creeping Ivy / Natasha Cooper. – 1st U. S. ed.
        p. cm.
     ISBN 0-312-20520-1
     I. Title.
PR6073.R47C74   1999
823'.914—dc21

                                                            99-15493
                                                            CIP

First published in Great Britain by Simon & Schuster Ltd.

First U.S. Edition: August 1999

10 9 8 7 6 5 4 3 2 1

FOR DOUGLAS McWILLIAMS

AUTHOR'S NOTE

All the characters, organisations, police stations, companies and partnerships mentioned in this novel are figments of the author's imagination and bear no resemblance to any in the real world. Only 'Daisy' is drawn from life.

The usual suspects have provided their customary help, support and advice. I should like to thank them all, in particular: Mary Carter, Gillian Holmes, Clare Ledingham, and James Turner.

As Creeping Ivy clings to wood or stone
And hides the ruin that it feeds upon.

—WILLIAM COWPER

PROLOGUE

She was sitting in front of a plate of slimy green stuff. She knew she was never going to get it down her throat. And she knew she would have to.

Her arms were sore under the blue and white dress. It was a pretty dress and she looked pretty in it. People said so. Some of them said she was good, too. But that didn't stop it.

Somehow she was going to have to get the slimy stuff down – and without spilling any on the dress – and she knew she wouldn't be able to do it. She knew. Tears started making her eyes all wet, and she tried to stop them because crying always made it worse.

The door opened. With the tears showing, she didn't dare look up. She just stared at her plate and waited.

'Pick up your spoon,' came the voice.

Her hands were shaking, but she did as she was told. She always did try to do what she was told, always. It was just sometimes she couldn't, however much she tried.

'Put in some spinach.'

She scooped some up and got it near her mouth. The

1

smell made her feel sick and she knew her throat would get shut like it always did. Even if she tried she wouldn't be able to swallow and it would be worse for her if she spat it out; it always was.

'Put it in your mouth.'

The voice was the most frightening thing that had ever happened to her, much worse than the sore arms. She still didn't look up. And she couldn't make herself put the spoon in her mouth.

'Put it in. You know what'll happen if you don't. Open your mouth. Open your mouth at once!'

At the sound of the voice getting louder and louder so it was nearly a shout, she got her mouth a little bit open and put the thin shiny spoon in. But her teeth bit shut on it. There'd be even more marks on the spoon after. She couldn't help it. She couldn't eat the slimy stuff. The voice was right: she did know what was going to happen, but she couldn't eat it. She waited in dumb terror.

CHAPTER ONE

The coffee was too hot. As soon as it hit her mouth, Trish knew what she was in for: little tassels of skin and a tongue like sacking, which wouldn't be able to taste anything more subtle than the local takeaway's prawn curry for at least two days.

'Bugger.'

She had been so keen to clear the night's thoughts out of her head that she had poured boiling water over the granules and taken a great slurp, without even bothering to stir the bitty liquid. But she had burned herself for nothing: memories of the cases she had been working on were still there, as vivid and unbearable as ever.

As she bent to drink some cold water from the tap, she half-saw a familiar face on the small television in the corner of the kitchen worktop. Straightening up, with the cool water held in her mouth to soothe the burn, she wiped stray drops from her chin with the back of her hand and looked more carefully at the screen.

Her cousin Antonia Weblock did occasionally figure on the news, but it was odd to see her on a Sunday morning when there couldn't possibly have been an announcement from the City or the Bank of England that might have needed one of her magisterial comments. And she seemed to be wearing a tracksuit under her long overcoat, which was even odder.

Trish moved towards the television to turn up the sound. Her bare feet spread a little as the soles touched the tacky coolness of the industrial-strength emerald-coloured studded rubber that covered her kitchen floor. It was a sensation she had come to dislike as soon as she had had time to notice it, just as she had begun to feel aggressed by the hard-edged, brightly coloured, echoing flat that sucked such enormous amounts of money out of her bank account every month.

'Antonia, this way – over here,' Trish heard in several different voices as she adjusted the volume.

The sight of aeroplanes landing and taking off in the distance behind Antonia solved one small mystery. She must have been at Heathrow, after a trip to New York or Tokyo, perhaps dealing with a crisis generated by unexpected movements of the Dow Jones or the Nikkei. Trish smiled as dozens of cameras flashed on the screen because she knew how much Antonia enjoyed her grow-ing fame, but then her lips stiffened. Instead of turning her head this way and that to give all the photographers a fair chance of getting a good shot as she usually did, Antonia kept wincing as though the flashes that hit her eyes were hard enough to hurt. Or perhaps she just had a headache. Her face was tight enough for that. Trish licked her lips and felt the burn on her tongue again.

'When did you first hear about your daughter?' asked a male voice as a microphone like a long, dirty grey mop was shoved over the heads of the avid journalists towards Antonia.

'Charlotte?' said Trish.

'I got the message at seven yesterday evening.' Antonia's

4

voice came breathily out of the television. 'New York time. They couldn't reach me any earlier.'

'And is there really no news?' asked a woman with an absurdly old-fashioned notebook in her hands instead of the much smaller cassette recorders everyone else was waving.

'None,' said Antonia, looking up at last and staring directly into the particular camera that fed Trish's television, almost as though she knew her cousin would be there, watching. Antonia's strong-featured face was grey and there was a heavy, defensive expression in her eyes, but she was still in control. Just.

'Charlotte was last seen in the playground of our local park yesterday afternoon with her nanny,' she said bleakly. 'She disappeared at about three-thirty. The families of her friends have all been contacted and none of them have seen her. The police are still searching.'

'No,' whispered Trish into the echoing spaces of her flat. 'Oh, please, God! No.'

She knew too much – that was the trouble – and understood exactly what an announcement like that could mean. Pictures from her own cases and other people's ran through her mind like a private horror film.

There was the six-year-old boy who had been kidnapped almost directly outside his parents' house, then found sodomised and dead months later; there was a girl, too, a year or two older than Charlotte, who had been raped by her stepfather and then murdered and buried in a nearby wood a couple of days before he went on television with his wife to plead for her return; and another, only a baby, so badly beaten by both her parents, and burned with cigarettes, that even though the social workers had found her while she was still alive, she had not made it.

Trish's eyes focused on the real screen again. Anxiety

5

for Charlotte and pity for Antonia started choking her until she remembered to breathe. It felt strange, working her lungs like bellows, forcing herself to breathe in through her nose and out through her mouth as though it was a skill she had only just learned.

Charlotte was Antonia's only child – a small, confiding, funny four-year-old with a terrible temper, utterly defenceless and far too young to be adrift in London.

'Is it true they've dragged the pond and found nothing?' shouted one of the journalists jostling Antonia on the screen.

She nodded without speaking, once more looking out of the television straight at Trish, who stared back, still breathing doggedly, as though Charlotte's safety might depend on that steady, rhythmic sucking in and exhaling of air that tasted as horrible as the burn in her mouth.

The thought of any child in such danger was unbearable, but that it should be Charlotte made Trish aware of layers of anguish that went far beyond anything she had experienced. She had only recently come to know Charlotte as a person, rather than simply Antonia's noisy, difficult daughter, and for a selfish instant she wished she had kept her distance.

It had happened about six weeks earlier, when Charlotte had appeared in the middle of one of the excruciatingly formal dinners to which Antonia still occasionally summoned Trish. Charlotte said she'd been woken by bad dreams and had a tummy ache and couldn't go back to sleep. Her jumbled dark curls and scarlet pyjamas had seemed wildly out of place in the over-furnished dining room. The sight of her had made her mother's face tighten in irritation, but to Trish it had brought a welcome hint of normality.

Bored with the grandeur of the food and plumb out of things to say to either of the pompous men sitting beside her, she had volunteered to take the child back to bed. Antonia had looked surprised by the offer but had accepted it at once. Robert, her current boyfriend, seemed to have hardly noticed either Charlotte's appearance or Trish's intervention. He was far too interested in explaining to the bored banker's wife on his right just how mega-successful his latest advertising campaign had been.

On the way upstairs, Charlotte had insinuated her warm little hand into Trish's and told her a long story about the huge wiggly pink worms that kept coming out from under her bed and waking her up so that it wasn't her fault she'd gone downstairs. Trish had enjoyed the inventiveness of the excuse and later indulged Charlotte to the extent of making a thorough search under the bed, the mattress and the bright yellow-and-blue cotton rug, as well as through all her bigger toys, to prove that there were no worms, wiggly or otherwise, waiting to threaten her.

Charlotte had eventually pronounced herself satisfied but she begged for a story before Trish abandoned her to the dark. Touched and amused as well as glad of an excuse to avoid the diners downstairs, Trish had obliged, sitting on the bed and reading from *My Naughty Little Sister*, a book that had given her much gleeful enjoyment in her own past.

The child's head had felt extraordinarily hard and her little body very soft as she pressed herself along Trish's thigh and wriggled in pleasure at the climax of her chosen story. Her highly original comments on the characters and their antics had made Trish laugh and kiss her silky black curls, wondering why Charlotte had such a reputation for obstinacy and tantrums. She seemed sweet and vulnerable behind the mask of sassy cleverness; and rather lonely, too.

'Could it be a kidnap? Have there been any ransom demands?' asked another of the journalists, a man who did not appear on the screen. His voice was nastier than the first and loaded with resentment. Trish remembered the announcement of Antonia's latest bonus a month or so earlier.

Antonia herself shrugged and at the same time shook her head, momentarily covering her eyes with her left hand. As she leaned closer to the man whose arm she was holding, the camera moved sideways, too. Trish, trying to think through all the implications of what had happened, was relieved to see that Robert was there.

A slight man with expressive dark eyes and flamboyantly ruffled black hair, he held up his free hand in a gesture of surprising authority. The buzz of questions quietened at once and soon died completely.

'There isn't anything more to say,' he announced in the light voice that had lost its malicious edge but still seemed quite inadequate to the scene.

The mass of journalists started muttering discontentedly to each other and occasionally shouting questions at Antonia, who flinched and whispered something to Robert. He raised his hand again, and his voice, to say with more authority than before: 'We're desperately anxious about Charlotte. As you can imagine, neither of us has had much sleep. We'd like to get home now.'

He urged Antonia forwards, directly into the crowd. After a moment's resistance it parted, allowing them to walk through unimpeded. Dozens of cameras flashed again. All it needed, thought Trish unhappily, was confetti. As the two of them left the terminal buildings, the television screen changed to show a line of police and civilians moving slowly but with dogged purpose across the manicured lawns, little copses and flat asphalt paths of a public park, obviously searching for clues.

'That was Antonia Weblock, mother of four-year-old Charlotte, who disappeared yesterday afternoon from the park near their Kensington home, where she had gone with her nanny,' said the newsreader dispassionately. 'The police say there are fears for the child's safety.'

Trish put both hands flat on top of the television and bent down until her forehead touched her knuckles. The hardness of her own bones began to help as she worked to dim the pictures her imagination was projecting in her mind. She reached for the telephone and tapped in Antonia's number.

Four rings later she heard the familiar message, dictated in Antonia's queenliest voice. It made not the slightest concession to anyone who might expect to be thanked for wanting to get in touch with her, and in the circumstances it seemed chillingly inappropriate.

'This machine can take messages for Antonia Weblock and Robert Hithe – oh, and for Nicky Bagshot. Keep your message as short as possible. Speak clearly after the long tone.'

'This is Trish, Antonia, on Sunday morning at . . . at eight-thirty. I've just seen the news and heard about Charlotte. I am so, so sorry. Look, I'm here all day so if there's any help you need – anything – I want you to ring. Just ring. *Please.*'

The newsreader had switched to the latest crisis in Africa, where there were millions of children at risk of death by starvation, disease, war, crime and genocide. Trish knew none of them and had no skills or knowledge that were relevant to their lives – or deaths. However terrible their fate might be, she could not help them. But she might be able to help Antonia; and she would do anything in her power. Anything.

They had not known each other as children, even

9

though their grandmothers had been sisters, because the family was neither geographically nor emotionally close. But when Trish's mother had run into Antonia's at a family funeral and heard that she, too, was going to the Inns of Court School of Law after university, she had arranged for them to meet.

Their characters and preoccupations were so different that they would probably not have made friends even then if they had not quickly discovered just how exclusive legal London was and how lonely outsiders could be. Most of their fellow students seemed to have had High Court judges for godparents and come to consciousness with their cots propped up on out-of-date editions of *Archbold*. Neither Trish nor Antonia had any legal connections, and they needed all the support they could give each other. The resulting alliance had eventually turned into a friendship that had flourished and survived even Trish's consistently better results.

Throughout all the adrenaline-driven years since then – and the inevitable spats – Trish had never forgotten the generosity of Antonia's reaction to her success. However regal Antonia had become as she earned more and more in the merchant bank to which she had retreated after she failed to get any offers of pupillage, Trish had always tried to be as generous in return. In fact, that had not been nearly as difficult as accepting some of the things Antonia had done to Ben, the quiet teacher she had so surprisingly married, or the way she had behaved since her divorce.

Trish reached behind her for her mug and drank, only to discover that the coffee was still disgusting. There seemed no point making any more. She tipped it down the sink, switched off the television and went up the black spiral stairs to the shower, pulling off the oversized T-shirt she wore in bed as she went. The shirt was one of several with slogans that had made her laugh when she first bought them but which by then she noticed only when someone else blinked in surprise.

Recently the only other person to see any of them had been her mother, an intelligently gentle woman who found the aggression of some of the slogans as worrying as Trish's inability to keep her fridge stocked with food within its sell-by dates or to put any kind of limit on the hours she worked or the emotion she expended on her clients.

Reaching her bedroom, Trish turned on the radio and thought about how differently her life had turned out from Antonia's.

As one of only two women tenants in her set of chambers, Trish had quickly found herself working in one capacity or other on most of the cases that involved children. They took up all her time and she had seen no way of getting any experience on the big fraud cases that were the reason she had chosen those particular chambers out of the three sets that had offered her pupillage. At first she had tried to protest to her clerk, saying that she did not want to be typecast as taking only 'girlie' briefs. He had stared at her, unregenerate misogynist and scourge of naive young barristers that he was, and started to tell her some of the facts of legal life.

When lowly devilling on matters of custody and access eventually gave way to advocacy in cases of neglect, cruelty and abuse, Trish had ceased to see her work as any kind of soft option and became passionately devoted to the cause of the damaged children whose miseries provided her living.

Memories of their sufferings latched on to everything she feared for Charlotte. She tried not to imagine the worst that could have happened as she dropped her

T-shirt on the bathroom floor and turned the shower to its most powerful setting. As she rounded her spine to the water, she felt the stinging jets hit her body and did her best to concentrate on the pleasure she usually felt as the water needled her skin, collected in the hollows of her spine and then cascaded down her sides, clinging to her breasts and dripping off her hardened nipples.

After a while she gave up trying to feel any of it and reached for the shampoo. She rubbed a generous puddle into her short dark hair. Foam seeped into her eyes, burning, and she turned her face up to the water. It streamed over her head and face. With her eyes stinging and her throat closing against the soapy water, she could not keep out the thoughts of all the children she had encountered who had been suffocated and starved, raped, beaten, or simply bullied and denied affection all their short lives. She wondered whether she would ever find a way of caring less.

Clean again, but unrefreshed, Trish emerged from the shower and wrapped herself in the biggest of the scarlet towels that hung over the hot rail. The whole bathroom was fogged with condensation, the mirrors already dripping so that she could not see her face in any detail. That did not matter; the blurred outlines were quite enough for her.

Her face, which had variously been described as beaky, predatory and magnificent at different stages of her last love affair, was all right, she had decided long ago, but it would never be beautiful. When she had rubbed the worst of the wet out of her hair, she ran her fingers through it to mould it roughly over her well-shaped head and left it at that.

Enough of the condensation had cleared by then to give her a glimpse of her dark eyes in the mirror, and she saw that they were full of all the fears she was doing her best to ignore.

'Oh, Charlotte.'

Grabbing the tail of her self-control as it whisked past her, Trish wondered aloud whether there was any point trying to go on working. She would never be able to concentrate, so she might as well do something else. The trouble was that she couldn't think of anything except Charlotte.

Having, as her mother had always said, worked far too hard for eleven years, Trish had begun to realise that she had become too involved with her clients, but she had not known how to free herself. Their anguish was so real to her, and her inability to change much for them so obvious, that she had been in danger of getting completely bogged down.

A series of minor but recurrent illnesses had kept getting in the way of her work and she had eventually gone to the doctor. Recalling their encounter, Trish was amazed at how patient and good-humoured he had been. At the time, all she had felt was outrage when he told her she was suffering from stress and advised her to find a way of managing it better.

Later, little by little, she had begun to see her resistance to his advice for what it was and had tried to do as he had suggested. She had learned how to snap less at people who did not understand her instantly, or asked stupid questions about the instructions she had given them, to eat more sensibly and drink in moderation, to take life a scrap more lightly and even – occasionally – to sleep the night through without pills.

It had been difficult because there was always another case, another ten- or eleven-year-old who, never properly fed since birth, had taken to stealing money as well as food and become uncontrollable by anyone; or perhaps a child who had been sunny and eager to learn until the age of six or seven, when she had suddenly changed – and only later told her teacher about what her uncle, or her stepfather, or her elder brother was making her do. With clients like those needing her to win them the protection of the law or defend them against cruelty or vengeance, Trish had not been able to take life much more easily.

Dry at last, she let the towel fall off her body on to the floor by her bed and rummaged in the cupboard for clean underclothes to wear under the crumpled jeans she had pulled off the previous night, and a daytime sloganless T-shirt. She shoved her feet into a pair of suede moccasins that had long ago lost whatever shape they had once had, and had turned from bright red to a kind of mud colour. They were supremely comfortable and she did not mind the slapping noise they made on the hard rubber and wood floors of her flat. And luckily there was no one else to object any longer.

Her salvation had appeared in chambers in the form of an invitation from the managing director of a small, progressive publishing house, who wanted her to write about children and the law. At first the letter had seemed to be just one more problem she had to deal with; but after it had lain in her in-tray for a couple of weeks she had begun to see that it might offer an honourable way out. If she accepted the commission, she could at least retreat for a time.

One of her most tormenting cases had caught the attention of the tabloids. As Trish battled in court to make the state provide appropriate care for a seriously disturbed eight-year-old who had been discovered trying to kill her six-year-old sister, she found herself more famous than most other barristers in their early thirties. She assumed that was what had interested the publisher in the first place. As far as she could see, there was no other reason for his approach and she was sure they had never met.

Eventually, when there had been a tiny gap in her diary, she had rung him up, agreed to meet for lunch in the Oxo Tower, and discovered that he shared her passion for justice for children and detestation of the way some of them were demonised in the popular press. Before they had finished their first course, Trish had agreed to write his book and gulped at the size of the advance he offered, which made even legal-aid rates seem princely.

She could afford to accept the commission, having earned well for the previous four years and spent comparatively little. For ages her only regular expenses had been her big mortgage, the bills, and the annual subscription to the gym she had begun to use as part of her stress-management campaign. She ate out with friends, drank in El Vino's after court, and occasionally gave parties at the flat, but there was rarely time for anything else. She could not remember when she had last been to the theatre; films often seemed alluring until the moment came, when there was almost always more work to be done; and concerts were something she did not even contemplate.

Back in the kitchen, she had just switched on the kettle for a fresh mug of instant coffee, which she hoped might taste better than the first, when she saw that her answering machine was winking. She pressed its buttons, assuming that Antonia must have rung back while she was in the shower, but it was a quite different voice she heard, lighter, younger and infinitely kinder.

'Hi, Trish? It's Emma. I was just wondering if you felt like meeting up for some food, or a drink or something – a walk, maybe. It's been days since we spoke, and it would be good to see you and hear how the work's going. I've got a great new case to tell you about – quite funny, too, for a change. Ring if you feel like it. But don't bother if you're busy. Lots of love. Bye.'

Trish smiled as she thought of Emma Gnatche, a specialist in lie detection and the psychology of false confessions, who was one of her closest friends. If it had not been for what had happened to Charlotte, Trish would have rung her straight back and arranged to meet at once. As it was, she thought she would have to wait in case Antonia had phoned.

With the television on again so that she could catch any news there might be, Trish sat down and tried to read the papers. She did not have long to wait.

'Antonia?' she said urgently into the receiver as soon as she had picked it up.

'Trish, thank God you're there. And thank you for your message. I should have known you'd ring. It's . . . it's . . . I can't . . . oh, you know.'

'I can imagine.' Trish turned down the sound on the television. 'Antonia, has there been any news?'

'No. Nothing. It's hell.'

'I can't tell you how sorry I am. Look, I don't want to get in your way or anything, but would it help if I came round?'

'Would you?' Antonia sounded so surprised that Trish wondered whether her increasing reluctance to accept invitations to her cousin's stultifying dinner parties had been misinterpreted as rejection. 'It's terrible here. The press are outside and they keep banging on the door all the time, wanting me to tell them how I feel. How the hell do they *think* I feel? I'm desperate and I could slaughter bloody Nicky. She's a fully trained nanny: how could she let something like this happen?'

'God knows. Look, I'll come straight round, but as

16

soon as it feels as if I'm in the way, you must tell me. OK? Promise?'

'All right. The police may be here when you arrive. They've rung to say they want to talk to me, God knows why. Apparently they haven't got any clues yet. Oh Trish, what am I going to do?'

'Is Robert with you?'

'No. He's got some crisis on at the office. He couldn't stay.'

For a moment Trish was speechless. No one's work crisis could possibly be more important than this.

'Hang on, Antonia,' she said tersely. 'I'll be round as soon as I can.'

Bloody Robert, Trish thought as she put down the receiver; that's absolutely bloody typical. As soon as there's any trouble, he's off. How could he? He may not care about Charlotte, but even *he* must have some idea of how Antonia's feeling. And he owes her. My God, how he owes her.

She grabbed her car keys and some money out of the jar that stood between the tea-bags and the dried milk powder, and was halfway to the door before she remembered the state in which Antonia lived. Dithering uncharacteristically by the front door for a moment, Trish told herself that her present sloppy get-up was irrelevant in the circumstances; Antonia probably wouldn't even notice.

Even so, she ran back up the spiral stairs to the gallery where her bed and clothes were, wrenched off her T-shirt and changed into an almost-pressed shirt, socks and boots, and a linen jacket.

CHAPTER TWO

'Come off it, Nicky. Charlotte didn't just disappear, and she didn't wander off into the pond like you said she must of, or meet up with one of her schoolfriends or anything.' There was real anger mixed in with the impatience in the older policeman's voice. 'We've checked everyone on your list, and it was a right waste of time.'

'I told you it would be.'

'Yeah, but you didn't say why. And you should've, you know. You should've told us everything you knew straight away. Still, better late than never. You'd best tell us the whole lot now, however bad it is.'

Nicky Bagshot felt her eyes go blank. She stared down at the grey plastic top of the table that kept him away from her and struggled to get herself sorted.

It was her fault Lottie'd disappeared. She knew that. There was no getting away from it, and she wasn't trying to. She shouldn't have turned her back; not for a minute. But it wasn't fair of them to accuse her of doing something to hurt Lottie. She could never do that, not in a million years. They must see that.

It was the sort of thing the police always did. When they didn't have anything on you, they forced you into saying something they could twist into evidence against you. But they shouldn't be doing it like this, not while Lottie was still lost. They should be spending their time out there, looking for her.

'P'raps she was nicked by aliens, Sarge,' said the younger of the two.

His sarcasm didn't bother Nicky. In a way, knowing he was stupid enough to make sneery jokes about something this important made her feel less bad.

'That it, Nicky? Come down in a UFO, did they, and kidnapped her?'

'I've told you all along,' she said, pushing back her fringe, which felt sticky with sweat from her forehead. 'Charlotte was quite safe in the queue for the big slide. When I heard another child fall behind me and start screaming, I looked round to see what had happened. Anyone would've done the same.'

'And then what?'

'Like I said before, it was a small boy who'd jumped off the swings and tripped. His knees were bleeding and no one was helping him. I did what I could for him – someone had to. When I'd finished seeing to him, I turned back to check on Charlotte and she'd gone. She hadn't made any noise at all, and everyone I asked said they hadn't seen anything – no little girl in trouble or upset, nor anyone struggling or protesting.'

'Sounds as though Dave's alien theory must be right after all,' said the older man with a stupid lying smile. 'You must've heard something, Nicky. Children don't just disappear in a puff of smoke, now do they? Come on, love, you must see it's not a very good story. It'll be easier for all of us if you tell us what really happened.'

'I have told you,' said Nicky. 'I've told you over

and over. It's not my fault if you don't believe me. There was no noise and no trouble and no one saw anything. There's no way I could've known anything was happening to her.'

'Yeah. You've told us. Trouble is, Nicky-love, it doesn't hang together, does it? You must see that. Clever girl like you.'

She put both hands over her eyes. As she pressed her fingers into the closed lids, she could see brightly coloured figures from the park. There was Charlotte in her blue skirt and red tights and shirt. The tights were too hot for the weather, but she'd been cross and wanted to wear them. It seemed silly to force her into something else just because it was more suitable, and anyway Nicky liked her to have what she wanted when she could. It made up a bit for all the other things she wasn't allowed to have.

Then there was the boy. She could see him, too, fizzing on the inside of her lit-up red eyelids. He looked about a year younger than Charlotte and he was wearing little thin brown shorts that left his bony knees bare. He would've been all right if he'd simply tripped over when he was running like most of them did. But he hadn't. For some reason he'd let go one of the chains of the swing at the furthest point of its arc. The swing seat banging into his back had probably bruised it and scared him, too, but what had got her going was his screams and the blood on his knees. She couldn't have left him like that, not for anything. Not screaming like that.

Antonia always made her take a bum bag with a first-aid kit whenever she went anywhere with Lottie, and so she had lots of antiseptic wipes and plaster in all different sizes. By the time she'd cleaned the scrapes and picked out the grit and little bits of bark, his short, shrill

21

screams had turned into pride-saving whimpers. She'd asked him to choose the plasters he liked and he'd got quite interested in the pictures of bears that were printed on the wrong side. She'd let him play with one while she fixed the other two firmly to his knees.

It was comforting, that feeling of strength and stickiness around the wounds. She could remember it easily. With the blood staunched and the scrape hidden, it was all much less frightening; and a big bit of plaster gave you a nice feeling of importance, too, when you were his age.

He'd got calm enough to smile at her by the time she'd told him she was done and set him on his feet. Before he'd said anything, a woman had come running up and pulled him out of Nicky's arms. He'd started crying again then, of course, and the woman had turned on Nicky and told her off in the most snotty voice – even worse than Antonia's.

She'd been a typical weekend mother, not knowing anything about what her child could manage or what he needed. She'd let him swing on his own when he was far too little for it. And she was so ignorant about who he really was that she didn't even recognise his screams when she heard them. Too busy gossiping with the other mothers, that was her problem, and probably saying how boring it was when your nanny had a day off. And how inefficient she was and ate too much, and used too much toilet cleaner. They all did that. Then she'd had the cheek to bawl Nicky out for helping! It wasn't fair. She should have felt grateful – and guilty. *Guilty.*

Nicky quickly took her hands away from her eyes.

'Why aren't you out in the park, asking people what they saw?' she said. 'It's Sunday so they'll be the same ones there today. And even if none of them noticed what happened to Charlotte, lots of them must've seen that mother slagging me off for helping her boy. She yelled at me like I was some kind of animal, and all I'd done was what she should've been doing. Ask them. They'll remember her. Then you might believe me. And one of them might've seen something that could help you find Charlotte. That's what you should be doing. She's lost and you're not even trying to find her.'

Her eyes felt hot and she clenched her hands together on the table to keep the tears well inside.

'We've got people out there,' said the sergeant, sounding a bit more reasonable and kinder, too. 'We just thought you might've remembered something yourself that would help us ask them the right questions.'

Nicky still didn't trust him in spite of his reasonableness. She'd read John le Carré's books and she knew why interrogators changed their tactics like that: it was to trick you into telling them things they thought you were hiding.

She hadn't ever thought she'd like books like his, but the principal of her training college had lent her a copy of *Tinker, Tailor, Soldier, Spy* once after they'd been talking about novels, and she'd liked it straight off for the secrecy and the awful quiet pain of it all. After that, she'd read his others, too, as soon as she could get hold of them, but she hadn't liked all of them; only the ones with Smiley in them. She really did like him and if she could keep thinking of him, she'd be all right, even if these two men went on shouting at her.

If she'd ever had a father, he might have been like Smiley: quiet and kind and not very happy, and so decent that it hurt. She'd go on thinking about him and not about the policemen shouting at her, pretending they thought she'd done something to hurt Lottie. She hadn't done anything wrong except turn her back for a minute or two. She shouldn't have done it, but that's all it was. Turning her back. Nothing worse, whatever they said.

'Well, love?'

'Well, what? There isn't any more to tell,' said Nicky, digging her short nails into the palm of the other hand and wishing it wasn't so sweaty. 'I've told you over and over. When I saw she wasn't there in the playground, I asked everyone there if they'd seen her, but because it was a Saturday of course they hadn't.'

'Saturday? Why does that make a difference?' asked the older of the two officers, looking really surprised. Nicky sighed; she couldn't believe he didn't know.

'In the week it's nearly all nannies there at that time in the afternoon, and we mostly know each other and each other's kids. We look out for them. If it had been a weekday, someone would have seen what Charlotte was doing and stopped her, or warned me. But the parents hardly know their own kids, let alone other people's. They're out working all day in the week; they leave before breakfast and don't get back till their kids are asleep. The nannies live with them and . . . and know them.'

Nicky paused to wipe her eyes with a grimy, hardened lump of toilet paper she'd found in her pocket. Antonia had ordered her to call it loo paper when she was talking to Lottie and she usually remembered, but she always called it toilet paper to herself and it felt like giving Antonia two fingers, which was great.

'Then at weekends the nannies go off and these mothers take over. They take their children to the park, dump them in the playground, and sit talking to each other and not paying attention. That's why none of them saw anything and why they were all so awful when I said she was lost. And it wasn't my fault. It wasn't!'

'OK, OK. Calm down. So, you saw that Charlotte

had gone. Fetch Nicky a cup of tea, will you, Constable?'

The younger one looked as though he hated being given orders like that and slouched out of the interview room to show how far above fetching and carrying he was.

'There, he's gone, Nicky-love. It's just you and me. We can sort it all now. What did you do next?'

'When I'd got nowhere with the parents?'

'Yeah.'

'I asked all the children I knew, but none of them could tell me anything useful. They'd seen Charlotte all right when we arrived, but none of them noticed what happened to her. And so then I just ran through the whole park, calling for her and stopping everyone I met to ask if they'd seen her. I went on and on till the gates were shutting and then I came here. There wasn't anywhere else to go.'

Nicky felt the tears again, hot and wet like blood, but she wasn't going to let them spill out in front of him. Not if she could help it. He was less awful than the other one, but even so she hadn't let anyone see her crying for years and years, and she wasn't going to start now.

'What about Charlotte's parents?'

'What about them?' She didn't even want to think about Antonia. Telling her in person what had happened was going to be awful. The thought of it made Nicky's stomach start boiling. Robert was all right; he'd understood she hadn't done it deliberately, but Antonia'd never see that. And if it came to a showdown, Robert would side with Antonia. Nicky knew that well enough. In a way he'd have to, even if it wasn't fair.

'Here's your tea, love,' said the sergeant. 'Thanks, Constable.'

Nicky took a sip, but it tasted awful.

25

'OK, love. Now tell me something. Why'd you come back here this morning? You reported what had happened yesterday. I reckon you came back this morning to tell us something. What was it?'

'Nothing,' said Nicky, pushing the plastic cup away from her. 'I didn't come to tell you anything. I came to ask if you'd found her, because I knew you'd never bother to phone someone like me, and Antonia isn't due home till later this morning. I wanted to find out straight away.'

'Are you sure you didn't want to tell us something? You see, I think there is something you can't bear to go on keeping to yourself.'

'No, there isn't.'

'I've been doing this job for years, love, and I've seen girls like you before. I *know* there's something nagging at you that you want to get off your chest.'

Nicky sighed. Round and round: they couldn't let go, could they? But however long they went on at her they weren't going to get anywhere. She was about to tell him so when she saw that there was a kind of pitying look on his face. And then she thought she understood.

'You've found her, haven't you?' The sick feeling in her stomach got worse. 'That's what all this is about, isn't it? You've found her, and someone's been hurting her. Is she . . . ? What's happened to her?' Her voice thickened in panic. 'You've got to tell me. You've got to.'

'Calm down, love,' said the sergeant. He looked as if he was enjoying himself. 'We haven't found her yet – nor any clues. But we will.'

Nicky looked at him. There wasn't any pity in his face any more, just creepy curiosity and gloating.

'And then we'll know what's been done to her and who's done it. You understand that, don't you, Nicky? It's not the sort of thing that can be hidden. Lots of people don't realise that. They think a bit of a shaking won't leave any marks, or that a slap or two just makes a little bruise; but it's not like that. That sort of thing damages little children much more than people think, and doctors can always spot it. Sometimes people looking after kids think they're just handing out a bit of discipline that won't really hurt, but then it goes too far. You know what I'm talking about, don't you?'

She stared at him, hating him. What he was trying to make her say was horrible. And he was horrible, too: a bully. She'd met plenty like him before.

'I've never laid a finger on Charlotte,' she said, making her voice less like her own and more like Antonia's. It was typical of creeps like the sergeant that he began to look at her differently after that.

'So if not you, then who? Her father ever hit her?'

'He's not her father. Her mother's divorced. Lottie never sees her real father.'

She saw the two of them look at each other and wished she'd kept her mouth shut. They'd probably start going after Robert now. The police always did that – treated everyone like suspects till they knew what was what. Still, Robert would be able to stand up to them better than her.

'When are you going to let me go?'

There was a funny kind of silence, and then the older one said, 'Whenever you want, love. You came here of your own accord, remember? We didn't bring you in and we're not keeping you here. You're not under arrest or anything, you know.'

The sweat on her face was much colder than it had been and the table seemed to be moving as she got up. She put both hands down on it, hating that she was leaving sweaty patches on its shiny surface. For a minute she thought she was going to pass out, but then she got it all under control and looked at them again. They were staring at her with even nastier curiosity than before.

'You all right, love?' asked the sergeant. 'You look very pale.'

'I'm fine.' She wasn't going to tell them about feeling so dizzy and sick. 'Except for worrying about Charlotte. Will you promise to phone me when you find her? I've given you the number.'

'Your boss's number,' said the sergeant, still staring at her. 'She's back already, you know, from New York. It was on the news before you got here. We saw her. She's furious.'

The table swayed again. Even Antonia couldn't make her feel any guiltier than she already did, but the thought of the things she was going to say was unbearable.

'How're you getting back, love?'

'I'm walking.' It might not be too bright outside. If it wasn't, the fresh air might stop the dizziness.

As soon as she turned into Bedford Gardens she saw a crowd of men and women at the bottom of the steps of Antonia's house. Lots of them had cameras and it was obvious what they were doing. Nicky stopped dead at the corner. She knew if she attempted to get back into the house they'd take pictures of her and try to make her talk to them and probably say all the things the police had just been saying. Worse, too, maybe.

She looked to see whether Robert's car was back outside the house, but there was no sign of it. If she'd known he'd be there in the house, she might have been able to force her way through the journalists. Robert would've helped her, whatever they said. Antonia wouldn't. Even in normal times she'd never help. She'd just say it was all Nicky's fault and probably laugh.

Nicky knew she'd have to face Antonia soon, but she

couldn't do it yet; not alone and not with the journalists to get through first. She just couldn't.

As the breathlessness came back and the top of her head started to feel floaty, Nicky leaned against the dark-blue sides of someone's BMW and tried to breathe through the dizziness and find some courage from somewhere.

CHAPTER THREE

Trish was sitting in a damask-covered wing chair, feeling even more suffocated by the pretentious grandeur of the drawing room than usual. All the windows were shut so that none of the journalists outside could hear anything that went on in the house, and the room smelled stale.

Antonia herself was a mess. She was still wearing the dark-blue tracksuit Trish had seen on the news. Like all her clothes, it was the most expensive version available and it fitted beautifully, but there was no getting away from the fact that it was a tracksuit. Her highlighted hair was tousled and needed washing, too, and yesterday's mascara was smudged down the sides of her nose.

But anyone would have agreed that she was a good-looking woman, bigger in every way than Trish. Her face, which was long and dominated by her direct grey eyes and firm chin, suited her better at thirty-four than it had done a decade earlier, before her achievements had caught up with her confidence. She usually held herself well and spoke firmly in a voice that had become rounder and plummier with each new success, but that morning she sounded vulnerable and looked as though the connections between her vertebrae had loosened in some way, allowing her whole body to collapse in on itself.

She was sitting hunched over her waistband and clutching her knees, tightening her hands whenever she had to say anything about Charlotte. The movement made her rings flash, accentuating the size and brilliance of the matching hoops of diamonds she wore on each hand.

They looked absurd with the tracksuit, but Trish knew that Antonia was so used to wearing them that it would never have crossed her mind to take them off. To her they were neither status symbols nor an advertisement of her latest bonus; they were merely toys she liked and felt she deserved after all her hard work.

She was trying to explain to the two plain-clothed detectives why Charlotte could not possibly have been kidnapped for ransom. Trish wished she had got to the house earlier and been able to hear everything they'd had to say from the start. As it was she had no idea whether the kidnap idea was a longshot or something they were taking seriously. She assumed they'd already discussed the possibility that Ben, Antonia's ex-husband, might have Charlotte with him. He could never have harmed her, Trish was certain, but the police wouldn't have known that, and his house must have been one of the first places they'd thought to look.

Although DCI Blake was watching Antonia's face as she talked so earnestly, Trish noticed that the much younger woman officer was staring at the rings and apparently trying to assess their worth. Constable Jenny Derring's expression suggested that she thought Antonia's wealth was quite enough to make the kidnap theory feasible.

'Anyway,' Antonia said as though she was summing

up a meeting, 'if they were after a ransom, they'd have been in touch by now.' Then her certainty wavered and she sounded like any terrified mother. 'Wouldn't they?'

'Not necessarily,' said the chief inspector gently.

He was about the same age as Antonia and he was treating her carefully. Trish had been impressed to see that although he was visibly sympathetic, he was not allowing his own emotions to leak into his voice and he had not offered any reassurance. That in itself would have made her trust him. There could be no honest reassurance for anyone until Charlotte was found.

'They could be trying to soften you up, Ms Weblock, to make you more receptive to their demands. Or you could be right and her disappearance has nothing to do with any ransom demand. What— '

He did not have time to put his question before Antonia had covered her face with her hands, muttering into them. Eventually Trish worked out that the words were: 'I feel so guilty.'

She ached to help, but there was nothing she could say or do. She could not even ask questions or offer advice until the police had gone. This was their interview and she was here only to be Antonia's silent support.

'Guilty?' repeated the chief inspector with no less gentleness. He had an attractive voice, deep and seductive. It would make confession almost easy, Trish thought.

'Why do you say that, Ms Weblock?'

'Well, it's all my fault. It has to be. If I . . . Oh, Christ!' Antonia must have been on the verge of losing control for she took her hands away from her face, pulled a handkerchief out of the open, sacklike leather bag at her feet and held it over her eyes for a moment. Then she blew her nose and stuffed the handkerchief up her sleeve.

The telephone rang. Antonia leaped to her feet, but Blake grabbed her wrist before she could run to answer.

'Wait a minute,' he said. 'OK – now. And take it carefully.'

'Hello?'

They all watched as her body sagged again.

'Yes. Thank you, Georgie. It's really kind of you to ring. No. No, there's no news. Yes. Of course. If there's anything, I'll ring you. No. No, that's OK. Right. Bye.'

She was breathing heavily as she returned to the fender stool.

'Just a concerned friend,' she said to Blake. 'Another one. They think it helps. What was it you were saying?'

'You'd just said you felt guilty and I couldn't understand why. You weren't even in the country.'

'That's why,' she said with an unsuccessful attempt at briskness. 'If I'd been here, it would never have happened. I know that. If I hadn't let my work take me away, Charlotte wouldn't have had to be with someone irresponsible enough to let this happen. She . . .'

Antonia couldn't go on and sat biting her lower lip and staring helplessly towards Trish, who got up at once and went to sit beside her on the wide fender stool. The fireplace behind them was empty and smelled faintly of soot and brass polish.

'Look,' she said quickly, 'that's not true, Antonia. Lots of mothers who've gone back to work have to be away at weekends occasionally. It's not your fault. You couldn't have known this might happen.'

'No, but it has, and I wasn't here to stop it,' said Antonia. 'And it was I who chose Nicky to look after Charlotte and so it *is* my fault. It has to be. You must see that.'

'Yes. Now, Nicky Bagshot,' said DCI Blake. Trish had the feeling that he was working hard to sound calm, almost uninterested. 'Tell me about her, Ms Weblock. Where does she come from?'

34

'There's not much to tell. She's only twenty-one, but she trained at the Wincanton School of Nursery Nursing, which has a wonderful reputation.'

'And was that how you found her? Directly from the training school?'

'No. She got herself on the books of Holland Park Helpers, who have one of the safest names in the business. They've got all her details. I'm sure they'll hand them over if you ask. She'd done a series of temp. jobs by the time she came to me, and she got good references from them all. She's always seemed reliable, and absolutely truthful. That's why I believed her.'

They were on to it at once, even before Trish had opened her mouth. It was the WPC who voiced the question.

'But you haven't spoken to her since you got back this morning, and you said it was Mr Hithe who telephoned you yesterday. When have you talked to Nicky?'

'I haven't. What d'you mean?'

'You said it was because of her truthfulness that you believed her. That sounds as though you've spoken to her.'

Antonia produced a smile of sorts.

'Not about this, Constable Derring. It was a few weeks ago. I was worried about something but Nicky reassured me and I believed her.' The smile disappeared as Antonia started to bite her lips, first the top and then the bottom, gnawing like a rodent trying to eat its way out of a trap. Trish briefly touched her hand just as the chief inspector said:

'What were you worried about?'

'I didn't think it was sinister, you see. She's a nice girl, kind. I'm sure she is. If anything she's usually too soft on Charlotte. I've noticed she can't bear to hear a child crying and so she tends not to be very strong on discipline and she gives in much too easily. But Charlotte loves her. I know she does – and she wouldn't have if they'd meant anything, would she?'

'If what had meant anything?' asked Blake before Trish could yell at Antonia to get on with it and tell them all whatever it was she was withholding. Then the telephone started to ring again.

After a moment it became clear that it was yet another sympathetic friend who wanted to offer support and help, rather than a kidnapper demanding a ransom. When Antonia had thanked her enough times, she cut the connection and then laid the receiver on the table beside the telephone.

'I can't stand it. If it's anyone important, they'll ring back.'

'Yes. Yes, I'm sure that's right,' said Blake, just as they all heard a series of electronic bleepings and a metallic voice ordering them to replace the receiver. Antonia got up impatiently to bury the telephone under a pile of cushions.

'Now, Ms Weblock,' said Blake as she sat down again beside Trish, 'you were telling us about something you had seen, something that Nicky Bagshot reassured you about. What was it?'

'Bruises,' said Antonia at last, looking at him with eyes that seemed huge and almost black, as though the widening pupils had obliterated her irises. 'There were bruises on Charlotte's arms.'

'Oh, Antonia,' said Trish, leaning sideways so that their shoulders could touch.

'Don't be kind to me, Trish, please,' she said. 'I can't cope with gentleness just now.'

'These bruises, Ms Weblock,' said the chief inspector. 'Could you tell me a bit more about them?'

'I was reading to Charlotte one evening a few weeks

ago, when she pushed up her pyjama sleeve to scratch her arm.' Antonia's voice was firmer but it was obviously costing her a great deal to make it so. 'I saw that there were some small bluish bruises around her bicep. I had a look at the other arm and there were more there.'

She was staring at the carpet ahead of her trainers and so she could not have seen the alertness in Trish's eyes, or the unnatural stillness of both police officers.

'Someone had obviously been holding her tightly by the upper arms. But the marks didn't look very bad and Charlotte wasn't distressed. On the other hand they were undoubtedly bruises. And they were on both arms at just the same height. You can see why I was worried.'

'What did you do?' asked the chief inspector. 'When you saw them?'

'Well, I didn't want to upset Charlotte by making a great fuss before I knew what had happened. I mean, Nicky was the obvious suspect but, as I said, Charlotte seemed to love her and I couldn't believe I wouldn't have known if Nicky was treating her badly, hurting her deliberately.'

'That seems reasonable enough, Ms Weblock. So what *did* you do?'

Antonia did not answer, just sat with her eyes down, looking guiltier than Trish would have imagined possible.

'You said you talked to Nicky, Antonia,' she prompted, remembering a few scenes she had witnessed in the past when people had fallen short of Antonia's expectations. 'What did she say when you tackled her?'

'I left Charlotte with the book and went to Nicky's room.' A little of Antonia's usual crispness of speech had returned. 'She said at once that she hadn't noticed any bruises herself, but that she had had to grab Charlotte earlier that evening when she was giving her a bath, and that might have made the marks. Charlotte had apparently slipped on the soap as she stood up to get out of the bath, and would have fallen if Nicky hadn't caught her. I told Nicky to stay where she was, and went back to Charlotte. I asked her if anything had happened at bathtime and she told me the same story. She also agreed that Nicky had hurt her arms that evening but she said it hadn't ever happened before. It all sounded all right, you see.'

'I do indeed,' said the inspector in what was obviously intended to be a comforting voice. Antonia's face did not suggest that she had found any comfort in it. 'Did they look fresh enough to have been made that evening?'

'Yes, I suppose so. I don't really know. What do bruises look like when they aren't fresh?'

'Yellowish rather than blue.'

'No. These were blue.'

'Did you take any further action?'

'Oh yes, of course. Even though I'd believed Nicky's story because of what Charlotte said, I didn't dare trust her completely, and so I started to come back to the house at odd times so that she would never know when I might turn up and be a witness to whatever she was doing. *If* she was doing anything, I mean. I thought if there was the slightest . . .' She stopped, apparently unable to put it into words.

Trish waited for the police to ask if Antonia had thought of setting up video surveillance in the nursery if she was worried about what Nicky might be doing to Charlotte. But they didn't.

There had been a lot of publicity in the past few months about the use of nursery-spy cameras in the States and the way you could have the pictures transmitted via the Internet to any computer terminal. Antonia must have read some of the articles, Trish thought, and seen how tiny the cameras were and how easy to hide. With her income, she wouldn't have had to worry about what they cost, and she could have had all the reassurance – or the proof – she needed without ever leaving her office.

'And of course I was with them every minute of every possible weekend. Whenever I could be. Even Sunday bedtimes when Nicky's back on duty. I thought it was all right, or I'd never have gone to New York, however important the deal. Oh, God! I'll never go away again.'

'But you said your husband had undertaken to keep an eye on Charlotte while you were in America,' said DCI Blake, still not asking any of the questions Trish wanted to hear.

'He's not my husband. We're just together.' There was something in Antonia's voice that made both police officers look very wary.

After a moment Blake crossed his long legs and said with an unconvincing pretence of casualness, 'Ah. Yes, of course. Does he get on well with Charlotte?'

'Reasonably, yes. But she's not his child, and he doesn't have much to do with her.'

Well, that's one mercy, thought Trish. But would Antonia necessarily know? She's always said she works far harder than him.

About four years older than Antonia, Robert was the creative director of a small independent advertising agency, and his hours were much more flexible than hers. Sometimes, if he were planning a huge presentation, he'd stay in the office half the night; but in less busy periods he was apt to get home by five-thirty, or so Antonia had once told Trish. She herself rarely left the bank until seven at the earliest and had begun to resent his greater freedom.

'I mean, he's just not that interested in children,' she was saying earnestly, 'and there have been times, I know, when he's felt tied down by my need to be with Charlotte as much as I can.' She twitched suddenly as though she had been bitten by a mosquito, quickly adding: 'Don't get me wrong, Chief Inspector Blake, Robert would never do anything to hurt or upset Charlotte. He's a kind man. Very kind.'

Trish caught the constable watching her suspiciously and hoped she had not shown any of her astonishment. She turned away to look out of the window and found herself staring into a camera one of the photographers had lifted to the window in the hope of catching some random but useful shot. Looking away, anywhere but at the journalists outside or the observant constable, Trish fixed on a dramatically lit studio portrait of Robert, which stood with a mass of others in silver frames on a round mahogany wine table.

'Kind' seemed one of the least appropriate adjectives for him. With his self-consciously trendy clothes, his sometimes cruel jokes, and his determination to tell everyone how successful he was, he had always seemed an unattractive man to Trish, and quite out of place among Antonia's other friends. She still could not understand why Antonia had fallen in love with him; or what it was he had seen in her to make him think he could be happy sharing her life. Trish had unkindly assumed it must have been Antonia's money, but now she was beginning to dread the possibility that Antonia's child had been her greatest attraction.

When Trish glanced back at the sofa, she was relieved to see that the constable was concentrating on Antonia again.

'But is he reliable? You did say he was supposed to be looking after Charlotte this weekend. And yet he went

40

out, having promised you he'd be here and stay with her, didn't he?' asked Blake.

There was no hint of disapproval in his voice, but Trish knew perfectly well what he was thinking and she assumed that Antonia must have a fair idea. After all, she was never remotely stupid even if there were times when she could be a trifle insensitive. She must know quite as well as Trish and the police that a stepfather would be among the prime suspects for any harm done to a little girl.

'Yes, but it was work,' Antonia said, as though explaining a self-evident truth. 'There's a crisis on. And he had no reason to think Nicky wasn't a safe person for Charlotte to be with.'

'Where is he now?' asked the inspector.

'In the office again. He went back as soon as he'd picked me up from the airport.' Antonia glanced away from his face, which for a second had betrayed real shock. Unfortunately she had then found herself looking directly at Trish, whose expression was even less encouraging.

'Don't look like that, Trish. I told him to go. He's got the crisis to sort out and there wasn't anything he could have done here. He'd just have hung about, feeling spare and saying all the wrong things. I knew we'd only quarrel if he stayed.'

Trish thought she could hear a note of hysteria in Antonia's hurried explanations and looked towards the police to say, 'I think my cousin could do with a short break. Could we stop for a while?'

'Yes, why not? That's a good idea. We haven't a warrant, Ms Weblock, and we're not equipped for a proper search in any case, but might we have a bit of a look around Charlotte's room while you have a cup of tea or something?'

'Look anywhere,' she said. The first tears Trish had ever seen Antonia shed were sliding down her face. 'Anywhere. I don't mind.'

'Right. Good. Thank you. And do you have Mr Hithe's office telephone number? I'd like to drop in and have a word with him after we've finished here.'

'Of course.' She recited the number. 'But he won't be able to tell you anything I haven't. Please don't disturb him for longer than you have to. Please. He's really busy.'

'We won't. But it may give us some clues if he can describe exactly what happened here yesterday morning before he left for work and what Nicky said when he asked her to work overtime – all that sort of thing. We'll give him a ring,' said the inspector, pulling a mobile out of his pocket as he led the way to the door.

Antonia went on sitting on the fender stool, her arms around her knees, as the two officers left. Trish didn't move.

'Antonia, where's Nicky now?' she asked after a while.

'At the police station.'

'You mean they've arrested her?'

'No, she went of her own accord. She hadn't left any kind of note for me and I had no idea where she was when I got here. Typical! But that man Blake said she appeared at the station first thing this morning, begging for news. Apparently some other officers there are going over the statement she gave them yesterday. If there are any discrepancies – or if there's anything she forgot to tell them that might give them a new lead – they'll deal with it.'

Antonia suddenly grimaced and drew in her shoulders, as though to make it clear that Trish was sitting too close to her. Trish obediently shuffled her bottom further along the stool so that there was more space between them. Neither said anything more and there was nothing to hear except after a while the clump of feet going upstairs and then moving from room to room. At intervals there was also the sound of voices, but it was hard to make out any of the words being used.

'Tea sounds like a good idea,' said Trish eventually. 'Shall I make you some or would you rather have a drink?'

'Shut up, will you? I want to hear what they're saying.'

Trish felt her eyebrows rising, but she did not protest. The two detectives seemed to be going up to the second floor, still talking. A door opened. There was more talk, so muffled by distance that it was the merest buzz. Then it stopped. Then there was nothing, not even footsteps.

The silence stretched out for a long time. Trish did not make the same mistake again and simply waited until Antonia might ask her for something. A little later they both heard footsteps coming downstairs again.

By the time the police returned to the drawing room, Antonia was on her feet and already moving towards the door.

'What is it?' she asked sharply. 'What have you found?'

'What makes you think we've found anything?' asked the inspector, holding out a hand as though to silence his colleague.

With an obvious effort, Antonia almost succeeded in controlling her wobbly voice. Her hands were twisting round and round each other. The diamonds crunched as they met when the rings slid round her fingers.

'It was the silence. It's like builders when they've broken something or drilled into a pipe. You always know that kind of silence matters. What have you seen?

Is it something that makes you think Nicky might have hurt her? You must tell me.'

'Please try not to worry too much. Can you give me some idea of what Nicky and Charlotte might have taken to the park?'

'Why? Sorry. I mean, of course I can. Nicky always took the first-aid kit: it's a kind of rucksack thing, made of red and yellow nylon with straps – black, I think – that go round the waist. I always made sure she had that in case Charlotte hurt herself while they were out. She probably put her keys and money in the bag with the first-aid stuff: I don't think I've ever seen her with a handbag. Why?'

'What about toys? Something to keep Charlotte amused on the way to the park, maybe?' asked the constable, earning herself a cold look from her superior.

'No, I don't think so,' said Antonia, looking puzzled. 'They were going to the playground. She wouldn't have needed any toys. But why? What is it you've found?'

'There's a little blood . . .'

'Blood? What d'you mean? Where?' gasped Antonia as Trish's mind shrieked, *No! No! No!*

'On some of the clothes in Nicky's room. It probably comes from the boy she helped in the playground. In her statement yesterday she said that he was bleeding from the knees and she cleaned the grazes and put plaster over them. She must have got blood on her hands then and probably wiped them on her clothes. We'd like to take them with us so the lab. can test them.'

'I see.' Antonia's eyes were blank, as though she had been suddenly blinded. Then they lit again and focused on DCI Blake. 'Why did you ask about toys? Is there some blood on those as well?'

'Just a little on the handle and under the hood of a doll's pram, which we'd also like to take with us.'

'But how could it have got there? I don't understand.'

'If they took the pram with them to the playground, then it's almost certainly the boy's blood there, too. If Nicky threw all her first-aid equipment into the pram when she realised Charlotte was missing, that would account for it.'

'And if they didn't take the pram to the park?'

Trish was impressed to see that Antonia was not letting terror overcome her ability to think logically, but she looked like death.

'There's probably a simple explanation either way, and we'll find out what it is. Don't you worry.'

'But how? How will you find out whose blood it is? Let alone how it got there?'

'We've officers out now, working to identify the boy and his mother. When they've been tracked down, we'll check whether the blood is his. In the meantime, Ms Weblock, could you give me the name of Charlotte's doctor? We'd like to have a word with him or her.'

Antonia dictated the name and address of the local surgery.

'But they won't have any samples of her blood there. It's not that kind of place. And anyway, I don't think she's ever had any blood taken; not since those tests just after she was born.'

'We wouldn't expect blood samples, Ms Weblock. It's just routine in a case like this. We always have a word with the doctor.'

In case the child has been taken in with unexplained injuries in the past, said Trish to herself. She could see from Antonia's grey face that there was no need to say it aloud.

'Will you tell me when you know?' she asked, staring at the floor. With what looked like enormous effort, she raised her head and met Blake's eyes. 'When you know if it *is* the boy's blood?'

'Of course. Now, I'll be off to have a word with Mr Hithe. And . . .'

'But what are you going to do about Nicky?' All the attempts Antonia had been making to sound calm had failed. Her voice was shrill and urgent. 'You can't go now. I mean, if there's any possiblity that she's been . . . hurting Charlotte, you must talk to her.'

'We will, Ms Weblock. Don't worry. I've just had a word with my colleagues at the station, and they said she's already left, intending to walk back here. I'm going to leave Constable Derring here to wait for her while I talk to Mr Hithe. Is that convenient?'

'Oh, I see. All right. Yes, if you like. Whatever you think's best.'

'Good. Thank you. I'd like her to start telephoning your friends and relations to check that none of them have seen Charlotte. You said you could give me a list.'

'Oh, yes.' Antonia put a hand to her forehead. She seemed to be having difficulty thinking. 'It's so hard to know . . . I mean, who . . . how many . . .'

'Look, why don't you just give them your address book?' said Trish. 'Then they can work their way through it, checking all the possible addresses.'

'Good idea, Ms Maguire. Thank you,' said Blake.

'All right. Will you wait? It's upstairs.' When he nodded, Antonia left the room.

'How hopeful are you?' asked Trish very quietly.

'It's hard to say,' admitted Blake. 'But it doesn't look good.'

Antonia came back and handed him a big address book bound in the softest black leather.

'Thank you, Ms Weblock. Now, where would you

like Constable Derring to wait? You won't want her disturbing you by telephoning in here.'

Antonia looked round the drawing room, a puzzled expression in her eyes, as though she did not understand the question.

'I don't know,' she said after a moment and then shook herself. 'Why not in the kitchen? Then you can have a cup of tea, Constable, couldn't you? I'll take you down and show you where everything is. Trish, you'll wait, won't you?'

'OK.'

Even from the drawing room Trish could hear the click of the cameras outside as DCI Blake let himself out of the house and the shouted questions. After a minute or so Antonia was back, still looking ill.

'Oh Trish, what am I going to do?'

'Try to hang on. They'll find out what's happened.'

'But they think she's dead, don't they? The constable wouldn't say anything just now, but that's why they went upstairs, wasn't it? To look for signs that she's dead. It must be.'

'I don't know, Antonia.'

'Oh, for God's sake, don't lie. You must have seen it in their faces when they came downstairs again, just like I did. And like I can see it in yours now. They've always thought she was dead and now they don't think it was a stranger who killed her. They think it was Nicky, don't they?'

'It may not be as bad as that,' said Trish.

'It nearly always is, though, isn't it? When the children are as young as Charlotte,' Antonia's voice was quivering again, 'and when they've been lost for this long?'

Trish put both arms around her.

CHAPTER FOUR

'Chief Inspector Blake?' asked Robert Hithe as he came running lightly down the spiral staircase into the atrium. 'What is all this? Didn't Antonia tell you I was busy? Couldn't you have waited until I was back at the house?'

Blake suppressed a sigh.

'Mr Hithe,' he said patiently, 'your stepdaughter has disappeared in exceedingly worrying circumstances. We have to find her. To do that we have to talk to everyone who saw her yesterday, however busy they may happen to be.'

'But Antonia knows exactly what I was doing for the whole day, and so does Nicky Bagshot. Either of them could have told you. You didn't need to come barging in here.'

'It's always better for us to hear evidence directly, sir. Is there somewhere we could talk?'

Robert Hithe tossed his black hair away from his face and looked round the gleaming glass and steel hall. Then he glanced back at Blake, a malicious little smile tweaking at the edges of his mouth.

'No gags that I can see, no scold's bridles either; not even "No Talking" signs. What's stopping you?'

'There must be somewhere less public we could go, sir,' said Blake, determined to take charge of the encounter.

'What – tea and biscuits in the boardroom? Is that what you're angling for?'

'The boardroom sounds fine.'

'Tough luck, old bean,' Hithe said, slipping so easily into a parody of Bertie Wooster that Blake assumed it was one of his party tricks. He resumed his own voice to add irritably: 'There's a meeting going on up there. A fucking important one, too, which you dragged me out of.'

'No meeting is more important than a missing child. Have you any idea what Charlotte could be suffering at this moment, sir? Would you like me to tell you what we've seen when we've finally tracked down abducted children in the past?'

Robert Hithe shrugged, but Blake thought he could detect a hint of shame behind the casual gesture.

'No, of course not. I know as well as you what may be happening. And it's . . . hideous. But I don't see what you think *I* can do about it. Still, if you're determined to waste your time and mine asking questions, you'd better get on with it. What is it you're so anxious to know?'

'Could we sit down?' DCI Blake gestured to the row of dark-green leather chairs ranged on the far side of the pool that took up an expensive amount of space in the middle of the atrium.

'No, we could not. There isn't time. Ask your damned questions and let me get back to work.'

He looked very nervous, Blake thought, but that could have been because of the meeting, whatever it was. His long fingers were constantly twitching, either adjusting his cuffs or smoothing the lapels of his jacket or else pushing back his dark hair. When you looked carefully at him, you could see his face was weaselly, but because of the flamboyance of his hair and the whiteness of his dazzling smile, as much as the in-your-face self-importance you didn't notice at first.

'Very well, sir. Could you run through everything that happened yesterday until you left your stepdaughter alone with her nanny.'

'I wish you wouldn't call her that. It's so laden with fairy-tale nastiness. I refuse to be anyone's wicked stepfather. She's my lover's daughter. Nothing to do with me.'

Blake could not think of a much more inappropriate tone for Robert Hithe to be taking in the circumstances, and he wondered what it was supposed to conceal. Well, he'd just have to find out. He hid his revulsion behind a polite smile and set about it.

'Very well, sir. Would you just tell me everything you did with them both yesterday.'

'I didn't *do* anything with either of them. I escorted them both to the swimming pool at eleven-thirty. Charlotte has a private lesson every Saturday morning. I then took them to McDonald's for an early lunch.' He directed a winsome grin in Blake's direction and added: 'Which is something I'd rather you didn't tell Antonia; she doesn't approve of feeding burgers and chips to her precious daughter. Can I rely on your discretion?'

He waited as though he really expected an answer. Blake stared him out. Robert shrugged and laughed.

'Have it your own way. Anyway, after lunch I drove them both home before negotiating with Nicky about how much I'd have to pay her to work overtime on Saturday afternoon so I could get back here. OK? Is that clear enough for you?'

'Remarkably straightforward, sir.' Blake saw with satisfaction that his little gibe had got through. 'What time did you leave the pool?'

'I'm not sure. The lesson's half an hour, then a shower and dressing, say twelve-fifteen; twelve-thirty.'

'And you went straight to the McDonald's in the High Street, did you?'

'Yes. I can't tell you precisely how long it took Charlotte to absorb her lunch.'

'I imagine you must have been home by about two o'clock.'

'About that.'

'I see. And how was Charlotte? Did she seem normal? During the swimming lesson, for example?'

'Perfectly. She's taught by a charming young woofter, who's done wonders with her. She used to be afraid of water, which is why Antonia insisted on the lessons in the first place, and young Mike Whatsisname has got her well sorted. He's good with kids. Charlotte swims like a little fish now.'

'She liked her lessons?'

'That's right. And they were useful for me too. It was sitting there, breathing in all that chlorine, that gave me the idea for the Fruititots bathing babies.'

'I don't understand.'

'It's only the most successful TV commercial this year. Haven't you seen it?'

'I can't say I have, sir.'

'Well, take it from me it's a small masterpiece. Fruititots are our biggest account, and fucking pleased with the way the bathing babies campaign has gone. I owe Lottie that.'

'It's beginning to sound as though you attend the lessons regularly.'

'Not regularly, but I go fairly often.' Robert's voice had

lost its self-conscious striving note. 'It's a way of giving Nicky a bit of a boost. She gets lonely with no one but Charlotte to talk to, and Antonia can be a bit sharp with her. I do what I can to make her feel loved and wanted. It's a small price to pay for domestic harmony. Nicky's very good with the little brat, you see.'

'Little brat, sir? That sounds as though you dislike your step— sorry, Charlotte.'

'Not at all, Chief Inspector Blake. Or no more than any child. But she's a demanding creature, given to tantrums. Perhaps they all are at that age; I wouldn't know.'

'Right, sir,' said Blake, making a note. 'Now Ms Weblock has told us she saw some bruises on Charlotte's arms a few weeks ago. Did you notice them yourself?'

'Bruises? No. I haven't seen anything like that. What are you talking about? What sort of bruises?'

'As though someone had been holding Charlotte too tightly about the upper arms,' said Blake, looking closely at him for signs of guilt, amusement, satisfaction or even fear. All he saw was surprise. 'You didn't see anything like that? Not even at the swimming pool? They must have been visible.'

Robert Hithe was silent for a moment as though genuinely searching his memory, but then he flattened his lips, squeezing them together in a horizontal pout and shook his head. 'No, can't say I did. But then I never get all that close to the brat – I never dry her or dress her or anything. I might well have missed them. Did Antonia say they were bad?'

'No. Could you give me the name of the swimming teacher, sir? And the address of the pool.'

'He's called Mike. I don't think I've ever heard his surname. But the pool's easy. Hang on, it'll be in my Psion.' He pulled the little computer from his pocket, pressed a few keys and then dictated the postal address and the telephone number of the pool. 'No. No record of young Mike's surname, though. But they'll be able to tell you at the pool.'

'Presumably, sir. Now, is there anyone who can confirm exactly where you were yesterday afternoon?'

'Why?' The sharp features twitched. It was a moment before Blake realised that Robert was laughing at him. 'Don't you believe I was working? That's a bloody good joke under the circumstances.'

'Why's that, sir?' Blake resented the way Robert kept trying to make him feel like the dullest, thickest plod on the beat.

'Because we had an almighty screaming match that could probably have been heard streets away. The whole cast is upstairs now. You'd better come up and meet them. You'll get to see the boardroom after all. Lucky old you. And lucky them. They'll be thrilled to know I'm being accused of child murder now.'

If he had been talking to the man in his private capacity, Blake thought he might have hit him at that point.

'May I remind you, sir,' he said, putting all the suppressed violence into his voice, 'that we're not asking these questions for fun. We're trying to find Charlotte before harm – or more harm – comes to her. It's no laughing matter.'

'Except that the idea that *I* could have done something to her is ludicrous. About as ludicrous as some of the things the dear colleagues accused me of yesterday. They'll love you. And you them, probably. Well, come on if you're coming. I haven't any more time to waste.'

Blake was coming to the conclusion that Robert was one of the most unpleasantly self-important, twisted little pricks he'd seen in years.

'Before we go up, sir, can you tell me why, if your

crisis was so important, you chose yesterday for one of your irregular visits to the swimming pool?'

Robert stopped with one foot on the bottom stair. After a second, he turned back. Only the anger was left in his face. All traces of nervousness seemed to have been wiped away.

'You really have got it in for me, haven't you? Who's been winding you up?'

'No one, sir. Would you just answer the question?'

'If you must know, my fucking fellow directors couldn't get their arses in gear in time to meet in the morning. Since that would have been a hell of a lot more convenient for me, I happen to think they must have done it on purpose to get me on edge. They want me out, but I'm not going without a bloody good fight. It's my ideas that have kept this place afloat so far. And if they'd done as I said and stayed in our old offices instead of committing themselves to this expensive monstrosity, we wouldn't be in the shit now. Every time they look at me they're reminded of how stupid they've been and so they detest me. That's why they'll love the idea that you think I'm a child murderer. Satisfied?'

'Very good, sir,' said Blake, wanting to kick him all the way upstairs and down again. He was beginning to feel even sorrier for Antonia Weblock. 'Let's get on with it. Will you lead the way?'

CHAPTER FIVE

Two other officers were walking up a short flight of steps outside a large red-brick Victorian house in Clapham at much the same time. They were pleased but a little surprised to find that there were no journalists hanging about there. As Sergeant Lacie knocked on the peeling black-painted door there was a barrage of frenzied barking from inside.

'Perhaps that's why the ratpack's not here. They hate big dogs as much as I do,' she said to her colleague. 'What about you, Sam? Are you scared?'

''Course not, Sarge.'

'Great – you can go in first, then. I'll—'

The door opened before she could finish telling him her plan, to reveal a tall thin man with one hand on the door and the other on the collar of the barking dog. Neither of the visitors paid any attention to the man. Both were too busy assessing the likely viciousness of the animal, a large black beast with a tan nose and a wildly flailing tail.

'Yes?' asked the man. 'Can I help?'

'Mr Benedict Weblock?'

'Yes.'

'We're police officers, sir. I'm Sergeant Lacie and this is Constable Herrick,' she said, showing her warrant card. 'We'd like to talk to you.'

'Fine. Come in quickly or I won't be able to hang on to Daisy and I don't want to have to chase after her down the road again. I take it this is about Charlotte. Is there any news?'

'Daisy?' echoed Sam Herrick in a voice of extreme disbelief as he hung back. 'Touch of Rottweiler in there, is there, sir?'

'So the vet claims. I'd have said Doberman myself. *Is* there any news?'

'Nothing yet,' said Sam, pushing the door back with the flat of his hand and keeping his gaze firmly on the dog. 'The park's being searched and we're talking to everyone who might have seen her yesterday. You sure that animal's gentle?'

'Definitely. Visiting children use her as a footstool and practise hairdressing on her. I'll put her in the kitchen. Go on into the sitting room, will you?'

Exchanging glances, the two officers walked into the long, dark hall, which was floored with the original tiles and papered with mustard-coloured Anaglypta below the dado rail and a lighter shade of yellow above. There were long claw-marks in the Anaglypta and a couple of adult-sized bicycles to show what had made them. A large pair of muddy green gum boots stood beside the door mat and three leather dog's leads hung from a hook beside a bunch of keys. There was a mirror on one wall beside the door through which the man and dog had disappeared, and two doors opposite. The nearest was open.

The police chose that one, only to find themselves in what was obviously a study. There were two flat-topped desks, one impeccably tidy with papers neatly arranged in a series of wicker baskets; the other had heaps of children's exercise books, papers, boxes, pens and computer disks piled higgledy-piggledy all over the top and balanced on the corners of several opened drawers below.

'D'you suppose this is the living room?' asked Sam Herrick.

'No. This is our study,' said Ben Weblock from behind them both. 'Come on through.'

Without the dog to distract her, Kath Lacie had a good look at him, rather liking his long, lined face with the tired gentle eyes and full lips. His floppy greying hair looked so soft that he must have just washed it, and he seemed to have cut himself shaving, or else scratched his neck on something. There were two fine red marks just below his chin, already scabbing over. She did not want to antagonise him by making notes, but she examined them carefully so that she could include everything about them in her report.

Apparently unaware of her interest, he turned and led the way into a pleasantly shabby room with a fitted carpet in a colour somewhere between beige and mushroom. Four soft-looking armchairs upholstered in a variety of faded prints and a sagging sofa were the only pieces of furniture, apart from a couple of ugly tables made of scarred dark oak. Along one wall was a fitted bookshelf crammed with hard-backed books and a serious musician's hi-fi system. That was the only expensive object in the room and, unlike the rest, it looked well dusted.

'Have you really found nothing at all?' he said as he turned to face them again. 'It seems extraordinary.'

'Nothing yet, sir,' answered Kath. 'And we wanted to ask you a few questions.'

'Why me? Oh, do sit down, both of you.'

'Thanks. You must see, sir, that we need to find out when you last saw Charlotte and where you were yesterday between, say, two-thirty and four in the afternoon.'

'Are you suggesting *I* had a hand in whatever's happened? That's ridiculous.'

'There's nothing ridiculous about it at all, sir. And you'd have to have a bloody strange reason not to tell us where you were,' said Sam Herrick with more aggression than Kath thought necessary. She suppressed a sigh at the thought of explaining to him yet again that you get more out of people when you make them feel comfortable with you than when you stamp and throw your weight about or insult them.

'When *did* you last see her?' she asked calmly.

'I've never met her.'

Kath stopped in the act of lowering herself into a deep armchair covered in heavy cretonne dimly patterned with parrots and palm trees.

'Never? But she is your daughter, isn't she, sir?' she asked, becoming conscious that her thighs were aching. She gave herself permission to sit down properly and smoothed her black linen skirt over her knees.

'Frankly,' he said with a bitter little smile, 'I've always doubted that.'

'So is . . .' Kath consulted some notes she had in her pocket . . . 'Robert Hithe the child's father then?'

'No. He was a later arrival.'

'Oh. Then who is? D'you know?'

'No. There was a fairly large cast of possibles. You'll have to get it out of Antonia. If you do, you'll be doing better than I ever managed.'

Sam Herrick opened his mouth, but Kath's frown stopped him saying anything. This was far too delicate – and important – for Sam to start trampling about in it.

'Was that why you parted?' she asked, not expecting to get anything but an ugly snap in reply.

'Not quite,' said Ben Weblock, surprising her with his willingness to answer. 'But I don't see how it's relevant to Charlotte.'

'Anything might be. We can't tell yet. You must see that, sir. No one's sensibilities can be considered in this kind of investigation, not when there's a child at risk.'

'No. You're right there, Sergeant. Sorry. It's all still rather raw, I'm afraid, even after four and a half years. And I don't like talking about it. I suppose in the beginning I put up with Antonia's affairs because supporting her seemed more important than anything else. Then, after I'd met my second wife, other things became important, too. That's when I stopped. OK?'

'Yes. Thank you. It's good of you to answer so frankly. When exactly did your first wife tell you she was pregnant?'

'When she understood I wasn't playing games,' he said reluctantly. Then, as though something in Kath's sympathetically encouraging smile spoke to him, he added: 'She came back here one evening after I'd got her to move out to say we were going to be parents. It was – technically – possible, but I didn't believe her then. And I don't now. She'd never expected me to find anyone else. I'm sure the announcement was revenge for that. In a way, you know, she gave up trying to make me believe the child was mine too easily for it to have been true.'

'Ah. Yes. I see. While we're here, would it be all right if Constable Herrick had a quick look round? Nothing formal like a search, but he'd better have a look, if you don't mind. I expect you can imagine the sort of report I have to give my superiors when we get back.'

'Sure. Nothing's locked except the garden door. The

keys are on the right of it behind the curtains. If you need anything, just shout, Constable Herrick.'

'Right you are.'

'So you've never talked to Charlotte at all, never got to know her?' said Kath as soon as Herrick was out of the way.

'That's right.' Ben Weblock shut his eyes for a moment as though they were hurting.

'Why does that upset you, sir?' she asked, trying to disguise the sharpness of her interest.

'Because for the first time I've been regretting that I was so stubborn.'

'Why's that?'

'If I had known her, I might have been able to help. Have ideas about what could have happened to her. It's . . .' He shook his head. 'How is Antonia? Have you seen her?'

'No, sir. Colleagues of mine are talking to her now.'

'God! I hope she's all right. Charlotte, I mean. Antonia could cope with most things, but any four-year-old facing . . .' His voice died. Kath watched him keenly as he struggled. After a moment he tried again. 'D'you think she's still . . . ?'

'I couldn't say, sir,' said Kath quickly. 'And I don't think it's a good idea to speculate. We've all heard too much these days of what can happen to little children who are abducted, and it may not be as bad as that. We'll get some news soon. It's usually quite quick.'

'Is it? Haven't there been cases when it's been weeks before a body's found, sometimes years?'

'Bodies, sir?'

'Aren't they usually killed when they're as young as this?'

Could any normal man, Kath asked herself, be able to ask a question like that about a child who might have been his own daughter? His voice had trembled badly earlier on and yet he had brought out that question as though he had been asking the price of tea. Even if he'd convinced himself that someone else had impregnated his wife, he must have wondered in the intervening years whether he had been wrong. And now that the child might be dead, shouldn't he be more upset?

'Where *were* you yesterday afternoon?'

'Here, working on next week's lessons, until I took the dog for her usual walk.'

'I see. And was anyone else here with you?'

'No. My wife was conducting a seminar – it was the first part of a weekend course that concludes today – and she didn't get back until nearly six. And as far as I can remember, no one phoned or called. So I haven't any witnesses, either. Sorry.'

'What about the neighbours? Might they have seen you?'

'They might. But we're a polite lot round here and don't go poking our noses into other people's business. And I didn't go into the garden or play heavy metal music or anything obvious like that. You may just have to take my word for it.'

'That's not something we ever do,' came Herrick's voice from behind Kath. She looked over her shoulder. He gave a small, disappointed shake of the head.

'Ready, Sam?'

'Yeah, Sarge.'

'Well, thank you very much, Mr Weblock. You've been very helpful. Here's my number in case you should hear anything or think of anything that might be useful. You will ring us, won't you?'

'If I have anything to tell,' he said with a warmer smile. 'But it's unlikely. I'm too cut off down here and much too far from Antonia's household to hear anything useful.'

'Maybe, but you never know. You're a teacher, aren't you, sir?'

'That's right. At the local primary.' He laughed in a modest way that made Sam Herrick look as though he felt like throwing up. 'One of the few men left. Unlike the rest, I still think getting kids happy enough at school to teach them the basic skills is the most important job in teaching.'

'You like children, do you?' asked Sam, not even attempting to sound sympathetic.

'Yes, Constable Herrick. I like them very much.'

'Then why haven't you any of your own?'

'I don't think that question is within your remit, is it?' He looked from Herrick to Kath Lacie and back again.

'In the circumstances, sir,' she reminded him quietly, 'I think just about any question is legitimate. Don't you?'

'Maybe. All right. My wife, my second wife, and I have not been able to have any yet. It's not something either of us enjoys talking about. But you can check with the local doctor if you need confirmation. He sees both of us and knows all about us.'

'Thank you,' said Kath. 'If you could just give me his name and address?'

Weblock dictated it and then stood up as though expecting them to leave.

'Any of the kids in your school ever disappeared or gone on the at-risk register, or had any unexplained injuries?' asked Sam, quite suddenly. 'Anything like that, sir, that we ought to know about? In your classes or any of the others?'

'No, Constable, nothing like that.'

'But you'll admit that it happens,' said Sam, sounding to Kath as though he were trying to needle Weblock. She decided to let him run a little longer before she reeled him in.

64

'According to the papers, sure. But I've never come face to face with anything like that and I've begun to think there's a lot less of it about than most people believe.'

'Oh, you do, do you? Know any paedophiles yourself, sir?'

'No, Constable, I do not.'

'Some people say they need treatment, sir, not punishment. What d'you reckon to that?'

Ben Weblock sighed and leaned against the ugly mustard-coloured wall, putting his hands in the pockets of his wide buff corduroy trousers.

'Everyone who breaks the law should be punished. But anyone who mistreats children needs education and therapy to—'

'Therapy, sir?' Sam Herrick's voice was disgusted.

'To make them confront their offending behaviour,' Ben said steadily, apparently unaffected either by the officer's voice or the contempt in his face. 'Come on, Constable, don't look so surprised. You must know they say things like: "she enjoyed it"; "she was flirting with me, asking for it"; "it didn't do me any harm, so why should it hurt him?". They have to be taught about that line no one can cross. And they have to be made to admit the damage they do when it *is* crossed.'

'You're beginning to sound quite passionate, sir.'

'Oh, I am, Constable. On that subject, I am a passionate man. Aren't you?'

'Yeah, well.'

Herrick opened his mouth and looked as though he might say something else, perhaps something unforgivable, and so Kath Lacie pushed him to go ahead of her out of the house.

'Thank you, Mr Weblock,' she said when they were alone again. 'I have to say that I agree with you.'

'Good. Will you tell me when the child's found? I can't rely on Antonia to keep me informed.'

'OK, if I can. But I expect you'll hear it on the radio before I can get to you. Goodbye.'

Sam Herrick was already in the driving seat of the car by the time Kath reached it.

'Well?' she said as she buckled her seat belt, aware that Ben Weblock was standing in the open doorway, looking down the steps at them. 'What did you find in the house, Sam?'

'Sod all, Sarge. No sign of any kids' things anywhere except for some paintings tacked up on the kitchen walls. It was a right mess upstairs, I can tell you. Women's clothes draped over all the chairs in the bedroom; clean, but they didn't look as if they'd ever seen an iron. Piles of towels and sheets, too, mixed in with them. Doesn't look as though his second woman is much of a housewife.'

Kath suppressed the obvious comment in the interests of getting the information she needed as quickly as possible.

'Nothing in the cellar neither, nor signs of digging in the garden. That was just as bad as the house: bit of ratty grass in the middle, unpruned roses with blackspot gone all leggy in the flower beds and all sorts of dead shrubs, too. My old man would turn in his grave. No one's dug any earth there in years. And the fence needed treating. It's nearly rotted through in places; be down in the next strong wind. Couple of sluts, if you ask me. But no sign of any kid or kids.'

'Right. We'll have to talk to the neighbours, but not, I think, just now while he's so aware of us. And to colleagues at his school. And the doctor. What did you think of him?'

'Big girl's blouse. I'm not surprised his ex fooled around.'

'Really? Why?'

'She was trying to get him to play the man for once, wasn't she? Put his foot down an' tell her that *he* wanted her and no other damned bloke was going to get his . . . get his hands on her.'

'What an interesting idea!'

'Why the sarkiness, Sarge?'

'I thought he might be a good man,' Kath said slowly, looking through the pristine windscreen but not seeing any of the traffic or the pedestrians. She was thinking about the worn, lined face and the kind smile, the warm voice, and the careful intelligence she had sensed in the man they had just left. 'I'd like to have been taught by him when I was at primary school. Wouldn't you?'

'Not sure I can remember that long ago,' said Sam with the realism that was his most admirable characteristic. 'But I doubt it. He'd have been too much of a creep for me even then.'

'I think he might be tougher than you give him credit for.'

'Come on, Sarge. He was a jellyfish. What d'you reckon? Could he have nicked the kid?'

'A man like that? I can't see it, can you?'

'Only if he'd done it to get back at his ex. Not to hurt the child; I can't see him doing that. But I can see him putting her somewhere safe so he could watch his ex squirm.'

'You've got a nasty mind, haven't you, Sam?'

'It's what they pay me for.'

CHAPTER SIX

'What shall I do, Trish? I can't sit here waiting – I'm not used to it. I don't know how to let other people run things any more.'

'You've got to, Antonia. The police know what they're doing. There'll be plenty for you to do yourself when . . .' Trish paused, reluctant to offer false comfort and yet unable to make herself correct her 'when' to an 'if'. 'Later,' she added feebly. 'Let's talk about something else. Tell me about Robert.'

'What about him?'

'How things are going with him. Whether you're happy. That sort of thing.'

'Why?' Suspicion stood out all around Antonia's head like the quills of a threatened porcupine. Trish could almost hear the rattle.

With the discovery of blood in Charlotte's toy pram and news of the marks on her arms, it was impossible not to believe that someone in the house had been hurting her. Knowing from the statistics that Robert was a much more likely suspect than the nanny, Trish wanted to find out a lot more about him. Antonia was the only person who'd be able to tell her anything useful, but she was looking so suspicious that she would have to be approached with care.

After a moment, Trish delved into her own private weediness and said, 'Because I'm so bad at relationships, and I don't understand why. I thought hearing about yours might give me a clue.'

Not all that convincing, she told herself as she waited for Antonia to answer. I know exactly why. It's because I hate the way men make you peel back all your defences until you've none left and then bugger off – or else use you for target practice. Either way you end up miserable, furious, and scared of the self you've found below the pith.

'I used to be able to keep an affair going for nearly a year but these days I can't stick it for more than about three months. I look at people like you and Robert and admire you like anything and then start wondering how you do it.'

'By not thinking too much.' Antonia's voice was dry but a good deal of the suspicion had gone. 'That's always fatal.'

'Why? I mean, what is it you're afraid you might find if you did start thinking about Robert?'

'Nothing awful, so there's no need to look so interested. I'm not a romantic like you and I've seen too much to believe in eternal bliss or even happy-ever-after; it's better to concentrate on the surface and not go digging for trouble.'

I've seen too much, too, thought Trish, but that's why I won't put up with any of it any more.

'Come on, Trish, you know as well as I do that no man ever stays as attractive – or as keen – as he was at the beginning. That's just life. But I'd say Robert's probably as good as they come. We still like doing the same things, and he makes me laugh.' Antonia's lips parted in a smile that was at least half a grimace. 'And he never *yearns* at me like Ben always did. That used to make me feel sick.'

'Yes, I know. I could see that you hated it.'

'Wouldn't you?' Antonia demanded sharply.

'Probably,' Trish said, hoping that her voice was as calmly affectionate as it ought to be to excuse what she was going to say. 'But perhaps he wouldn't have yearned so much if he'd had more confidence in what you felt about him. He always did need a lot of bolstering, didn't he, poor Ben? And you were a touch niggardly in handing that out.'

Antonia smiled, some of the familiar queenliness returning to her posture and her eyes. 'You were pretty keen on him yourself, weren't you? I used to wonder at one stage if you might be trying to cut me out.'

'You didn't, did you? When?'

'Oh, ages ago,' Antonia said vaguely.

'You must've been mad. I was always fond of him, of course I was, but in a cousinly kind of way,' said Trish, before adding more truthfully: 'He was yours from the beginning and you know what I think about people who break up other people's marriages.'

'I ought to, you've told me often enough. Do you ever see your father these days?'

'No.' Trish would have talked happily about almost anything to keep Antonia from tormenting herself with pictures of what might be happening to Charlotte, but she still found it hard to discuss her father with anyone.

He had disappeared with brutal suddenness when Trish was eight. Looking back, she was amazed how well her mother had managed, refusing to panic and finding both a job and a cottage she could afford to rent on her meagre salary within a month. She had had no financial help from her husband until she eventually forced him into court five years after his desertion, but even so she had managed to give Trish nearly everything her schoolmates had. It must have been extraordinarily hard for her, and yet she had never once criticised him in Trish's hearing. In retrospect that seemed positively saintly.

In fact, it could have been a bit too saintly. There had been times when Trish felt that a little criticism might have helped. Her father had never bothered to get in touch with her. She'd had no letters from him, no Christmas or birthday presents, no congratulations on any of her exam successes, no contact at all until she had appeared in the papers as a rising young barrister, and by then it was far too late. She was too angry to let him anywhere near her, and she was damned if he was going to take the credit for any success she might have achieved. Her mother had a right to that; but no one else.

'Sorry,' said Antonia, looking curiously at her. 'I didn't realise it was such a sore subject.'

Trish shrugged. 'Just one I find difficult to talk about. Tell me about Robert instead.'

'He didn't break up my marriage to Ben, so you can stop looking so disapproving. It was that American bitch of Ben's who wrecked it, as you very well know. I didn't meet Robert until later.'

'Yes, I do know,' said Trish, keeping her thoughts about Antonia's many affairs to herself.

'And life is much easier with him than it ever was with Ben.'

'Is it? Good. In what sort of ways?'

'Oh, lots,' said Antonia with a peculiar smile. 'If I'm honest . . .' She paused and then a moment later nodded as though either she or Trish had said something. 'Yes, I think a lot of it has got to do with the way

Robert loathes all the things Ben always thought were so wonderful.'

'Like what?'

'Oh, come on, Trish. You must remember how Ben used to bang on about the wonders of family life. He was forever fantasising about clean nappies drying on one of those old nursery fireguards with the flames flickering behind them and a clutch of dewy naked babies playing with hand-carved bone rattles on a hearthrug woven by his devoted wife during long winter evenings while he did manly work in the fresh air somewhere else. There'd be apple pies in the oven, smelling of cinnamon, and me being plump and aproned, smiling adoringly whenever he chose to come home to pay my bills and keep me safe and tell me what to do. Ugh!'

Trish had never seen evidence of so much imagination from Antonia before and hoped she was not goggling in astonishment.

'Robert would detest all that as much as I do. He likes decent restaurants and adult company and a much more sophisticated kind of life altogether. And he's not in the least threatened by my success. Ben couldn't ever hack that. It was weird, you know; I'd always earned infinitely more than him even at the beginning, but he insisted on paying for everything. I suppose it was some kind of power trip, but it drove me mad. Robert's completely different. He loves the fact that I make such a lot and positively encourages me to lavish money on him.'

'And that's a good thing?'

'Sure. Can't you see why? He's confident enough to take, which Ben never was. And it's a hell of a lot easier to live with a confident man than a dribbling wimp.'

'Oh. Good,' Trish said, thinking, Poor Ben. What a life you led him.

'And then Robert likes me as I am. Ben was always trying to make me different, less than I am, so that he wouldn't feel inferior.'

Did he? Trish asked herself, looking back into the past. Surely not. Didn't he just want you to go on caring about him in the way that you seemed to at the beginning? Wasn't that all it was?

'Well, I'm really glad it's working,' she said aloud. 'By the way, what was Robert's reaction to the bruises you saw on Charlotte's arms?'

'He didn't know anything about them.'

Trish stared. She would never understand Antonia. In her position, Trish would have told everyone anywhere near so that she could involve them all in policing Charlotte's life.

Was it possible that at some level Antonia had always known that Nicky was unlikely to have made the marks? Could she have been afraid it was Robert? So afraid that she hadn't been able to admit it to anyone, even the police?

'Why didn't you tell him?' Trish asked as gently as possible.

Antonia shrugged. 'He's not all that good at pretending, and I didn't trust him not to alert Nicky before I'd got some evidence one way or the other.'

'Right. I see – at least I think I do. Antonia?'

'Yes?'

'Did the police give you any idea of who saw Charlotte last yesterday?'

'Nicky, of course.' Antonia looked at Trish as though she was a complete fool. 'And before that Robert when he left for the office at two-thirty. And before that Mike, her swimming teacher. But they will have left the pool at about twelve as usual, so he can't have seen anything useful. Who's that out there?'

They'd both heard the journalists coming to life out-side the closed windows.

'It must be Nicky,' said Trish, hearing an anxious female voice amid the reporters' aggressively excited babble. 'Shall I rescue Constable Derring from the kitchen and let her get started?'

'Not yet. I want a word with Nicky first.'

'But the inspector specifically said . . .'

'Sod that. There are things I need to know before they get their hands on her.'

Antonia left the room, to return a moment later with a slight fair-haired young woman at her side.

Trish looked at her with interest. She had never met the nanny before and knew of her only from Antonia's impa-tient descriptions and Charlotte's affectionate prattle on the night of the wiggly worms. It seemed from her account then that Nicky, too, had been pretty good at proving that they didn't exist.

She was said to be twenty-one, but Trish thought she looked younger, possibly because she was so small. Barely five feet two, she was slim and dressed in black jeans held up with a blue elastic snake belt and a tight stretchy shirt of blue and green stripes. Trish was too far away to see the colour of her eyes, but the skin around them was puffy with crying and there were raw patches on either side of her nose.

Her naked face looked surprisingly pasty for someone who, if Antonia's description of the household routine had been true, must have spent the greater part of every afternoon out of doors. The only bright colour about her was the emerald-velvet scrunchy with which she had pulled back her hair.

'Antonia, I'm so sorry,' she was saying in a hesitant voice with more than a hint of the north in it. 'I'm really, really sorry.'

75

Antonia shut the door carefully behind them as though to make sure no sound reached the basement kitchen, where Constable Derring must be still obediently drinking her tea.

'Don't even try to apologise,' she said in a voice that made Nicky wince. 'Just tell me what happened.'

Nicky did not answer. She just stared at Antonia, looking stupid and obstinate. Trish was surprised. Charlotte's description had suggested someone both intelligent and sensitive.

'Come on, come on,' said Antonia impatiently. 'It's ludicrous to pretend. The police may have swallowed this story of yours about Charlotte disappearing into thin air, but I won't. I want to know exactly what happened yesterday.'

'But, Antonia, I'm not pretending about anything,' said Nicky, finding her voice and looking less obtuse as soon as she spoke. 'I told Robert exactly what happened yesterday and I've been telling the police again all morning: I was bandaging up another child and when I'd finished I saw that Charlotte had gone.'

'A complete stranger? You turned your back on Charlotte, who was in your sole charge, and put her at terrible risk in order to look after a child you'd never seen before? I can't believe that even of you.'

Trish glanced sideways at Antonia. Such open hostility did not seem to be the best way of getting information out of Nicky.

'Antonia,' Trish began tentatively and got no answer.

'I had to, Antonia. No one else was there for him. He was only little and he was bleeding. Scared, too. Charlotte was safe . . .'

'Not according to this story of yours. Quite the opposite.'

'She should've been,' said Nicky passionately, her voice beginning to shake. 'There wasn't any reason to think anything would happen to her. There were other children there. No one was watching *them*.' She had taken a well-used paper handkerchief from the pocket of her jeans and was twisting it between her hands, ripping it and dropping little sodden balls of greyish tissue on the unspotted cream carpet like beads from a broken necklace. 'You must believe me, Antonia. I didn't see anything.'

'Because you took care not to, is that it? Were the other child's screams some kind of signal? Or a decoy to distract everyone's attention while Charlotte was snatched? Is that what it was? Come on, Nicky, answer me. You'll have to tell me in the end. You might as well do it now.'

'But I haven't got anything to tell. I've told the police everything that happened. Why won't you believe me?'

Nicky's face was even paler than it had been when she had arrived, which made the redness around her eyes and the bottom of her nose stand out like flags marking her guilt; her constantly twisting hands were trembling.

'Antonia,' Trish began, 'I think—'

'Be quiet, Trish. Nicky, I don't believe you because I don't believe even you would be as ludicrously irresponsible as that. I want the truth and I'll do whatever's necessary to get it out of you.'

'Antonia, you can't do it like this. Whatever's happened, you must—'

'This is none of your business, Trish. Keep quiet.'

'I can't let you—'

Antonia's voice exploded into fury. 'It's not for you to *let* me do anything. You have no right to interfere. If you can't hold your tongue, you'd better leave.'

Aware that more protest would merely drive Antonia to greater fury, Trish got to her feet. As she moved,

Nicky produced a strangled word that sounded like 'Please.'

'Shut up until I tell you to talk.' Antonia's voice cracked like a bullwhip. Nicky flinched and put up her hands as though to ward off a blow. When Trish passed her on the way to the door, Nicky looked at her, obviously begging not to be deserted.

After an infinitesimal pause, Trish turned her head to say as calmly as possible, 'I'll wait in the hall until you've finished, Antonia.'

'As you like. Now, Nicky. I want—'

Trish left the room before the demand had been made, wondering whether she ought to go down to the basement to warn Constable Derring that Nicky was back. If she had been certain that would help she'd have been quite prepared to brave Antonia's fury, but she was not sure.

Wondering how DCI Blake was getting on with Robert, Trish sat down to wait on an uncomfortable if beautiful old fruitwood chair, which stood to one side of the cold radiator in the hall. The edge of the seat cut into her thighs however she arranged herself. After a while it got so bad that she stood up and started to walk the length of the hall and back again.

As she walked she tried to think through everything she had heard, wishing she had access to whatever the police had discovered. It seemed to her then that of all the things that could have happened to Charlotte, there were only three that were even remotely likely. She might have been picked up in the playground and taken away by a complete stranger for some so-far unidentified reason; she might have been murdered by someone close to her; or she might have been taken by Ben Weblock in a bizarre custody snatch.

The thought that Charlotte might be in Ben's hands

was reassuring, but Trish could not make herself believe it. She had not seen him since the divorce, but everything she had ever known about him before that told her that he could not be so devious or so cruel as to kidnap Charlotte. However angry he might still be with Antonia, he would never try to take revenge on her like this. And if he had wanted custody of a child he had never known, he would have gone through the courts to get it. Of that Trish was sure. Almost.

No, she told herself. It's got to be worse than that. Could it be Nicky?

If I could see her eyes I might be able to tell. There might be that blankness in them, the blankness that comes from cutting the link between what's done to you and what you feel about it.

I wish I could see her eyes. Hers and Robert's. I've never looked at his. I wish I had.

The drawing-room door opened and Nicky emerged. By then it was not only her hands that were trembling but her whole body.

'I'm sorry,' said Trish quietly from the far end of the hall, moving towards her.

Nicky started as though a thousand volts had been passed through her body.

'I'm sorry I left you to face that on your own, but I thought it would only make Antonia fiercer if I stayed.'

Nicky shook her head, clinging on to the bannisters with one hand and knuckling her eyes with the other.

'Nothing could make her worse. I know it's my fault, but she didn't need to say those things. She must know I'd never hurt Lottie. I feel . . .' She stopped as though there were no words to describe it.

'Yes, tell me, Nicky: how *are* you feeling?'

'I can't bear it.' Nicky looked straight at Trish. 'I can't

bear thinking about what they could be doing to Lottie, what . . .'

The red, thickened lids closed over Nicky's eyes then, but Trish had seen enough to feel some reassurance.

'And I can't stop it. I'd give anything to go back to before. Antonia doesn't understand. She thinks I hurt Lottie, you know, like . . .'

'Yes, I do know. But you must see that she's so frightened just now that she'd say anything. Try not to feel too hurt – or too angry. Can't you put up with it, knowing what she must be going through?'

'It's not that different than usual. She's always accusing people of things. And she doesn't even know Lottie or understand her. She never hugs her or anything. Children need to be hugged and stroked. If they're not they grow up thinking they're bad, dirty. But she'd never bother to hug Lottie because she doesn't love her. Not like I do.'

'Nicky! You mustn't say that. She's Charlotte's mother. She's terrified for her.'

Nicky snorted. 'Haven't you seen them together ever? Never watched how Lottie tries to play? She brings Antonia toys and offers them to her. But all she gets back is lectures about being noisy or clumsy or not paying proper attention. She's a little child.' The anger had gone from Nicky's voice and she was crying again.

'What's worse is that she loves her mother so. She didn't want to go to the park yesterday because she was hoping to make sweets for when Antonia got home from the States. "Merica", she always calls it. "When's my Mummy coming back from Merica?" She kept asking it all morning, in the swimming pool and everything. "Why's my Mummy gone to Merica?" On and on.'

'That must have been difficult for you,' said Trish, alert to a danger she had not suspected.

'I didn't mind,' said Nicky. 'That wasn't why I wouldn't

let her make sweets. It was because Antonia makes us go out every day, whatever the weather. Often when I think Lottie'd be better off warm in bed, she insists we go out. Well wrapped up, but out. I didn't dare not go on Saturday, even for something like making a welcome-home present. She'd have been so cross if she found out, and she would; she always finds out everything. I said we'd make the sweets this morning. But if I'd let her do what she'd wanted Lottie would've been safe.'

'Was she still upset when you set off for the park?'

'Only for a minute or two. I let her wear her tights, you see, and take her pram with her favourite doll, and that cheered her up. It was a treat because she's usually only allowed the pram in the house. She soon forgot to be cross. But we could've been safe at home if I'd listened better. That's what's so awful: seeing all the times when I could've stopped it if I'd done something different. It didn't need to happen, you see.'

Trish heard footsteps coming up from the basement.

'Did Antonia tell you that Constable Derring is waiting to ask you some more questions?' she said more loudly. The door at the top of the stairs swung open. 'Hello, Constable Derring. This is Nicky Bagshot.'

'So I hear,' said the young officer. 'Will you come downstairs with me please, Nicky?'

Nicky sighed, but she did not protest. She looked as though she would do whatever she was told by anyone because she was too tired and miserable to resist. Derring waited for her to go ahead and then turned to look at Trish with an expression of contemptuous reproach.

Trish looked back at her, smiling politely, until the door had swung shut. In the drawing room, Antonia was leaning on the mantelpiece and apparently staring down into the empty grate.

'Derring's got her now,' said Trish. 'Was it really necessary to attack her like that?'

Antonia straightened her spine and shoulders as she turned to answer. Her face was quite composed and she looked very hard.

'I think so. She must know more than she's telling. And there must be a way to get it out of her. I know Blake didn't want me questioning her, but I had to see what I could do. And I didn't say a word about the pram, did you?'

'No. But she volunteered that they did take it to the park. Did you get anything useful?'

'Not a thing. I could—' Antonia broke off, looking at her hands as though they belonged to someone else. They were clenched into fists.

'Honestly, Antonia, I think she's genuinely miserable.'

'So she sodding well should be.'

'Look, why don't you try to rest for a bit? I can stay here if you like while you go to bed, and then wake you when Blake's back. You must be jet-lagged as well as all the rest.' Trish paused. It had always been important to avoid seeming to give Antonia orders. 'Would you like me to do that?'

'I couldn't possibly sleep. If I only shut my eyes, I see . . .'

'OK, then d'you want to talk?'

'I haven't got anything to talk about. If you're trying to ask me something, then for God's sake come out and ask it. I can't bear being manipulated into saying things.'

'OK. I wasn't trying to manipulate you, but it's true, I did want to ask if you might be able to tell me a little more about the bruises on Charlotte's arms.'

'Oh, for God's sake! I've told the police. You were here – you heard. Let it go.'

'I just wondered what sort of size and shape they were,' said Trish, who had never been afraid of Antonia's anger. Unlike poor Ben.

'Shape? What is this, Trish? What are you on about now?'

'The bruises: were they small and round? Or big? Or like a band – or a kind of strip – around her arm? Or blotchy with little dark-red speckles?' Trish found a way to laugh. 'But I shouldn't be asking leading questions.'

'Oh, for Christ's sake! Why not ask it straight out? You want to know whether Nicky could have been digging her fingers into Charlotte or tying her up, don't you? Or, what's the other – blotchy with speckles? Giving her love bites? Is that right?'

'Yes, Antonia, it is. Although from the little I've seen of Nicky, I do find it hard to imagine her deliberately hurting Charlotte. But since I didn't see the bruises myself, I—'

'Perhaps if you had, you'd feel less sympathy for Nicky and be on my side in all this.'

'Antonia, *of course* I'm on your side. I know exactly what you're going through.'

'You couldn't possibly,' said Antonia, looking at Trish with almost as much hostility as she had shown Nicky. 'You've got no children.'

'True. But I'm not devoid of imagination, and I've had a certain amount of experience with this sort of case.'

'"This sort of case". If you mean child abuse, why the fucking hell won't you say so? I've told you, I hate this pussy-footing around. We all know what this is about, and you're pretending—'

'Antonia, I'm not pretending anything. I just want to help,' said Trish steadily. 'Try to tell me, if you can. What were the bruises like?'

'They were clearly fingermarks. That's why I believed

83

Nicky when she told her story of Charlotte slipping in the bath. I'm not stupid. If they'd been made by some kind of ligature, I'd hardly have accepted Nicky's version. But I didn't measure the marks against her hands, if that's what you're going to ask next.'

Trish nodded. 'I did wonder. I noticed that Nicky has peculiarly small hands.'

Antonia shook her head. Her lips were clamped together. Her eyes were like stones.

'Oh, Christ! I wish I'd never believed her. I should have sacked the little bitch on the spot. I must have been mad.'

'No, you weren't. Don't punish yourself, Antonia. You had plenty of reasons to trust her, and none – or very few – to doubt her.'

She must see that Robert's a serious suspect, thought Trish. *She must*. How could she not?

'It didn't seem such a terrible risk at the time,' Antonia was saying, as though Trish had never opened her mouth. 'She was so bloody plausible, and Charlotte seemed so happy with her, but then perhaps that was her way of defending herself against the horror. Could that be it? Oh Trish, what am I going to do? I thought I could force Nicky to tell me the truth, but she didn't give in at all. If the police can't get it out of her and I can't either, what am I going to do?'

'The police will find out the truth, whatever it is. But I honestly don't think Nicky can be guilty of anything except sloppiness. She seems to care much too much for Charlotte and be too . . . too kind altogether.'

'That's what I used to think. Now I'm not sure. In any case, mustn't all child abusers be able to make themselves seem likeable? I mean, they've got to be able to charm the children into trusting them, haven't they?'

'Yes, they have – but even so Nicky doesn't fit the

profile of any child abuser I've ever met – or heard of. Look, Antonia, is there anyone else who might have wanted to snatch Charlotte? Not for any of the things we both dread so much, but for something comparatively trivial?'

'Like what? Like who, for God's sake? And how could anything to do with this be trivial?'

'Well, maybe Ben, for instance. I wondered if he might have had some kind of brainstorm and decided he wanted her to live with him for a bit. I mean, he is her father, after all. Isn't he?'

'Oh, don't be ridiculous. Of course he's her father. You're as bad as he is. And anyway, you're just making complications for their own sake. I wish you wouldn't. He's never shown the slightest sign of wanting to take on any of the responsibility for Charlotte. Which is typical. And even if he did, this isn't his style at all.'

'I wondered if maybe you'd like me to go and see him.'

'There's nothing you can do that the police can't.' Antonia shook her head, struggling for self-control. After a tense moment she added: 'I know I asked you to come today, but it wasn't so you could play amateur detective. I just wanted someone with me. I didn't know you were going to start grilling me and criticising me and threatening to cause all sorts of trouble.'

'I'm sorry,' said Trish, fighting to feel the necessary sympathy. 'Perhaps I'd better get out of your way. When will Robert be back?'

'God knows. Now that the police have been wading in and taking up his time, I probably won't see him till midnight. Why? I suppose you want to start tormenting *him*, now.'

'I'm just concerned that you shouldn't have to bear this on your own and hoped he'd be back soon,' Trish said steadily, trying not to react to Antonia's heavily sarcastic emphasis.

'To hold my hand, you mean? That'd be a first. Look, get out, will you, before we start quarrelling?'

Trish got to her feet without another word. Almost at once she felt Antonia's damp hand on her wrist.

'I'm sorry, Trish. I can't be ordinary or polite, not with Charlotte in . . .' Antonia's voice broke. She stared straight ahead, digging her teeth into her lower lip. After a moment she let go of Trish's wrist and covered her ears with her hands, as though she were hearing some terrifying sound she had to block out. Shuddering, she let her arms fall to her sides and opened her eyes again and eventually sounded almost normal as she said, 'Not with Charlotte in such danger.'

'I know,' said Trish at once, thinking how odd it was that even the sharpest terror a woman could feel seemed theatrical when it was put into words. 'I'll get out of your way now, but will you ring me if you hear anything – or if you want me back here? I'll come straight away and do anything you want – just sit and watch whatever's happening in silence if that would help. Whatever.'

'All right. Thanks. I'll ring.'

Trish left the house, doing her best to block out the journalists' questions and not glare too furiously at the cameras that flashed all around her.

She tried to remember which of the bridges across the Thames was likely to be emptiest on a Sunday and plumped for Chelsea. Driving through streets that seemed almost more crowded with shoppers than they were during the week, she thought about Ben, and about the light he might be able to shed on what had happened.

CHAPTER SEVEN

'Sir?'

John Blake looked up from his desk to see Kath Lacie standing by the door of his office.

'Yes, Kath?'

'Jenny Derring said you wanted to see me.'

'So I do. What did you make of Benedict Weblock?'

'Haven't you got the report? I put it on your desk myself.'

'Did you? I must have missed it.' Blake privately acknowledged yet another of the stratagems his subconscious kept devising to bring her into his office. He shuffled through the heaps of paper on his desk. 'Yup. Here it is, all tidy and official. Still, you might as well give me the flavour of the man while you're here. Come on in and sit down.'

'I thought he was honest,' she said, smoothing the black linen skirt around her knees and giving no sign that she knew what Blake's subconscious had been up to.

She was as tall as he, taller than most of the men in the squad, but she always managed to look feminine in her simple clothes. As well as the black skirt, she was wearing a T-shirt-shaped thing made of thin cream-coloured silk, a string of pearls and a straight black jacket. They probably hadn't cost all that much; he was sure the shirt came from Tie Rack because when he'd first seen it he'd tried to get one for his wife. But Kath looked a million dollars in hers. She always did, whatever she wore, even jeans. And it wasn't as though she flaunted it either. Her smooth hair was bunched tightly at the back in a bit of black velvet and she had hardly any makeup on her slightly moon-like face.

'Careful of people's feelings, too, intelligent and self-aware,' she went on. 'The last man in the world to hurt a child, sir, I'd have thought. But to be fair, Sam didn't get the same impression at all.'

'No, I can imagine not.' Blake had been skimming her report as she talked. 'You've put here that Weblock claimed he'd never seen the child. D'you believe that? It seems unlikely.'

Kath took a moment to think. It was one of the habits he most valued in her. She never bothered to say anything to fill a gap and she never made things up to please anyone.

'I did. But I've no evidence to back it up. I liked the man and so I was inclined to trust him.' She looked at Blake, half-smiling, and then added: 'I don't trust many people, sir, and so far I haven't been wrong.'

'Fair enough,' he said, trying not to read into that what he shouldn't even have hoped she felt.

'Sir?'

'Yes, Kath.'

'I heard that you brought a doll's pram away from the ex-wife's house.'

'Yes, I did. I'll be giving all the details at the next briefing. Why d'you ask?'

'I just wondered what you'd seen in it to make you bring it away.'

'Mainly blood and hair. It's possible there's an innocent explanation for both, so don't jump to conclusions.'

'But you have, haven't you?'

'Well, it doesn't look too good.'

Kath said nothing, just sat controlling the tiny shudder that had made her silk shirt ripple against her skin. The outline of her plain, unembroidered bra was clearly visible for a moment. He told himself savagely to get a grip.

'Would a four-year-old fit into a toy pram, sir?'

'Not easily.' It was odd, he decided, how your brain could split into the professional half that minded like hell about the child and the other half that could not think about anything much beyond Kath Lacie's skin under her clothes. 'But Charlotte Weblock was small for her age, and if she was dead when she was shoved in, it's possible. Some of her joints would've had to be smashed to make her fit, but it could've been done.'

Kath sat watching him for a moment. Then she said with a pretence of calm, 'You're pretty sure that's what happened, aren't you?'

'Yes. There were traces of soil caught in the seams at the sides of the mattress as well as the blood and hair. And signs of wiping all round the inside.'

'Suggesting,' said Kath, who always liked to have everything as clear as possible, however unpleasant or difficult it might be, 'that after she was dead, the killer stuffed her body in the pram, wheeled it out of the house, looking all innocent, dug a grave somewhere and then picked the body out to bury it, spilling soil from his hands as he did so. That it?'

'Broadly.'

'Got a suspect?'

'The obvious one's the mother's boyfriend, but there's the nanny, too, and anyone else who had access to the house.'

'Except the mother.'

'Yup. For once the mother's in the clear, Kath. No way of getting back from New York in time.'

'I suppose we are sure she was there, are we?'

'Yes. The fax came through an hour ago.' Blake knew that however obvious fathers and stepfathers might be as suspects in such cases, there had been an unpleasant number in which mothers had assaulted their own children, even murdered them. It was one of the things he still found hard to accept.

'Has the boyfriend got an alibi?'

'He was being shouted at by five of his fellow directors and watched by a secretary taking the Minutes yesterday afternoon. I'd have said none of them liked him anywhere near enough to lie for him. They've convinced me he wasn't in the park then, but that doesn't mean he's innocent. He could have involved the nanny, in which case I think we may be able to get him through her. She looks much more likely to break than him. Anyway, so far we've only her word for it that Charlotte was ever in that damned playground. But we're trying to get confirmation.'

'You mean you think the boyfriend could have killed Charlotte and then persuaded the nanny to get the body away in the pram? And then while she set up a scene in the park to establish some kind of alibi for herself, he did the same for himself in his office?'

'Something like that.'

· 'He'd be taking a hell of a risk, wouldn't he?'

'Maybe. We don't know enough about either of them yet. We'd have a better idea if the Superintendent wasn't so sold on the idea of a random snatch by a stranger.

If we'd had a proper search of the house done and been able to give the lab. boys a chance to look for blood in samples from the drains and so on, we'd be far further on.'

'But he could be right, sir. You must see that. There've been a fair number of stranger-abductions, haven't there?' said Kath, her face full of pity.

'Yes. But it'll take days to track down all the known paedophiles who might have been in the area. And we haven't got days. That child's . . . Christ! I hate these cases.'

'How's the mother bearing up, sir?'

Blake shrugged. 'Hanging on by her fingernails.'

'What's she like?'

'In normal circumstances I should think she's a smug bitch,' he said frankly. 'Lots of diamonds. Expensive hair. House worth a cool million and a bloody good job. But not now. She's all over the place and looks like shit warmed up. She cares about that kid all right.'

'What sort of terms is she on with the boyfriend?'

Blake smiled a little. Talking to Kath always helped to clear his head. She knew the right questions to ask.

'Hard to say. I wouldn't have thought they were a natural pair. But then how would I know? I've never seen a natural pair in my life.' He thought of Kath's husband, who'd seemed like one of the biggest turds he'd ever met. 'Except at weddings and sometimes not then. But he wasn't with her at the house; I had to see him in his office.'

Blake nodded as he caught Kath's expression. 'Interesting, isn't it? But there was an explanation of a sort, and a cousin of hers did arrive halfway through our interview as a kind of stopgap.'

'Any idea who she was, this cousin?'

'Introduced as Trish Maguire. I don't know much

more than that, except that she hasn't seen Charlotte for weeks.'

'What sort of age?'

'Maguire? Oh, thirties, I should think. Thin, distinctly thin, short spiky dark hair, amazing face – you know, all bones and flashing eyes. Ferocious eyes, come to think of it. Eagle-like, maybe. Clever, too.'

'You liked her,' said Kath, beginning to smile at his description.

'I suppose I did,' he said, his face creasing in amusement to match hers. 'More than Antonia, really. They were unlikely-looking cousins. Maguire's not the diamond type at all. Sensible clothes – jeans – and no makeup.'

Blake saw Kath snatch a glance at her watch. It was a very ordinary quartz watch on a plain black-leather strap. He found himself thinking of Antonia Weblock's rings again and then realising that for a woman who looked like Kath – was like Kath – flashy gold or jewels would be way over the top. He thought too of the white band there must be around her wrist where the watch-strap had blocked the sun from touching her.

Get hold of yourself, Blake.

The order seemed to work and he suddenly saw her properly, her self as well as her body, and noticed how near the edge she was. She'd been in the nick since dawn and he knew she had trouble at home, too. With a turd like that, who wouldn't?

'You'd better pack it in for the day, Kath. You look knackered.'

She nodded. 'I hate these cases, too,' she said with uncharacteristic passion. 'I wish . . .'

'I know,' he said, suddenly remembering – far too late – that she'd had a miscarriage only last year. It had been her first pregnancy, too. No wonder she'd shuddered at the thought of a child's body being broken to make it fit into the toy pram. Shit, he thought, and for a moment forgot about protecting his own delicate sensibilities and the not so delicate ones, too. 'What about a drink, Kath? Just a quick one to take away the taste.'

She smiled at him, her calm face regretful and so aware of him that it wasn't fair. 'Better not, sir.'

'No, perhaps you're right. Pity, though.'

She nodded and stood up in a single easy movement that most dancers would have envied. 'Sometimes I think I ought to shift to another nick,' she said. 'Nearer home. Good idea – or not?'

Blake thought about all the things he ought to say, the sensible comments about her career and about her husband, who was some kind of lawyer, and then he said, 'I'd hate it.'

Without looking at her, he picked up the file again and heard her walk away. He did not trust himself to watch her go and stared blindly at the file until the door clicked shut behind her.

CHAPTER EIGHT

'Hello, Trish,' Ben said when he saw her standing outside his house. His voice was as warm as ever, but his face was much less easy to read than it had been in the old days. After a moment he pulled the door open as far as it would go.

'I wish it hadn't taken something as bad as this to make you come back. Come on in.'

'You don't mind?' She hovered on the step, very conscious of the four and a half years since they had last met and everything she had thought about him then.

The rage she had felt when she heard he was insisting on divorce even though Antonia was pregnant had shaken Trish so badly that for a long time she had not wanted to see him. Whatever there had been between him and Antonia, the child at least was innocent; and yet it was she who was going to have the worst punishment if she had to grow up never knowing her father.

Even so, Trish's greatest fury was reserved for Ben's new wife. If it had not been for her, he'd never have behaved so far out of character. Trish was sure of that, if of nothing else.

Bella was a child psychotherapist – said to be good at her job – and that seemed to make it even worse. She of all people should have known what effect her selfishness would have on Ben and Antonia's child. In Trish's view, Bella should have given him up as soon as she heard about the pregnancy, however much it cost her.

'Having you in the house again?' said Ben cheerfully. 'Far from it. Come and meet Bella. You'll like her. Bel? We've got a visitor.'

Mad Daisy came flying out of the kitchen, barking her head off, ahead of a comfortable-looking woman in a large flowered skirt and loose cotton sweater. Trish, who had forgotten quite how terrifying the dog could look and sound, shrank back.

'Daisy, hush up, will you!' said Bella in an accent that was still distinctly American in spite of the nine years she had spent in London. She tucked her artfully straggled blonde curls behind her ears and looked up at her tall husband. In her tilted head and questioning smile as much as her pink cheeks and meadow-like skirt, Trish recognised the embodiment of the fantasy Antonia had described earlier in the day and wondered if it was as fake as it looked.

'Bella, this is Trish Maguire, the lawyer. You've heard me talk about her.'

'Sure,' Bella said, straightening her head at once. Her expression did not suggest that what she'd heard had made her want to meet Trish. 'The legal expert in dysfunctional families who's seen too much of what happens to children to trust herself with any of her own. Hi, Trish. How are you?' Bella held out her hand.

Stunned by the cheek as much as the inaccuracy of Bella's diagnosis, Trish was glad to be able to go on hating her. Ben was looking distinctly embarrassed.

'I'm sorry to interrupt your evening, Bella,' Trish said

sweetly, shaking hands as though she did not mind the touch of Bella's skin on hers.

'That's OK. I have the makings for a pitcher of iced tea. Will you have some?'

'Well, yes, thanks,' said Trish, who did not much care for cold sweet tea with half the garden in it, like some poor-man's Pimms, but wanted to have a chance to talk to Ben alone. It was not that she would have preferred Pimms. She hated that, too, for absurdly obvious reasons: it had been her father's drink.

'Daisy, come on,' said Bella, demonstrating fearless mastery over the animal she had known for a much shorter time than Trish had, as she went back to the kitchen.

'We don't drink alcohol any more,' said Ben, leading the way out of the hall, 'hence the tea. D'you mind, Trish?'

'Not in the least. But don't you miss wine? You used to get through a fair amount.'

'Bella's helped me give up a lot of destructive habits.' He pushed open the drawing-room door.

The room looked shabbier but otherwise exactly the same as it always had done, with piles of newspapers on the floor beside each of the squidgy chairs and heaps of books on every available surface, the dust marks showing which of them had been recently read. Only the hi-fi system was new. Bella had made none of the changes second wives usually insisted on to mark the change of ownership.

'Has Antonia sent you? You do still see *her*, don't you?'

'Yes, I do,' said Trish, ignoring Ben's emphasis and trying to stop her mind filling with memories of the hours the three of them had spent in the big room when it had all begun to go wrong. She had to admit that the atmosphere was a good deal sweeter than it had been then. If that had been Bella's work, then maybe she wasn't all bad.

'But no, she hasn't. In fact, she virtually ordered me *not* to come.'

'Then you've been amazingly brave. Although, come to think of it, she never did frighten you, did she, Trish?'

'No. There've been lots of times when she's made me go completely bananas, but she's never frightened me. Not many people do.' Except myself.

Ben laughed but quickly sobered again as he asked for news.

'Of Charlotte? There isn't any. That's why I came. I wondered . . .'

'Whether I'd got her?' The pleasure had gone out of his face, and she could feel him withdrawing from her. 'Oh, Trish.'

'No. I knew you couldn't have had anything to do with it,' she said at once. 'But I thought you might be able to tell me things I couldn't possibly ask Antonia.'

'I doubt it, but I'll try,' he said, adding with an effort, 'But it would have been a reasonable question to ask. Don't think I don't know that. You could have suspected me – the police do. And I haven't got an alibi. But I'm glad you don't. After everything . . . Anyway, I can promise you I haven't got her. I wish I had. I'd know she was safe then.'

I wish you had, too, thought Trish. And I know what Bella would make of that if she knew anything about me. I want all fathers to make a real push to see their children and take care of them. That's why I was so angry when you told Antonia you'd never have anything to do with her baby. I dumped on to you all the fury I'd like to have poured over *my* father. I'm sorry about that. It wasn't fair and it hurt you when you were so hurt already by everything Antonia had done, but I didn't know what I was doing. I couldn't help it. I'm sorry.

'You always were a forgiving bloke, Ben.'

'You've never done anything that would need forgiving.' He took off his spectacles and rubbed his eyes with a familiar gesture that brought the past back far too vividly. 'Anything. I've missed you, you know, Trish.'

'I . . . It seemed so difficult when . . . you know. I can't think now why it was quite so tough.'

'It was an odd time,' he agreed. 'None of us behaved very sensibly. Have you been happy since?'

'That's a tricky one. I've been busy, excited, triumphant, enraged . . . powerful and then got scared of the power; in love once or twice. You know, more of the same, really. You?'

'I have been happy.' His brown eyes, unprotected without the hornrims, looked so much more at peace than they had ever done in the old days that Trish believed him and tried to think more charitably of Bella.

'Good. Ben, do you know anything about Robert Hithe?' she asked, grabbing the opportunity before she had to start being polite. A cannonade of barking from the passage suggested that she didn't have much time left. 'I tried to ask Antonia about him, but she wouldn't talk.'

'I've never met the man. I know even less about him than I know about poor little Charlotte. Sorry, Trish.'

'Shit,' said Trish.

'That's not a word I permit in this house,' said Bella calmly as she bent down to put a neatly laid tray on the table in front of Ben. Her hips looked enormous as she bent forwards, and the pleats of her flowery skirt spread apart to make room for them.

Trish caught sight of her own legs in the straight indigo jeans and enjoyed the sharpness of her wrist-bones, too.

'"Shit" is as nothing to the words in my mind,' she said casually, and then felt ashamed of herself. There was probably nothing seriously wrong with Bella, or nothing much, and there was no reason to wind her up.

'And why is that, Trish?' Bella asked, looking and sounding just like a patronising schoolmistress.

'Because she hoped I could give her some information about Antonia's new man,' said Ben, smiling first at one of them and then the other, 'but I can't.'

'The child's stepfather?' There was more hostility than curiosity in the question, and in Bella's face, but Trish was an old hand at dealing with hostility. She had always found that much easier than patronage.

'Why should you know anything about him, Ben? And why should she force her way in here to ask you?'

'I hoped he could tell me something,' said Trish pacifically. 'That's all. Any man in Robert Hithe's position – particularly without children of his own – who has to act as father to another man's child comes into the category of people most likely to do that child harm.'

'Yes – so? What's that got to do with you? She's not your child. Aren't the police dealing with it?'

'Of course they are. They've been talking to him today, and they'll probably get the truth out of him soon enough, but I thought if I could find out a bit more, myself, then if he is implicated in what's happened, at least I'd be in a position to help Antonia, perhaps even warn her in some way.'

'And you'd want to do that, of course.'

'Bella,' said Ben, as he leaned forward to give Trish a misted glass of iced tea. There was a warning in his voice. It did not seem to have much effect on his wife.

'Look, Ben, this is a woman you haven't seen in years, who you've no reason to trust, coming here pretending to ask questions about your ex-wife's lover. Anyone but you would know she's got an ulterior motive. She's trouble. Can't you smell it? You don't have to answer anything she asks you. You have rights here.'

Trish felt better as she realised that she was not the only one with childish feelings. But once again she wondered just what Ben had told Bella about her.

'Don't, Bel,' he was saying. 'I'd answer anything Trish chose to ask me. She couldn't possibly be trouble for either of us. Trust me.'

'She sided with Antonia. And it sounds as though she hasn't changed.'

'No, she didn't side with Antonia,' said Ben, turning his head to smile at Trish. 'She just got out of the way of the flying plates. Didn't you?'

'Something like that,' Trish admitted.

'And Antonia's her cousin, her blood relative, and she's a loyal soul,' he went on, his voice bathing Trish in reminiscent approval. 'As I have reason to know.'

Bella's eyes could have shrivelled a heavyweight boxer at a hundred paces, but she said nothing.

'I wish I could help you, Trish,' said Ben, 'and poor Charlotte, too, but I can't see how. I may have met Robert Hithe at some stage in the past, but I don't remember him. All I know is that he's a hotshot advertiser, and that's not a world I know anything about. I hardly ever cross the river these days. I don't see Antonia. I've never even spoken to Charlotte. I had nothing to tell the police – or to show them.' He laughed unhappily. 'They looked round the house, you know.'

'You never told me that,' said Bella sharply, her attention switching away from Trish.

'It wasn't important and I knew it would make you angry.'

'It's outrageous. Did they have a warrant? They can't have. I wish you'd remember that you don't always have to do what everyone tells you, Ben. No, really, that was dumb.'

So, thought Trish looking at her boots, he's picked another bossy wife. I wonder why.

Ben laughed at Bella's vehemence. 'Sometimes it's easier to do what people want. And when it doesn't matter, why try to resist?'

'Principle?' suggested Trish quietly, remembering how difficult it had been to hang on to hers in the days when she and Ben had discovered that there was more to their feelings for each other than the cousinly affection she had admitted to Antonia.

It had been almost impossible to refuse the happiness they could have given each other, but they had managed to do it. They had not betrayed Antonia. They had never made love. One evening they had come very close to it, and Trish knew that she would never forget the feeling of absolute emotional security coupled with dizzying, utterly destabilising physical pleasure that she had felt then. But they had resisted it.

'I don't have principles any more,' said Ben. 'They lead to a lot of unnecessary misery.' He looked at Trish and she knew that he was remembering, too. She hoped that Bella did not understand what was going on. After a time Ben lowered his eyes.

Later he said: 'Where will you go next, Trish, now you know we can't help with Charlotte – or Robert Hithe?'

'I haven't a clue, unfortunately. I feel helpless – and hopeless.'

'Does that matter?' asked Bella sharply. 'You have no official role here.'

'True.' Trish got to her feet. There was no point trying to explain why she had to do everything she could to help Charlotte – and Antonia. 'Look, it's late and I've kept you too long.'

Too right, said the expression on Bella's round face.

'The iced tea was delicious,' said Trish. 'So often it's sickly.'

'Not mine. I always use a lot of lemon and fresh 'erbs. I'm glad you liked it,' Bella said. She produced a smile, perhaps in pleasure at Trish's impending departure. 'It was good to meet with you at last. We'll see you again, I hope.'

'I hope so, too. Goodbye.'

Ben left Bella alone in the drawing room while he walked Trish to the front door. Then, standing on the step, breathing in the warm evening air, he said, 'Don't get Bella wrong. She's not usually that aggressive. She just feels protective of me where Antonia's concerned. All this business with Charlotte has stirred up a lot of old emotions.'

'I know, but . . . Look, don't get *me* wrong, either. I'm not doubting anything you've said, but have you really no ideas about what could have happened to Charlotte?'

He shook his head. 'Like you, Trish, I feel hopeless. If I had anything useful to contribute, I'd have been on to Antonia at once. Whatever there's been between us, I'd never have wished something like this on her. Or Charlotte. If I could've helped, I'd have done it straight away. You must know that.'

'Yes, I do know it. Ben . . .' She stopped herself and then asked whether he had any suggestions about who else she might ask for help.

'None. But listen, Trish. No one who cares about children could do something like this. You should be looking for a child hater, not a child lover.' He shook his head, obviously impatient with himself. 'No. "Lover" isn't the right word. Someone who minds about children and *their* happiness. But that's obvious enough.

I'm sorry – I can't think of anything even remotely useful.'

'Pity,' she said, trying to work out why she felt so convinced that he must be able to tell her something that would help. 'Ben, are you and Bella . . . ? No, sorry. I know that's a question one should never ask.'

'I meant what I said when I told Bel I'd always answer anything you chose to ask me, Trish. Didn't you trust that?'

'I don't want to trespass, that's all.'

'I know. You never did; you couldn't. Out with it, Trish, whatever it is.'

'I just wondered why you and Bella haven't started a family of your own, that's all.'

'We're still trying. But there are problems.' His voice told her that he had been wrong and she *had* succeeded in trespassing where she was not wanted. 'It was nice to see you, Trish. Don't stay away so long next time. Good night.'

She took her dismissal quietly – there wasn't much option – and went back to her car, her mind racing. The trouble was that her brain was fuddled with a whole lot of odd feelings from the past that she thought had been rationalised long ago.

The telephone was ringing when Trish got back to her flat. Tempted to let the machine answer, she changed her mind when she saw the time.

'Mum?'

'No, it's me again, Emma.'

'Oh, Emma. Look, I am sorry I didn't call you back this morning. It's just that I didn't want to risk missing her if she tried to ring.'

'Who, your mother? Has something happened to her, Trish? What is it? You sound very peculiar.'

'My mother's fine. But haven't you seen the news?'

'No.' Emma's voice sounded unlike her, edgy and somehow artificial. 'Hal's away – some local-government-corruption frolic – and I've had a completely news-free day: no papers, no radio, no telly. World War Three could have broken out for all I know, or care. Why?'

'Antonia Weblock's child has disappeared. I've been with her most of the day. The police haven't found anything yet, and it's looking . . . well, pretty bad.'

'Oh, damn! Trish, I'm sorry to have been so frivolous. I didn't know. You must be feeling like hell. I am so sorry.'

'It's fairly grim. And hard not to let one's imagination make it grimmer. But, look, Emma, I wanted to ask your advice.'

'Go ahead. Anything I can do.'

'Antonia's trying to convince herself that her nanny's involved, but I don't think she can be. The account she's given of what happened just before the child disappeared seems quite believable to me. I've nothing more than intuition to go on, but . . .'

'I'd have said yours was better than most. Could I help? I mean, d'you think it's a suitable case for a polygraph test?'

'Well, I do in fact. I've been thinking about that all the way back. The nanny's account is crucial. If it's true, then it means she's not guilty of anything but carelessness, in which case the police should be concentrating on finding someone else with a motive to harm Charlotte, or a complete stranger who picked her at random. If it's a lie, then she is involved, either on her own or with someone else. Listen.'

Trish repeated everything she had heard from Antonia, DCI Blake, and Nicky herself about what had happened in the playground, adding at the end: 'If you could prove it one way or the other, then at least we'd be further on, and if she's definitely innocent it'll be much easier for Antonia. Imagine having to live in the same house as someone who might have—'

'I don't think I could bear it, Trish. Why hasn't she sent the nanny somewhere else?'

'Knowing Antonia, I should think she wants to keep tabs on Nicky until she's sure.'

'Yes, I see. Are there any other suspects, apart from the random stranger?'

'If it's not Antonia's new man,' said Trish reluctantly, 'then as far as I can see, the only other possibility is Ben Weblock.'

'It can't be him.'

'Why not?'

'Oh Trish, come on. Everything you've ever told me about him – and you've told me a fair amount – makes that impossible.'

'But he did throw Antonia out when he fell for bloody Bella, and he's never even tried to see Charlotte. I know it's technically possible that he's *not* her biological father, but legally she's his child. He has responsibilities for her, and yet he's always ignored them. Doesn't that make him seem a bit weird?'

'Are you sure he hasn't had a DNA test done? In his place most men would. Honestly, Trish, I bet he has and knows that she's not his. That would explain it all. Men get very twitchy about taking on someone else's child.'

'Yes, I know,' said Trish, smiling a little at Emma's characteristic understatement. 'I hadn't thought of that. You're being much brighter than me.'

'No. Just less involved and perhaps able to see a bit more clearly. Has Ben got an alibi for whatever the relevant time is?'

'No. But he did tell me that quite freely.'

'Well, that's encouraging. We can put him on the back burner and start with the nanny. And then go on to Robert Hithe if you can think of any way of persuading him to take a test.'

'You mean you really will test the nanny?'

'Trish, how can you ask?' Emma's gentle voice had become quite crisp. 'You know I will. When would you want me to do it? ASAP, I presume.'

'Yes. But obviously I'll have to clear it with Antonia first – and the nanny. Have you got a lot on at the moment? Sorry, silly question. Of course you have.'

Emma's growing reputation among defence lawyers meant that she was usually booked up for weeks in advance. Polygraph tests were not admissible in court and many lawyers and police officers distrusted them, but Emma's expertise was wider than simply lie-detection. She had appeared in court quite often as an expert witness, testifying on the vagaries of memory and the mechanics of deception to prove that someone could have been manipulated into making a false confession, or that identification evidence was flawed, or prosecution witnesses had to be disbelieved for one reason or another.

'A fair amount. Hang on.' There was the sound of rustling paper down the telephone. 'No, tomorrow's completely clogged, but actually there is a gap on Tuesday morning. I've got a meeting with some solicitors first thing, but then I should be out by eleven-thirty. If Antonia would agree, I could go round to her place after that and see the nanny. Since it won't be competing with any other work, my accountant can hardly complain if it's *pro bono*. Anyway, it's none of her business.'

'Oh Emma, you are wonderful.' Trish had never seriously doubted that Emma would be prepared to use her expertise in such a cause, but her readiness to offer her skills – and without charging for them – was the one

107

bright spot in an otherwise dreadful day. Antonia could easily afford to pay top rates, but it might be easier to persuade her to agree to the test if it could be presented as a freebie. She'd always liked a bargain.

'And, you know, Trish, it's not just a question of whether or not the nanny's been telling the truth about what happened in the playground. It's quite possible that the right questions will elicit memories she's not aware she has.'

'I hadn't thought of that. I'll tell Antonia.'

'How is she?'

'As you'd expect: desperate with terror for Charlotte, and expressing most of it as aggression. I found that tougher to take than I should have done. She must be in torment.'

'Do you think there's any hope for Charlotte? I mean that she could be still alive.'

'I keep trying to believe it, but I don't actually see how, unless it's like that awful Belgian case. You know the one, where that man's thought to have kidnapped young girls and kept them in terrible conditions in secret cellars until he had a buyer for them.'

'Oh, Trish. Please God, it's not like that. D'you want to talk about it? Would it help? I could come to you or you could come here. Whatever.'

'I don't think so, Emma. But thanks. The only thing that's going to help is getting some good news. Or maybe any news at all. At least if we knew for certain what had happened, we could all start trying to cope, but as it is . . . No, I think I'll stay here on my own. Sorry to be churlish.'

'You're not. And ring me if you change your mind. Would you like me to cancel Willow?'

'What?'

'I'm not surprised you've forgotten, but you and I were

due to go to the Worths' tomorrow night. Would you like me to cancel it? Willow would understand. God! Anyone would, and she's always been better than most at knowing how one feels.'

Trish had completely forgotten the long-standing arrangement for dinner with a novelist friend of Emma's, who was married to a senior police officer.

'No, I don't think so,' she said. If the invitation's still open, I'll go. I like them both so much and Tom might be able to help.'

'Good. Eight o'clock then. And don't worry about dressing up.'

'Fine. I'll see you there.'

'OK. But if you change your mind – or if something happens – ring me and I'll sort it. Bye.'

Trish dialled her mother's number. 'Hi, it's me.'

'Trish, darling. How are you? I haven't rung because I've assumed that you'd be with Antonia. How is she? Has there been any news of Charlotte?'

'Not yet. I'm glad you know about it. I don't think I could have gone through the whole story again.'

'No, I should think you need to forget it – if one ever could. *You* were lost once, for about twenty minutes, and I nearly exploded with terror. What Antonia must be going through! I wish her mother wasn't dead. She must need her so much at the moment. I've written and offered to help, but I didn't want to ring. I thought she'd have enough to deal with, and I knew you'd be there.'

'Yes, I was,' said Trish as she fell into the familiar comfort her mother had always managed to give her. She felt even sorrier for Antonia than she had done all day. 'I don't remember ever being lost. How odd! You'd have thought something so frightening would stick in the mind.'

'Or be buried as too painful. You were four or five, I

think. One of your schoolfriends' mothers had taken you to a fair and turned her back. She wasn't a bad woman and she rang me the instant she realised you'd gone, but I could have killed her. And I never did manage to forgive her. We might have been friends, I think, looking back – but not after that.'

A fair? Noisy – bangy – very colourful and what felt like millions of people washing around her like a sea? Yes, Trish thought, I do remember something. And Charlotte's even younger than I was then. And I was only lost for a few minutes. It's been more than twenty-four hours now. What have they done to her? Is it over yet? Oh, God! Would it be easier if we knew for sure that she was dead? Then at least they couldn't be hurting her any more. Oh, Charlotte.

CHAPTER NINE

'You look as though you haven't slept, Mike,' said Stephen as he leaned across the polished slate worktop to help himself to coffee from the Alessi espresso pot on Monday morning. 'What's the worry this time?' Mike looked up from his huge breakfast cup, brushing his moustache first one way then the other, as he always did when he was in a state. His perfect skin was paler than it should have been, and he was biting the inside of his cheeks. His round khaki eyes were full of blank, mindless terror.

'I'm all right.'

Stephen suppressed a sigh as he recognised all the signs. He mentally ran through his diary for the morning, relieved to remember that he had no meetings scheduled until well after eleven. If Mike really lost it, and it looked as though he might, there should be time to get him reasonably stable again and still not miss anything too important in the office. There was not much point in asking questions while he was still hanging on; the outburst would come soon enough as it was.

Stephen reached for the newspapers. The *Daily Mercury* was on top of the pile and he looked at it with disdain. Mike insisted they took it, but really it was the most dreadful rag.

'Isn't that one of your pupils?' he said, catching sight of the headline. 'Charlotte Welbock? Daughter of the rich banker?'

There was a gasp from Mike and Stephen looked up at him again.

'Yes,' he said. 'And see what it says: someone's killed her. Look, Steve.'

Accustomed to Mike's dramatics, Stephen carefully read the article under the screaming headline, picking out the truth without difficulty.

'Not necessarily,' he said, when he reached the end of the account. 'She's disappeared and there are fears for her safety, that's all. What are you in such a state about? All right, she's one of your pupils, but you can't know her that well.'

Mike shook his head, but his eyes were still full of horror. 'She's such a sweet little thing, Steve. If you'd seen her, you'd understand. She started her first lesson all white and quivering on the edge of the pool but too brave to cry. And now she just leaps off the edge into my arms, miles out of her depth, squealing with pleasure. She's so trusting, you can't imagine. And so sweet, Steve. I wish you'd seen her.'

Stephen softened his voice and his expression until no one, not even Mike-in-a-panic, could possibly read criticism in it.

'It's horrible for her and her parents, and I can see you don't like thinking about what might have happened to her, but there's nothing here to make you all of a doo-dah like this. What's the problem? Come on, Mike, out with it.'

Tears welled in Mike's eyes, making them even more lustrous and appealing than usual; the long lashes looked like black silk. 'She's only four, Steve.'

'So?' he said. His voice was still not unkind or even cool, but Mike started biting the inside of his cheeks again. 'I know it's sad, but it isn't really anything to do with you, now is it?'

'No. No. Of course it isn't. How could it be? But will they believe me? The police. You know what the police are like. They'll come to the pool. I had her for a lesson only a couple of hours before it happened. They're bound to think I . . . You know.'

Stephen walked round to the other side of the worktop and put both hands on Mike's head, smoothing the thick hair away from his face, and then dried his eyes with a perfectly ironed fine linen handkerchief. Mike looked up at him with a nauseatingly familiar mixture of fear, gratitude and begging.

'Don't get yourself in such a state. Listen, Mike, you might conceivably have a reason to panic if the child had been a boy, but even the stupidest, most ignorant police officer isn't going to think a man like you could do anything to a four-year-old girl.'

'But most of them don't think there's any difference between gay and paedophile. They'll come after me and and then probably you, too, and make our life hell. It's not only me I'm worried about. It's you too. You'll hate it if they start accusing me and it gets in the papers. I'd do anything not to make trouble for you, Steve. You know that.'

Stephen sighed. He and Mike had lived together for nearly three years. He loved Mike beyond reason – and would have done almost anything for him – but there were times when the boy's irrational terrors drove him to the brink of fury. Long experience had told him that any sign of anger would only make the panic – and his own impatience – worse. Breathing deeply to instil calm into his mind, he fetched them both more coffee and poured out a bowl of the special muesli Mike concocted from little bags of seeds and nuts he bought in secret health-food shops all over London, added cranberry juice and put a spoon in Mike's hand.

'Eat,' he commanded as gently as the necessary firmness would allow. 'And while you eat, listen. Carefully. For one thing I don't suppose they will even bother to ask what this child was doing in a swimming pool on Saturday morning if she was lifted from a park in the afternoon. For another, I cannot imagine you were ever left alone with her at the pool, were you?'

Mike shook his head, a dripping spoonful of muesli halfway to his mouth.

'Who was with you?'

'She has individual lessons. The nanny brought her and stayed beside the pool all the time with the step-father. He's not always there through the lessons; sometimes he just comes to collect them at the end. This time he was there all the time.'

'Did you see them leave the pool?'

'Yes.'

'All three of them together?'

'Yes.'

'There you are then. What on earth are you worrying about? Eat.'

Mike obediently chewed a mouthful of oats, pumpkin seeds and chopped hazelnuts doused in juice.

'But what if the police come here and start asking questions?' he asked when he had swallowed.

'Even if they do, so what? We're not doing anything illegal here. At least I'm not,' said Stephen. He was an administrative civil servant in the Home Office and

114

several times in the past had had to explain to Mike with as much ferocity as he thought the boy could bear that he would not have drugs of any kind in the flat. 'Are you?'

Mike did not answer. After a moment, Stephen saw his cheeks begin to flush.

'Mike?' He did allow some of the heavily suppressed irritation into his voice at that point.

'How can you ask?' Mike said, looking desperately hurt. 'I promised I wouldn't, and I haven't. Not here, not at the pool, not at the gym – not anywhere. I'm clean. I've told you.'

'Good. Because I warn you, if you do – for whatever reason – it's curtains.'

'Oh don't, please, Steve. Not now, not while there's this horror hanging over me. I can't take it now. I can't.'

'It's not hanging over you,' said his lover unmoved by the hysteria, 'and your promises haven't always been kept.'

'I know, Steve. I'm sorry. I . . .' He looked up at Stephen again like a wounded fox. Stephen was perfectly well aware that he was supposed to offer a forgiving hug. But foxes, wounded or otherwise, can bite; they can also disappear to lick their wounds in dangerous company. Stephen put down his coffee cup, fetched the jacket of his suit and his briefcase, and slipped *The Times* and the *Financial Times* into it.

'I wish you'd let your lunatic terrors about things you couldn't ever have done teach you a bit of sense about the misdemeanours you do commit,' he said without much passion as he checked the contents of the case. 'Are you at the pool today?'

'Yes, all morning: group lessons. And then I'm training at the gym this afternoon. It's adult non-swimmers at the pool this evening. OK?'

'OK. Well, take care.' Stephen started for the door and then relented. Mike leaned against him and Stephen felt his arms moving round the boy's back in spite of himself.

'You drive me mad sometimes, you fool,' he said affectionately as he removed himself.

'I know,' said Mike, smiling at him once more with all the radiance that had been dimmed by fear and apology, 'but you love me, don't you?'

'Don't wheedle and don't trade on it. Are you going to be all right now?'

Mike nodded and apologised again, as he always did. Stephen patted his cheek, well aware of the aspects of his own character that allowed – or perhaps even encouraged – Mike's chosen games and left the exquisitely appointed flat. As he walked towards South Kensington tube station, he was considering whether it would be worth asking around at the office in case anyone had heard anything about the kidnapped child. In spite of the reassurance he had given Mike, Stephen knew that there were in fact still plenty of people ignorant enough to make just the kind of idiotic assumptions that had frightened the boy.

It was not the police that bothered Stephen as much as the journalists. They could be much worse, and the last thing in the world he needed at that moment was any publicity. Certain people in the office knew about him, of course; it was stupid to lie about your sexual orientation when you were being vetted. But provided there was no scandal, nobody seemed to mind too much these days. Photographs in sleazy newspapers and tabloid taunts would be something else entirely, and would completely scupper any hope of promotion. He'd probably be offered early retirement or – worse – be moved to MAFF.

CHAPTER TEN

Trish was reading her way through a whole heap of newspapers in case there was anything helpful in any of them, and trying not to look at the photographs of herself apparently rushing furtively out of Antonia's house with an astonishingly unpleasant expression on her face. She could not stop staring at one photograph and hoped it was a bad likeness. She was sure that she did not have such sneering, hooded eyes, such a beaky nose or such a cruel-looking mouth. Having checked in the nearest mirror and seen only her vulnerabilities, she returned to the paper, wondering whether the editor had taken a dislike to her and decided to 'improve' her portrait, as some had done to other notorious women in the past.

The different papers' articles ran the whole gamut, from a sober analysis of the chances of Charlotte's being found alive to liplicking excitement and a barely disguised outpouring of satisfaction that a rich working mother should have been so adequately punished.

Becoming aware that the sun was blazing in through the huge windows of her flat and that the atmosphere was fuggy, Trish pushed the offending tabloid away from her and opened every single one of the windows, letting in comparatively cool, fresh air.

'There are compensations to working at home,' she said aloud as she went back to the papers. In the old days she had never been able to air the flat fully because she was rarely there in daylight and Southwark was not an area in which anyone would want to leave open windows after dark.

She was still wearing last night's T-shirt, inviting the reader to dip her in honey and throw her to the lesbians, her teeth were unbrushed and her long legs were bare and more bristly than they should have been. When the front-door bell rang, she made sure the shirt, which almost reached her knees, was not rucked up and opened the door cautiously.

The postman handed her a package that was too large to go through the letter box.

'Thanks,' she said, daring him to comment. His face split into a delighted smile between the dreadlocks.

'Great shirt, man.'

'Thanks,' she said again, but in a quite different voice. 'Good, isn't it? Bye.'

He was already halfway down the iron steps and raised a hand in casual acknowledgment. She took the heavy package back to the table and began to pick the brown tape off it. Inside the well-used Jiffy bag, there was a letter from her publisher on top of a heap of laser-printed paper.

Dear Trish,
How's it going? I know you've been trawling the Net, too, but I wasn't sure you'd have come across this lot. Don't worry; I haven't lost my marbles printing it off for you. I know it would have been quicker and cheaper to

send you an E-mail, but I hit the wrong key by mistake and before I could stop it, half this stuff was already spewing out of the printer. At that stage I thought I might as well finish the job.

I don't want to nag, but have you any idea when you can let me see some material? We've got the sales conference coming up next month and I'd like to give the reps something. With a book this difficult, I shall need to get a real buzz going if we're to get it into the non-specialist trade.

The design department have come up with a few sketches for the cover. Could we make a date for you to come and see what you think about the ideas? I want you to be happy with whatever we do decide to put on the cover, really happy. Authors are so often bamboozled into accepting something they feel misrepresents their work and I don't want that happening to you on this one.

I know you hate the telephone, but will you ring me? Christopher.

'How do you know I hate the telephone?' asked Trish aloud. 'I've never told you. I've never told anyone. And I've rung you as often as I had to.'

Her gratitude for his percipience faded as she reread the letter and understood that in spite of its friendliness, it was in fact a demand for the three chapters she had said she would deliver by the beginning of May. They were still in draft form, heavily edited, rewritten about sixteen times, but still not right. Writing for publication was so different from planning opening and closing arguments for court that Trish was amazed any author ever managed to let a page out of her sight. At least in a trial, on your feet, you could tailor what you had written to the reactions you saw in the jury's faces – or the judge's. You could correct and embellish as you went.

With the book, she had only one chance to say every-thing as she meant it and, which was even more difficult, to work out exactly what it was she *did* mean. All the questions she hoped she would have been able to answer as she researched other people's cases and drew on her own seemed to get more difficult with every extra hour she spent on them.

Would it have been better for a maltreated child to have been aborted? Were there some people who were so inadequate or perverse that they should never be allowed to have children? And if so, who should decide? The courts, obviously, but who should bring the cases and would there ever be enough court time to deal with them? And how could the prospective parents be prevented from having children, short of forcible sterilisation, which was not an option in a civi-lised state?

What should you do with a woman in her very early twenties who had five children already, none of whom she fed properly or was able to control? Would they be better off in so-called care? Should they be taken by social workers for adoption by intelligent, well-meaning, wholesome infertile couples who longed for children and would give them everything the more fortunate took for granted? Was parental love (and in that particular case, it had been very clear that the mother did love her children even though she could not look after them) better than clean clothes and regular meals? And were any adopted children truly happy?

Should children who had been physically or sexually abused by a parent be removed from the family home or should the abuser be exiled? And if you forcibly removed a parent, how could you make the child believe that it was not his or her fault that the family had been smashed and probably driven into poverty?

How could you stop parents resenting their children, ill-treating them, corrupting them, exploiting them, or simply hurting them? Who should draw the lines between what was unpleasant but no business of the state's and what was intolerable in any civilised society? And how should the lines be policed? And how could you ensure that children taken into care were given absolute safety as well as all the things their families had not been able to provide, and later sent gently into the world instead of being hurled without resources into a jobless, hopeless, homeless existence, in which they were prey to the worst sort of exploiters?

Trish knew by then that the questions were not answerable. Very few of the suggestions thrown up by what had happened to her clients or by her own memories, needs and ideas were usable. However much her instincts might scream at her that no woman should be allowed to give birth unless she was self-aware and intelligent enough to avoid punishing the child for her own frustrations and shortcomings, or that all men should have their fertility controlled until they were in an emotional and financial position to be adequate fathers to their children, she knew they were wrong.

Trish was going to have to come to terms with that if she were ever to produce a book that would be worth anything to anyone. If she did not get down to it soon, she would have to give up and get back to her real work. Perhaps Christopher's letter would force her to finish the sixty-odd pages she had chewed over for so long. Or perhaps it would not. Until Charlotte was found, it was going to be hard to concentrate on anything else.

Even so, Trish leafed through the pile of printout Christopher had sent and saw that it was the report of a particularly difficult Australian case, which only confirmed her own doubts about allowing the inadequate to bear and care for children.

Pushing the printout to one side and trying not to think about the two maltreated children it described, she went back to her newspapers. One of them had a large photograph of Antonia and Charlotte on the front. Antonia was wearing a severely tailored black suit, with her hair newly highlighted, and her makeup discreet. Charlotte was wearing dungarees; there seemed to be chocolate around her mouth, and she was brandishing a sticky-looking spoon.

Trish recognised the photograph as one that had originally been published in an article about high-flying businesswomen who manage to keep their humanity and care deeply for their children. To anyone who knew Antonia it was obvious that the photograph had been carefully posed. In ordinary circumstances she would never have risked holding such a messy child anywhere near her suit – or allowed the child to eat chocolate in the first place. Antonia had always had unrealistically high standards of both cleanliness and nutrition where Charlotte was concerned.

Beside the double portrait was a shot of the playground. There was a tall row of swings for older children hanging from a gibbet-like wooden structure and a smaller set of bucket-seated ones for toddlers. The big slide for which Charlotte had waited reared up in the background of the photograph like a surfacing sea monster. There were no children in the picture, which must have been taken at dawn before the park opened, but it was clear enough that the queue for the slide would have stretched along the fenced side of the playground at the opposite side from the entrance.

The height of the fence was about half that of the

slide. Without any humans in the shot for scale it was difficult to estimate its exact height, but it did seem too high for someone to reach over and pluck a child from the other side. That must mean that whoever had taken Charlotte had persuaded her to leave the queue and walk the whole width of the playground to the gate.

'The dog that didn't bark in the night,' Trish said, with a vague memory of a Sherlock Holmes story her mother had read aloud during one of their shared crazes. The Sherlock Holmes one had lasted for nearly three months when Trish was nine or ten, some time after her father had left.

Thinking about the people Charlotte might have trusted enough to let them take her out of the queue without protesting, Trish realised that her bare legs were covered with goose pimples and she was beginning to shiver. She abandoned the newspapers to shower in very hot water and dress.

That afternoon she drove across the river, up through the City and then west to Kensington, where she miraculously found an empty parking meter close to the park. Having collected her camera and locked the car, she went to see the playground for herself. On the way she noticed several yellow signs asking for information about a child abducted on Saturday and, later, she was stopped by a uniformed constable with a clipboard who wanted to ask a long series of questions. She answered them as fully as possible, giving her name and address and explaining her connection to the case; then she left him.

The newspaper's picture had given a fairly accurate impression of the playground, she saw as she soon as she got there. Pacing the distance between the slide and the gate, she decided that it was at least thirty yards. She also discovered that the fence was far too high to allow any child to be lifted over without a ladder on both sides. But the slide was nowhere near as tall as she had expected. Surprised at herself, she realised that she had been remembering the big slides of her childhood and picturing it from the perspective of someone of three-feet-six.

'Trish! What are you doing here?'

She turned from her contemplation of the fence to see Hal Marstall, Emma Gnatche's boyfriend. Liking Emma so much, Trish had always tried to warm to Hal, but she had not succeeded so far. He was attractive enough and good company, but Trish didn't feel at ease with men of such conspicuous charm and good looks. His job got in the way, too, and she had the feeling that he was never off-duty and would sacrifice any friend for a scoop.

To Trish, it had always seemed that journalists like Hal, working for newspapers like the *Daily Mercury*, used crimes against children to whip up and focus the frustrations of not very clever people who did not have enough to do or think about. When they were roused to outrage, the damage they could do was appalling. That the outrage was often wholly reasonable did not affect Trish's disapproval; in her view, lynching was never right, whatever the provocation.

'Much the same as you, I imagine, unless you've changed jobs, Hal.'

'Me? No, I'm still with the *Mercury*.'

She saw that he was about to ask another question and hurried to get her own in first. 'Why are you on this? I thought you were doing some local-government corruption story.'

Hal raised an elegant dark eyebrow. 'Is that what

Emma told you? Yes, I see she did. Odd. I'd have thought she'd know better by now. I don't go round tattling about her work.'

'She knows I'm trustworthy, Hal, and she didn't give me any clues about which local authority,' she said, noticing that his attitude to Emma seemed to have changed considerably since she had first seen them together, when he had treated Emma as a cross between a goddess and a particularly delicious meal. Even more wary of him than before, Trish asked what he believed had happened to Charlotte.

Hal looked back over his shoulder so that he could survey the whole playground. 'It was someone she knew.'

'Unless she just grew bored and wandered off and got lost – or run over. Perhaps her body was trapped under a lorry and dragged. It's possible that no one would have noticed.' She saw an expression of derision in Hal's dark eyes, and added slowly enough to keep her dignity: 'Unlikely, but possible.'

'Hardly. No, I'm sure she was nabbed and by someone she trusted.'

'That's what it looks like,' Trish agreed, 'unless there was some kind of invisible pulley that whisked her up over the fence.'

'So that's what you were staring at so beadily. I thought you must have seen something on the ground outside. My money's on the nanny.'

'I'll bet it is.' A lot of the pent-up anger sounded in Trish's voice. It seemed to amuse Hal. 'It would make a good story, wouldn't it? "Nanny from Hell strikes in Kensington".'

Hal grinned engagingly and pushed back his soft dark hair as though he had seen too many charming English actors being winsomely self-deprecating on the big screen.

'Not half as a good as "Selfish Superwoman Abandons Child to Psychopath".'

'Don't, Hal. Even as a joke. Antonia's in agony. Don't twist the knife just to get a few extra readers.'

'She's news, Trish, and she made herself into that deliberately. She uses us when she wants to stir up a profile-raising bout of controversy to boost her career; she can't complain when we go after her over something like this.'

'Oh, I expect she can,' said Trish as she thought with satisfaction about how much and how power-fully Antonia would probably complain. 'It's a game to you, isn't it, trying to catch celebrities out? You all want photographs of famous beauties looking like dogs and pieces about the ultra-successful getting their comeuppance. It's a good way to feed the jealousy of people who are never going to be successful, isn't it? Why can't you leave them alone in their misery?'

'I don't make the rules about what sells newspapers, Trish. I just report crime.'

'But only crime that affects the rich and famous or titillates your readers.'

Hal shrugged, looking rather less charming but more interested.

'And there's nothing so titillating to the British people as the abduction or seduction of a child, is there?' said Trish, disliking him more than usual.

'Is that a quote from your so-far invisible book?' he asked with a sneer.

'Part of what I'm writing covers the reasons why people get so excited when there are crimes against chil-dren, yes,' she answered steadily, 'and crimes committed *by* children, too. It's a strange contradiction that reading about both should give people so much pleasure.'

'Hal!' A shout from the far side of the playground

126

from a man with a selection of cameras slung across his chest made Hal wave and yell something about 'being right with you'. He turned back to Trish.

'I think you're misinterpreting the excitement. It's not sexual, but—'

'I never said it was. I said it was titillating. It gives people a frisson. It may be a frisson of horror, but there's enjoyment in it, too. Admit it.'

'I still think you're wrong. Look, Trish, if you hear anything, will you—'

'No, Hal. I'm sorry, but I won't tell you anything.'

'The interest the press stirs up will probably be what gets her back – if she's still alive.'

'I doubt it. The press has never saved any other abducted child, has it?'

'You've been getting cynical, Trish, these last few months. You want to watch that. It's a right turn-off. Good to run into you.'

'And you,' she said automatically as she watched him lope off to the other side of the playground to collect his photographer. She wondered what exactly Emma saw in him, and then caught herself up as she recognised a familiar reaction. When not doing his job, Hal was probably as sensitive as he was undoubtedly intelligent, and with luck he valued Emma as she deserved to be valued. That was a great deal.

'Aren't they awful?' said a voice from some way off.

Trish looked quickly to her left and saw a pleasant-looking young woman coming towards her with a scarlet ball in one hand and a tricycle in the other. Releasing the frown between her eyes, Trish smiled politely.

'Awful,' she agreed when the woman reached her side. 'Had he been asking you questions, too?'

'Yeah, about a friend of mine. What did he want from you?'

'Anything I knew about the child who was abducted here on Saturday,' said Trish, assuming Nicky was the friend in question. 'I've met him before and he knows I'm close to the family, so I suppose he thought it was worth trying to pump me. Is your friend Nicky Bagshot?'

'Yeah. Poor Nicky,' said the young woman. 'He told us she's getting all the blame for what happened to Charlotte. That's not right, you know. It wasn't her fault.'

'How d'you know? Were you here on Saturday?'

'No,' she said obstinately. 'It's my half day, but I know she couldn't have anything to do with it. She's a good nanny, responsible, and lovely with Charlotte. And she can be very difficult, you know.'

'I know she can. And I know she's fond of Nicky. She told me so. Look, my name's Trish Maguire.' She held out her hand.

'Susan Jacks,' said the young woman, putting down the trike to shake hands. 'Nicky's a good friend of mine, and I don't like what they're saying. It's too easy to blame the nanny and we don't have any protection, none of us. We had the police here first and now all those journalists. We thought you must be one of them till we saw you looking so cross at that man.'

'No,' said Trish, still smiling. 'I'm not a journalist. I'm a lawyer. But I did come to see how it could have happened, so that I could understand.'

'Do you think it was Nicky's fault?'

'No. From everything I've heard, I think she was just unlucky. It must've happened because she wasn't watching, but I think that was a horrible chance. I don't think she was responsible for it.'

'Great,' said Susan energetically. 'That's just great. D'you want to come and meet the others, then?'

'Others?' said Trish, looking in the direction of Susan's

pointing hand. She saw a group of young women sitting on benches arranged around a large sandpit in the corner of the playground furthest from the slide. 'Yes, I'd like that.'

Susan introduced her to six or seven nannies, all of whom in the intervals of calling instructions to their charges, breaking up fights, and picking up the children when they fell, reiterated their belief in Nicky's innocence of anything and everything.

'Susan said Charlotte can be difficult,' said Trish impartially to all of them when they had stopped telling her what a brilliant nanny Nicky was and how gentle with Charlotte. 'D'you agree with that?'

'Can't they all?' said a strapping New Zealander with a mop of black curls and a big pretty face. 'But Lottie gets it from her mother. Have you ever met her?'

'Once or twice,' said Trish, smiling. The friendly atmosphere cooled distinctly.

'Oh,' said the New Zealander, having exchanged glances with some of the others. 'You'll know about the hereditary temper then.'

'Yes,' Trish admitted in the interests of regaining their confidence. She knew all about it, and hated it. 'But what about Robert, Charlotte's stepfather? Have any of you ever met him?'

It seemed they had all seen him quite often, because he made a habit of collecting Nicky and Charlotte from the playground whenever he could. That seemed odd to Trish, considering how busy he was supposed to be.

'What's he like?' she asked.

'He's all right,' said the New Zealander. 'And much nicer to Nicky than Antonia ever was. Not that we saw much of her, except when she was checking up on Nicky. Honestly, that poor girl. Nothing was good enough for Antonia, not the way Nicky made Lottie's bed nor the food she gave her for lunch nor the stories she told her or the toys she let her play with. They always had to come here in the afternoons although Lottie liked Holland Park better.'

'I know,' said Susan. 'Antonia even used to check up on that – where Nicky'd brought her in the afternoons. I ask you!'

'She was a right cow,' said the New Zealander. 'It must've been a hard job keeping her sweet, but Nicky did it as well as anyone could have. Rupie!' she shouted suddenly. 'Stop it. Give it back.'

Trish looked behind her to see a small boy with bright brown hair dragging a large, beautifully dressed doll round and round the edge of a puddle while a small girl pleaded tearfully for its return. As his nanny reached his side, he deliberately flung the doll into the middle of the water and then started to howl as though he was being tortured, although she had not even touched him by then.

As the little group around the sandpit watched Rupie and his victim being sorted out with a firm hand, Trish asked the other nannies whether they had ever noticed anyone odd hanging about the playground.

'No one,' said Susan, who seemed to be their unofficial leader. 'Not that I noticed anyway. There are always people about, and sometimes tramps wander in and scare the children, but no one regular.'

Most of the others shook their well-washed heads, but one, much taller than the rest and with a shock of bright-pink hair that must have given her employer pause when she first saw it, said, 'Except the guy with the dog.'

'Yes,' said another of them, who was relacing the red-leather boots of a cheerful girl of about two, whose face was liberally smeared with strawberry jam. 'But he wasn't odd. He was just a dogwalker like any other.'

'Although he did use to hang about outside the fence and stare at the children. He didn't look pervy, but he'd stand and watch for as long as the dog would put up with it. D'you think he could've had something to do with Charlotte?' said Susan.

'No,' said Pink Hair. 'He couldn't. He was only ever here on Wednesdays.'

'But then none of you are around at the weekends,' Trish reminded her. 'He might have come back then. What did he look like?'

Tall, they agreed, tall and quite old – in his forties probably. No, Pink Hair thought, he was more than that. Not very good-looking, they said, and shabbily dressed.

'A tramp?' suggested Trish hopefully, trying hard not to recognise the man they were describing.

'No, just shabby. You know, old brown corduroy trousers and a tatty waxed jacket and desert boots. A long face with lots of lines and those round glasses. Tortoiseshell.'

'What about the dog? What was that like?'

'Mad and noisy,' said Pink Hair. 'It was a big black thing and it hated waiting around and always made a noise. That's why I don't think he was odd. If he'd been a perve, he'd have left the dog behind. It always made people look at him. He just liked watching kids. People can do that without being weird.'

'Yes, it sounds like it,' said Trish, fairly sure of the dog's identity. 'Was it plain black, the dog?'

'No. It had one of those orangey noses, you know?'

'Yes, I do know. Well, thanks. You've all been very helpful.'

'D'you think we should have told the police?' asked Susan, looking worried. 'About the Wednesday man and the dog?'

'Probably,' said Trish, quite glad they had not. Everything they had said made him sound like Ben, but there must be other men in London who would fit the description – and even be walking a dog like Daisy. Trish wanted to get more evidence before the full horror of a police investigation was unleashed over Ben's head. 'It's generally a good idea to tell them everything they ask.'

'That's all right then,' said Pink Hair. 'They didn't ask. They just wanted to know about Nicky – like the journalists – and if we'd been here on Saturday. And if anyone had ever been seen approaching any of the children. The guy with the dog never approached anyone.'

'Well, you'd probably better tell them if they do come back and ask,' said Trish, wondering what on earth Ben could have been playing at – if it had been him – and how she was going to get him on his own to ask without risking Bella's intervention.

She said goodbye to the nannies and found a telephone box on her way back to the parking meter. Dialling Ben's number, she noticed that her hands were sweating.

'He couldn't have had anything to do with it,' she said aloud as she listened to the clicks on the line as the number registered with the exchange's software. 'He couldn't have. He's honest, I know he is. He's not my father; even though he kicked Antonia out and wouldn't have anything to do with Charlotte, he's nothing like my father. He couldn't have hurt her. But if he isn't involved, why has he been lying? Why didn't he tell me he came to the park to watch her? What the hell's going on?'

'Hello, this is Ben and Bella Weblock's number. Neither of us can come to the phone right now, but if you leave a message we'll get back to you. Or if it's urgent you could try Ben at school or Bella at her consulting rooms. The numbers are . . .'

Trish listened, planning her message with care. When she heard the beep, she said clearly: 'Ben, this is Trish. I need to talk to you. It's very urgent. Could you ring me at the flat as soon as you get in? If you're not back before I have to go out, will you leave a message saying when I can get you tomorrow? I really need to talk to you. Thanks. Bye.'

CHAPTER ELEVEN

'How's Hal?' asked Tom Worth as he poured more white wine into Emma's glass.

Trish, who had noticed that Emma was getting through the wine much more quickly than usual, watched her friend with interest mixed with a certain amount of pity. It seemed that Willow had been watching, too, for she held out her own glass, which was still half-full and said meaningfully, 'Don't be stingy, Tom. I want more as well.'

He looked at her in surprise and then, tactlessly, back at Emma.

'It's all right, Tom. There's no mystery. I just don't talk about it much. Hal's playing silly buggers at the moment, and I'm not quite sure where I stand.'

Oh hell, thought Trish. And I've been so worried about Charlotte that I didn't even notice she was upset. No wonder Hal was aggressive in the playground. He must have thought I was about to savage him for whatever he's doing.

'Put my size twelves in it there, didn't I, Em?' said Tom. 'Sorry.'

'Smack in the middle of it, Tom, but don't worry – I'll live. After all, we've had three good years and a lot of fun. Not many people get more than that – or as much. And anyway, it's nothing to what Trish is going through.'

'No,' agreed Willow, a tall stylish woman with a smooth bell of dark-red hair and wonderfully simple clothes. 'It must be unspeakable, Trish. She's your goddaughter, isn't she, Charlotte Weblock?'

'No. Second cousin once removed. That sounds more distant than it is. She . . . she means a lot to me.'

'I'm sorry. Tom said there's been no news since she disappeared.'

'None,' said Trish, wishing that she had not allowed herself to spend the afternoon fantasising about what it would feel like to arrive at the Worths' pretty mews house to be greeted with some good news of Charlotte that the police had been keeping secret from everyone else. It had been a silly thing to do; now she was feeling worse than ever. 'And I don't see how there can be, not now, after so long. Do you, Tom?'

'It's a tough one, Trish. Previous cases would suggest it's unlikely that she's still alive, but it has happened. You know they've been stepping up the house-to-house enquiries all round the park?'

'No, I didn't,' said Trish. 'I haven't any line to the police, and I can't keep ringing poor Antonia for news. We did speak this afternoon, and she told me then that all the known paedophiles in the area have been checked and cleared. Why are they doing more house-to-house interviews?'

'Apparently your cousin said that Charlotte gets bored very easily and the current theory, as I understand it, is that as the playground was so full and the queue for the slide so long, she got fed up waiting for her turn, wandered out of the playground and got lost.'

'But then what?' asked Willow as they moved into the dining room and sat down.

Tom shrugged. 'Who knows?'

'Have the house-to-house enquiries turned anything up?' Trish asked.

'Not by the time I left the office this evening. I checked because I knew you'd want to know.'

'You are kind, Tom.' Trish thought again of the suggestion she had made to Hal and wondered whether she and everyone else had been getting so hysterical over what might have happened to Charlotte that they had missed something obvious. 'Do you know what they think happened after Charlote wandered off, if she did?'

'Not in detail. They've decided she couldn't have run into the road and been knocked down. All the casualty departments have been checked.'

'And anyway, it was the middle of a busy Saturday afternoon. Wouldn't that kind of road accident have been witnessed?' said Willow.

'You'd have thought so, yes. At the moment they're working on the possibility that she pottered out of the park and was picked up so unobtrusively that no one noticed.'

'In a car, presumably?' Once again it was Willow who asked the question.

'Probably, Will. Hence the interviews with every-one who lives or works on the park's perimeter. And of course the searches of all the films from the CCTV cameras. There are lots of cameras round there, and I understand all the films have been col-lected.'

'That sounds as though they've given up suspecting the nanny,' said Emma, obviously thinking about her polygraph test.

Tom piled the soup bowls together and stood up. 'Let's say that they're still keeping an open mind.'

'Presumably on both the nanny and the stepfather,' Emma went on, as though she knew how hard it was for Trish to talk and yet how much she wanted to know everything Tom could tell them about the police investigation. He did not answer, just smiled slightly and carried the soup plates out to the kitchen.

'Your poor cousin,' said Willow, looking at Trish. 'She must be going through hell worrying whether her boyfriend could be involved and thinking about all the signs she might have missed, the hints that he was interfering with the child, or hurting her.'

Trish thought of the bruises, but she said nothing.

'She must be having to weigh up her own past happiness with him against what he may have done to her child and realising that they couldn't ever balance.'

'Steady on, Will,' said Tom, returning and reaching for the wine bottle. 'There's no evidence he's been doing anything whatsoever.'

'No,' she said, crunching the last of the hot salty biscuit that had been served with the cold pea soup. Trish was pleased to see that in spite of Willow's style and her riches, she talked with her mouth full. She probably said 'shit', too, and maybe even worse. It would be interesting to see how she would deal with Bella Weblock.

'But it must be him, mustn't it? It's silly to pretend otherwise.'

'Antonia told me on the phone this afternoon that he's got an alibi,' said Trish. 'It must have checked out or the police would have arrested him by now. They're not stupid.'

'It's always good to hear a spontaneous tribute,' said

Tom, making her laugh unhappily. 'Will, shall I get the meat?'

'No. It's OK, I'll do it.'

'D'you know the officers doing the investigation?' Trish asked him as Emma got up to help Willow.

'Not personally, no. But the whole force is aware of the case. Everyone gets in a state where children are concerned. They're working round the clock, Trish,' he said, touching the back of her hand in a surprisingly comforting gesture. 'They know what may have happened. They're not fools, and they want her found as much as anyone.'

She nodded, too surprised by his touch and moved by his concern to trust her voice.

. 'What about your cousin's ex-husband, Charlotte's father?' Willow asked, returning with a charger edged with roasted artichoke hearts and filled with sliced lamb fillets cooked with olive oil, lemon and garlic and covered with green olives and faggots of fresh thyme. 'Could he be involved?'

'Not possibly,' said Emma so firmly that Trish did not have to say anything, which was a relief.

Until she had heard why Ben had lied about not knowing Charlotte and found out what he was doing in the park, she could not bear to talk about him.

'We should really be drinking retsina with this,' said Willow, handing the plate of lamb to Trish.

'Over my dead body,' said Tom. He closed his eyes briefly as the inappropriateness of the image struck him.

'Help yourself, Trish,' Willow said. 'Weren't the papers awful, the way they reported what's happened to Charlotte?'

'Yes,' Trish said as she obediently spooned a tiny slice of meat and two olives on to the hot plate Emma had slid on to the table in front of her. 'As I said to . . . as I was saying to a journalist this morning, there's nothing like a child-abduction case to get everybody tickled up.'

'It's vile,' said Willow, clearly understanding exactly what she meant. 'A kind of collective wallow in excitingly delicious outrage.'

'Isn't that just because it's the worst thing they can imagine?' said Tom quietly. 'They're terrified for their own children and they can also remember the complete powerlessness they felt at that age. It doesn't take much imagination to go that one step further. Couldn't it be that?'

'Partly,' said Emma, who had been so badly bullied by her elder half-brother that she still had vivid memories of the horrible powerlessness of childhood. 'But don't you think there's also an element of . . . not so much *Schadenfreude*, because they're not actually enjoying other people's distress, but a feeling of: If it's happened to someone else's child, then it's less likely to happen to mine?'

'That's very charitable,' said Willow in a voice that made it clear that in that instance she did not much value charity. 'No, I'm with Trish; I think people like it. And that is revolting. What's your view of the nanny, Trish? You must know her.'

'Will,' said Tom severely.

'I'm interested,' said his wife, smiling at Trish. 'But we can talk about something else if you'd rather.'

'To tell you the truth, I can't really think about anything else at the moment.'

Willow shot a triumphant smile at her husband.

'I don't know the nanny well. But I do know that Charlotte loved her, and I quite liked her myself when we met yesterday. I can't see her as guilty. I really can't.'

'How did Antonia find her in the first place? Recommendation, advertisement, what?'

'Through Holland Park Helpers, apparently.'

'But they're good,' said Willow, sounding surprised. 'One of the few agencies that make thorough checks in the girls' backgrounds: police, medical and all that. That's why I get our temps from them when Mrs Rusham's on holiday. You know, it always amazes me that childminders have to be licensed before they can look after children, but there's no regulation of nannies at all.'

'Really?' said Emma, putting down her knife and fork. 'That seems almost incredible.'

'I know. Anyone can claim to be trained and some of the agencies don't even check that much, let alone the references or any criminal record they might have. They must—'

She stopped talking as she saw the slow, silent opening of the dining-room door. She nodded to Tom and, ignoring the door, started to talk loudly about the holiday they had planned near a Finnish lake later in the year.

Trish watched the door, waiting to see what would happen. When it was fully open she saw six-year-old Lucinda Worth, dressed in a pristine long, white nightgown edged with blue gingham. There was not a single crease in the fine cotton and her golden-brown hair was very smooth and obviously freshly brushed. She had blue velvet slippers on her feet. Although she had her thumb in her mouth, she looked in charge, assured and ready to join the party.

'Yes?' said Tom as severely as he could. Lucinda took her thumb out of her mouth and smiled at him, the large gaps in her front teeth adding considerably to the charm of her appearance.

'I had a nightmare,' she said, sidling towards Emma's chair. 'Hello.'

'Hello,' said Emma to her goddaughter, not even bothering to disguise her amusement or her affection. 'And what are you doing out of bed, madam?'

'I had a nightmare,' Lucinda repeated slowly and clearly as though to a foreigner or a fool. And then she spelled it out, letter by letter. Trish was impressed, but she could not help remembering Charlotte and the night when she, too, had interrupted dinner. Lucinda was only two years older, but she seemed decades more confident and able to take care of herself. Trish could hardly bear the contrast.

'So what?' asked Emma.

'So I need to talk about it,' Lucinda said, leaning against Emma's side and gazing beatifically at her parents, who were doing their best not to laugh.

'Do you, though?' said her father. 'Well, before you start, you'd better say good evening to Trish Maguire.'

'Good evening, Trish,' said Lucinda obediently.

'Good evening,' she answered, hard put to it to decide whether she found Lucinda's precocity amusing or irritating. It was all too clear that she had everything in that house arranged just as she wanted it.

'Now,' said Tom, 'what about this nightmare?'

'People were chasing me,' said Lucinda readily, but then it took her a moment to think what to say next. 'And I couldn't get away. And then there was a huge crane and the only way to flee was to jump off. But I woke up before I got to the floor.'

'Flee, eh? I see, and you were so upset by it that you brushed your hair and changed your nightie, were you?' said Willow, not managing to hide her pleasure in Lucinda's ease with words.

Lucinda paused for thought again while Trish thought

142

how lucky she was to be so at ease with her parents and able to have such absolute confidence in them both. The contrast between Lucinda's life and Charlotte's hit Trish even more sharply.

'No,' Lucinda went on eventually, 'but I knew you were having a dinner party and I thought it wouldn't be polite to be messy, so I changed first.'

'Lulu, stop telling porkies,' said Tom, sounding more severe than he felt. 'It's jolly nice to see you, even though you should be fast asleep, but I'd rather you just came down and said you wanted to join in than told lies about dreams you haven't had.'

'I have had it,' she said, climbing up on to Emma's lap and helping herself to an olive from Emma's plate.

'Just not tonight, eh?' said Emma from behind her. Lucinda pushed a strand of gleaming hair behind her ears and admitted it, adding, 'Rusty says nearly everyone has chasing dreams and it's not true if you hit the floor you wake up dead.'

Willow frowned. 'Who said it was?'

'A girl at school. So I asked Rusty. She knows everything,' said Lucinda, watching her mother from under her long dark lashes. Trish thought she must be expecting some kind of strong reaction, but all Willow said was: 'Do you ask Mrs Rusham lots of things?'

'Yes,' said Lucinda impatiently. 'I said Rusty knows everything.'

'A fair amount,' said Tom, 'but not quite everything. Your mother knows quite a lot too, and so do I.'

'Yes.' Lucinda rejected the olive she had just removed from Emma's plate and chose another one. 'But it's not the same.'

'Lucinda,' said Trish suddenly. 'Are all your nightmares about people chasing you?'

'Oh, no. Sometimes there're dogs and sometimes

143

there's a garage with lots of cars and a man in uniform and I get lost in it. And sometimes I don't know what it is; I'm just frightened.'

'And does being frightened ever make you think there might be something in your room? When you're awake, I mean?'

Trish became aware that Willow was getting restive, but Lucinda seemed quite happy to talk about her fears to a new and interested listener.

'Not now. When I was little I thought the dogs might be there. So I had a nightlight so I could see they weren't.'

Later, when Tom had managed to persuade his daughter to leave the party, Trish said, 'Willow, I'm sorry I did that. I didn't mean to frighten her or worry you.'

'Oh, I'm sure she was fine. But what was it all about?'

'It's just that the last time I saw Charlotte, she told me about a monster nightmare that had been frightening her. I'm not sure I took it seriously enough. I mean, with all this having happened, I've been wondering if her fears were only to do with the nightmare.' She frowned. 'I suppose I wanted to find out whether they were normal for her age. Lucinda's dogs did sound pretty much the same. How little was she when they were bothering her?'

'I don't know,' said Willow, her face looking tense. 'She's never told me anything about them before. Clearly she prefers to confide in Mrs Rusham.'

'Will,' said Tom, looking worried.

'No, it's OK. It's the price one pays for handing the boring bits of childcare over to someone else.'

'Don't let it get you down, Willow,' said Emma with a glinting smile. 'Lulu was trying to wind you up. She

144

had one good go about the chasing dreams and when you didn't rise she had another. She's far too sharp for her own good.'

'Or mine. You're probably right, Emma. But it's a worry, all the same, how you can think you know your child through and through, and then discover something important that she's kept from you. What else might there be?'

'In Lulu's case?' Tom said robustly. 'Nothing. No one could eat so well, organise her friends and both of us so firmly, and do as well at school if there was anything wrong. Don't start getting neurotic about her.'

Even in her misery Trish was amused to see the dignified, rich, middle-aged novelist stick her tongue out at her important husband. Then she turned to say, 'Trish, you're not eating. More lamb?'

'Honestly, I don't think I can manage any more. It's amazing, but I'm not tremendously hungry.'

'That's Mrs Rusham for you. Amazing is exactly what she is, and at everything she does. Help yourself, Em. You're not eating anything.'

'I'm not fantastically hungry either, actually.'

Emma left as soon as they had finished coffee, saying that she was going to walk home. Trish would have given her a lift, had it not been for Willow's unmistakable signal that she wanted Trish to wait.

While Tom was seeing Emma out, Willow said, 'I'm bothered that she's not talking about Hal. D'you think she's OK?'

'No,' said Trish. 'But I don't see that there's anything much we can do about it. She told me you're feeding her a lot at the moment. I'd have thought that was all you could do until she wants to talk.'

'I just wish I could help.'

'Sometimes it's easier not to be helped or asked questions.'

'Don't I know it.' Willow, who had spent most of her life hiding her feelings and her real character from everyone around her, had the grace to look ashamed of herself. 'But I'm so fond of her that I worry. If you think of anything I could do that might be useful, will you let me know?'

'Of course I will,' said Trish, relieved that she was not going to be grilled about Hal and what he might or might not be doing.

'And I did wonder whether you'd like me to talk to my contact at Holland Park Helpers and find out what they've got on Nicky Bagshot. It struck me that if you knew a bit more about her background, you'd have a better idea of where she fits in with what's happened to Charlotte.'

Trish looked at her in surprise. Willow seemed faintly self-conscious.

'You were very discreet, but it was plain enough to me at least that you've been digging to see what you can find out about them all. I thought that could be my contribution. I can't bear the thought of what might be happening to that child. Ah, that sounds like Tom's step. I'll give you a ring if I find anything. It was wonderful to see you this evening, Trish.'

'Sweet of you to have me, Willow,' she said, unable to believe that someone of Willow's age and apparent confidence did not want her husband to know of her offer of help. 'And you, Tom. It was great to get away from the flat for a bit. I spend the whole time longing for the phone to ring and then hoping it won't because I know the only news we're likely to get is bad. Then it reaches the point when any news seems better than this not knowing.'

'And then we made you talk about it,' said Tom, putting his arm round his wife's waist. 'I'm sorry. You must want to forget it.'

'Except that I can't. No one could. Charlotte's in my mind the whole time. It's agony not being able to do anything about it and looking at first one person and then another, thinking that all of them must have had something to do with it and yet knowing they couldn't. Look, I . . . I'd better go before I lose control. Thank you for this evening.'

'I hope there's some news soon. Good news, I mean. Good night, Trish,' said Willow, her severe face softened by pity. 'Keep in touch.'

It wasn't until Trish was almost back at the flat that she realised she had been driving much more slowly than usual. When she had locked the car and opened her front door she realised why: she was reluctant to know what response Ben might have made to her message.

Her joints seemed to have stiffened as she walked across the hard floor to her answering machine. The flat seemed bigger and emptier than ever, and more lonely. There was a red light flashing on the machine. She pressed the button.

'Trish? It's Ben. You sounded awful on our machine. Has something happened? I mean, is there some news? I'm so sorry we weren't here when you rang. We'll be back ten-ish this evening. Ring whenever you get in. Whenever. We won't be asleep until much later.'

Rubbing her left eyebrow with the ball of her thumb, Trish dialled Ben's number. When she heard Bella's sugary, languorous voice, she almost cut the connection. But it was too important for that.

'Bella? Hi, it's Trish Maguire here. Sorry to bother you so late. Ben's left a message saying I should ring at any time. Could I have a word with him, please?'

'He's in the bath. Is there some news of Charlotte?'

'No. It's just that I need to talk to Ben about something I heard today when I was questioning some of Nicky Bagshot's colleagues.'

'I don't see how he can help you, but if you tell me what you want to know, I'll ask him.'

'I'd rather ask him directly, Bella. Could you be very kind and ask him to ring me back later? As soon as it's convenient. I'll wait up.'

'No. I . . .' Her voice was muffled, as though she had put her hand over the receiver. A moment later a different voice said, 'Trish? Ben here. I was in the bath – sorry. What's up? How can I help?'

'Ben, I was in the park today, talking to some of the other nannies who knew Nicky and Charlotte, and they told me about a man they saw every Wednesday afternoon.'

'So?'

'He was a tall, tired-looking man in his forties, usually dressed in beige corduroy trousers, a waxed jacket and desert boots. He used to stand at the fence of the playground every Wednesday to watch Charlotte.'

There was a short silence. Trish thought she could just hear breathing in the silence. It was not the same rhythm as Ben's. Bella must be listening.

'Have you told the police, Trish?' he asked, trying to sound casual.

'Not yet.'

'Well, I think you should, don't you?'

'Probably. I just wanted to know what you thought about it first.'

'I can't see why. I think you should talk to the police. I saw a very nice woman sergeant called Lacie. Kath

148

Lacie, I think. Get in touch with her. She'll follow it up. I'd better let you sleep now, Trish. You must be so tired. Bye.'

Trish put the receiver very gently back on its cradle and stood looking at it, wishing that she could understand what he was trying to do.

CHAPTER TWELVE

'Why did you want to meet with *me*?' asked Bella Welbock of the two police officers who had come to her consulting rooms at eight-thirty on Tuesday morning.

She was dressed in her usual working clothes of a loose natural linen jacket over a plain cream round-necked shirt and a chocolate-brown skirt. They were, she had decided when she first went into practice on her own, formal enough to give her clients' parents confidence, but not so authoritative as to inhibit anything the children themselves might want to say.

The room was decorated to the same ends in three different greys and white. There was a large red, cream and grey kilim on the polished floor and the furniture was simple. All the toys she used in her work with the youngest children were kept in a tall glass-fronted cupboard. A long desk made of a red-painted door slung across two low-level grey metal filing cabinets stood under the window. Her computer weighted down one end of the door and the other held a rack of the reference books she used most. In between were wicker baskets of letters to be answered, bills to be paid, and filing. At the other side of the room was a long couch, where the woman sergeant was sitting, and two armchairs. Her constable had one; Bella, the other.

She was angry that they had the right to interrupt her day, but grateful that they had at least made a specific appointment so that she did not have to force one of the children to wait. They hated that; any interruption or distraction affected them like a deliberate rejection and it could take weeks to overcome the resulting obstinacy and hostility.

'What is it you've come to ask?' she said, as usual rephrasing a question that had apparently been too hard to answer.

'Whatever you can tell us about your old man's relationship with his ex, the rich banker.'

Disliking the constable's lack of subtlety, Bella glanced at the woman sergeant and was interested to see that she, too, disapproved but had not bothered to intervene.

'There's not a great deal I can tell you,' she said frostily. 'And I don't see that it's relevant. I hear you've found a witness who walked by our house and saw him through the window, working in the study on Saturday afternoon.'

'Yes, we did,' said Sergeant Lacie. 'He was there at one-thirty. We haven't found anyone who saw him any later than that. What we need now is some indication of his relationship with his ex-wife.'

'He doesn't have a relationship with her. That ended when they divorced.'

'He told us that he had put up with her infidelities for years before he divorced her,' said the sergeant. 'It would help us fill out our picture of her and the child if we had a better understanding of the whole relationship. Do you know why he was so complaisant?'

'Isn't that privileged information?'

'No, Ms Weblock, I'm afraid it isn't. Even if he were your client, it wouldn't be. And he's not, is he – at least, not now?'

'No, and he never was,' Bella said, outraged that they could have thought her capable of an affair with a client. In her opinion that was the grossest abuse of the therapist-client relationship, and it was typical of the British cops that they could accuse her of it in that devious way. They hated all Americans, she knew, and professional women, too, so she'd be losing out both ways. 'My practice is entirely with children these days.'

'Fine. Then please tell us anything you can, Ms Weblock.'

'May I ask why?'

Bella felt a blast of hostility from her right and followed it to its source in the constable. If he'd been an American he'd probably have told her to quit stalling by then. But the Brits were different. They just could never say what they wanted. And not only the police either. Everyone did it. Ben was one of the worst, going right around a subject instead of getting straight to what mattered. It made her mad.

'Quite frankly, Ms Weblock,' said Sergeant Lacie, 'I don't understand why you're reluctant to talk us. A child is missing. We all know what may be happening to her. We need to find out everything we can about her and her background so that we can have some idea where to look for her. You can help us do that.'

Bella briefly raised her eyebrows and nodded to indicate her willingness to receive questions on those terms.

'Her mother claims that your husband is the child's father; he told us that he doesn't think he is. We need to find out who else it could have been. D'you know?'

'No. And I don't believe that's why you're here. You want to know whether Ben was lying and she is his child and he had a hand in her abduction.' Bella was so angry that her voice was shaking as though she was scared. 'Isn't that why you've been interrogating my neighbours and searching my garbage?'

'Yes,' the sergeant said with all the directness Bella could want.

'Right.' She wished she'd rung the US embassy to find out what her rights were here. 'I have no way of knowing anything about their relationship or Charlotte's paternity except what my husband's told me. And I have no reason to think he's lying. As far as I know, there's never been a DNA test. Ben didn't dispute paternity during the divorce because he's not a vindictive man.'

'Sure of that, are you?' said the constable.

'Perfectly,' said Bella, amazed to hear how much like Bette Davis she could sound. 'He's generous, more generous than any man I've ever met. That has always been his problem. It's the reason he put up with Antonia's affairs for so long. He'd have done anything to make her happy. He'd have accepted Charlotte as his own if he'd thought that would help. But when he finally acknowledged that Antonia was never going to open up to him, that she'd turned him into part of the problem, he knew he had to get out.'

'Why did it take him so long?'

'He has a big problem with self-esteem, Constable Herrick,' said Bella, looking at him in disdain. 'A different problem than yours.'

She turned back to the sergeant, whose lips twitched in a smile. So, sisterhood does cross the Atlantic, thought Bella.

'You see, Sergeant Lacie, he's a man of very little—'

'Brain, I should think,' said the constable as though he'd made a great joke.

'Sam,' said Sergeant Lacie unemotionally, 'I left some notes in my briefcase in the car. Could you fetch it for me, please?'

As soon as he had gone, looking mad enough to shoot someone, the sergeant apologised for him, adding: 'How far do you think your husband's generosity would take him?'

'I don't get you.'

'Forgive me. If he believed the fact that you and he are unable to have children was poisoning your life, would he be capable of—'

Bella got to her feet. Her whole body burned with fury. All her inclination to like Sergeant Lacie had gone.

'No, he would not. That's an awful suggestion. You're right out of order.'

'There are a great many more awful things being done at this moment than an unpleasant suggestion being put into words, Ms Weblock. I can imagine how you feel about not being able to have children. I had a miscarriage myself last year and we've been trying for another baby ever since without success. I know how it can come to loom larger than anything else – almost – and make the idea of happiness like something designed only for other people.'

She paused as though to give Bella a chance to contradict or agree, but Bella was so locked into her rage that she could not feel even sympathy for another woman who shared some of her suffering. At least the sergeant had gotten as far as a miscarriage. She herself hadn't ever conceived.

'For a man like your husband – as you have described him – generous and longing to give, your distress might have been too much to endure without taking some kind of action,' said the sergeant. There was compassion in her big, dark eyes. 'If he had come to believe that Charlotte was his child after all, the temptation might have been too much. Mightn't it? Don't you think he could have taken her?'

Recognising the fairness of the question with difficulty, Bella gave it only a moment's consideration. She was still angry, but she was a just woman and had to admit that the sergeant couldn't know Ben; couldn't know how unlikely he would be to do anything as evil as that.

'If he had, which is more unlikely than you'll ever know, he would have brought her straight to me,' she said, trying to choose a form of words the detective might understand. 'And he hasn't, as you must know from the questions you've been asking round here and at home.'

The constable returned at that moment with Kath Lacie's briefcase. She did not even make a pretence of looking in it.

'Fair enough. If you think of anything that could help us, Ms Weblock,' she said, 'will you get in touch with me?'

'What kind of thing?'

'Anything your husband might have said or done recently or in the past to throw any light on who might have had an interest in the child or a grudge against her mother.'

Bella laughed. She couldn't help it. The question was really dumb.

'If you've been destroying her reputation with her friends and neighbours in the way you've been doing to us, you'll know that half the world has a grudge against her.' Thinking about Antonia and everything

156

she had done to Ben, Bella suddenly lost her temper.

'She's an evil woman,' she said. 'If it weren't that there's a child involved, I'd say she deserved everything she's getting now.'

'Why d'you say that?'

'She uses people and gives nothing back. She almost destroyed my husband, and from what I've heard, she does that to everyone who comes into her orbit.'

'I see. Well, thank you for being so frank, Ms Weblock. Come along, Sam.'

Bella watched them both go, gave them time to get well clear of her building and then pulled the telephone towards her.

'Ben?' she said, when he had been fetched from the staffroom. 'Ben, I've had the police here asking more questions.'

'They've been here, too. But don't worry, Bella. They'll go on talking to both of us and everyone else who's even remotely involved until they've found Charlotte. You can't blame them. We'll just have to hang on in there until it's over. I can't stop now, my darling, I've got to take my kids to the library and they're clogging up the lobby and making an awful din. Will you be home this evening?'

'Sure. My last client's due at five-thirty, so I'll be home by a quarter of seven at the latest. Shall I bring some takeout with me?'

'Great. Bella, I'm sorry about all this. I know it's vile. It'll be over soon; one way or the other. We'll just have to keep our peckers up until they lose interest in us.'

'Unlike you, Ben,' she said, remembering her amazement the first time she had heard him use the phrase, 'I don't have a pecker.'

He laughed. 'In England you do. It's a chin on this side of the Atlantic, as you well know.'

She laughed with him and put down the phone feeling the littlest bit better. So long as she could believe in Ben's laughter – and not be faced too often with melodramatic phone messages from Trish Maguire or questions like the ones Sergeant Lacie had just asked – she'd survive until Charlotte Weblock was found. If she ever was found.

CHAPTER THIRTEEN

'Get that, will you, Nicky?' Antonia called as the sound of the door bell died away.

She waited until she heard Nicky's acknowledgment and then closed her bedroom door again. It was important to keep Nicky in the house where the police could get their hands on her whenever they needed to, but that didn't mean Antonia wanted to have to look at her.

Antonia returned to the important business of applying the glossy surface she needed to keep between herself and whatever the day was going to turn up. She had known all along that she would not be able to work until Charlotte was found, and so there was no real need to have set the alarm so early, but she was not sleeping much anyway and it seemed absurd to change her routine. Besides, a later start would have allowed Nicky to slack off and Antonia wasn't going to allow that. As it was Nicky skulked in her room for most of every day instead of doing anything useful.

There must be the most awful fug in there. Nicky hated fresh air, and so she never opened the window.

What with the cigarette smoke – and probably worse – the room must be disgusting. In normal times Antonia would have gone storming upstairs to catch her in the act and nip it in the bud, but these were not normal times and the less she saw of Nicky or her room, the better. Antonia thought yet again of the way the police had searched it and gone so ominously quiet, and whether they were likely to come back again for another go. They ought to.

Hearing a quiet knock on her door, Antonia checked the perfection of her makeup in the dressing-table mirror, tightened her dressing-gown cord around her waist and went to see who was outside.

'Yes, Nicky?' she said, noticing that the girl was red-eyed again, as though she had been crying more useless sympathy-inviting tears, and she looked even less healthy than usual. Antonia shuddered and turned her head away so that they did not have to meet each other's eyes.

'It's the police, Antonia,' she said, sounding properly scared. 'They want to see you.'

'Tell them I'll be down in a minute and offer them coffee, will you? Or tea. I suppose that sort might drink tea at this hour.'

Antonia shut the door without waiting for an answer, and stripped off her dressing gown. The beige suit she would have worn to work was hanging in its Tuesday position in the long cupboard and she reached for it automatically, taking the top shirt off the pile in the adjoining shelves with her other hand. She put them on, examining the effect with care and then added a gold pin to her lapel. Her fine Lycra tights were exactly the same colour as the taupe leather shoes into which she pushed her wide feet. Walking towards the door, she noticed a single blonde

160

hair on the shoulder of her jacket and picked it off, frowning.

Then, at least looking as though she might be able to deal with whatever had to be faced, she went slowly downstairs to find out what the police had come to tell her.

As she pushed open the door, she saw that DCI Blake was standing in the kitchen with a mug in his hand, talking to Nicky, while his pretty constable was staring out of the open French windows towards the expensively landscaped garden. Antonia deliberately slowed her heart-rate by looking out, too, and noticing even from that distance that the *Acer japonicum* was thriving and that the last few camellia flowers were turning brown and dying. Almost certain of her self-control, she shut the door loudly behind her, making them all jerk to attention.

'Good morning, Chief Inspector Blake.' Her voice did not tremble at all and her back was very stiff. 'Constable Derring.'

Blake handed the mug to Nicky without looking at her and came towards Antonia with his right hand outstretched. It seemed absurdly formal, but she shook hands with him, glad that his grip was firm. She waited to be told to sit down and, when she was not, tried to smile and asked for news.

'There isn't any yet, Ms Weblock. Nicky?'

Nicky looked stupidly at him and then obeyed the jerk of his head and left the kitchen without looking at her employer again.

'Ms Weblock, would you like to sit down?'

'No, I don't think so,' she said, twisting her hands together and feeling the sharpness of her diamond rings as they slid around her fingers. 'What are you going to tell me?'

He pulled out one of the Italian rush-seated chairs she had been so pleased with when they were delivered, but she ignored it.

'What, Chief Inspector?'

'We need to dig up part of the garden.'

She did sit down then, her legs crumpling beneath her. She felt his hand under her elbow, easing her down, and hated the brush of his coffee-scented breath on her cheek and nose. It would have given her a lot of satisfaction to push his face away, but naturally she did nothing of the kind.

'Why?' she whispered, leaning away from him.

'We need to eliminate the possibility that—'

'That Charlotte's body is buried there. I understand that,' she said, quite proud of the way she kept her voice just the right side of collapse. 'But why have you got to eliminate it? Is it something to do with what you found in the pram?'

'Not entirely. We haven't had the results back from the lab. yet.'

'Then have you identified the boy Nicky claims to have bandaged up on Saturday, is that it? Why won't you tell me? What's the matter? What are you hiding?'

'We're not hiding anything.' Blake looked as though he'd have liked to put an arm around her. She shrank away from him. She couldn't help it. 'And yes, we have found him.'

'And? Is that story of Nicky's true?'

'Mainly.'

'Mainly? What does that mean?'

'His mother agrees that she became aware that a strange young woman, whom she's since identified from photographs as Nicky, was sticking plaster over her son's knees in the playground on Saturday.' He stopped as if he thought she'd want to make some kind of comment. She didn't.

'So that much is true. But she showed us the wounds on his knees and they don't look quite bad enough to account for the amount of blood I saw in the pram.'

Antonia gasped as though she'd been punched.

'We will, of course, be testing the blood to see whether it matches the boy's. The mother's given permission and the blood will be taken this afternoon.'

'Why haven't you arrested Nicky?'

'Because we've no firm evidence that she's hurt Charlotte in any way.'

'But someone has, haven't they? That's why you want to dig up the garden.'

'We think it's possible, and that's why we have to do everything we can to get the necessary evidence.'

'But why must you dig?' Antonia asked, making herself think of the time it would take them to remove all the carefully laid paving and dig up the laboriously chosen and trained maples, camellias and azaleas, because that was easier than thinking about anything else. 'Can't you use one of those heat-seeking machines? Wouldn't that be quicker? The sooner you—'

'Ms Weblock, we are going to dig, but not under the paving; it's obvious that's not been disturbed since Saturday, but the earth beyond has been turned fairly recently. We don't need your permission, but I wanted to warn you before the men got here and started work. Do you understand?'

'Yes. Yes, of course I do. Is it the neighbours? I know you've been talking to them. Did they hear people in the garden, see someone digging on Saturday? Who? Who did they see? You must tell me.' She grabbed his sleeve and pulled him towards her. 'You must tell me. Who was it? Who was it they saw in the garden?'

'Where is Mr Hithe?' he asked in his most soothing voice.

'He's not here. Why? Who did they say they'd seen? Who was it who told you it was him?'

'No one saw anything, Ms Weblock. And no one has seen Mr Hithe doing anything.'

'Then why do you want Robert? You talked to him again yesterday, I know. What did he tell you?'

'I want Robert because I don't think you should be on your own while we're digging. Where is he? Can we collect him for you?'

Antonia shook her head. 'There's a crisis at work. He had to go in early.'

'Another crisis? There seem to be rather a lot of them at the moment, don't there?'

'It's the same one,' she said impatiently. Noticing his immediate suspicion, she moderated her voice to add: 'The bank's got scared because the company has lost their two biggest accounts, and it wants to withdraw their loans. They're trying for a white knight and putting together a big presentation. It's very important for them. The bank's deadline is close of business on Friday and this is Tuesday. Please don't interrupt Robert because you think I need help here. I can manage.'

'What about your cousin, then, Ms Maguire? I really don't think you should be alone. Why not call her?'

Antonia shook her head. 'She's busy, too. Look, just get on with it, will you? Stop worrying about me and dig. Do whatever you have to. Just find her quickly. That's all that matters, isn't it?'

She sucked in a huge breath and held it for some time before turning her back on them to reach the drawer where the kitchen paper was kept, tearing sheets off and scrubbing at her eyes.

'Ms Weblock,' said DCI Blake, 'please let me—'

'Leave me alone for Christ's sake and just get on with it, can't you?' she shouted as she ran out of the room.

Upstairs she hung over the basin in her bathroom, gasping loudly and coughing. Then she washed her face in very cold water and blew her nose several times.

The bedroom looked slovenly, she thought, with the unmade bed in such a mess. Her nightdress and dressing gown lay across the bunched duvet and her slippers and her book were still on the floor, and there was no air. She had been keeping all the windows shut in case the pack of journalists got round the back of the house into the garden and started recording any noise she made or anything she said.

In normal circumstances she never saw the room like that. She got ready each morning in the twelve-and-a-half minutes she allowed herself and left without a backward glance. By the time she returned, Maria would have cleaned, tidied and aired it.

Now that the police were in the garden, at least she wouldn't have to worry about the journalists. She flung open both the windows, kicked off her shoes, and lay down on the unmade bed to wait.

The men who were digging were discreet, but the knowledge of what they were doing made every sound sinister. After ten minutes the thud of their spades and the low-level talk were too much and she got up to pace about the room. Then she stripped the bed, carefully folding the linen and laying the neat heap on her dressing stool before picking up her book and putting her slippers away.

That done, she risked a glance out of the window and saw a group of men in shirtsleeves huddled around the far end of the garden. They had stopped digging and were just standing, looking down. Ignoring her naked face, she put her shoes back on and ran downstairs.

She was about to open the kitchen door when she heard the constable's voice, saying, 'I wouldn't have believed it, sir.'

'What, Jenny?'

'That anyone in her position would have got herself up like that – all that makeup and an Armani suit. I know you've got to be hard to do her job, but to have that sort of self-control with your child lost, probably dead? I think it's horrible.'

'It could be for protection. You know, like a spinal corset to hold her together.'

'Maybe.'

'You don't like her, do you, Jenny?'

'No, sir, I don't. If the child had been a year or two older I'd have suggested we started looking at runaways.'

'Maybe, but not at four.'

'And what about this bloke of hers? D'you buy that story of a crisis with the bank?'

'It fits with what the other directors told me when I interviewed them on Sunday. And they all swore he didn't leave the Saturday meeting until Bagshot rang his office hysterically from the nick. Look! Come on, Jenny, we'd better get out there and see what they've got.'

Antonia, who had been listening in outrage outside the door, knew that she shouldn't have minded any of it. The police always suspected the worst of everyone, especially when a child was involved. If she hadn't been in New York they'd probably have been accusing her by now. She knew that. She mustn't lose her temper. So far the police were on her side. Just. She didn't want to jeopardise that while Charlotte was missing. Antonia waited for two more minutes and then went in. She was standing with her back to the fridge when they came back.

'What have they found?'

'Nothing, Ms Weblock. Nothing yet.'

'But they thought they had, didn't they? Somebody thought they'd found something.'

'Were you watching?'

'Of course.'

'You and your nanny both. She's still up there, looking at them.'

'What did they find?'

'A big piece of polythene. Probably irrelevant, the sort of thing builders tend to bury in gardens because it's less trouble than carting it away.'

'But not necessarily?'

'No. We'll take it away and let the lab. have a look at it.'

'Why?'

'Let us worry about that.'

'Oh, please don't keep trying to protect me,' she said with all the quick anger that was most easily sparked by junior staff in the office making stupid, careless mistakes. 'Why are you interested in the polythene?'

'In case her body was ever wrapped in it,' said DCI Blake quietly, reluctant to put it into words.

'But wouldn't the body have been there in that case?' asked Antonia, wondering if he understood the effort she had to make to keep her voice sounding calm.

'Not necessarily,' said Blake, noticing that Constable Derring was looking disgusted. 'Burial in the garden might have been a temporary measure.'

'I don't believe it,' said Antonia. 'I won't.'

'Good. You hang on to that.' He smiled at her and appeared to be waiting for her to leave her own kitchen. She did not know what to say or where to go, how to spin out the time until they had found everything there was to find. Eventually she went upstairs to ring Trish. That at least would take up a little time.

When Trish's answering machine cut in, she said, 'It's Antonia here. They're digging up the garden.'

Then she dialled the number of her office's direct line and was answered by her own voicemail. Surprised and angry that her secretary was not there, she looked at her watch and discovered that it was still only nine o'clock. She put down the receiver and paced up and down her bedroom and bathroom, wishing that there was something she could do to hurry the police.

Luckily Trish soon rang back, to say that she had just been out buying the newspapers when Antonia rang.

'Have they found anything in the garden yet?' Trish asked.

'Only some old polythene. They're taking it away, but they don't think it means anything.'

'Right. Good. How are you?'

'How d'you think?'

'I meant in detail,' Trish said with irritating patience. 'But don't worry about it if you'd rather not talk. Antonia, there is something I wanted to ask you. I tried yesterday, but—'

'What is it?'

'Do you still think Nicky's responsible for whatever's happened?'

'Of course.' She would have told Trish about the fact that there was too much blood in the pram for it to be the boy's if she'd asked, but she didn't.

'It's just that I've been wondering if you'd let me arrange a polygraph test – you know, so that you could catch Nicky out in whatever lies she's been telling you and the police.'

A polygraph test. Why hadn't she thought of that? It stuck out a mile, but she hadn't seen it.

'The police don't much like them, I know,' Trish was saying. 'But they can be useful and I'd have thought it would be well worth it. I have a friend, I'm not sure if you've ever met her, called Emma Gnatche, who's something of a specialist. She's said that if you approve she will administer a test to Nicky, and she won't charge for it.'

'That's generous, but hardly the point.'

'No,' agreed Trish. 'So may I fix it? It seems the obvious thing to do next.'

'Yes, I think you'd better. When?'

'Well, Emma said she could come later this morning, say about twelve or half-past. Would that be any good to you?'

'Yes, I suppose so. I'll make sure Nicky's here. What exactly will she be asked?'

'Emma and I have talked about it and decided that she'd better go through the playground story, stage by stage, to check that each bit of it is true, and then ask about Nicky's treatment of Charlotte in general and the bruises in particular.'

'That sounds all right.'

'Fine. I'll tell Emma to meet me at your house then, so that I can introduce you.'

'No. Don't bother. Let her come on her own. The house is too full as it is with police crawling all over it. I'd rather you didn't.'

'Oh. OK. Whatever you want.'

'Will this friend of yours have some kind of identification? I don't want to go letting a journalist into the house by mistake.'

'I'll warn her. Thanks, Antonia. And if you change your mind, send for me.'

'I will. Goodbye, Trish.'

Antonia put down the receiver and thought about polygraph testing and how she should have realised that Trish would know all about it and asked for it sooner.

CHAPTER FOURTEEN

U p in Buxton, in Derbyshire, at almost exactly the same time, a couple in their late sixties were at breakfast. They were eating fried bread, eggs, bacon and grilled tomatoes, as they always did. Harold liked it and Renie was sure it must be good for him, whatever all those London papers said about cholesterol and animal fats and all that. She wouldn't have wanted Harold going out of the house without a hot breakfast inside him. That cereal-stuff they ate nowadays was no use to a grown man, not soaked in cold milk like it was. And wasn't milk animal fats anyway? Stuff and nonsense, if you asked her, all these newfangled food rules. She saw that Harold was cutting into his egg and waited to make sure that the yolk was right. He liked it runny, but felt sick if the white wasn't cooked. Pleased to see she hadn't lost her touch, she unfolded the paper she'd laid neatly beside her plate and cut her fried bread up into tidy squares before slicing into the egg, carefully adding a square of fried bread and a small piece of bacon to the forkful for contrast before raising it to her lips.

It never got there. She sat with her mouth open,

staring at the newspaper as the egg-yolk ran down the fork. Not until the cooling yellow stickiness had reached her fingers did she start and remember where she was. She put the fork down and carefully wiped her hand on the serviette.

'What's the matter with you, then?' Harold asked, looking up from the racing page of his own paper.

'It's our Nicolette, isn't it? I'm sure it is. Have a look.'

He put out a hand for the paper and she passed it over to him, just as she always had done whatever he wanted. That was how she'd been brought up and she was proud of it, even when it was difficult. Specially when it was difficult.

'So it is,' he said when he had wiped his lips with his serviette and read the accompanying article to make sure Renie hadn't got it wrong as usual. 'Who'd have thought she'd be capable of something like that?'

Renie, remembering the child she'd known between the ages of nine and thirteen, shook her head. Nicolette was one of the few she could think of with more than dutiful affection.

She'd been a good child, Nicolette, and nice with it once she'd got over the trickiness they all had when they'd just been moved. She'd been helpful, too, much more helpful than any of the boys they'd had before. That was why she'd always asked for girls after Nicolette, but it hadn't been the same; and lots of them had been just as violent and swearing as the worst of the boys. She hadn't minded it so much with the boys, but when it was girls she hated it. That was why she'd wanted to give up in the end, why she'd told Harold she couldn't take it any more. He hadn't believed her at first, but when she'd got ill even he could see she couldn't do it. It was the girls calling her a fucking wanker – and worse – that'd done it. She could've put up with the mess and the truanting and the banging music and staying out late and being cheeky, but she wouldn't stand for being called a fucking wanker and a dirty cunt in her own house by an angelic-looking twelve-year-old girl.

Oh, Renie knew it wasn't the child's fault, not really. Someone'd taught the girls words like that. Babies weren't born knowing them. But somehow she couldn't feel the same about what she and Harold had always done after. And if you couldn't forgive the children and want to try to like them, then it wasn't any good going on, was it? That's what she'd said to the lady from the Social, and she'd said she understood and it wasn't surprising. And by then she and Harold were both over sixty, and it was nearly time to stop in any case. They'd got their pensions, too, so the money didn't matter so much, what with Harold not having been in work since the factory shut. Harold had wanted to go on but it wasn't any good once Renie got ill. It was nice to know she'd never have to have another foul-mouthed little slut-in-the-making in her house again.

But Nicolette was different. She'd been such a nice child. Not pretty, mind, but ever so gentle when she stopped being scared, and always willing. If she'd been able to have her own kids, Renie'd have liked a daughter like Nicolette. She would.

Harold gave her the paper back when he'd finished with it, and she read the whole of the article, feeling tears rising in her eyes at the thought of the child being in such terrible trouble.

'Where did she come from?' asked Harold, not commenting on her tears. 'I can't remember.'

'I can't either,' said Renie after ransacking her unreliable memory. The things she forgot these days; sometimes she'd go down to the shops and only find she'd left her list behind when she got there and would have to walk all the way back up the hill to get it. She'd forget her own name one of these days, just like Harold said. It riled her sometimes when he said it, but it was true enough. But anyway, she'd never forgotten Nicolette. 'There'd been a tragedy of some kind, hadn't there? There usually was.'

'Or plain neglect,' said Harold, who'd never had much time for the parents of the kids they'd been sent to foster. Lot of wastrels, he'd always said, having kids they couldn't afford to keep decent and then hitting them black and blue. Some of them had come to the house with shocking bruises. And if there was one thing Harold always said he didn't hold with, it was hitting kids. There was other ways to make them mind you, as he'd told her often enough.

'It must be ten years since they took her away,' said Renie when she had blown her nose. 'Nearly.'

'She's done all right for herself by the look of it. Stuck in a fancy house in London.' He stabbed his yolk-painted fork towards the front page of the *Daily Mercury*. 'Paid a fortune, too, I shouldn't wonder by a woman like that.'

Renie was surprised at the edge in his voice, not having realised that he did not share her friendly memories of Nicolette.

'I think it's good she's got herself a steady job,' she said bravely. 'Not many foster-children manage it. D'you think we ought to go up to London and see her? Try to help?'

Harold, who didn't see he'd been bullying Renie ever since they got married – or how hard she had to work to keep from minding about it – shook his head.

'You don't want to get involved in something like that. It's nothing to do with us and mud sticks, you

174

know. You start going down there and getting involved and they'll start saying it's our fault she's gone bad. Look what's happened to all sorts of carers and foster-parents. It's not safe. That poor little kid.'

'Yes,' agreed Renie, assuming that, like her, he was thinking of Nicolette.

He picked up his own paper and turned to the football results. Renie finished her bacon and egg. She didn't much fancy it, but she didn't like waste. Never had.

Later, when Harold had gone to meet his friend down the pub like he always did on Tuesdays, she disobeyed him for the first time in her married life and sat down to write a letter to the child. At the end she wrote:

> *I often think of you, Nicolette, and miss you. I remember the way you used to like helping make the butterfly cakes for that Mrs Smith's stall at the church fête. Do you remember those, and the way we cut the tops in half to make the wings and stuck them in the icing? Oh, I remember as if it was yesterday. But you've probably forgotten, it was all so long ago.*
>
> *I'm glad to see you got a good job, but I'm that sorry you're in this trouble now. You were never in trouble here. And I know you didn't do anything to that baby.*
> *Renie Brooks.*
>
> *PS Harold would've sent his love if he'd known I was writing, but he's not here just now.*

Renie did not much like the implied lie in the post-script, but it was better than confessing that he'd told her not to make contact. She did not know where to send the letter and re-read the piece in the paper to see if it said. But it didn't. In the end she wrote Nicolette's name on the envelope and then put *c/o Antonia Weblock, Kensington, London* and hoped it would get there.

Then she thought about that poor woman whose child had gone missing and she picked up her pen again. It was funny how good it could make you feel to be writing to people who weren't going to tell you you were stupid or couldn't remember your own name or weren't worth anything. And that poor woman would probably like to know people were thinking about her and taking the trouble to tell her so.

Renie took both letters to the post office to buy stamps and was back at the house in good time to make Harold's dinner. She'd do the kitchen floor when he went to the Lodge later. He'd never know the difference and it was better not to tell him anything about the letters.

CHAPTER FIFTEEN

Trish tried to work while she waited for Emma, who had promised to come straight to Southwark to report after she had tested Nicky, but it was impossible to keep her mind off Charlotte – and Ben.

When Emma eventually reached the flat, she looked worn and irritable, but Trish could not be sure whether that was because of what Hal was doing to her or the things she had learned from Nicky. Trish kissed her, took her briefcase, and offered tea, coffee or wine.

Snatching a quick look at her watch, Emma said, 'Would you be shocked if I said wine? It's past lunchtime.'

'Of course I wouldn't be shocked. Don't be an idiot. Red or white?'

'Oh, I don't mind. Anything. Red please,' said Emma.

Trish fetched a bottle of Rioja from the rack, collected glasses and a corkscrew and a bag of crisps she'd found at the back of one of the cupboards. If Emma was going to drink at the rate she had the previous evening, she'd need something to sop up the alcohol.

'OK,' she said when they were sitting with their glasses in front of them. 'What did you think of Nicky?'

'I'm not sure she's the most interesting one,' said Emma with rare harshness. 'That cousin of yours was something else.'

'Antonia? Oh, nonsense, Emma. I know she can be a bit robust, but it's just her manner. And she's not at her best right now, for obvious reasons.'

'No. But I'm glad I don't work for her.' Emma took a sip of wine and then another. Then she put the glass down and opened her briefcase, saying, 'She took me up to Nicky's room, flung open the door without knocking and told her in the most appallingly bullying voice to get up and pull herself together. Then, while Nicky was surreptitiously trying to wipe her eyes and nose, Antonia told her who I was and ordered her to answer everything I asked, saying that there was no point trying to lie any longer, because I was trained to see through lies told by people like her.'

'Oh God,' said Trish. 'It does sound embarrassing. I'm sorry, Emma. I didn't realise she'd be as bad as that or I'd have warned you.'

'I wouldn't have cared less about embarrassment. But it was damaging, what she did. Nicky was so jangled by it that her physical responses to my questions were all over the place. I did what I could to calm her down before I started the test, but I'd say your cousin probably scuppered all my chances of getting anything useful.'

'Shit. But, look, Emma, you can't really blame Antonia. She's desperate about Charlotte.'

'Yeah, maybe. But . . .'

'And she's sure that the whole thing is Nicky's fault.'

'She's not the only one,' said Emma drily.

'What?'

'Nicky's not stupid, Trish, and as far as I can tell she's a thoroughly decent human being. No one could

178

blame her more than she blames herself for what happened. Now, here are the charts. I'll go through them more stringently later, but I've had a preliminary look. Here, here and here are where I was asking the control questions. These smooth outlines are the ones for questions that didn't trouble Nicky, and these – mainly about Antonia – are the ones I asked in order to provoke a reaction. Clear?'

'Yes,' said Trish, staring down at the long graphs with their rearing, crossing lines in different-coloured inks. She was reasonably familiar with such charts by now and knew that the different-coloured lines represented the changes in Nicky's heart-rate and breathing and the electrical conductivity of her skin as she gave answers to each of Emma's questions. The theory was that the reactions would sharply increase when she was under the kind of emotional pressure that lying brings. It took great skill to design the questions for successful polygraph tests and to interpret the results, but Trish had faith in Emma's capabilities.

'I'm not very good at reading the charts. What have they told you?'

Emma reached into her briefcase for the list of questions she'd asked and the notes she had made beside each. There were also a pair of cassette tapes and a small recorder.

'Shall I play you the tape I recorded?'

'No. Don't bother. It would take too long. Just give me the gist.'

'OK. As I say, I'll go through the whole thing properly later. But the obvious conclusion is that everything Nicky's told you and Antonia about what happened in the playground is accurate.'

'And Ben? Does Nicky know who he is?'

'She doesn't know his name,' said Emma, as though

trying to control some emotion she mistrusted. 'But she identified the photograph you gave me at once and agreed with the other nannies that he was there, watching the playround every Wednesday. Her reactions to the questions about whether he was there on Saturday are mixed, but on balance I'd say he was.'

'Shit.'

Emma drank the rest of her wine. 'I'm sorry, Trish.'

'No. You shouldn't be. We needed to know. Was there anything else?'

'Just one oddity. When I was trying to find out what else Nicky might have seen that she hadn't consciously remembered, she mentioned Charlotte's swimming teacher, a man called Mike. When I tried to check the memory, she got confused but, again on balance, I'd say it's possible – likely even – that he was there, too. I don't know if that helps.'

'It might,' said Trish, feeling a faint hope again. 'It just might. More wine?'

'No, thanks. I've got a late afternoon meeting. I'll sort through all this tonight, and if I come up with anything else, I'll ring you, OK?'

'You've been wonderful, Emma. Thank you.'

'That's OK. Sorry I couldn't reassure you about Ben.' She shut her briefcase and stood up. 'I'll be off.'

'Emma, wait.'

'What's the matter?'

'I just wondered how you are. It can't just be dislike of Antonia's manner that's making you like this.' For a moment Trish thought that Emma was going to retreat into anger, which would have been very unlike her, but then she shook her head.

'Hal's definitely gone,' she said eventually. She sat down again with her hands clamped between her knees. 'I got a letter this morning.'

'It does sound as though it's been on the cards for some time,' said Trish to keep the conversation going.

'Yes. What got to me . . .' Emma's big blue eyes filled with tears and Trish refilled her wine glass. She drank a little. When she looked up again she had herself back under control. 'What got to me was that he accused me of trying to play power games with him. Power games!'

'Isn't that a typical kind of cop-out? Don't they usually say that sort of thing when they're buggering off?'

'Do they?' For a moment Emma looked almost hopeful. She also looked astonishingly young. 'Do they really, Trish?'

'They have to me,' she said drily, wanting to help but knowing that all she had to offer was her own experience. There was nothing she could do to lessen Emma's soreness except give her the chilly kind of comfort that comes from knowing one is not unique in one's inadequacy. 'It's that or misunderstanding them or demanding too much commitment from them or behaving like their mother. Very few seem to come out with it honestly and say "I've gone off you" or "I've met someone else". Let's be fair: perhaps it's not cowardice – perhaps they think that sort of reality would hurt us too much.'

'I'm not sure anything could hurt more than this,' said Emma, staring down into the wine in her glass. 'I'd really come to trust him, you know. I must be an incredibly bad picker.'

'You and me both.'

'Weird, isn't it?' said Emma, reaching after the kind of cheerfulness she had not felt for months and months. 'Two such gorgeous girls as us?'

Trish laughed obediently, although the disguised

sadness in her friend's voice cut into her like cheese wire. 'From what I can see, gorgeousness doesn't have anything to do with it. Has Hal said what he wants to do about the flat?'

'Oh, flog it, of course. He wants his equity out. Thank heavens the market's begun to pick up. At least we might make a profit. I'm supposed to be ringing an estate agent this morning.'

'Oh, I see,' said Trish, revelling in the hot rage that efficiently pushed aside most of the sadness in her. 'He's dumping you *and* expecting you to do all the work to make it easy for him. What a shit!'

'Well, he's always earned the most and paid most of the mortgage. I suppose that gives him—'

'That's the way Antonia thinks, Emma. It's not you. You've never thought like that before, so don't start now. Money doesn't excuse anything. And anyway, half the deposit was yours, wasn't it?'

'Yup. I'll have to think about what to get next, where to look, where I can afford.'

Thoughts rushed through Trish's mind faster than she could produce words for them. The most generous was that Emma needed help; she had trusted Hal with difficulty and then been betrayed. Someone had to make up to her for that. The least, that the mortgage on the Southwark flat was enormous and a little rent might help; and there was so much space that a temporary tenant need not be too much of an incubus.

'Look, while you're thinking, Emma, would you like to move in here? Only until you make a decision, of course, but if you need somewhere to tide you over . . .'

Emma put her glass on the floor, got up and flung both arms around Trish, laying her head on Trish's shoulder for a second, before standing back to say,

'You are the kindest and the best, Trish. And if it comes to it, I'll take you up on your offer. I can't tell you how much it means. I've been waking up out of nightmares about sleeping in a cardboard box in the Strand for days now.' She tried to laugh. 'I'd better be off now before I start snivelling. I've done too much of that these last few months as it is. What are you going to do next? Apart from asking Ben Weblock what he was doing in Charlotte's park?'

'I'm not sure.'

'Trish?'

'Yes?'

'Why haven't you already asked him?'

Feeling her cheeks heating, Trish shook her head.

'I have in a way, but his wife was listening on the extension and I felt I couldn't press it. Then this morning, I suppose I hoped you'd discover enough from Nicky so that I wouldn't have to. I'm not sure if it's that I'm terrified of what I might hear, or that I don't want to upset him by suggesting he's capable of . . .'

She looked at Emma and saw that she understood.

'I was vile to him when he sacked Antonia nearly five years ago, and he looked so hurt when he thought I'd gone to ask if he knew where Charlotte is, I was wary of wading in again without better evidence. You've now provided it and I'll have to bite the bullet.'

'Fair enough. Although couldn't you just tell the police? After all, it's not exactly your responsibility to chase up suspects, is it?'

'No.' Trish sounded doubtful. 'But I want to do everything I can, for all sorts of reasons.'

'Like what?'

'It's absurd, but since this started, I've been feeling almost as though she were my child. It's partly because I like her so much, and partly because I've seen quite a lot of myself in her, too. Everyone says she's inherited the family temper, like me. And she hasn't got a father, either. If Ben's . . . If he's hurt her, then I have to know.'

There was a pause until Emma said lightly, 'Trish, I don't believe you've ever been bad-tempered.'

'Then I must've got better at hiding it than I knew. Thank you for that, Emma.'

'It's true. Good luck with Ben. And don't forget you know him well. You were sure at the beginning that he hadn't touched Charlotte. Robert's always sounded much more likely. This new evidence can't have changed that completely.'

'Maybe not. It's a pity Robert's so bloody elusive. I know the police keep grilling him because Antonia's told me so, but I'd be happier if I'd managed to talk to him myself.'

'Why can't you?'

'Because I have no official position. If he were ever there at the house when I rang up, I could have a go, but I don't see how I could make him talk to me if I rang him cold at the office. I'd drop in one evening if I thought I'd get anywhere, but Antonia seems determined to keep me away from the house now.'

'D'you think she realises what you're afraid of?'

Trish nodded. 'She's much too intelligent not to. But she's either convinced that Nicky's guilty or desperately trying to make herself believe it. Anyway, she hasn't admitted to the slightest hint of suspicion of Robert. Maybe that's because she knows I think she should've stayed with Ben. Perhaps she thinks I might crow.'

'If she does,' said Emma, picking up her bag, 'she doesn't know very much about you. Goodbye, Trish, and thank you. For listening as well as for your offer of asylum.'

Trish stood at the top of the iron steps, waving as Emma walked to her yellow car. She thought how much more they had in common than she had ever had with Antonia, even in the early days.

Trying to get rid of the feeling of disloyalty, Trish went to the kitchen to scuffle among the out-of-date food packets in the fridge in case there was anything edible. After a while she fetched a black bag and scooped the whole lot into it before dumping it in the dustbin and taking the car to Sainsbury's. There she stocked up with enough nourishing provisions to satisfy even her mother.

Once everything was stowed, she ate a watercress-and-goat's-cheese sandwich, drank some health-giving cranberry juice and settled down to a solid afternoon's work on the book before finding enough courage to do what she knew must be done.

There was no answer to her knock at Ben's door at four o'clock, and so she sat in her parked car, waiting. At about quarter to five she heard mad Daisy's barking and got out to meet him.

'Hi, Trish!' he said, kissing her cheek and then having to pull back to restrain Daisy. 'I suppose I expected you. Come in.'

She followed him into the kitchen and watched him fill the kettle.

'Tea? Proper PG Tips, I mean, not Bella's iced stuff.'

'Thanks.'

'Great. I'll bung Daisy in the garden and then we can talk undisturbed.' She watched him unlock the back door. Daisy was out like a rocket, bucking and leaping and barking as though she had not been allowed even to smell the air for weeks.

'There,' he said, coming back to wash his hands at

the sink and then putting tea-bags into two large mugs. 'So what's the problem?'

Trish breathed carefully and stood up straighter.

'Ben, I want you to tell me what you were doing in Charlotte's park on Wednesday afternoons when you were watching her and Nicky Bagshot in the playground. And what you were doing there on Saturday.'

He blushed. That was what was unbearable. He didn't say anything. He didn't move. He just stood there, blushing. And he would not look at her. The kettle boiled and the steam must have burned his hand for he winced and moved sharply back, but even then he didn't say anything.

'Ben?'

At the sound of her voice, he did look up. She was shocked to see shame in his eyes.

'Ah, Ben. No. Please.'

'It's not what you think, Trish,' he said with difficulty.

'How do you know what I think?'

'I know that you must think I've hurt her, but I haven't. I promise. And you know that I never promise what isn't true, don't you, Trish?'

'Then why did you lie to me, Ben? And about something so important. How could you?'

'I didn't lie.'

'You told me you'd never seen her,' said Trish angrily.

He shook his head. His full but beautifully shaped mouth, which had always been his most expressive feature, twisted. Trish could not persuade herself that there was not a hint of satisfaction in the grimace. She felt that she could not bear to discover that Ben – gentle, decent, intelligent, kind Ben, whom she had thought she could have loved – was none of those things.

'What I told you,' he said, 'was that I no longer see Antonia and that I've never even met Charlotte. It's what I told the police, too. I suppose I knew I might one day have to come clean and so I was particularly careful with my words.'

It was almost impossible to ask the question, but Trish knew she could not avoid it. She leaned on the edge of the worktop and looked at him, willing him to meet her eyes. At last he did so and she thought she could see misery in his and fear, but also enough shame still to make her worst fears seem stupid.

'Come clean about what, exactly?'

'That I have been there, watching her, every Wednesday for the past six weeks. It's my half-day, Wednesday. I've taken Daisy there instead of to the common.'

'That was why I knew you'd been there. I doubt if anyone would have noticed you if it hadn't been for Daisy barking her head off.'

'But you must see that I had to have her with me. A dog is the only reasonable excuse for a middle-aged man to be hanging about in a park full of children.'

'Ben, don't! Sorry, I didn't mean that. Why did you go?'

'Here. Tea.' He found some bags and a carton of milk and proceeded to make the tea so slowly that Trish was almost screaming by the time he pushed one mug towards her. 'It was when the results of Bella's last tests finally came through. She can't ever have a child naturally. And we're both too old for fertility treatment to be a reasonable option. I . . .'

He looked at Trish, his mouth moving but not producing any sound. Seeing that he was in real diffculty, she reached over the wide worktop to touch his hand. He turned his palm upwards so that he could grip hers. That seemed to make it possible for him to speak.

'You know how much I've always wanted children,' he said, not making a question of it. 'So, being you, you'll understand. I'd always told myself that Charlotte wasn't mine. There was so little chance of it, wasn't there? You know, given what Antonia had been up to. But I . . . I began to want her to be. Even though I wasn't ever going to try to have anything to do with her . . .' He stopped and looked so self-conscious that Trish removed her hand.

'Sure about that, Ben?'

'Almost,' he admitted. 'You see, what I wanted most was to know that there was a child of mine alive in the world. I thought I'd know if I saw her . . . If I could see what she looked like, hear her, watch her playing, then I'd know if she was anything to do with me.'

'And did you?'

He shook his head. 'Sometimes I'd think she was and then sometimes I'd be certain there was nothing in her I recognised as being mine at all. She was a quick child, Trish, bright and clever and she made the other children laugh. I loved that. She was a real entertainer and popular, too. Nothing like me, you see.'

Oh don't, thought Trish. Don't go all weedy and self-critical on me, Ben. It's just about the only one of your moods I've never been able to stomach.

'Didn't you think she was like that, Trish?'

'Yes,' she said, noticing that he was using the past tense and hating it. 'Look, you must have watched the nanny as well. How did she strike you?'

Ben shrugged. 'She seemed nice enough. I never saw her hit Charlotte, or even shout at her, if that's what you mean. In fact, she always seemed remarkably gentle, always there if Charlotte fell over – or any other child, come to that. I'd believe this story she told about the other child falling off a swing. It'd fit with everything I saw during those six weeks.'

'But you must have seen that too, since you were there on Saturday,' said Trish angrily. 'Don't play games with me, Ben. This is much too serious.'

'I'd gone before that happened, Trish, if it did happen. I got there at about five to three, just as they were arriving. Charlotte was pushing her toy pram and chattering away to Nicky. I didn't stay longer than about five minutes. It seemed too risky.'

'OK. Then what about other people? Did you ever notice anyone else hanging about, watching?'

He shook his head. 'Trish?'

'Yes?'

'What are you going to do about this?'

'You mean, am I going to tell the police?'

She looked straight at him and thought she could still see traces of most of the qualities she had once believed he possessed.

'Only if you don't,' she said as gently as she could. 'You must see that they'll have to know.'

'OK.' He breathed heavily. 'But you know what I'll be risking, don't you? As far as my job's concerned.'

She shook her head. 'Not if you're innocent.'

'Don't be naive, Trish. You know how it goes. Someone in the police station rings a mate in the press and there are snide little articles, full of innuendo, not enough to sue on, but enough to put a blight on any primary teacher's career.'

'I think you may be being unfair to the police, Ben. And you must see that they have to know. Look, I'd better go. I can't . . . When it's all over we can talk properly, can't we?'

'If we can ever trust each other again.'

By that stage Trish was beyond wanting to know

what he meant. She found that she could not see properly and stumbled as she went up the three steps to the hall. He was behind her, very close. She tensed in case he touched her and hurried towards the door. Her hands were slippery as she struggled to turn the knob of the Yale lock, but she got to grips with it eventually and managed to escape without having to look at him again.

CHAPTER SIXTEEN

A t six-thirty the following morning Trish was pulled out of yet another nightmare by a tremendous banging sound. With the echoes pushing away the remains of her dream, she realised that she had not really been dragging Charlotte's bleeding, mangled body out of a cellar. The banging came again, and a shrill ringing with it. She tried to get out of bed but found her legs were tangled up in the duvet.

'Open up! Police! Open the door!'

She kicked herself free, thinking of film footage she'd seen of the police battering their way into suspects' flats on the evening news. Out of bed, swaying a little, she reached for something to cover her long legs. In her hurry, she could not find any kind of dressing gown and so she wrapped a bathtowel around her waist. She was still tucking in the free end of the makeshift sarong as she opened the door.

'You took your time,' said a man, who flashed a card at her. 'Constable Herrick.'

A peculiarly unpleasant smile widened his thin lips as he looked at her. Noticing the direction of his gaze, she glanced downwards and was not sure whether his prurient smile had been aroused by the sight of her breasts pushing out the thin cotton of her T-shirt or by its slogan. She was relieved she had changed the one about the honey and was now sporting nothing more surprising than: *I suppose you want me to be assertive. Well I'm not going to, OK?*

'Yes?' she said. 'How can I help you?'

'We'd like to ask you some questions, Miss Maguire. This is Sergeant Lacie.'

Trish, who had not been able to focus on anything except the stout young constable's unpleasantly leering expression, looked behind him to see a tall, well-dressed woman about five years older than him. The woman's expression was one of faint distaste. Her smoothly pressed clothes put Trish at even more of a disadvantage, with her tousled hair and crumpled nightshirt.

'You'd better both come in,' she said, standing back to let them walk past her into the flat and almost tripping over the towel. 'I'll just get some clothes on.'

'Yes, of course,' said the sergeant in a pleasant voice. 'Take your time.'

'Do go and sit down,' said Trish firmly, pointing towards the two vast black sofas that squatted on either side of the open fireplace. 'I won't be long.'

With memories of some of her clients' complaints against unscrupulous police officers ringing in her mind, she hurriedly stripped off her T-shirt and towel and substituted knickers and her usual jeans and a pink-and-white quartered rugger shirt. Socks and bra could wait, she thought as she scrubbed her teeth and slooshed crimson mouthwash around her gums, before running her fingers through her hair until it stood up in confident-looking black tufts.

Her eyes were pressed back in their sockets by lack

of sleep, and the rims were red as cayenne pepper, and so she stole another minute to draw black lines round them and then had to add a puff of powder blusher and a smear of lipstick to stop herself looking like a drunken panda. The final effect was not particularly enticing, but the last thing she wanted to do was entice either of the police officers.

Shoeless, she ran down the spiral staircase to see the constable poking about among the papers on her desk. With anger roughening her voice, she said, 'What are you doing? I asked you to wait for me over there.'

He turned lazily and smiled with so much offensiveness that she wondered what he and the tall sergeant could possibly have come for and decided not to offer them coffee. She was longing for some herself, not least to jump-start her brain, but that would have to wait. The constable was making no effort to obey her instructions and Trish was damned if she was going to leave him to make free with the papers on her desk while she went to the kitchen.

'Do go first,' she said, pointing once more to the sofas.

Slightly to her surprise he went, smirking, and sat at the far end of the sergeant's sofa. Trish herself took the opposite one, bunching up the scarlet, emerald and purple cushions behind her aching back.

'Well?'

'We understand,' said the sergeant, 'that you have been several times to Antonia Weblock's house since her daughter was taken and also to her ex-husband's.'

Since no question had been asked, Trish made no comment even when the silence stretched out too long.

'Isn't that right?' asked the sergeant, looking surprised.

'To be specific: I've been to Antonia's house once

and telephoned several times, and I've been to her ex-husband's twice. I hadn't realised you wanted confirmation. Why didn't you say so?'

The sergeant smiled, making her flat face look almost beautiful. 'Could you tell us why you went to see them both?'

'Why d'you think?' Trish rubbed her forehead and then her burning eyes. The last wisps of the nightmare were still floating about in her brain. 'Charlotte has disappeared. Of course I went. Wouldn't you?'

'Know Charlotte well, do you?' asked the constable, butting in as though he found his superior's manner too dilatory.

'Yes. Her mother's my cousin. Of course I know her.' Trish turned to glare at him.

'When was the last time you saw her?'

'Six weeks ago. Why?'

'Sure of that, are you?'

'Yes,' said Trish, feeling the familiar deep line pulling her eyebrows together. 'Why shouldn't I be?'

'What was the occasion of your meeting?' asked the sergeant, still sounding polite and detached, unlike her sidekick.

'I was at a dinner party held by Antonia and Robert Hithe. Charlotte came down talking of a scary nightmare, and I volunteered to put her back to bed.'

'I see,' said the sergeant, consulting a note in her little black book. 'When exactly was this party?'

'Give me a minute to look it up and I'll tell you,' said Trish, increasingly puzzled. It had, of course, occurred to her that they might suspect her of having done something to Charlotte, but she had dismissed the idea at once. It was too absurd. They could not possibly have had any evidence.

Conscious of their gaze following her to her desk,

she found her diary and checked the date of Antonia's party.

'Let me have a look,' said the constable from just behind her, making her jump.

Trish whirled round, with the diary pressed to her shirt.

'Don't creep up on me like that,' she said, taking a moment to suppress her jumpiness. 'No. There's no reason for you to see my diary. What is all this?'

If he had asked politely and without trying to startle her into co-operation, she would probably have let him see it. There were no secrets in it. But it was not a good policy to let the police get into the habit of thinking they had a right to anything they wanted. And besides, she didn't like him.

'Nervous, aren't you, Miss Maguire. Why would that be? Little private notes in it, are there? Things you wouldn't want strangers to know about you?'

As she looked at him, trying to understand why he should want to make her angry, Trish saw him pushing his lips a little forward in a proto-kiss. She made a face; she couldn't help it.

'What's all this then?' he asked, pointing at the jumble of papers, books and photocopied articles that were spread across the surface of her big trestle desk.

'I am working on a commission for Millen Books about crimes involving children.'

'Interested in that, are you?'

'Yes.' She raised her eyebrows, still feeling the ache of the frown between them. 'I'm a barrister. I've been specialising in cases involving children since I finished pupillage.'

'Why's that then?' he said, looking unimpressed. That didn't surprise Trish. She knew that most police officers loathed lawyers, just as most barristers were determined never to let the police get away with anything. Both sides had heard too many horror stories of trials that had gone wrong, bullied suspects, and convictions thrown away because of mishandled evidence.

'Because I'm a woman, Constable Herrick. When I started at the Bar, women tended to be given such work.' She was determined not to use the word briefs and see him laugh at the pun. 'As I understand was once the case in the police force.'

He wandered away from her towards her computer.

'You on the Internet at all?'

'Yes,' said Trish warily. 'Why?'

'Ever come across pornography on it?'

'Yes, Constable Herrick. I do. It's part of my work.'

'Like it, do you?'

'No. I find it repellent, as I find the way you're asking these questions. If you have nothing else to say to me, I'd like you both to leave now. I certainly have nothing to say to you.'

'You're wrong there, Ms Maguire. You've got a lot to tell us. For a start, what exactly you did with Charlotte Weblock when you were up in her bedroom during her mother's dinner party. And how many other times you were alone with her, and how you made her—'

Trish stared at him, appalled. The brief time she had spent with Charlotte had meant a great deal. To have a man like Constable Herrick licking over it revolted her.

'That's enough,' she interrupted. 'I have said that I would like you to leave. Please do so now.'

The constable tried to bluster and demand an account of everything she had done since the previous Saturday morning, but Trish was too angry to give him anything he wanted. When he tried to bully her, she recited the law relating to the questioning of suspects who were not under arrest. She had meant to keep her voice cold and low, but she found herself shouting before she had reached the end.

The sergeant came to join in.

'Ms Maguire,' she said, smiling gravely, 'you must understand that in our efforts to find Charlotte Weblock we have to ask all sorts of apparently impertinent questions of everyone who could possibly tell us anything that might be useful.'

'I'm well aware of that,' said Trish through her teeth.

'Then please could Sam have a look round your flat?'

'Not without a warrant,' she said, moving towards the front door. 'Unless you're going to arrest me, I'd like you both to go now. This is outrageous.'

'I'm sorry you see it like that. Everyone else we've been to interview has been very co-operative. Are you sure . . . ?'

'Will you please leave. *Now*.'

'Sam?'

He looked as though he might protest, but after a moment he followed the sergeant quite meekly. Having shut the door on them both, Trish stomped towards the kitchen, swearing as she went.

She cursed the constable and herself for having lost her temper and even Ben for having worried her so much the day before that she hadn't slept properly. If she'd had a better night, she'd have handled the police much more sensibly.

Banging her hands against the worktop and crunching one of her mugs on the edge of the sink, taking such a huge chip out of it that she had to throw it away, she eventually managed to make herself some vaguely drinkable coffee. She ate some toast, too, hoping the carbohydrate would calm her down. When she could trust herself, she rang Antonia, who sounded preoccupied and unfriendly.

'What d'you want, Trish?'

'Just to tell you the preliminary results of Emma's polygraph test.'

'Oh, yes? Did she find out anything useful?'

'Only that it seems likely that everything Nicky said about the playground was true.'

'Well, that's not much help, is it?'

'And that there's a possibility that she caught a glimpse of Charlotte's swimming teacher there. She did get very muddled when Emma tried to confirm it and said what she must've meant was that she'd seen him at the pool earlier in the day, but I thought you might want to tell DCI Blake. It could be useful for him to know the swimming teacher could have been there.'

There was silence.

'Antonia? Are you there?'

'Yes, of course I'm here. I'll tell him, all right, but I don't see what good it'll do. The swimming pool's only about four minutes' walk away. There's no reason on earth why he shouldn't be walking through the park.'

'No, I suppose not. Antonia?'

'Yes? What now? I'm very busy and Blake's due any minute. He's insisted that Robert wait here to answer yet more questions.'

'Oh, I see. Right. Well, I won't keep you then.'

'Before you go, Trish, if you're talking to your mother, will you thank her for writing to me? It was really kind of her, and luckily her letter arrived before I started burning the mail.'

'What?'

'I've been getting anonymous filth by every post.

"Serves you right, a bitch like you." "If you're not prepared to look after children, you shouldn't have them." "Mothers like you should hang." That sort of thing. I couldn't go on reading them. Now I just pick out letters with writing I recognise – or obviously official stuff – and burn the rest without even opening it. Robert's and Nicky's, too. They've had some revolting stuff, both of them. It's better burned before they even see it.'

'Don't the police mind?' asked Trish, worried.

'It's none of their business. Goodbye, Trish.'

Well, that didn't do much good, thought Trish, as she made another mug of coffee. She took it to her desk, where she started to tidy up the mess. When she had relabelled a whole boxful of floppies and filed heaps of letters, she had given herself at least an illusion of control over her work.

That done, she switched on her computer to re-read what she had written in the draft introduction to the book. As she read, she was surprised by the clarity of the aims she had set out and began to feel happier until she came on the description of the murder of a four-year-old girl.

That child had been strangled. It was impossible not to see Charlotte, with her pale face still and her dark curls tumbled, lying with a great purple bruise spreading around her neck like some macabre necklace.

'Oh, God,' said Trish as she leaned forwards, resting her face in her hands.

CHAPTER SEVENTEEN

'Well, Kath?'
        'I'm not sure, sir.'
    'Why?' Blake knew he sounded impatient, much more
so than he usually was with her. He couldn't help it.
    None of the house-to-house enquiries near the park
had produced anything; none of the bus drivers on
the relevant routes had caught even a glimpse of
the child. The closed-circuit televisions had produced
nothing useful. None of the known paedophiles had
been anywhere near the playground at the operative
time. The expensive second dragging of the park's pond
had been as useless as the first. All the budgets had been
crashed; none of the team had come up with anything
yet, and he was being hassled by the superintendent
because *he* was being hassled by the media and the
politicians. You had to get a result quickly in a case
of child-killing.
    'Maguire seemed OK,' Kath told him, unfazed by
his spurt of temper. 'It's true she looked as if she was
living in a nightmare, but then she would, wouldn't
she? I mean, anyone involved with Charlotte would

be. And I know it's not proof of anything, sir, but her eyes looked honest to me.'

'You're right, Kath,' he said unpleasantly, 'it's not proof of anything. And you should know better than to make silly judgements like that. Anyway, if she's so honest, why wouldn't she answer Sam's questions or allow him to look at the stuff on her desk? She was obstructive, not just uncooperative, from what he's told me.'

'That's true, but you know how Sam can be. I always thought it was a mistake to let him loose on her.'

'Then why the fucking hell did you agree to it?'

She didn't remind him, as she could have done, that he had ordered her to give Sam his head. After a moment she said quietly, 'I should have insisted on following my first instinct and asked the questions myself. I have a feeling she might have answered them. I'm sure she's on our side. But she is a brief; and you know what they can be like when they get angry.'

'You could be right,' he said, trying to match her fairness. 'On the other hand, it's all a bit too suggestive, isn't it? Come on, for a minute, Kath, forget feminist sympathy or whatever it is and use your head. There's a lot about Maguire that's bloody suspicious.'

Blake thought of the tall thin woman he'd met on Sunday, whose harshly magnificent face and anguished eyes had softened as she tried to comfort Antonia. Could a woman like that really be capable of what had been suggested?

'What was it the mother said about Charlotte's bruises, sir?'

'What? Not a lot more than I've already told you, Kath. She was reluctant to say anything much on Sunday. That's partly what worried me when I started to think about it, but even when I got her on her own she wasn't very forthcoming. When pressed, she had to admit that she did first see the bruises on the day after Maguire'd been there in the house, and alone with the child in her bedroom.'

'Still. It could be coincidence, couldn't it? And Bagshot did provide an explanation for the bruising that had nothing to do with Maguire.'

'I know. And I believed it for a while, until I'd heard all the rest and discovered how long Maguire had had up there alone with Charlotte. They were up in that room together for nearly twenty minutes, which is a long time in the middle of someone else's dinner party, don't you think?'

Kath shrugged. Her face was unhappy.

'I can't get this picture out of my head,' said Blake, wishing he could, 'of the child terrorised into silence, not daring to call out for help because she couldn't be sure that Maguire had gone. After all, she must've thought her mother had handed her to Maguire.'

Kath frowned, shaking her head. 'Any news from the lab. yet about the pram, sir?'

Blake nodded and handed her the report. Kath read it, her tender mouth tightening and her eyes anxious.

'So there *are* two sorts of blood in the pram: one lot belongs to the boy with the scraped knees; but the other is quite different.' She looked up. 'Did the GP have any samples of Charlotte's blood?'

'No. Antonia was right about that. But the hair in the pram matches that on Charlotte's brush and the soil *is* from the garden.'

'But they didn't find anything when they dug up the garden, did they?' said Kath.

'Only that piece of thick plastic. But it seems to be irrelevant. It looks as if it's been there for a while, probably ever since the landscaping was done. I don't think it's got anything to do with Charlotte. But there had been recent digging near it. It looks as though someone started off by trying to bury the body in the garden and then panicked when they heard something, and decided it would be safer to get it right away from the house.'

'Then Maguire couldn't have had anything to do with it, sir. There's been no suggestion that she was anywhere near Kensington on Saturday, has there? None of what you've got on her is more than gossip – and the coincidence that Antonia saw the bruises the day after Maguire was with the child in her bedroom. It's not enough to hang a cat on.'

He looked at her and then, without answering her question, said, 'There is more. Nothing helpful like hard evidence, but one or two suggestive things. I know you liked Maguire, but we've been checking up on her and it's clear she's unstable. She's even had to leave chambers for a spell because they were afraid she was cracking up. And there are serious questions over her sexuality, too. We have to pursue it, Kath. *Someone* took Charlotte Weblock. We've got to explore every possible suspect, however unlikely.'

'Yes, I know. But no one saw Maguire anywhere near the house at any time on Saturday, did they?' she said doggedly.

'Nope. But then Bagshot was here, crying all over the desk sergeant, telling him the kid had gone missing; the stepfather was in his meeting; the cleaner's never there on Saturday; and all the neighbours were in their country cottages. It's entirely possible that Maguire snatched the kid from the park and then seized her chance to bury the body in Antonia's garden when the rest of them were safely out of the way.'

'I don't believe it, sir. I just don't believe it. And it doesn't fit anyway. If it was Maguire, then the pram and the blood and the hairs are all irrelevant because Nicky had the pram with her when she came to make her first report here, didn't she?'

'True,' said Blake, annoyed that Kath was determined to make complications for their own sake. 'But they could be in it together. I've always thought it unlikely that Bagshot was the whole answer. At first I assumed she was in cahoots with Robert Hithe. Since I heard about Maguire's background, she's seemed an even likelier accomplice. Nothing makes sense unless there was a conspiracy between at least two of them. Bagshot must be in it and either – or possibly both – of the others. We've got to find out which.'

Kath took a moment to think about it.

'Maybe. But I find it hard to believe. You know the hairs in the pram, sir? They've been worrying me, too. Couldn't they have got there naturally? I mean, little girls do bend right into their toy prams when they're laying dolls to sleep. I've seen them do it.' She smiled. 'I even did it myself. It would be easy to get one's hair caught and tug some out as one pulled away. Couldn't it be that?'

'Possibly, but the lab. boys don't think so.' The thought of her playing with her dolls and the smile had taken the edge off his irritation for the moment. He smiled back. 'The suggestion was made quite early on and dismissed. And then there's the blood, which must be Charlotte's: not quite enough of it for us to be sure, but it's rubbed into the creases and seams of the mattress, as though someone had cleaned the rest off.'

'What about prints?'

'Several all over the pram, of course. Antonia's,

Charlotte's, Nicky's. None of Robert Hithe's, but quite
a few still unidentified. I'd like to print Maguire, but
I can't see her giving her consent, and we're not
going to get an arrest warrant without more evidence.
You'll—'

'Sir?'

At the sound of a third voice from the doorway, Kath
and Blake looked away from each other with difficulty.
Blake saw from the newcomer's face that he'd heard all
the gossip about them in the nick, and he wished he'd
hidden his feelings better. It wasn't fair on Kath. He
could see that. He didn't want them to start treating
her like the relief bicycle. He'd seen what that did to
women.

'Yes, Martin?' he said coldly.

'The superintendent wants a word, sir.'

'OK. I'll go straight up. You'd better go ahead then,
Kath, and get a warrant to search Maguire's place –
and her car. There's no real evidence yet, but somehow
I don't think the magistrate will cavil at a search warrant,
at least not in the circumstances. The way she's been
trawling the Net for paedophile pornography could be
enough in itself. Some of the stuff she's been looking
at is . . . it's the worst, Kath. There's something very
odd about her. You must accept that.'

'The pornography could be for the book she's writing,
though, sir,' said Kath, hoping that she was right. 'I
thought I'd get on to her publishers to find out what
they know about the work she's done so far.'

'OK. Not a bad idea.' Then, as though sensing DC
Martin's impatience, Blake put both hands flat on
the desk and pushed himself quickly into a standing
position.

He'd hated the case from the beginning and it looked
as though it was about to get very nasty indeed. He

found himself wishing he could have kept Kath out of it and then realised he was on the point of losing it completely. She was a police officer, heading for a good few promotions yet; if she couldn't take something like this, she shouldn't be in the job.

Oh, fuck it! Somehow he was going to have to get her out of his mind, her and the gloomily atmospheric Leonard Cohen songs that kept running through his head whenever he tried to sleep at night and found her image sliding into bed between him and Lydia. He'd even bought himself a thin green candle in an access of sentimentality the previous lunchtime and then had to chuck it away in a street litter bin before anyone saw it and decided he'd flipped.

'OK, Martin, I'm with you. Get on with it, Kath. Bring back everything that might have any relevance at all, and we'll see if we can get enough to have Maguire in and start interviewing her. Don't take Sam with you this time. That was an error on my part. You're right – Maguire obviously responds better to women. Take Derring. Between you, the pair of you may be able to get what we need out of her.'

'Will do, sir.'

Blake checked to make sure her eyes were calm enough and then nodded to her and went up to answer to the superintendent for his part in the failure to turn up a body. It was a pig of a case.

CHAPTER EIGHTEEN

A nd so it is essential that the emphasis of any punishment
is weighted towards rehabilitation and away from retri-
bution. Education is what is needed; not revenge, Trish typed
carefully. *It is necessary . . . important . . . crucial that
offenders be made aware of the effect they have had on their
victims. That is of infinitely greater importance than adding
to their sense of being unfairly persecuted for something that,
in their minds, 'doesn't matter all that much'.*

She re-read the paragraph, saw all its imperfections,
and then realised that her brain had gone fuzzy and
was not going to allow her to improve anything she
had written just then. When she had saved a copy of
the edited document, she put both hands behind her to
stretch away the aches in her back and arms, but she got
that wrong, too, and set up a screaming pain down the
back of her neck. Long experience had told her that she
would have to hold it in both hands, breathing deeply,
until it was bearable again.

About halfway through the process, she heard more
knocking at the front door.

'Hang on a sec!' she called through the pain and then,

still holding her neck with her left hand, the arm pressed in a V-shape between her breasts, she got up to open the door.

At the sight of the good-looking sergeant, this time accompanied by a second woman instead of the unpleasant constable of the morning's visit, Trish let go of her neck.

'I thought I told you that I had nothing more to say, Sergeant Lacie,' she said coldly, standing in the narrow gap between the door and the jamb to guard the way into her flat.

'We have a warrant, Ms Maguire.'

'A warrant? What kind of warrant?' Trish put out her right hand and received the familiar-looking piece of paper. She read it with care. After a moment she looked up at the police in astonishment.

'You suspect that *I* have Charlotte Weblock *here*? Why didn't you say so this morning, instead of letting that oaf you brought with you get up my nose so badly. You're mad if you think I've got her, but you're at liberty to look wherever you want. You didn't need a warrant for that. I'd have let you in.'

'But I asked you to let us look,' Sergeant Lacie said in surprise. 'This morning.'

'Did you?' Trish remembered the shameful surge of temper that had overtaken her in the morning and eased her conscience with the knowledge that there had been provocation. 'Sorry. But you should have asked first instead of setting him on to accuse me.'

She opened the door wide without another word and stood back to let the two women into her flat. As they moved past her, Trish added quickly, 'But I should like to file the document I've been working on. I don't want to risk losing a day's work if one of you hits the wrong button.'

'We'd like you to print it out first. Constable Derring will come with you,' said Kath Lacie calmly.

'I don't see,' said Trish out of principle rather than any kind of anxiety, 'anything in your warrant to justify that. You're not allowed to ransack the place, you know. You have permission to search for a child. That's all.'

Kath Lacie took a second warrant out of her bag and handed it to Trish. It was as she read that one that she began to worry. The warrant gave Sergeant Kathleen Lacie the power to search for and remove indecent photographs or pseudophotographs of a child under Section 4 of the Protection of Children Act, 1978.

Nothing that Trish planned to use in her book came anywhere near the definition of such material – she would have hated to publish any such thing – but she had searched the Internet for examples of the indescribably degrading pornography she was convinced was the cause of some of the cruellest crimes against children. She had downloaded some of it, too, for use as examples if she had to persuade doubters in the publishing house of the seriousness of the material that was so easily available.

'Very well,' said Trish, moving to her desk.

As the printer clunked its way through twenty-five pages of the still inadequately written third chapter, Trish watched the women moving through her flat in search of Charlotte. They went through her cupboards, touching her clothes; they probed for loose floorboards and false panels in the walls; they insisted on pulling down the loft ladder that led up into the roofspace so that they could check there, too. They opened every door and lid; they touched everything they saw.

Trish stood and watched them and knew that it was irrational to think she'd have to scour the place before

211

she could bear to live in it once they'd gone. After a while, leaving Constable Derring to her work, Sergeant Lacie came back to Trish's desk, where the printer was chattering out the last page of her chapter.

'Thank you,' Lacie said when Trish silently handed her the pages and turned away to file the document. 'When did you last see Charlotte Weblock?'

'I've already told you that. I have nothing to add to what I said this morning. I have not seen Charlotte Weblock since her mother's dinner party six weeks ago. That's all you need to know. Now do please get on with your job and find her. It's been nearly four days. You know what that means as well as I do. But she could still be alive. If she is and you're fiddling about here while she's being . . .' Trish breathed with extreme care to keep everything working normally. 'You won't be able to live with yourself if that's the case.'

'That cuts both ways, Ms Maguire. If you have nothing to hide, you have no reason to object to any of our questions. We need your answers if we're to find her.'

'You're wasting time. Can't you see that? I've told you I haven't seen her for six weeks,' said Trish, wondering how she was ever going to get through to them. She could feel the anger beginning to tighten at the base of her brain.

'Every citizen has a duty to help the police in their enquiries.'

'Only a moral duty,' Trish reminded her automatically. 'There's no law that says I *have* to talk to you. But, as you must know, if there was anything helpful I could tell you, I'd have done it days ago. I want Charlotte back more than anyone.'

'Well, that's something. You're sure you haven't seen her since the dinner party?'

'How many more times? Yes, I'm sure.'

When pressed, Trish impatiently repeated the whole story of Charlotte's appearance and added all the details of how she had persuaded the child back to bed, and denied all knowledge of the bruises Antonia said she saw the following evening.

'You have a certain amount of experience of caring for little children, haven't you?' said Sergeant Lacie suddenly.

'I don't know what you mean,' said Trish, puzzled. 'Unless you're talking about my legal experience.'

'No.' Sergeant Lacie was talking as quietly as ever but with rather less gentleness. 'I'm talking about the babysitting you used to do and your experience with your godchildren. You have four, I understand, three girls and a boy.'

Trish said nothing, wondering where Lacie had got her information and why she had bothered.

'Is that right?'

'Certainly, Sergeant Lacie. But I do not see how it is relevant.'

'You were taking care of your godson . . .' she looked down at her notebook, 'your godson, Philip Clark, when he suffered a serious cut in his head. Isn't that right?'

'Yes,' said Trish, the cleft between her eyebrows deepening. 'Nearly five years ago. He fell from the climbing frame in his parents' garden and caught his head on the edge of a toy lorry he had left there earlier.'

'He needed stitches, didn't he?'

'Yes.' Trish could not imagine how the police had got hold of the story. Unfortunately she could see exactly where they were planning to go with it. She remembered his screams, rhythmic bursts of shattering sound that had frightened both of them even more than the blood and pain. 'I took him to the local casualty unit and they stitched him there. He was fine then.'

'And your goddaughter, Patricia Smith-Cunningham, suffered a burn when she was here in this flat, two years ago, didn't she?'

'A tiny little burn, yes.' The memories of that incident were much less worrying. 'We were cooking toffee and she got over-excited and dropped a smidgeon of boiling syrup on her hand. It scared her and she howled, but I had some Acriflex in the kitchen cupboard and she calmed down as soon as I'd put it on.'

'You've never been married, have you?' said Sergeant Lacie, switching subjects with an abruptness that would have told Trish exactly what she was trying to do if there had ever been any doubt about it.

'That's enough,' she said. 'I do not know what it is you are trying to suggest, but whatever it is, you'd better stop.'

'You have had a series of affairs with men, have you not?' pursued the sergeant, not looking as though she were enjoying her job. 'But each one lasts less time than the one before.'

She waited but Trish said nothing. Her rights were clear: she had no need to answer anything.

'Each one becomes less satisfactory than the one before,' the sergeant went on. 'Perhaps because, as I believe you once announced at a party, the trouble with men is that they tend to behave like children given half a chance, and yet have none of the charm of children and are not nearly as attractive.'

Trish controlled her impulse to fling up her hands in frustration. There seemed no point trying to explain the circumstances in which she had made that frivolous remark or exactly what she had meant by it. Lacie sounded so convinced by her fantastic theory that she probably wouldn't listen. 'May I ask where you've got this extraordinary picture from?'

'You know better than that, Ms Maguire,' said Sergeant Lacie with what was beginning to look like pity mixed in with the disgust in her eyes. That was almost the worst of it all: the pity. It suggested that someone had managed to convince her that Trish was capable of that most dreadful crime: damaging a child.

'You said, I believe, on another occasion, that there is no physical sensation as satisfying as holding a newly bathed child on your knee.' That was a remark Trish could not remember making, but she could well believe that she had said it to someone, the mother of one of her godchildren, probably, or to one of the women for whom she had done babysitting in the days before she had earned any real money at the Bar. It was the kind of spontaneous comment anyone might make, she thought. And it *was* a charming sensation – a firm, wriggly body wrapped in its towel sitting on your knee and a cajoling young voice begging for a story or for another game.

Trish could feel the blood thumping in her cheeks, making her teeth ache, and wished she could control her reactions better.

'You find it hard to get satisfaction from sex with adults, don't you? So do you find it easier with children?'

'Don't be ridiculous.' Emotion had affected the nerves that controlled Trish's voice and made it sound almost violent.

'Children are easy to control, aren't they, when they're a little frightened? Do you hurt them a bit first to show what power you have over them and then make them—'

'That's enough,' said Trish passionately as her fingers

215

curled into the palms of her hands. 'You must know that what you're saying is rubbish.'

'Perhaps you didn't let yourself go all the way to begin with. Perhaps you stuck for a while at the point of teasing yourself with it; you'd do the hurting and then you'd hold back: the cut in Philip's head, the burn on Patricia's hand, the bruises on Charlotte's arms. Perhaps you hadn't ever tried anything else until last Saturday. Perhaps until then you'd managed to get all the satisfaction you need from pornography. Was that it? You'd excite yourself first with real children and then avoid the worst risks by letting them go at that point and switching to pictures on your screen. And then when you did let yourself go on Saturday, you found yourself going further than you meant.'

As Sergeant Lacie went on making her fantastic, appalling allegations, it became clear that she and her colleagues had been searching through the whole of Trish's past, talking to her friends and relations, building up a picture of her as a wildly dysfunctional, dangerously obsessive woman, weirdly interested in the damage done to little children and capable of mind-numbing cruelty.

Trish stood, and kept the sergeant standing, while the tide of innuendo, accusation, and misinterpreted fact flowed over like a stinking mud slide. She felt filthy and degraded and bitterly humiliated. In a way, she thought as she listened to it all going on and on, it would have been less terrible coming from the constable who had been so unpleasant that morning. At least he would have made it easier to dismiss the accusations as the ravings of a lunatic. Spoken in Kath Lacie's pleasant, educated voice, issuing from her calm, attractive face, they sounded almost credible.

When Sergeant Lacie eventually ceased to speak and

stood waiting for a comment, Trish dashed the back of her hand across her eyes. There were no tears there, she told herself, just the scalding pain of fury.

'You can't possibly believe any of that,' she said, her voice shaking with the effort of control. 'Look, I pity you for what they've made you do. I have no comment except to say that it is all completely ludicrous. I have no idea what has happened to Charlotte. If I had, I should have told you as soon as I heard she was missing.'

As Trish spoke, she remembered Ben saying something very similar and the sensation of standing under a stream of shit changed to one of dreadful cold. There were very few people who could have told the police so much about her. But one of them was Ben. She remembered threatening to tell the police about his expeditions to Charlotte's playground if he did not confess them first.

'What is it, Ms Maguire?'

'What?'

'What are you thinking? You look . . .'

'Yes? How exactly do I look?' asked Trish with far more aggression than she usually allowed to escape into her voice. The harshness of it shocked her, but she was damned if she was going to apologise to anyone who had said such things to her, however reluctantly.

'As though you might pass out. Is that perhaps because we have come so near to something you thought you would be able to hide from us?'

'Oh, stop it!' Trish had stemmed most of her anger by then and felt merely tired of the whole idiotic situation. 'You must know this is all rubbish. Look, if you're not going to arrest me, get out. If you are, get on with it.' She held out both hands as though to allow the sergeant to clap handcuffs on her.

'You don't seem to understand how serious this is.

We are trying to trace a very young, very vulnerable child.'

'Of course I understand. Christ Almighty! Do you think I haven't spent the last four days and nights in constant terror for Charlotte? I just wish I knew who hated me enough to have tried to make you believe this crap about me.'

It was Sergeant Lacie's turn to stand in silence, an obstructive expression in her eyes.

'Who was it, Sergeant?'

'You can't expect me to answer that – even if I knew, which I do not.'

'Sarge?' The constable who had been riffling through the papers on Trish's desk and the files beneath it, was standing straight up again. There was a large pile of computer printout in front of her and a box of floppies.

'Yes, Jenny?'

'I'm ready.'

'Fine. We can leave you in peace now, Ms Maguire, but if . . .'

'I'm glad to hear it,' said Trish. 'In that case, I should be grateful if you would give me a detailed receipt of everything you are planning to remove and then leave me alone.'

Kath Lacie made no protest and Constable Derring sat down at the desk and laboriously wrote out on two pieces of lined paper sandwiched around a creased and patchy sheet of carbon paper provided by Trish a list of all the papers, disks and photographs that had been packed in the black bag for transport to the police station.

Trish watched in silence and then at the end, as first she and then Kath signed both copies, she said, 'I should like to make it clear that if anything is mislaid or damaged in any way I shall sue. And if anything quoted from the material you have taken, or any of the ludicrous allegations you have made against me, reaches the newspapers I shall sue over that, too.'

'How can you say that?' asked Sergeant Lacie, looking hurt. Trish knew perfectly well that the pain was synthetic.

'That, Sergeant, is as nothing to the allegations you have been making against me. Even if you yourself have never given the press any information, you must admit that other members of your force have done so in the past. Goodbye.'

They went, carrying the black bin bag, without another word. Trish was left feeling scoured by fury, misery and a shame she did not deserve. She felt useless and sick. She did not think she would ever again be as she had been before Sergeant Lacie's visit, and she could not believe that none of their suspicions would leak out of the police station.

If they did she was in for a bad time. Ben's earlier comment only underlined what she already knew of the gullibility of the public. The thought of the shock – and distress – her friends and relations would suffer if they came to hear even the most minor of the accusations was vile.

Trish thought of her mother, too, and reached for the telephone. She would have preferred to get herself under some kind of control before they spoke, but she could not bear to wait. The telephone rang in the Beaconsfield cottage until the machine cut in.

'Hello, this is Meg Maguire. Thank you for ringing. I'm sorry I haven't answered your call myself, but if you will leave a message, I'll get back to you as soon as I can.'

'Mum? It's me, Trish. Can you ring me back? I need to talk. I'll be here when you ring. Bye.'

She put down the telephone and saw the devastation of her desk all over again. With tears prickling in her eyes, she shook her head and went upstairs, hoping to wash away some of the filth that still seemed to cling to her.

After fifteen minutes of standing under the hot, needle-like jets, she felt very little better. She rubbed the water out of her eyes, wondering why they were stinging so much more than usual, and reached for a towel. It was then, as she was standing with one foot in the shower cabinet and one on the floor outside that she became aware of the one huge omission in the questions Sergeant Lacie had asked. Not once had she suggested that she wanted to know where Trish had been on Saturday afternoon, or with whom. During the first interrogation of the day Constable Herrick had asked for an account of her movements, but Trish had been too angry to answer. Kath Lacie had forgotten to ask. It was an extraordinary mistake and could have been made only, Trish thought, because she had, after all, hated what she had been sent to do.

Catching sight of herself in the mirror and smiling for the first time that day, Trish understood the reason for her stinging eyes. She had completely forgotten the eyeliner and mascara she had put on that morning and had been laboriously rubbing them into her eyes. Looking more like a drunken panda than ever, she tore a bunch of cotton wool off the thick roll, soaked it in oil-free eye-makeup remover and set about wiping off all the marks. When it was done, her face was pale and undefended but also, she thought, marked by the accusations they had made.

Tempted though she was to let the police run with

their suspicions and make serious fools of themselves, she knew she could not do anything so irresponsible. Charlotte still had to be found.

Dressed again in the same clothes as before but with the addition of bra, socks and shoes, Trish fetched a jacket and drove to the Kensington Church Street police station. She did not want to risk any telephone message being incorrectly relayed.

'Yes, miss?' said the officer at the desk with a fine disregard for political correctness.

'I'd like to see Sergeant Lacie, please.'

'In connection with what, may I ask?'

'The Charlotte Weblock case.'

'If you have information, miss, you can give it to me and I'll see the sergeant gets it.'

'Constable,' said Trish, having checked his uniform, 'will you please call up to Sergeant Lacie at once and tell her that Trish Maguire is here and would appreciate a word. If she is not here or is busy, please tell Chief Inspector . . .' for a moment she could not remember the name of the man who had treated Antonia so sensibly on Monday morning, and then it came back to her. 'Chief Inspector Blake instead.'

'I'll see, miss. Would you like to take a seat at all?' He waved to a plastic-upholstered bench, on which a fat woman hung about with rags and bags was sitting, muttering to herself.

Trish caught a whiff of the strong ammoniac smell of ancient dirt and urine, which rose from the old woman's clothes and, in a surge of pity, almost forgot Charlotte. There was too much to be done, she told herself. You had to ration your compassion; you could not help everyone who needed help. You'd beggar yourself and wear yourself out and you still couldn't do it all. The only way to live with any kind of ease was to help the people you knew, your friends, your relations and your clients, and leave it at that. Otherwise you would have nothing to give yourself – or anyone else.

'Ms Maguire?'

She looked away from the dirty, mumbling, frightened woman on the bench and saw both Sergeant Lacie and DCI Blake. Their faces shared the same hard expression that did not completely hide their excitement.

'Would you come in here, please?' said Blake seriously, holding open the door of one of the interview rooms.

As soon as Lacie had shut the door and Blake had started fiddling with the built-in tape recorder, Trish said, 'Look, I haven't come to confess to anything, if that's what you think. You won't need a tape recorder.'

They both stopped what they were doing and looked at her and then at each other.

'I came to say, Sergeant Lacie, that you never asked where I was last Saturday afternoon and it didn't occur to me until after you'd gone. But I was with two friends,' said Trish calmly. 'We all lunched in full view of about fifty people in the Oxo Tower brasserie and then went to an exhibition at the Hayward, before watching the five-thirty showing of a film at the National Film Theatre. You'll want to get hold of my companions,' she added before dictating their names, addresses and telephone numbers.

'Why on earth didn't you say all this earlier?' asked Kath Lacie, apparently too angry to think.

'Because the constable you brought with you this morning was so gratuitously offensive that I lost my temper. I shouldn't have, but I did. And then this afternoon, I was so shocked – and disturbed – by the accusations you made that I couldn't remember anything as simple as the need to offer an alibi. And you never asked for one.'

'That's not a very likely story, is it, Ms Maguire?' said Blake. 'From some people I'd accept it, but you're a barrister. You're far too experienced to make a mistake like that.'

'You underestimate the effect of a police search and attempted interrogation,' said Trish drily.

'I see. Or perhaps you've spent the intervening hour setting up this alibi with two complaisant friends?'

'I realise that you'll have to check it. But although I didn't settle the bill at the Oxo Tower, I did buy the cinema tickets and I put them on my credit card. Access will have evidence of the payment.'

'That hardly proves you saw the film. You could easily have left the cinema once you'd paid.'

'True enough. But I think you'll find that the two people I went with are acceptable witnesses – acceptable to the court, that is. They are both barristers, too, and neither is going to lie to give me an alibi. Besides, they're well known at the Oxo Tower. Talk to the staff there. I think you'll find someone who remembers seeing all three of us.'

'What time did you leave the National Film Theatre?'

'I can't remember exactly. I should think it must have been about eight.'

'And then?'

'I went home. But you don't need to know all this. Hadn't Nicky come to report Charlotte's disappearance hours before?'

'The disappearance was only the beginning of the story,' said Kath Lacie drily. 'As you must know.'

'You think I might have commissioned someone to pick Charlotte up for me. Is that it?' Seeing what looked like confirmation in Blake's face, Trish shrugged. 'Then I give up. Poor Charlotte.'

'What d'you mean?'

'To have one's fate dependent on people prepared to waste so much time on such ludicrous fantasies . . . if it wasn't so tragic it would be almost funny.'

A dark flush seeped into the skin under Blake's cheekbones.

'We'll need to check this information,' he said, completely po-faced. 'I'd like you to wait here while we do it.'

'I'm sure you would,' said Trish, smiling politely. 'But I'm not going to. I'm going home – unless you choose to arrest me. You know how to get hold of me. I'm not going to disappear.'

'I'd rather you waited.'

'I'm sure you would,' she repeated. 'But there's only one thing that will keep me here.'

He had no option but to let her go. She was aware that if he and his colleagues decided to be vindictive they could still try to have her prosecuted for possessing pornography. It wouldn't be difficult to defend herself against the charge, particularly not with the backing of Millen Books, but it would be time-consuming and might have unpleasant repercussions.

Once again she asked who it was who had provided the spiteful information about her godchildren and her past disastrous love affairs. Blake refused to tell her anything.

When she gave up trying to make him talk, she left the police station to look for a public telephone. Since she was in Kensington it seemed a good opportunity to see Antonia, but her call was answered by the machine. Trish left yet another affectionate message, as usual offering help and support.

Back in Southwark, she discovered that the front door to her flat was no longer double locked and she began to smile. There was only one other person who had keys. In the past her unsolicited visits and unwanted deliveries of nourishing one-pot meals for the freezer and bumper supplies of vitamins had sometimes been irritating, but that afternoon the thought of her presence was a boon.

Trish pushed open the door, calling, 'Mum? Are you there?'

'Trish, darling, how are you?' called her mother from the far end of the enormous room. She came towards Trish with her arms extended. Feeling about twelve again, Trish walked forward and let herself be hugged.

'Thank you,' she said a moment later as she let go. 'I needed that.'

'You've been having a hellish time, haven't you? I thought you could probably do with a bit of company.'

'You've been having a bad time, too, by the look of it,' said Trish when she had examined her mother's face. 'They've been at you, haven't they, the police? Oh Mum, I am *so* sorry. What did they ask?'

Her mother shook her head, making the blunt-cut gleaming grey hair swing freely.

'Nothing I couldn't answer with absolute confidence. Don't look like that, Trish. You don't need to worry about anything the police said to me.'

Trish looked directly into her mother's clear blue eyes and was amazed to see unshadowed trust in them.

'If they said to you a tenth of what I had to listen to today, then I am really touched that you came here and that you hugged me like that.'

Tears seeped into her eyes. Meg reached forward to brush away the one that spilled.

'Oh, Trish. You can't have thought I'd believe you ever deliberately hurt any of your godchildren or . . . or abused any child in any way, or that you had anything whatsoever to do with what's happened to Charlotte. I remembered all the incidents the police talked to me about quite well, and I know that every one was an accident, the kind of thing that happens to anyone who looks after children.'

'Thank you. I can't tell you how much it helps.'

'Heavens, I had a friend whose baby rolled off the changing table and cracked her skull. That's infinitely worse than any of the injuries that happened to children in your care, and no one ever accused her of doing it on purpose.'

'That must have been some time ago,' said Trish sadly. She sniffed. 'Nowadays any child that badly injured would be on the at-risk register at once.'

'Go and get something to blow your nose with,' said Meg as though Trish were indeed twelve again, 'and I'll put the kettle on.'

Trish went up the spiral stairs to wash her face. Then she put some more mascara on and went back downstairs, feeling a little more in control.

Meg presented her with a steaming mug. Trish caught the scent and said, 'Marmite! That takes me back.'

'Drink up. I'll make you some supper later. You've obviously not been eating again, in spite of all the food you've got here. Honestly, you are hopeless, Trish! It's not surprising you've got yourself in such a state.'

'I forget sometimes,' she said, before obediently sipping the delectable liquid. It was what she had always been given to drink as a child whenever she was ill or miserable. 'And then when I try to eat, I think about

Charlotte and what could be happening, and I find I can't swallow much. But this is great. I should've thought of it before. Thanks, Mum.'

'Pleasure,' said Meg, who had made herself tea. 'Now, tell me. Haven't the police found out anything about what's happened to Charlotte?'

Trish shrugged. 'They can't have, or they wouldn't have gone after me today.'

'She must be dead, mustn't she?' Meg blinked several times to get rid of the unshed tears. 'By now?'

'I think so. Unless someone's keeping her somewhere – like in that awful Belgian case. I'm sorry, Mum.'

Meg put her hand over her eyes for a moment. Then she smiled resolutely and drank some tea.

'It's just that she looks so like you did, Trish. I've only met her once, I think, but the photographs Antonia sends at Christmas are just like you were at that age. I . . . I come over quaggly whenever I think of you then and what she might have had to . . . Sorry, Trish. This doesn't help.' She blew her nose. 'What have the police been doing to find her, d'you know?'

'Everything they could've done – even I can see that. All the neighbours and all Charlotte's close friends were contacted right at the start in case she'd found her way to any of them. None of them had seen her. Each building around the edge of the park has been visited and the inhabitants questioned. There've been officers at strategic points in the park all week, interviewing passers-by. Antonia's garden's been dug up and I suspect her house searched, too, although she hasn't told me so. I don't see what more they could've done.'

'No. If they've been digging, it sounds as though they think she's dead, too, doesn't it? Oh Trish, why would anyone kill her, a little child like that? I know they think it's a paedophile, but is that likely? A girl as young as four – could anyone . . . ?'

Trish shrugged. 'It's what we've all assumed from the beginning – the papers, too. It's what everyone always does assume nowadays when a child goes missing.'

'We know too much, don't we?'

'Yes. But that has to be better than the old days when children with terrible stories to tell weren't believed; were even punished sometimes for trying to tell someone what was being done to them. Although I do think maybe we leap to conclusions too quickly now. I mean, murdered children aren't always victims of paedophiles. Sometimes they were just there in the way when an adult lost her temper and hit out or shook them much more violently than she meant.'

'Would shaking do that much damage?' asked Meg. 'I know very young babies can be brain-damaged by it, but I'd have thought Charlotte's too big now.'

'Probably, I'm not sure. No, you must be right. But that doesn't rule out hitting. And someone might have hit Charlotte.' Trish smiled unhappily. 'Everyone agrees that she's inherited the family's temper, poor little thing.'

'As you say, poor child.'

They were both silent as they thought about the past and the struggle Trish had had to curb her rages.

'Have you got a suspect?' asked Meg after a while.

'At the beginning it looked as though the most obvious was Robert Hithe,' Trish said, pushing away pictures of herself as a furious six-year-old swearing at her ever-patient mother. 'And Antonia's told me that the police were interviewing him on a daily basis, but they must have cleared him now.'

'I suppose so, or they'd never have gone after you, would they?'

'No, probably not. But he still seems much the likeliest to me. He really is the most ratlike man, Mum. Even you'd find it hard to like him.'

Meg frowned, and in the flattened shape of her eyebrows Trish was glad to see something of herself. It was reassuring to know she didn't share everything with her father.

'Trish,' said Meg, looking unnaturally serious, 'I know you've never liked him, but has it ever struck you that you may be being unfair?'

'To Robert Hithe? No. He trivialises everything other people care about, almost as a matter of principle. And he's so bloody pleased with himself. And—'

'And, let's face it, my darling, you don't like the idea of single mothers having men in their lives.'

Trish looked at her mother. In spite of the familiar gentleness in her lined, pretty face, there was also an unusual implacability. Facing her without any of the self-protective assumptions about a mother's duty to her young daughter or the slightly patronising kindness of a successful burdened professional to the mother who can never have experienced anything like the exciting, terrifying life she herself is living, Trish began to feel a powerful tug of shame.

'Did I get in the way of your marrying again?' she asked after a long pause.

In retrospect it had always seemed that her whole childhood had been ruled by her father's desertion and her assumption that it was her bad temper that had driven him to it. Once she had grown up and discovered that most children of divorce take on the responsibilty for their parents' failures and cruelties, she had battled to think more rationally about what had happened. But she was beginning to understand that there were yet other points of view she should have taken into account.

'Not quite,' said Meg, watching her with undeserved love. 'I don't think I'd have wanted to risk it again, but you could have made it easier for me to have friends – male friends.'

'I'm sorry,' said Trish, frowning hard. 'Look, Mum, I'm *really* sorry. Except that it wasn't deliberate. I mean, at the time, I didn't understand.'

'No, I know you didn't. Thank you,' said Meg, without any suggestion that no apology had been necessary. In spite of what she had seen about herself and her role in her mother's life, Trish was a little shocked.

'Now, darling, why don't you go and have a shower and change? Wash off all the memories of the beastly police, while I cook some of those chicken breasts you've got in your fridge before they go off. I saw you've got grapes and shallots and crème fraiche, too, so we can have quite a nice sauce with them.'

'And some wine. There's a good dry German white at the back of the fridge. We could have that.'

'Fine. I'll open it while you're having your shower. Go on, Trish. Off with you.'

Trish felt all her muscles softening as she smiled. Her mother's face, so different from her own, so much rounder and kinder and more tolerant, looked back with the old steadfast affection.

'Thank you, Mum. You don't know how much I owe you, but I do.'

CHAPTER NINETEEN

'Miss Nicky! Miss Nicky!'
Maria's hoarse, clotted shriek reached Nicky from one flight below her attic bedroom. She was lying fully dressed on her bed, looking up at the ceiling, thinking about Charlotte, and trying hard not to cry any more. Crying didn't help. It made her feel ill and stopped her breathing properly. And the signs of it made Antonia even crosser on the few occasions when they couldn't not look at each other.

'Miss Nicky! Miss Nicky! Come!'

What's the point? she thought. Maria and I can't tell each other anything. I can't even pass on Antonia's orders or make Maria read the notes Antonia leaves her, but still I get into trouble when she doesn't. It's not fair.

'How extraordinary!' Antonia had said at the first interview. 'I didn't know anyone left school these days unable to speak at least *one* other language. Well, it'll be a nice project for your days off: you can learn Spanish and it'll be useful to us both. It'll look good on your cv, too.'

'I bloody won't.' Nicky had not said it then, but she said it loudly in her own bedroom with Maria bellowing away downstairs. If it hadn't been for Lottie and how sweet she'd been at that first interview, Nicky wouldn't ever have agreed to do the job. She'd known straight off that Antonia would be a cow. And she was. But even Nicky'd never thought she could be so awful as she'd been since Lottie was lost.

'Miss Nicky! Come!'

She could hear a heavy tread on the last flight up to the attic and rolled off the bed. There was no way she wanted Maria coming in and seeing her on the bed. Every bit of her ached and all she wanted to do was crawl back under the duvet and not think or even see anything.

She hated looking at her room. It had always been bleak, and Antonia had said she wasn't ever to put up any posters or stick anything to the white walls. But she'd got her books with her and photos of Charlotte in frames and there was usually a vase of flowers, so it wasn't too bad. But now, since she'd noticed signs that people had been in her room whenever she left the house, looking through all her things and moving them around, she'd detested it. But there was nowhere else to go. And anyway she couldn't have gone until Lottie was found. She couldn't.

Suddenly she realised the footsteps weren't Maria's at all. And they were more than just one person's. She stumbled over to the white-painted chipboard dressing table to look at herself in the mirror. Her eyes were squidgy and swollen and her nose was all red again. She pulled a comb through the tangles in her hair and stuffed it all into a scrunchy just in time to turn to face the door when someone knocked on it.

'Come in.'

'Nicolette Bagshot?' said a strange woman Nicky had never seen before. 'I am Sergeant Kathleen Lacie.'

Nicky stared at her. She couldn't have been more different from the officers Nicky had seen each time she went to the police station, and she seemed much grander than that Constable Derring who'd made her go down to the kitchen to answer all those questions on Sunday morning.

'This is Constable Sam Herrick. We have a warrant to arrest you on suspicion of the murder of Charlotte Weblock. You do not have to say anything. But it may harm your defence if you do not mention when questioned something you later rely on in court. Anything you do say may be given in evidence. Do you understand?'

'No,' said Nicky, holding her stomach as though someone had punched her. She thought she was going to be sick. When she dared open her mouth again, she said, 'No, I don't understand. Have you found her? I mean, her . . . her body?'

'No.'

'Then why did you say about suspicion of . . . I can't say it. What have you found?'

'I want you to come down to the station now. Bring what you need with you: underclothes, washing things, but no belts or sharp objects. OK? You don't have to bring anything with you, but you might be more comfortable if you did. Tampax if you need them – that sort of thing.'

'No.'

'Come on now, Nicolette. Don't make a silly fuss. You have to come with us and you might as well make it as easy for yourself as you can. You'll be able to ask all the questions you like when you're down at the station. Have you ever been arrested before?'

'No.' Her voice was still dull, she realised, not outraged like it should've been.

'Well, come along now then. It won't be nearly as
frightening as you think.'

How do you know? Nicky asked silently. She had
had far too much experience in the past of hiding her
hopes and terrors to say anything aloud. There was
sweat creeping coldly about behind her knees like wet
little worms, and down her armpits, too. Her throat felt
rasped, as though she had swallowed a whole carrot
wrapped in sandpaper, and there was a whining sound
in her head.

'Come along now, Nicolette.' The sergeant's voice was
brisk but kind, quite different from the expression on the
man's face. He looked snotty and hard, too, as though
he'd like to hit someone, Nicky thought, specially her.
'Get your things together quickly, please.'

Nicky had turned away to scuffle in the drawer where
she kept her underclothes before she realised she was
obeying the order. She'd like to have rebelled, but she
nearly always did obey orders; it was safer. Even when
they were wrong.

She fetched her toothbrush and flannel from the
basin in the corner and stuffed them into her red
nylon washbag. As she hesitated, planning to ask a
question, the sergeant told her to hurry up again. She
sounded less kind; more like Antonia.

'I'll have to leave a note.'

'Very well, but I shall have to read it,' said the
sergeant.

'OK.' Nicky stuffed her few things into a small
rucksack and then sat at the table in the window
to write.

'Please be quick.'

*   *   *

Dear Robert,
The police have arrested me for murdering Lottie. I
didn't. You know I didn't. They're taking me to the
police station. Will you tell Antonia?
Nicky.

She folded the sheet of plain paper in half and wrote
Robert Hithe on the front, before handing it to Sergeant Lacie, who unfolded it, looked interested as
she read it, and then said brightly, 'We'll just leave
this downstairs then, shall we? Come along; bring
your bag.'

With the silent but snotty constable leading the way and
Sergeant Lacie blocking off any exit, Nicky went down the
four flights of stairs to the ground floor. It was funny she
could manage the stairs, that her legs and feet still worked
properly in spite of feeling so weird.

Maria was waiting at the bottom, leaning on the
Hoover. There was an excited look in her nasty little
black eyes.

'You go out, Miss Nicky?'

'Yes. Please give this to Mr Hithe,' Nicky said,
handing her the note.

'Come on,' said the sergeant, applying the lightest
pressure to Nicky's back. She stumbled and for a
moment thought she'd fall, but she managed not to.

As soon as the front door opened, people started
shouting and flashing cameras. Nicky put her arm
over her eyes, ignoring all the questions, and heard
the sergeant asking politely to be 'let through'. Two
minutes later Nicky was being helped into the back
seat of an unmarked, dark-blue car. The sergeant got
in beside her and the constable sat at the wheel.

Nicky looked back at the house to see some of the
journalists clustering round the open front door, talking

to Maria. They probably couldn't speak Spanish. She hoped they couldn't. Maria hated her and would've said anything.

Nicky sat quiet in the car, hating Maria back, and Antonia, and the police. She could not think of anything else except the questions they were likely to ask her once they got going. She should have been thinking of Charlotte and the reasons why they were sure enough she was dead to start arresting people, but she couldn't. All she could think about was what was going to happen to her. She tried to think of George Smiley and what he would've done.

It would be better if the questions got asked by the sergeant. Women were easier to talk to than men. Not Antonia, of course. But other women.

The car turned into a gap between the police station and the row of shops and pulled up outside a barred doorway. Sergeant Lacie got out and pulled Nicky after her. Again with the constable leading the way, they walked up to the barred door, waited while he tapped a number into the keypad beside the door and watched the heavy bars rise, and then walked through into the station.

The smell hit the back of Nicky's nose and made her cough. It wasn't disgusting or anything – just disinfectant and floor polish – but it frightened her. She thought of the men who had been digging in Antonia's back garden and of the nightmares she had had ever since of being pushed face down into wet soil and held there till she suffocated.

She was told to stop in front of a desk, where a man in uniform was standing. She tried to stop coughing so she could listen properly.

'This is Nicolette Bagshot,' Sergeant Lacie was saying to him, still speaking in the same briskly kind voice she had used to Nicky herself. 'She has been arrested on suspicion of the murder of Charlotte Weblock.'

'I see. Now, Nicolette, would you turn out your pockets and give me that bag of yours.'

While Nicky laid her few possessions on the table in front of the custody sergeant, surprised by the ordinariness of his voice, he wrote a list of them all. Then he gave her back everything except the money and the spare tights she had brought with her. He also told her to take off her snake belt and give it to him. And he asked whether she was wearing tights under her jeans. She told him she had socks on, but he didn't believe her and told her to pull up her jeans so that he could see. She should've shaved her legs. It was embarrassing to see how hairy they were. He didn't say so; he just seemed puzzled that she had brought clean tights with her. She tried to explain that she hadn't been thinking straight when Sergeant Lacie told her to bring some things and she'd taken what was on top of her drawer. Just the first handful of clothes.

Then she realised: they were expecting her to hang herself. They thought she'd killed Lottie and now they thought she'd kill herself. She stared at the floor, so scared she couldn't bear to let them see her eyes.

When the custody sergeant had folded up the tights and the belt and put them in a plastic bag tagged with her name, he told her that she had the right to have one person informed of her arrest and asked who it should be.

Then, for the first time since Sergeant Lacie had come into her bedroom, Nicky felt her eyes go prickly and wet again. She blinked several times, hating the thought of crying in front of all these people who could think her capable of killing anyone, anyone at all, let alone the one person she'd ever been allowed to love. The tears spilled out and she had to start sniffling and wiping her sore eyes. But the more she tried to stop crying the worse it got and then the sobs started choking her. She couldn't stop them, or her voice going on and on: 'I didn't. I didn't. I didn't. I didn't.'

The custody sergeant fetched some paper tissues in the end and a plastic cup of water and they helped a bit. She managed to stop howling in the end and sipped some water. Then the suffocating feeling started up again and she had to give the cup to the sergeant so she could blow her nose. When it was clear again, she took back the cup and finished the soapy-tasting water. Then she saw Constable Herrick watching her with a nasty look in his sneery eyes and knew she had to stop crying altogether.

'Sorry,' she muttered to the custody sergeant.

'That's OK, love. It happens. Now, who would you like us to call for you?'

Nicky shook her head, still unable to think of anyone. She couldn't disturb Robert, not with the trouble in his office, and anyway, she'd left him a note. She didn't know anyone else. The other girls from the park wouldn't be able to help. They were just like her and not nearly important enough. The principal of her college would've been all right, and she'd always been kind and given her a really good reference, but Nicky couldn't bother her. Anyway, it was more than two years since they'd met. She'd probably forgotten who Nicky was.

'What about one of your parents, love?'

'I haven't got any,' she said, having to use the snotty tissue again. She thought of Renie Brooks, who'd been good to her while she lived up there in Buxton, the nearest she'd ever got to a real mother, but that was even longer ago. Renie'd never even tried to get in touch after the social workers had moved her, so perhaps she hadn't been much like a real mother after all. There wasn't anyone she could think of who'd help. Antonia would be awful, and with her being accused of murdering Charlotte, Antonia wouldn't come anyway. Why should she?

Seeing pity in the custody sergeant's face, mixed with growing impatience, Nicky tried to think. There was the woman at the nanny agency, but she wouldn't come. She'd probably be furious, and anyway she was the last person in the world Nicky would have wanted anywhere near her if there were questions going to be asked. Remembering what those questions might include somehow sharpened Nicky's brain and she thought of the only person with a bit of authority who had been kind to her since Charlotte had been lost.

'There's Trish Maguire,' she said shyly. 'Could you tell her, d'you think?'

'I expect so. Who is she?'

'She's a cousin of my boss.'

'Of Antonia Weblock?' asked the custody sergeant in surprise. He obviously knew more about the case than Nicky had realised.

'Yes. But I don't know her phone number.'

'It's all right,' said Sergeant Lacie from behind Nicky's shoulder. She sounded surprised, too, but interested as well, and almost scared in a way. 'I know it.'

'That's OK then. Come along now, Nicky, and we'll call her for you.'

Beginning to shake, Nicky followed him, looking back at Sergeant Lacie, who suddenly seemed almost friendly.

The custody sergeant took Nicky to a long corridor of yellowish-painted iron-looking doors with small gratings in them. She knew what they were from hundreds of television shows. He unlocked one and held the door open for her.

It ought to have been less frightening to have seen it so often on the telly, but it wasn't. Nothing she had ever seen had prepared Nicky for the feeling of walking past the sergeant into that small room with the bed in it so low it was nearly on the floor and a toilet in the corner. He did not say anything else, but he looked at her quite kindly as he pulled the door shut. She heard it bang as it hit the door frame and then the click of the lock.

She didn't know what to do next. She hadn't thought to bring a book with her and there wasn't a television nor even a radio. After a moment she went to sit on the edge of the bed, staring at the locked door. Somehow the thickness of it she'd seen as she walked past it into the cell made it worse. She was locked in and there wasn't anything to do but wait until they came for her to start the questioning. She was in prison. She could hear the shrill voice of one of her early foster mothers when she'd been found eating a biscuit from the kitchen cupboard between meals.

'Prison, that's where you'll end up, a little thief like you. Dirty, you are. Horrible little slut. Little thief.'

Her eyes closing as though that might shut off the memories, Nicky lay back and let her legs swing up on the bed.

CHAPTER TWENTY

'M s Maguire?'

'Yes?'

'This is Sergeant John Hinksey from the Church Street police station in Kensington.'

'What now?' Trish demanded. The previous day's confrontation with Kath Lacie and DCI Blake ought to have stopped any of them ever bothering her again.

'I'm the custody officer. Nicolette Bagshot has been arrested,' he said, sounding only mildly surprised at her tone, 'and she has asked us to let you know.'

'Me? Why?'

'We're required to offer all detainees the chance to nominate one person to be informed of their arrest.'

'Yes, yes, I'm well aware of that,' said Trish. 'But why me? I hardly know her.'

'I have no idea. It took her some while to come up with your name and she was quite distressed,' he said, sounding a little less like an automaton.

'What's the charge?'

'She hasn't been charged yet.'

'OK, Sergeant, then what are the grounds for the arrest?'

'Suspicion of the murder of Charlotte Weblock.'

'Oh, no!' Trish felt her throat closing. She coughed to clear the airways. 'You've found her, then? Charlotte, I mean.'

'I understand that no body has been found as yet.'

Think like a lawyer, Trish told herself. Don't think about Charlotte; not now. There'll be time for that later. Concentrate. Don't feel.

'And yet you've arrested Ms Bagshot,' she said, sounding quite as detached as she wanted. 'On what evidence?'

'I'm not at liberty to give you any more information, Ms Maguire. She asked us to inform you and that's what I've done.'

'Has she got legal representation?'

'The duty solicitor has been sent for.'

'Has she been questioned yet?'

'No. Since she has asked for legal representation, the officers are waiting to start the interview until the duty solicitor gets here.'

'Right,' said Trish. Once they started to question Nicky they could hold her for only twenty-four hours without charge unless the station superintendent sanctioned a further twelve. If they had not managed to get anywhere by the end of thirty-six hours, they could apply to a magistrate to keep her for another twelve hours. Once that was up, they would either have to charge her or let her go.

Trish had seen enough clients so bewildered and scared by their first experience of custody and police questioning that they would have agreed to whatever crime the police suggested they might have committed. And she had also heard of plenty of young solicitors

and clerks who did not have the experience or the drive
to offer enough protection.

'Look, I'd like you to cancel the duty solicitor. I'll
get someone to her as soon as I can. Will you let her
know that you've told me where she is and that I am
sending her a lawyer?'

'Very well,' said the officer, tightly enough to convince
Trish that he'd been told who she was and what a fool
she had made of Lacie and Blake the previous day.

'But make it quick,' he added officiously.

'I'll do my best. And please call me at this number
if Ms Bagshot needs anything.'

'Very well. Goodbye.'

Trish put down the telephone receiver, at the same
time turning her Rolodex clumsily with her left hand.
There was no doubt about the solicitor who would
best protect Nicky's interests, and Trish only hoped
that he would be available. It did not occur to her
then that Antonia might think her guilty of disloyalty
by wheeling him in to help Nicky. Later it struck her
with some force, but by then it was much too late.

She found the number and was soon answered by
the usual crisply efficient secretary.

'Good morning. It's Trish Maguire here – could I
speak to George Henton, please?'

'May I tell him what it's in connection with?'

'A client of mine urgently needs a solicitor. I'm a
barrister. George has briefed me in the past and I should
like to ask his advice.'

'Oh, I see. Of course. I'll see if he's in, Ms Maguire.'

While Trish waited for George, she thought about
their last bruising run-in over one of his clients, and
about some of their happier dealings in the past.

An unusually tall man and built like a megalith, he
was known among the younger barristers in Trish's

chambers as 'The Great Bear' for his size and the super-ficial cuddliness that masked formidable speed and ferocity in attack. He was almost universally admired, but also feared for the sarcasm with which he greeted any sloppiness or mistakes.

What Trish valued most was the passion with which he protected his clients and the way he never tried to protect himself from anything. He did not take on much criminal work, but she knew Nicky would be safer in his hands than in most.

'So Trish Maguire, is it really you?' came his voice down the telephone into her ear.

It was a voice that could not have belonged to anyone else, she thought, deep but extraordinarily invigorating, as though the anger that propelled him through every day was matched by the warmth of sympathy he could give to those who needed it.

'It's really me, George. How are you?'

'Fine. More to the point, how are you? I gather you've been ill.'

'Is that what they're saying?' She was suddenly seized with a rage almost as powerful as his and was surprised she could still see clearly.

'Yes. I tried to brief you for an important case a couple of weeks ago, but your clerk said you were ill and taking some months to convalesce. It sounded serious. What was it – an op?'

It took a moment or two for Trish to control herself. When she did speak, she was glad to hear that her voice sounded almost normal.

'In fact I've taken a sabbatical to write a book on children and the law for Millen Books.'

'Ah. That sounds much more like it. And more like you. Now, what can I do for you? This is a tough morning.'

'It's a bit of a cheek, but I wondered whether you could go – or send someone you trust – to Church Street police station for a sort-of client of mine, who's been arrested on suspicion of murdering a child. I'm afraid it'll be legal aid, but she'll definitely get that. She has nothing except her wages. She's called Nicky Bagshot.'

'The nanny in the Weblock case?'

'That's right. Have you been following it?'

'Hard not to when it's been on the front of every newspaper. That was another reason I believed your clerk's illness story: the pictures of you were hardly flattering. Have they found the body?'

'No. But they've obviously got something that's justified an arrest. I don't know what.'

'OK, I'll check it out. But, Trish, why are you doing this? I thought you were Antonia Weblock's cousin. I'm sure that's what the caption to the photo said.'

'Yes, we're second cousins.'

'And you're trying to get help for the nanny who at the very least allowed the child to be snatched and at worst caused her serious harm? Is that right?'

'Yes,' said Trish, not wanting to go into a long explanation and yet knowing that she would have to give him one if she wanted him to take on Nicky's case. 'For lots of reasons. One, I don't think Nicky's guilty; two, she's so alone in the world that she asked to have me, of all people, informed of her arrest. I couldn't *not* help after that. Look, I know it's not exactly your line, George, but will you help?'

'I'll have a go,' he said again but more lightly. 'She can't have a record, or she'd never have got a job like that.'

'No,' said Trish, dragging out the vowel as she remembered that Willow Worth had volunteered to

245

pump her source at Holland Park Helpers for anything they had on Nicky's background. 'But I am trying to get more information on her past. I'll chase it up this morning and let you know what I get later, if you'll take charge down at the nick. Is that possible? I know it's asking a lot.'

'Why don't I get down there and see what's what and draft in one of the troops if it looks like being too time-consuming. As you say, she's bound to get legal aid. OK?'

'Wonderful. George, you are good to do this.'

He laughed, sounding friendlier and much less caustic than usual. 'Not at all. I'm glad you came to me, if a touch surprised. We didn't exactly part on good terms.'

'No,' said Trish, remembering how angry she had been when he criticised the way she had handled the summing up of his client's case. 'But you are the best. And you, after all, were trying to get me again a couple of weeks ago.'

She rang off without waiting to hear what he had to say to that, and dialled Willow's number.

Mrs Rusham, the housekeeper, answered and told Trish that Willow was out for most of the day. She offered to take any message, but Trish did not feel inclined to leave anything more than her name. She put her finger on the telephone cradle and then tried to think what else she could do. It was only later that she realised that if anyone knew about the evidence that had justified Nicky's arrest, it would be Antonia. Trish picked up the phone again and punched in the number.

'Robert Hithe.'

She was so surprised to hear his voice that she almost dropped the telephone. She realised that his work crisis – whatever it had been – must be well and truly over.

'Hi, Robert. It's Trish here, Trish Maguire. How are you?'

'You're not usually that stupid. How the fucking hell d'you think I am? Have you got Antonia there?'

'Here? No – why?' Trish was accustomed to ignoring his hostility. 'I assumed she'd be at home. That's why I rang.'

'No. It's like the *Marie Celeste* here, and I need to get hold of her. Lottie's dead.'

Trish felt as though a hand had closed about her throat and started to squeeze. She'd always suspected him, but that didn't make it any easier to take.

'Trish? Are you there, Trish?'

'Yes.' She coughed twice. 'Yes, I'm here, Robert. Why did you say Charlotte's dead?'

'They've arrested Nicky Bagshot for her murder. She left me a note and that's all she said in it. I've rung the bloody plods, but they won't tell me anything else, not where they've found the body nor what was done to Lottie. Nothing. It's a shambles.'

'There isn't a body. They haven't found it yet.'

'And just how do you know that, Trish?' The suspicion in his voice did not sound convincing.

'Because Nicky got them to inform me about her arrest and I asked when they rang me,' said Trish, trying to keep her own voice free of everything she felt. 'I've fixed for a solicitor to go down and make sure she knows her rights and has all the protection she needs.'

'*You've* got her a solicitor? But why? What's it got to do with you?'

'Nicky asked to have me told.' Why couldn't Robert grasp the simplest thing that was said to him? 'I did what I could for her.'

'I'm gobsmacked, Trish,' he said, sounding warmer and more human than usual. 'And grateful. I wouldn't have believed it.'

She decided to take advantage of his new softness. 'Look, Robert, could I come round? There are things I need to know, and it'd be a lot easier to ask you than Antonia. Can we talk?'

'Fine. But not here. There's no point my kicking my heels round here if Antonia isn't coming back for lunch. I hate this fucking house anyway these days. Let's meet near my office. What about The Iced Pear? D'you know it?'

'Just off Charlotte Street? Yes, I know it. I can meet you there in about half an hour.'

'Make it three-quarters. I'll leave Antonia a note in case she does deign to roll up. See you, Trish.'

Amazed that it was going to be so easy to talk to him, Trish ran up the spiral stairs to change. The Iced Pear was a newish, amazingly chic bar and restaurant mainly used by people in television and advertising. She did not want to risk distracting Robert by looking obviously out of place.

Ten minutes later, dressed in a cream lycra body, short black skirt and very long jacket, with much more mascara on her eyelashes than usual, she hurrried out of the flat, pinning a long silver brooch to her left lapel as she went.

Robert was sitting on a high stool at the bar, gloomily drinking the latest ultra-fashionable beer from the bottle, when she got there, only ten minutes late.

'Hi,' said Trish.

Robert nodded. 'Drink?' he said by way of greeting.

'Thanks. Um.' She could not think of anything she

wanted to drink with all the questions buzzing around her head. 'Oh, a spritzer please.'

'OK.' He waved to the bartender and gave the order. Trish saw from the man's expression that her chosen drink was appallingly old-fashioned. She should probably have ordered something like a Sea Breeze, unless that was already passé; but she'd never liked that sort of mixed drink.

'Cheers,' said Robert inappropriately. He looked shocked and as ill as the rest of them; unhappier, too, than she had ever seen him. His black Armani jacket exaggerated the yellowness of his skin, and his lips looked chewed as well as dry. He seemed to have lost weight, too.

Trish, who had been rehearsing her questions all the way from Southwark, found it hard to begin.

'You said Nicky left you a note?' she said eventually.

He nodded and scooped a handful of roasted almonds from a silver bowl on the bar, pouring them into his mouth. Three dropped into his lap. He brushed them on to the floor with enough vigour to hurt himself.

'Saying what?'

'Just that she'd been arrested,' he mumbled through the half-chewed nuts. 'It wasn't sealed and I assumed Antonia'd read it and that's why she'd buggered off. But when I rang the plods they said there'd been no sign of her. She hadn't left any message with Maria – at least not as far as I could discover.' His voice sounded irritable. 'Why Antonia needs to employ a woman who only speaks Spanish, I've never been able to understand. It's ludicrous. On a par with . . .'

'With what, Robert?'

'What? Oh, nothing. What is it you wanted to ask that she couldn't hear?'

'Ah,' said Trish, wishing he had not remembered the pretext she had used to get him on his own. 'It's really to do with how Nicky behaved with Charlotte. I've been told you saw quite a lot of them together.'

'Who told you that?' His thin face was clawed with suspicion. Trish smiled as soothingly as possible. It had no noticeable effect.

'I went to the playground to talk to some of the nannies there the day after I first met Nicky. Antonia's been convinced all along that Nicky's guilty, but I wasn't so sure. I wanted to talk to someone who liked her.' Trish smiled. 'I hadn't realised you'd qualify, or I'd have rung you days ago.'

Robert didn't comment.

'Anyway, the nannies told me that you quite often picked up Nicky and Charlotte from the playground in the afternoons,' Trish went on, wondering whether she'd ever get him to say anything useful. 'They seemed to think a lot of you, Robert, unlike most of the parents they talked about.'

'So that's it, is it?' he said unpleasantly before tipping some more beer into his mouth. 'I wondered what had made her do it.'

'I don't understand.'

'You passed that little titbit on to Antonia, I presume?'

'I haven't a clue what you mean, Robert. I haven't seen Antonia since I was at the playground. She's furious with me about something and doesn't return my calls any more. Why should it make her angry to know you'd been there?'

The barman put Trish's spritzer in front of her, and substituted a second bowl of nuts for the empty one. Trish thanked him and turned back to Robert, her eyebrows raised.

He shrugged. 'It bugs her whenever I knock off work earlier than she can. And she loathes me fraternising with Charlotte, and she thinks I shouldn't even talk to Nicky unless it's to give her orders. Being friendly to "staff" makes them uppity in her book. Silly cow.'

'Robert!'

'Well, she is sometimes. You must know how she treats people she despises.'

'I suppose so. But forget Antonia for the moment. Robert, there's something I can't understand.'

'The brilliant Trish Maguire at a loss? Good God!'

'Oh, stop it, Robert. Isn't what's happened to Charlotte bad enough to make you take at least that seriously? Must you fart about like a child all the time? It drives me bonkers.'

He looked at her, the wary malice and suspicion in his eyes joined by sheer surprise.

'What's got into you?'

'I want to know what's happened to Charlotte,' she said through clenched teeth.

'So do we all, Trish. What gives *you* the right to be so fucking holy about it?'

'Sorry,' she said, catching a hint of desperation in his voice. 'It's just that I don't understand.'

'What, for Christ's sake?'

'Why everyone keeps talking about this crisis you've got in the office. You seem to me to have all the time in the world: time to go to the playground, time to go swimming on Saturday morning, time to go home for lunch today . . . What's going on, Robert?'

He hunched his shoulders.

'You were too busy to stay with Antonia on Sunday, but—'

'Hah!'

'What does that mean, Robert?'

251

'Do you really think I wouldn't have stayed on Sunday, if Antonia had let me?'

'What?'

'My meeting was important all right, but I'd have stuck to Antonia like glue if she'd allowed it, whatever the cost at work. But you know what she's like; she can't bear being helped, or having anyone near her when she's miserable. It makes life bloody difficult.'

Trish remembered that Antonia had told the police that she knew she and Robert would have quarrelled if she'd made him hang about waiting for news of Charlotte.

'Perhaps I ought to apologise,' she said slowly.

'Good God! The great Trish Maguire apologising to me. Halleluja, Mary!'

'Oh Robert, I wish you wouldn't. But look, quite apart from the meeting on Sunday, if this crisis is so awful, why have you got so much spare time now? It doesn't hang together. You must see that.'

'So you suspect me of killing Lottie, too, do you? Christ! You women. I could've been Doctor Mengele from the way Antonia's been treating me. Ever since the airport. And she's been giving it to them. I'm sure it was her. There isn't anyone else. And it's just the sort of thing she would do.'

'What is?' asked Trish, wishing that he would talk in complete and sequential sentences. She assumed that his habit of cutting from one subject to another without finishing any of them must have something to do with the fractured, flashy techniques he used in his advertising campaigns. Accustomed to the rounded wordy sentences of the courts, she found his tricky style exasperating. 'What has Antonia been doing?'

'Giving the police all sorts of irrelevant facts about me,' he answered much more clearly. 'They've put it all together and added it to their own prejudices and turned me into Suspect Number One.'

Trish's guts contracted in sympathy – and suspicion.

'Hasn't Antonia told you?' asked Robert curiously.

'No,' said Trish. 'She's been incredibly loyal to you all along; hasn't said a word against you that I've heard.'

'You do surprise me.'

'But if you're Suspect Number One, why have they suddenly arrested Nicky?'

'God knows,' he said, his narrow face looking even more ratlike than usual. 'They laid off me yesterday. I thought they'd seen the light. Now I'm not so sure. It'd be par for the course if they'd planted some evidence so they could get an excuse to bag Nicky and try to force her to say she saw me killing Lottie.'

'Did she?' asked Trish before she could stop herself. To her astonishment, Robert coughed and bent his head, putting his thumb and forefinger either side of his nose, almost as though he was trying to push back tears. It was absurd. Nothing she'd ever seen or heard of him could make her believe he was upset.

'Robert? What is it?'

'For Christ's sake! Can't you tell? Why is Nicky the only person bright enough to grasp the fact that I liked the little brat?'

'Did you, Robert?' Trish had noticed his use of the past tense and looked even more coldly on his performance. 'Why?'

He looked up and blew his nose on a paper napkin from the bar. Trish thought she could see real tears and felt even more confused.

'She had guts and she could be fun, great fun. She was the first kid of that age I'd ever known.' He drank some more and then went on with almost idle antagonism: 'You are a bitch, you know, Trish. I didn't see it till now.'

'What d'you mean?'

'You tricked me into meeting you, didn't you? You said you had things you couldn't ask Antonia, but you just wanted to accuse me and see what happened. Even Antonia hasn't gone quite that far. Yet.'

'Robert . . .'

'Or is she behind this little frolic of yours – is that it? Did she think the police plan with Nicky wasn't going to work and decide that her precious, brilliant Trish might do better?'

'Absolutely not,' Trish said, working hard to hold on to her temper. 'I told you, I haven't spoken to Antonia today. And I haven't accused you of anything. All I wanted to know was about your work crisis. It was you who raised the rest. I can't think why you're being so cagey about the office.'

For a while she thought he was going to refuse to say anything more as he signalled to the barman for another beer.

'Oh, why not?' he said, when he had drunk nearly half of it. 'If it'll get you off my back I might as well tell you. The news is going to ooze out soon anyway – the bank'll see to that. And it doesn't matter a toss compared to Lottie. We're up shit creek, Trish. Our biggest account has been poached and the cash-flow's been dire for the past six months. The bank's given us until close of business on Friday to get another backer or a crunchy new client. There – satisfied?'

'Couldn't Antonia help?'

'Rich though she is, Trish,' he said in a patronising tone that set her teeth on edge, 'she's a minnow compared to the sharks circling about our pool. We have got pretty big in the last four years, as you'd know if you ever listened to anything anyone said to you. I distinctly remember telling you all about it nearly a year ago. You looked bored to buggery at the time, but I hadn't realised you weren't taking any of it in.'

Trish remembered both the occasion and her dislike of Robert's remorseless insistence on informing everyone he met about his successes.

'Anyway, I wouldn't ask Antonia even if she wasn't such a minnow.'

'Although as a banker,' said Trish, 'she must be in a position to know of lots of potential backers you could have approached, isn't she?'

He shrugged, trying to look unconcerned. For the first time Trish caught a hint of hard anger in his petulance. After a moment he swung round on the stool to wave his empty bottle at the bartender to ask for yet another beer. He stayed with his back to Trish. She could see how tense he was.

Oh no, she thought. He did ask for help and Antonia refused. No wonder the atmosphere in the house is so peculiar. And no wonder she's been so suspicious of him. Does she think he took Charlotte out of revenge? Or to get a ransom that would pay off his bank? Is that what she's afraid of?

Or is it worse? Are the police right about the paedophilia? They could be. Stress is one of the best-known triggers for child abuse. Is that what this crisis was for Robert? Did Nicky really believe she could have made the bruises Antonia saw on Charlotte's arms, or was she trying to cover up for Robert?

Suddenly the questions that were rushing through Trish's brain gave way to a clear memory of what Charlotte had said about her nightmares during the dinner party.

'Did Charlotte ever talk to you about bad dreams?'

'No,' said Robert without turning to look at her.

'Dreams about "huge wiggly worms"?'

He did shift a bit then, and glanced at her over his shoulder.

'Worms?' he said in a voice much higher than usual. The shrillness could have come from surprise, but Trish thought fear was more likely and struggled to keep a tight grip on her imagination.

'Yes,' she said as firmly as she could. 'Big, pink worms.'

He shook his head and looked back towards the bartender. Having given his order he swung back to face her.

'You look awful, Trish. What is it?'

'Nothing. Why? What?'

'You're white as a sheet and you look as though you might throw up.'

'I do feel a bit weird,' she admitted. She sipped her white wine and soda water, but it did not help. 'It keeps happening whenever I think about Charlotte and what someone may have done to her.'

But it didn't. Or not quite as badly as that. Not usually.

'Not pregnant, are you, Trish? Is that it?'

'What?' she asked, angry at the idiotically irrelevant question. 'No, of course I'm not.'

'That's what it sounds like. You look it, too. And if you keep feeling sick . . . Natural assumption. And the biological clock must be ticking away pretty loudly for you these days.'

That's just the kind of tone the police took, thought Trish. So was it you, Robert, who briefed them about my past? Out of revenge for the way they'd been grilling you? Biological clock indeed!

'You'd better get one of those test things from the

chemist to find out before it's too late to get an abortion.'

Trish glared at him, not prepared to dignify his various insults with a protest. He raised his eyebrows and looked as though he was prepared to enjoy himself.

'You're sure she never mentioned the worms?' she said.

'How many more times? I'm quite sure. She never talked to me about bad dreams of any kind.'

'Well then, did Nicky ever mention the dreams? She knew all about them.'

He seemed surprised, completely unaware of her suspicions.

'Look, at that dinner party of Antonia's when I took Charlotte back up to bed, she asked me to search everything in the room, even through all her toys in case there were worms there. She said Nicky always checked to make sure there weren't any before she turned the light out, but that Antonia hadn't had time that night. It seems bizarre that neither of them should have mentioned it to you.'

'Well, they didn't. You're on a wild-goose chase here, Trish. And a bloody silly one, too. Neither Lottie nor Nicky ever said a word to me, and one of them would have done if it was half as important as you seem to think. I'm off.' He drained the remains of his third beer and slid off the tall stool.

Without making any attempt to pay for his drinks, he walked to the door with the stiff, strutting gait Trish had always assumed was supposed to make him seem taller than he was.

She watched him go, almost able to feel Charlotte's hand curling round hers as her small breathy voice confided the terror of the huge wiggly pink worms. The possible significance of the words she had chosen seemed so obvious that Trish could not understand why she hadn't seen it sooner. The thought that Charlotte might have been asking for help that night – help she did not get – was agonising.

CHAPTER TWENTY-ONE

'Hello, Trish,' said Willow Worth's voice on the answering machine. 'Mrs Rusham said you'd rung. I fear you must be chasing me for the stuff on Holland Park Helpers. I'm sorry I haven't rung before, but I've been round at Emma's rather a lot. What a shit Hal is! She says you've been wonderful. Thank you for that. I'll try you again later. It was good to see you the other night. Bye.'

After that message there was just a beep; nothing yet from George Henton. Trish rang Emma to find out how she was. Hearing only her recorded voice, Trish scrambled out an affectionate message after the beep.

'Emma, how's it going? I've made up your bed here ready for when you want it. But it doesn't matter if you decide you don't. Whatever. Up to you, as you know. Things are looking grimmer and grimmer for Charlotte. As soon as I've got any real news, I'll ring. But if you feel like a chat – or a meal or something – in the meantime, let me know. I hope you're coping.'

Trish put the receiver back on the telephone, wishing that she'd organised her thoughts into a more effective message, and then made some coffee. She took a mugful to her desk. There she sat, watching the coffee cool and thinking about Charlotte's nightmare worms and the ease with which anyone could fall into child-abuse hysteria if they knew enough and feared enough.

Anyone involved in protecting children was at risk of exaggerating the significance of what they heard. It was a tricky balancing act. If they ignored hints of real abuse, children could suffer terribly and even die, but if they gave in to hysteria, it could bring disaster on everyone involved. A client of Trish's had once been accused of sexually abusing his three-year-old daughter, even though the police surgeon could find no physical evidence. The social workers who suspected him refused to say why they were suspicious, for months interviewing and re-interviewing his daughter and her two older brothers about how Daddy played with them and what he said to them, and whether he touched them or asked them to touch any bits of him. His marriage broke up under the strain and the children were traumatised.

When the social workers eventually produced their 'evidence', it turned out to be no more than a report from his daughter's playgroup leader of an involved story she had told him about Daddy's special rocket that she could only touch when he said and that she wasn't to be frightened of even when he made it go up and burst.

The absurd story was easily explained. The family had had a Guy Fawkes-night party the previous November, when it had rained so much that they had decided to save some of the fireworks for a drier evening. The biggest and best was a rocket, which they kept until Trish's client's birthday. Then the family trooped out into the garden for a ceremonial launch.

Remembering how scared his daughter had been of the bangs at Guy Fawkes, he had taken great trouble to show the rocket to her before it was lit. He let her touch it and look at the pictures on it, saying firmly that once it had been taken away to be lit she mustn't go anywhere near it. Then he told her that he knew exactly what he was doing with it, and that she didn't need to be frightened even when he made it whizz up and explode.

The disproportionate damage that the social workers' well-meaning but over-excited interpretation had done could still make Trish angry, and she did not want to make the same mistake herself. Even so, the more she thought about the huge wiggly pink worms, the more significant the words seemed.

She was still uncertain what to do and who to tell when there was a knock at the front door. It was a much gentler, less peremptory kind of summons than the police had achieved.

'George,' she said as she opened the door and saw the Great Bear waiting for her, not looking at all ferocious. 'How wonderful! Come on in and tell me how it went. Would you like some tea? Or coffee?'

'Cup of tea would be great. Thanks.' He was opening his briefcase as he walked in and did not look up until he was standing in the middle of the main room. 'Golly, Trish, this is a magnificent flat.'

Golly, she repeated to herself on her way to the kitchen. Golly? Can a man of forty with a brain as sharp as guillotine really use a word like that except as a joke? She looked back over her shoulder to see him gazing around at the flat, and she smiled at his awed expression.

'Haven't you seen it before? I thought . . . Oh no, of course – you wimped out of my party last Christmas, didn't you?'

'As you know perfectly well,' he said, his tone answering the gleam in her dark eyes rather than the words, 'I had the 'flu, and I was furious about it. I . . . You know, I'd always assumed you lived in a dark book-lined basement. I can't think why.'

I can, she replied silently. You thought I was a kind of troglodyte, burrowing my way through mountains of work and never looking up at anything – or anyone – else. Charming. No wonder I went a bit mad.

'It's stunning,' he went on. 'So light and huge. Yes, perhaps it is a likely place for you, after all. A kind of eyrie from which to soar.'

'Thanks, George,' she said, pleased that he hadn't seen the flat as her departed·and unlamented lover had done. His parting words had been that the place was 'as cold and empty as you, Trish. I should've known you couldn't give anyone anything as soon as I saw it. You're the most soulless woman I've ever met.'

'Ordinary tea or something herbal or Chinese?' she said brightly, banishing the memories of Jack's voice. Perhaps the police had somehow got on to him and dug all their spiteful innuendos out of his many resentments. Perhaps their information had had nothing to do with Ben or even Robert. In some ways that would be a comfort, except that she'd hate Jack – of all people – to know anything about the police's accusations. 'I've got most things for once.'

'Ordinary, please. And as strong as you can get it.'

She squished the tea-bag against the side of the mug until the liquid was the colour of dark mahogany, flipped the bag into the bin, added a little milk to turn the brown liquid orange, and brought it back, collecting her cooling coffee on the way.

'Here, George. Look, do stop prowling and sit down.'

'I can't get over this place,' he said, moving from her

books to the long desk and then standing in front of a big painting she had bought one year at the Royal Academy Schools Degree Show. It had surprised a lot of people at the time, but she had loved it as soon as she saw it.

Smoothly painted in a mixture of buffs and greys, it was a bleak urban landscape, showing nothing but the space under a motorway junction. But it had something that had spoken to her as soon as she saw it, a kind of speed and space that gave her a much-needed sense of freedom.

'You're a bit of a mystery in some ways, Trish. Intriguing.'

'Me? Nonsense. Clear as mud.' She could not think why she was suddenly enjoying herself and tried to concentrate on what mattered. 'But, look, this is about Nicky Bagshot, not me. What happened at the police station?'

'Trish,' he said seriously, putting his mug on the floor as he stretched his long legs luxuriously on her deep-seated sofa, 'listen to me.'

'I am. What's the matter?'

'I know how upset you can get when people you believe in turn out to have been stringing you along.'

'So?' she said, surprised that he had noticed.

'So I want to warn you that Nicky's innocence may not be quite as clear-cut as you thought.'

'Why not?' she asked after a long silence, thinking about the bruises and the worms and the various reasons why Nicky might have covered up for what Robert had been doing. The most obvious was that they had been having an affair, but she found it hard to believe that anyone as young as Nicky would really want to bonk Robert, a man nearly twenty years her senior.

'Two quite different reasons,' George was saying.

'They don't have anything to do with each other but, in their separate ways, both are worrying.'

'OK. Now you've warned me. I can take it. What are the reasons?'

'The first is that she's admitted she's epileptic.'

'Well, I don't see how that makes her either a paedophile or a murderer,' said Trish, almost relieved.

'Has she said anything to you about paedophilia?' he asked with sharp suspicion.

'Nicky? To me? No, of course not. Why should she?'

'So why did you mention it?'

'Oh, come on, George! What are you being so peculiar about? It's what all of us have been afraid of all along. And anyway, it was entirely clear from the way the police questioned me yesterday that they're convinced there's a paedophile involved.'

'They questioned you?' He sounded so outraged that Trish had to smile, in spite of everything. She pushed both hands through her hair, making it stand up even more tuftily than usual.

'Why shouldn't they? I hated it, but I can see they had to.'

'Trish,' he said as he reached for his tea, 'you were prepared to wheel me in for someone you hardly know. Why didn't you call me when they started in on you?'

'Because, unlike poor Nicky, I know how these things work and what my rights are and where to make a stand. Anyway, I wasn't arrested. If I had been, I'd probably have rung you.'

'I should hope so.' He drank some tea and then put the mug down on the floor beside his feet. As he straightened up and looked at her again, he smiled. It was a different smile from the hard polite version he had always offered during conferences in her chambers. 'I hate the idea of you having to deal with all that on your own.'

'I was fine.'

'OK. But if it happens again – ever – call me at once. Anyway, this bombshell about the epilepsy puts a different complexion on Nicky's possible responsibility for what happened.'

'I still don't see why.'

'Don't go cold on me, Trish,' he said, watching her as though she were a dangerous and ill-maintained machine that might explode at any moment. 'It's stupid to ignore facts. First of all, she's kept her condition secret from everyone.'

'Except you. How did you get it out of her?'

'It's my job, Trish. It was obvious from the minute I saw her that she was terrified of something and longing to make a confession. I thought I'd better find out what it was before the police picked up on it. Even they usually get on to that sort of thing in the end. I made it clear I was completely on her side, whatever she'd done, and that anything she said was sacrosanct. I'm not sure she believed me, but she poured out everything about her fits, poor little devil.' He paused for a moment and then added: 'You were right, Trish – she is very much on her own.'

'I know.' She looked at him and saw how comforting he must have seemed to Nicky with his size and the warmth he could offer so freely when he chose. 'But why does her epilepsy make you think she did something to Charlotte?'

'I don't think she did anything deliberately. But there could have been an accident. I don't know enough about it yet but, as I understand it, when someone has a *grand mal* seizure, their whole body becomes rigid and they fall heavily to the ground. They often damage themselves – cut their scalps open, bruise themselves severely, that sort of thing – which means it must be possible for them to hurt someone they happen to hit.'

'Ah. I see. And did Nicky have a fit on Saturday?'

'She swears not. In fact, she says she hardly ever has them, hasn't had any for more than five years. But she could be lying. She looked terrified enough for that.'

'But could she have done serious damage even in a fit? She's so tiny.'

'I'd have thought so if Charlotte hit her head, broke her neck perhaps. Or she could have been suffocated. There must be lots of ways it could have happened.'

'OK. Say she did have a fit and damaged Charlotte – killed her – what then?' Trish remembered Nicky's strange, greenish pallor on Sunday and began to wonder whether that was what people looked like twenty-four hours after a major seizure. 'She would have had to get rid of the body somehow. Oh, Christ!'

'What is it, Trish?'

'The pram. The doll's pram the police took away on Sunday. I'd forgotten it. Is that how they think she got the body out of the house?'

Trish stared at the wall, trying to remember the size of the pram and work out whether any child's body would have fitted into it. Only by thinking about straightforward things like the pram's dimensions could she stop herself seeing pictures of Charlotte dying, and imagining what she might have felt.

'It's what their questions suggested, yes,' said George, unaware of what her imagination was doing to her. 'They think Nicky put the body in the pram and wheeled it to the park, where she took an opportunity to make herself noticed by a large bunch of potential witnesses, before pretending to discover that Charlotte had disappeared. After that the police scenario meshes with everything Nicky's always claimed. She rushed about the park like a mad thing, pushing the pram as she went.'

Trish thought of everything she had seen and heard of Nicky and tried to dredge up something – anything – that might make George's suggestion seem as unreal as she wanted it to be.

'What about surveillance cameras? There must be millions in that area of London. Haven't the police looked at the films? There could easily be one that shows Nicky with Charlotte alive on the way to the park. That would knock this theory on the head straight off.'

'It would. But unfortunately there are no cameras on the route Nicky and Charlotte always took from the house to the park. Although there is film of Nicky rushing about the park with the pram later, there's no record of her arriving with or without Charlotte.'

'Shit.'

'As you say. It's seriously inconvenient.'

'But look, I can't believe Nicky would have thought up something as clever – no, not clever – as devious as getting the body away like that. I don't mean she's stupid, but I think she's too straight for that kind of pantomime.'

'She could have been working to someone else's script, Trish, and persuaded by . . . him that the risk was worth taking.'

'Robert Hithe, you mean?'

'He seems the likeliest from everything I've read about the case and what I heard behind the questions the police were asking Nicky. You must know him quite well, Trish. D'you think he could have dreamed up a script like that?'

'Easily. But would he? I have been wondering whether he and Nicky could be having an affair, but even if they are I'm not sure I can see him protecting her after she'd killed Charlotte, even accidentally during an epileptic fit.'

'There are other reasons why he might be involved, nothing to do with Nicky's epilepsy.'

'Ah. All right – go on.'

'The police have found a quantity of pornographic magazines under the floorboards of Nicky's bedroom.'

'What?' Trish was so surprised that her voice came out in a kind of yelp, like a puppy whose paw has been crushed by a heavy shoe. 'I find that very hard to believe. What sort of pornography?'

'Pretty bad.' George reached down for his mug and drank some more tea. 'Mainly involving both adults and children. You know the sort of thing as well as I do. And to make it more damning, there were also a lot of photographs of Charlotte Weblock naked. Nicky says the photographs are the sort of thing everyone takes of little children in the bath and at the seaside, but that she never put them under the floorboards, and that she's never seen the magazines before in her life – but then . . .'

'That's what she would say,' said Trish, finishing his sentence without trouble.

'Exactly. That's why I was curious when you seemed to be saying that Nicky had talked to you about paedophilia.'

'Ah. I see,' said Trish vaguely as she remembered Robert's wild suggestion that the police were trying to fake evidence of Nicky's guilt. 'Could the magazines have been planted on her?'

'They could. But I'd have thought it was more likely that Robert persuaded her to hide them for him, or just conceivably that he hid them there without her knowledge because it was such an unlikely place for anyone to search.'

'Which would mean that he *is* turned on by the thought of sex with children and could have tried something on with Charlotte.'

'That's right,' said George, looking nearly as ill as Trish felt. '*If* they do belong to him. We don't know that they do.'

She told him about the worms dream, adding sadly, 'D'you think she was trying to tell me about it that evening?'

'It's beginning to sound as though it's possible, isn't it?'

'And I jollied her along and told her she'd been imagining them and they were nothing to be afraid of. Oh God! If it's true, I could've helped her, George. I could have, but I didn't.'

'Trish . . . I . . . If she was trying to tell you, it's unlikely you were the only one. After all, you said you didn't know her particularly well before that. And we may be wrong. It's an ambiguous way of describing a penis, you must admit.'

'Oh yes. But it could've been her only way, couldn't it? She was only four, George. She probably didn't have the vocabulary for anything more specific. It's not as if she had a brother. I suppose she must know some boys at playgroup, but even if she'd seen them showing off their willies, they wouldn't have been erect. She might not have made the connection. "Huge wiggly pink worms" could have been the only words she could think of to describe what frightened her.'

'Maybe. And if she was telling people,' George said, 'then that could be why she's been silenced.'

In spite of her determination to think rationally and

not leap to hysterical, unwarranted conclusions, Trish couldn't do it. Charlotte's terror filled her mind.

'It may not have happened, Trish. Don't . . . don't . . .'

'Don't worry?' she asked sharply. 'Don't upset myself?'

'Not more than you can take,' he said reasonably. 'That wouldn't help Charlotte, or you, or anyone.'

'True enough.' Trish tried to get her brain working ahead of her emotions. She drank some of her cold coffee and grimaced. 'Ugh. I need something else. Would you like more tea?'

'No, thanks. It was great, but it was enough.'

'I won't be long.'

'Can't I come with you?'

'OK.' She led the way into the kitchen, saying, 'Supposing Nicky did push Charlotte's body through the park in the pram, what did she do with it then?'

'Took it somewhere she was sure she'd be alone, somewhere well away from her boss's house, dumped the body and took the pram back home. In Robert's place, I think I'd have told her to put the body in a skip, or in the river, or even in someone's dustbin. In a way a dustbin's the likeliest. After all, hardly anyone re-opens a black bag they've put out for the binmen, and they just sling them into the back of the lorry when they collect the rubbish. After that, the bags are crushed or dumped in a landfill site and buried under the next load. A small child's body could easily disappear like that with no one any the wiser. It wouldn't be that surprising if the police haven't found it.'

'It does make sense of a sort, but I still can't make myself believe it,' said Trish, unaware of the tightening of her forehead until George reached over and drew his thumb down the deep line between her eyebrows.

'Don't look so tormented, Trish.'

'I am tormented,' she said. 'Charlotte was – is – a wonderful child.'

He moved closer to her and stroked the growing space between her eyebrows. She did not know how to comment on that or deal with what it made her feel. After a moment she turned away to make her coffee, saying into the kettle, 'If your theory about Robert is true, Nicky's epilepsy would be irrelevant.'

'Yes. If it is true.'

'So, what do we do next?' she asked, leaning back against the kitchen worktop and holding her coffee mug tightly between her hands.

'Wait until they charge Nicky or let her go. There's no point even thinking about the future until we know that much.'

The telephone rang, chirruping like a hungry fledgling. Trish stared at it, wishing she had never asked George to help. If Nicky and Robert had done what George suggested, she did not want him orchestrating their defence. If Nicky were guilty, then Trish wanted her behind bars, not saved from a conviction by clever lawyers arguing technicalities.

'Aren't you going to answer?' said George so gently that it seemed he must know what she was thinking. She shook her head.

'The machine will pick it up; I can deal with it later, whatever it is.'

'I ought to go soon, Trish, but I hate leaving you like this. You mustn't tear yourself apart over something that may not have happened.'

'No. But I am beginning to wish I hadn't asked you to see Nicky. If she's—'

'I know,' he said, stepping forwards to take her in his arms. 'But you did and she may still be as innocent as you hope. Oh Trish, I'd do anything to save you from all

271

the things you most dread. I've . . . You know, I've been trying to get up the courage to ring you here ever since we quarrelled that day, but I couldn't. When Penny told me you were on the line this morning, I nearly sang.'

She leaned against him, amazed that in the middle of her anguish for Charlotte, she could feel such comfort.

'Trish,' he said as he kissed her hair.

'George, I'm very bad at this sort of thing.' She pulled herself out of his arms and felt him tensing up. She smiled, trying to show how muddled she felt and how much she had liked being hugged.

His face relaxed and the lines of anxiety – or anger – around his eyes and mouth turned briefly into laughter. 'That makes two of us, then, Trish. Corny, isn't it?'

'Why?'

'We can talk ourselves and everyone else into an early grave on almost any subject but this. Why are you bad at it?'

'That's corny, too,' she said, not even smiling as she remembered Bella Weblock's infuriating diagnosis of the state of her psyche and emotions. 'My father walked out on my mother and me when I was eight. I've been bad at trusting people ever since. A bit loopy on the subject, I suppose. Whenever I've thought I was what you might call in love, I've positively looked for reasons to prove I wasn't, and generally found them. I've more or less given up trying now; it seemed so unfair on the lovers – and on the wearing side for me, too.'

'Ah, not so corny, then,' he said, surprising her. He stroked the frown lines between her eyebrows again. 'Worrying about being unfair in those circumstances is much more like you than being afraid of being hurt – which is the usual excuse, isn't it?'

'There's been plenty of that, too,' she said, not having noticed the compliment. 'But, you see, I'm too much like my father for comfort. I look exactly like him; I've inherited his fiendish temper. And I've never yet managed to be in love with anyone without wanting to get free again quite soon.' She shivered and then quickly added: 'I couldn't bear to do to anyone else what he did to us. Look, now it's your turn. What's your excuse?'

'I've never met anyone who didn't want to cling and domesticate the Great Bear,' he said, pretending to be serious. Then, as he saw a faint blush warming her cheeks, he laughed. 'Come on, Trish, you must have known I'd have heard about that. I've always taken it as something of a compliment. It was you who invented it, wasn't it?'

The blush deepened, but so did the laughter-lines around her mouth and eyes.

'I suppose I did. I'm glad you didn't misunderstand.'

'I'm glad too. We've got lots to say to each other, Trish.'

'I know,' she said quickly. 'But not yet. Not while Charlotte's . . .' He reached out to take her face between his hands. 'I'm a bad-tempered sod, too, you know. Your fury won't frighten me.'

The florid grandfather clock, the only antique piece she had in the whole flat, startled them both by striking four with all the sonorous solemnity of a passing bell.

'Blast! I really must go now, Trish. Can I ring you?'

'Whenever,' she said. 'You've been . . .' She wanted to leave it to his imagination, but he wouldn't let her.

'Try, Trish,' he urged. 'It doesn't commit you to anything, but it would be nice if you could say it. Or some of it anyway.'

'You've been wonderful, and I've loved you hugging

me like that. And I . . . I think I'd almost dare risk trying again – with you.'

He kissed her then, grabbed his briefcase and ran, leaving her standing in the kitchen, feeling the first intimations of happiness she had known for a long time. A very long time.

It came to her later, as she was pottering about, collecting their mugs and checking her face in the mirror, making sure that her bare feet had not been disgustingly dirty all along, that the afternoon's revelation almost justified her sabbatical in itself. Perhaps she really had managed to look at herself and other people more clearly since she had stepped back from her work. Perhaps she was slowly recovering her strength.

Hugging herself, she began to remember too the pleasure of being touched, of letting down some of her defences. She also recognised an impatience to get on to the next day so that she could talk to him again.

At last she remembered that someone had left a message on the answering machine and went to listen. It turned out to have been Willow, telling her that Holland Park Helpers confirmed that Nicky had never been in any trouble, but that she had had a difficult background. Apparently she'd been taken into care at the age of three months when her unmarried mother proved incapable of looking after her. Since then she'd been fostered. Because it was an unusual background for one of their nannies, the owners of Holland Park Helpers had taken more than usual trouble to check all her references. In spite of the police suspicions over Charlotte's disappearance, they were holding to their confidence in Nicky. Willow hoped that that would be of some use to Trish. If she wanted anything more, she was to ring Willow at once and she'd do her best to provide it.

Trish listened to the tape whirring back to its starting point, torn between sympathy for Nicky's past and present solitude, and suspicion of what it might have made her do.

The telephone rang again while she was still standing there. It turned out to be Emma, answering the message Trish had left that morning. They agreed to have an early dinner in a tiny Italian restaurant Emma had discovered and then go to a film.

Back in Southwark, having admired Emma's attempts to rationalise away the misery Hal's desertion was drilling into her and tried to help, Trish saw that there was another message waiting for her. Turning on the black halogen lamp with one hand, she pressed the buttons on the machine with the other. After the usual whirrs, clicks and whistles, she heard George's voice:

'Trish, it's me. I meant to say, but funked it this afternoon . . . can't think why except that . . . Blast! Listen, Trish, I know you gave the police an alibi for Saturday, but it seems that they haven't completely wiped you from their list of suspects. *I* know you weren't involved, of course. But it's possible they'll come back to you – even likely. Will you promise to ring me when they do, whatever time it is? Day or night. I mean that, Trish. You've got my home number as well as the office one, I know.'

She sat down heavily on the black-leather swivel chair and caught her coccyx on the hard arm as she went down.

'Shit!' she shouted, partly at the pain and partly out of fury. All her sensible appreciation of the reasons why the police had had to try to interview her disappeared in a tide of pure feeling.

If they pursued their idiotic, slanderous suspicions

much further, someone would talk, and some people would mutter things like 'no smoke without fire'. The thought of going back to the Temple to face the covert contempt of the people who had never liked her, or the outright condemnation of her few real enemies was bad enough. But what if some of the people she had counted as friends began to turn away?

The generosity of George's declaration suddenly seemed even more valuable than it had done that morning. Trish knew that she would have to speak to him that night.

'*Qui s'excuse s'accuse,*' she reminded herself as she turned the Rolodex until she came to George's card. She pressed in his number, not realising that her fingers were touching the buttons far more softly than usual, almost stroking them.

'George? It's—'

'Trish. Thank you for ringing. Sorry to have been so pusillanimous this afternoon.'

'You should have said.'

'Somehow I couldn't. Wet of me, I know. But it was so glorious seeing you today, I couldn't wreck it with police nonsense.'

'Ah, George. But look, let's be sensible for a minute: what is it they think they've got on me?'

'I'm not sure in detail, but the questions they were asking Nicky made it clear they think she had a partner, and that it was either Robert or you. It sounded to me as though they've got no evidence against you and are hoping that Nicky will give them something.'

'So obviously it can't have helped that it was me she asked to have informed of her arrest.'

'Precisely.'

'I should have seen that coming after the things Sergeant Lacie said to me. But at the time the only thing that struck me was the sadness of Nicky's having no one else.' Trish frowned. 'Although it would've been more logical for her to use Robert. I can see why she might have balked at giving Antonia's name, but why not Robert? Particularly as they're so friendly.'

'But perhaps she was clever enough to see how that would look and decided to protect him. Trish?'

'Yes, George?'

'It's not late. Would you like me to come round?'

She stood holding the receiver to her cheek, thinking about the possibility and the temptation, but after a moment she said, 'No. I think . . . I think, as we said, we ought to get all this out of the way. If you came tonight, I might . . . we might . . . No. George, I can't mix us and Charlotte.'

There was a long pause, as though he was trying to decide whether to argue.

'No. I can see that. OK, darling,' he said at last. 'But I'm here if you want me.'

'Thank you, George.' She probably shouldn't have been surprised by the endearment, but she was.

When he had gone, she put the receiver back and thought how vast the flat seemed and how empty, and how stupid she had been to tell him not to come.

CHAPTER TWENTY-TWO

'What have you got for me, Blake?' The superintendent looked perfectly calm as he sat behind his ugly desk, but Blake had known him for years and understood all the frustration he was feeling.

'Nothing like enough, sir. I'm sorry.'

'You've had the nanny . . . what's her name?'

'Nicky Bagshot,' said Blake irritably, knowing that the superintendent knew her name as well as he did.

'That's the one. You told me Bagshot was the key and demanded a free hand. I gave it to you. You've had her in here thirty-three hours already, and you've still got nothing to charge her with?'

'No, sir. I was sure she'd crack. She has to have had something to do with it. Nothing makes any sense unless she's involved. But she's a tougher little nut than she looks. Even so, if it hadn't been for her brief, I'm sure we'd have had her. George Henton of all people!'

'Yes, how the hell did she know to get him? And why did he come for a little thing like her? Has she had dealings with the law before?'

'Not so far as we've discovered, sir. It was Trish Maguire sent him.'

'Did she now? How deep *is* she in all this?'

'I'm still not sure, sir. She keeps cropping up all over the place. I know she's involved somehow.'

'Well, of course she is. She's Antonia Weblock's cousin.'

'Yeah, but none of the other relatives have been behaving like that. And some of the prints on the doll's pram – the ones inside the hood and on the bottom of the mattress – are hers.'

'Maguire agreed to be printed?' The superintendent sounded astonished.

'We didn't even bother to ask. We knew she wouldn't. So we lifted her prints off the computer disks she handed Lacie and Derring,' said Blake with some satisfaction. 'I know it's not enough, but it's another oddity that adds to all the rest.'

'It certainly isn't enough,' the superintendent said coldly. 'Nothing like. If she's involved, she'll have thought up a story to explain the prints away. It wouldn't be hard. She's probably in and out of that house all the time; she'll claim she tidied the toys one day and left her prints on the pram then, or something similiar. It could even be true. Anything else?'

'Only the circumstantial stuff you've already heard – her breakdown, the fact that so many small children who've been in her charge have had injuries of one sort or another . . .'

'Minor injuries, John.'

'True. But still injuries. Then there's her interest in child abuse and pornography. I know she claims it's for this book she's writing – and Lacie's got the publishers to confirm they have commissioned it – but that could be a very handy excuse for someone who knows their progress over the Internet can be monitored. And Maguire would know that. She could have provided the stuff we found under Bagshot's floorboards. As you know, there are no identifiable prints on any of the magazines, which suggests someone pretty knowledgeable put them there.'

'That's ridiculous. You don't need to be "knowledge-able" to be fingerprint-conscious. Everyone watches *The Bill* these days. And aren't you forgetting Maguire's alibi?'

'She's involved somewhere. I'm sure of that.'

'You could be right, but it's hard to see how we're going to get any evidence,' said the superintendent.

'Unless we put her under surveillance, sir.'

'We could do that, but why should it turn anything up? She's hardly likely to lead us to the body, and that's the only thing I can see that would tie her to the case.'

Blake couldn't think why the superintendent had been able to impress promotion boards so much better than he had. They'd started in the job at the same time and he had a much more substantial arrest record. Why should that shit on the other side of the desk have forged ahead of him like this?

'We might find her interfering with someone else's child, sir,' he said, holding on to his dislike. 'That would be strong corroboration. I'm sure she's involved.'

'So you keep saying. But you haven't convinced me.'

'She sits there so quiet, watching all the time, waiting. When she does speak, even when she's angry, she sounds reasonable. But she's . . . There's something sharp about her, dangerous almost. It's hard to put a finger on it, but I know there's fury in her somewhere. It's tightly controlled, too tightly perhaps, but it's there.' Blake gritted his teeth in frustration. He couldn't even hold the idea long enough to find words to express it, although he knew exactly what he meant.

'And she enjoyed making an arse of me when I showed too clearly that I assumed she'd come in to confess,' he added.

'Wouldn't anyone who'd been a suspect, especially in a case like this? Come on, Blake, I think you're letting your ego get in the way of your judgement on this one. Why d'you dislike her so much?'

'I don't, sir. Quite the reverse. I thought she was great at first – until she started to make me so damned suspicious. Look at the way she's behaved the last couple of days: refusing to answer reasonable questions and then tipping up all cool and innocent-like an hour or two later to say she couldn't have had anything to do with the case because she was eating in a trendy restaurant you and I couldn't afford in a month of Sundays, and being well and truly noticed by all sorts of influential people.'

'But it was true, wasn't it?'

'Oh, sure. But it's too pat. And then she turns up as Bagshot's only friend and provides a top-flight solicitor for her. It's all wrong, sir. There's something about it that stinks.'

'Maybe, but it's flimsy stuff. If you were a woman I'd accuse you of an overdose of intuition.'

Christ, what an insult! thought Blake.

'Come on, John, you must admit you've got nothing on her that would stand up in court. What about the rest of your suspects? Got anything on any of them yet? Robert Hithe, for instance?'

'Not enough. There is one missing hour, though. He and Bagshot left McDonald's just before one-thirty and went back to the house. He stayed there until two-thirty when he left to go to his office. Bagshot

claims she took the child to the park a few minutes later.'

'And what does she say they were all doing during
that hour?'

'She claims – as he did each time we asked him – that
she put the child down for a rest because she's always
tired after her swimming lesson, that Hithe read the
papers for his meeting in the drawing room, and that
she herself read a book on her bed. It could be true.'

'Unless they were having sex.'

'As you say, sir. If so, they're both keeping that very
quiet. They both say that Hithe didn't see the child
between getting back after McDonald's and leaving for
his meeting.'

'You've got bugger all, Blake. You must see that. It's
a random snatch by a stranger like I always said, and
we're not going to get any further now until someone
stumbles on the body or we get something through
Crimestoppers or one of the TV appeals.'

'If there'd been a forcible abduction, someone would've
seen something,' said Blake, as he had done so often
before. 'That park was a circus on Saturday, stuffed
with potential witnesses.'

'You never heard of strange men offering little girls
sweets, Blake? Come on.'

'It's got to be either Hithe or Maguire with Bagshot,'
Blake said obstinately, as though it was the mantra that
was going to get him to heaven. 'It's got to be.'

'Maybe you're right, but without a witness or a cough
from Bagshot we haven't a thing. And now you're
going to have to let her go. It's not good enough,
John. It'll—'

'I know you're being leaned on, sir,' said Blake, all
the muscles in his throat tightening with the effort of
not yelling at the man.

'All we need is a nice juicy body we can get to work on and then we'll be fine.'

Christ! You really don't care, thought Blake. You really have no feelings whatsoever for that poor kid. She's just a case to you, something that'll help the clear-up rate look good if we get a result or pull us down if we don't. You are a shit.

'Don't look at me like that, John. Face it, she can't be alive. Not after this long and all the searches we've done. There isn't anywhere else she could be.'

'Unless someone's got her in a cellar, pending a purchaser, like in that Belgian case.'

'There is that, but I doubt it. And even if you're right, the only thing that's going to turn that up now is accidental or direct information from a member of the public. We've done all we can, checking out the locals.'

'We can't give up. Not yet.'

'Of course not. But we need some new lines of enquiry. Or a body. Something for the lab. boys to work on. Pity that toy pram didn't give them more.'

'Only the fingerprints and the two kinds of blood, sir; one matching the boy with the scraped knees and one that's almost certainly Charlotte's. There's nothing in the sample we took from her mother to rule that out.'

'Well maybe we had better get a costing for surveillance. Sort something out and bring it to the briefing tomorrow morning and we'll take it from there. But limited, straightforward surveillance, mind. I'm not having officers cosying up to Bagshot in clubs all over London or trying to take Maguire out dancing to seduce her into a confession. Understood?'

'Yes, sir.' Blake turned to go, but the superintendent's voice stopped him as he stood with his hand reaching for the door.

'Now, on to something else: how's Kath Lacie shaping up?'

Blake stood facing the door for a second that felt like minutes before getting his face in order. Then he turned.

'Well enough, sir. She has a knack of getting witnesses to talk and she's an efficient officer.'

'Not putting it about, is she, John? Inside the station?'

'No, sir. Not as far as I know.'

'Glad to hear it. When they look like that, and talk so sweetly, they can be useful enough for getting round suspects and pleasing juries, but they're a damn nuisance if they can't be trusted to keep their legs together. But then maybe it's less their fault than the idiots' who risk good promotion prospects for a quick tickle. You know that as well as I do, don't you, John?'

Blake did not answer.

'OK. Get on with it.'

With the fury making his eyes feel like hot corn about to pop, John Blake left the superintendent's office for his own. He'd probably deserved the warning, but coming from that jumped-up prat, it left him wanting to hit someone.

He was still furious more than two and a half hours later when Sam Herrick put his head round the door.

'Yes?' he snarled as Sam opened his mouth to ask a question. 'What do *you* want?'

'The custody sergeant sent me to find you, sir. We've got to get Bagshot out of here in fifteen minutes. Twelve and a half now. And that Henton creep's been on the phone again to remind us of the time.'

'I know, I know. I'm on my way.'

He walked down to the cells, sorted the necessary bits

of paper, and stood by while the custody sergeant went to unlock Bagshot. He could have let her go without seeing her again, but he wanted her to know that he hadn't finished with her.

She came slowly up the sick-coloured corridor between the closed doors, looking very small and very stubborn. He knew she'd been holding out on him about something, but he hadn't been able to work out what. He thought again of the neighbour who insisted she was certain she'd seen Bagshot and the child setting off for the park on Saturday afternoon. Bagshot had had the doll's pram with her, but the neighbour was convinced she'd seen the child, too. Howling and shouting and very much alive as they walked along the pavement. Blake knew how easy it was for old biddies like his witness to muddle one day with another, but he couldn't get her to see that. It was a pain in the arse he hadn't managed to shake her and get her to admit she might have seen Bagshot and the pram, but *not* the child. He'd tried hard enough.

He also thought of the gay swimming teacher who'd been so jumpy when they interviewed him until it became clear they were asking about Bagshot and her treatment of the child, not about his own activities. The jumpiness had made Blake highly suspicious until he'd probed a bit further. Then the bloke had broken down and admitted he had a record for drug dealing and had done time in Feltham as a juvenile. Blake had sent an officer to check it out and the reasons for the jumpiness had become entirely clear. It wasn't only anabolic steroids they were dealing in the health club he belonged to; it was smack and coke and amyl nitrate and God knows what besides. He'd passed the information over to the Drugs Squad. The swimming teacher was probably already up on a charge, but that wasn't Blake's concern.

The bloke had been quite clear in his assessment of Bagshot once he'd calmed down; said she was on brilliant terms with the child, who adored her and had never shown any signs of injury. Blake had pressed him on that, even mentioning bruises on Charlotte's arms, but he stuck to his story, said he'd never seen any bruises on her arms or anywhere else. Antonia had first spotted them on a Sunday evening, so it was possible that they'd faded by the next swimming lesson nearly a week later. But it was a right pain all the same.

'Well, Nicky?' Blake said as she came to stand in front of him. 'How're you feeling?'

'Tired,' she said without obvious resentment. 'Like I said earlier, there was a drunk in the cell next to mine and he was singing half the night and throwing up the other half. What do you want to ask me *now*?'

'Nothing, love. We're letting you go,' he said, and watched hope breaking over her face like sunlight.

'You've found her then?'

'No. Not yet.'

The brightness died out of her face, leaving it stony.

'Why not?' She stared up into his face as though the answer might be written there. 'There can't be that many places she could be. You should be looking. She could be—'

'You're managing to sound as though you care,' he said, trying to be offensive and succeeding. He could see the custody sergeant out of the corner of his eye looking restive, but he was not going to pass up the chance of one more crack at Bagshot.

'Of course I do. Can't you get that into your thick skulls, any of you?' she said, her voice rising.

So, he thought, we're maybe getting somewhere at last. He was about to ask how far the so-called care had taken her when she lost it completely and broke into hysterical tears, beating both fists on the custody sergeant's table again and again until Blake was afraid she might draw blood and then try to get them for brutality. He nodded to the custody sergeant to restrain her and went away as quietly as he could. It had been a long day and there was still a hell of a lot to do. Lucky, really, that he didn't want to go home.

First thing in the morning he'd have to get someone – Kath probably – to sort out the best way to use a limited surveillance budget, and he needed to get hold of Antonia Weblock again. It was a definite plus that he'd established such good communication with her and she was talking so freely. Even the superintendent had been impressed by that. But there were still one or two things that needed clarifying, and he had to check on this business of her burning the mail. She'd promised to hang on to that day's post to show him what she'd meant, why she'd had to destroy the rest. It hadn't been hard to imagine the sort of things people had been writing to her, but she shouldn't have done it without his say-so.

She'd laughed bleakly when he'd told her that and explained that when you did her sort of work at her sort of level, you'd forgotten how to ask permission of anyone. He might've been angry, but she'd got serious again at once and recited one of the worst of the letters. As she'd spoken, her face had grown visibly paler and her voice had shaken so much she'd had to stop talking. She'd looked at him then, her eyes swelling up with tears she was too proud to shed, and begged him to understand.

She was being bloody brave, and in a way it was that courage of hers that was making him so angry with Maguire. What a bitch she must be, to be so cool and manipulative when her cousin was in such hell. How could Maguire have dug out one of the most expensive lawyers for the chief suspect in the abduction of her own cousin's four-year-old daughter? What a bitch!

CHAPTER TWENTY-THREE

Trish heard of Nicky's release from George's secretary, who had been working late. He had had to go to a conference with counsel, which he hadn't been able to reschedule, the secretary told Trish, and he'd asked her to hang on in the office until she had confirmation that Nicky was out. He'd also asked her to pass on the news to Trish as soon as possible.

Trish thanked her warmly and then tried to ring Antonia. Yet again she got the answering machine with its regal message.

It seemed impossible to Trish that Antonia could believe her guilty of any of the things the police had alleged, but there was no other explanation for her determined silence. She was probably furious that Trish had sent George to help Nicky, but she had stopped returning the calls long before that. Trish decided that she would have to go to Kensington, force Antonia to admit her suspicions and somehow persuade her that they were nonsense. Otherwise, even when the truth of what had happened to Charlotte had been discovered, the two of them would never be able to salvage what was left of their friendship. They had lost too much of it already to risk the rest.

She had forgotten the press pack until she got to the calm-looking, white-stucco house, over which the wisteria was hanging like streams of lilac-blue water. There were fewer journalists there than had been on Sunday, but still quite enough. And some of them recognised her.

'Trish, this way,' shouted one of the remaining photographers, as a woman pressed close to her and said, 'What's your theory of what has happened to Charlotte, Trish? You know all about cases of this sort, don't you? D'you think she's still alive?'

'Unfortunately,' said Trish, picking her words with care because she knew she would have no control over what appeared in the headlines, 'I have no idea. The police are doing all they can. We can only hope.'

'When did you last see her?' asked another journalist. Trish ignored the question, arranging her expression with care. She did not want witch-like photographs of herself all over the next day's tabloids.

She pushed her way through the crowd and rang the bell, hoping that if Antonia was in she would have enough self-preservation to avoid a quarrel on the doorstep. But it was Robert who flung open the door with a blinding smile, which dimmed as soon as he saw Trish.

'Oh, it's you,' he said. 'You'd better come in. Don't say anything you don't want that lot to overhear.'

When he had shut the door behind her, he leaned against the wall as though he was too tired to stand upright without support.

'I thought you might be Nicky. She's bringing back a takeaway.'

'Oh. I'd heard that the police have released her. Is Antonia here?'

He shook his head. 'Poor Nicky. They really put her through it, you know. She said if it hadn't been for you and that lawyer you got her, she'd never have survived. That was good of you, Trish. I'm not sure I thanked you properly yesterday.'

'That's all right, Robert. I couldn't have left her on her own, with no help,' she said, searching his face for signs of sincerity. Seeing plenty, she thought she had most of the confirmation she needed that he had been having an affair with Nicky. But she still wanted to know why. 'When will Antonia be back?'

He shook his head. 'Not till after dinner. She hardly ever eats here now. Can't stand the sight of me at the moment or Nicky. And she's not overly pleased with you either, Trish.' He smiled a little slyly. 'You'd better come and have a drink.'

Trish followed him into the frowsty drawing room. Cushions were heaped at one end of the sofa and there was a long dark-grey mark on the cream damask, where Robert must have put his shoes. A glass of whisky rested on the floor by the sofa, next to a heap of jumbled newspapers. The state of the room, more than anything, showed that Antonia was avoiding the house. Perhaps she had not heard all ten of the messages Trish had left for her.

'Whisky, Trish, or something else? I can't remember what you drink.'

'Nothing for me, thank you, Robert,' she said, deciding that if she couldn't confront Antonia, at least she could try to find out more about what motivated Robert and what he was capable of doing.

'I oughtn't to stay long,' she went on. 'D'you know why Antonia's so angry with me? I haven't been able to get her on the phone for days now.'

'She wasn't best pleased that you'd been fraternising

with her dreary ex, old Ben the blackboard-monger. And she didn't like your little polygrapher-friend proving that Nicky's story about the playground was true, or some of the questions you've been asking. But worse than everything was your getting the lawyer for Nicky. She's never going to forgive you for that, Trish. She's been muttering about betrayal ever since she heard. And you know what she's like when she thinks someone's done the dirty on her.'

'Yes. I don't suppose she will forgive me for George Henton. But how did she know I'd been seeing Ben?'

'He told her the last time they met.'

Trish gaped at him.

'I know. Weird, isn't it? She doesn't tell me much these days, but she was so angry with me this morning that she threw that one out to try to make me hit back. Needless to say it didn't work. I learned a long time ago that there's no point joining in when Antonia's in a rage. She always wins.'

'Why is she seeing him?' Of all the things Trish had expected to discover, that was the least likely.

'I haven't the foggiest. Unless she's trying to do some amateur sleuthing just like you, Trish. Got any further, have you?'

'Not a lot,' she said, deciding that the time for caution was past. She and Robert were never going to be friends, whatever happened. She might as well take advantage of his gratitude for what she had done for Nicky to try to bounce him into an admission. If she was wrong, it would hardly matter. 'Except about your affair with Nicky. I have found out about that.'

His face did not move and his smile suddenly looked like the rictus on a corpse. Then he relaxed and laughed.

'You think you're so clever, don't you? What makes you believe that then?'

'It's the only credible explanation for your attendance on Charlotte.'

'But I told you: I liked the little brat.'

'Yes, but you'd never have got to know her if you hadn't been hanging around Nicky. Come on, Robert. There's no point pretending. It's hardly the crime of the century, after all.'

'Maybe not. But it's not the sort of thing you want said about you – that you're bonking the nanny.'

No, thought Trish, but you did it, didn't you? Were you turned on by Nicky's vulnerability? Or was it a way of getting back at Antonia that didn't involve confrontation? You've just admitted you're too much of a coward to stand up to her; were you sliming away behind her back, getting your satisfaction out of doing her down by bedding Nicky? You're such a revolting little rat, I could believe that. But is that all it was? Or did you seduce Nicky to blind her to what you were really after?

'Even so,' she said aloud, trying to talk as unemotionally as George had done when all her instincts were yelling at her to peg Robert out in the blazing sun and force him to tell her the truth. 'And what about Charlotte? Where did she fit in?'

Before she could get any further, they both heard the journalists coming to life outside.

'Good,' said Robert, apparently not having heard what Trish had said. 'That must be Nicky with our supper. There's bound to be enough for three. I told her to get a lot. D'you want to stay, Trish?'

The thought of eating with him disgusted her. She shook her head, saying, 'But I would like to talk to Nicky.'

'And I know she wants to thank you,' he said, sounding almost friendly again. 'I'll go and lay the table while you have a word with her up here. I'll send her in.'

It was a couple of minutes before Nicky came in, looking tousled and well-kissed.

'Oh, I'm so glad you're here,' she said, smiling like a child faced with a pile of Christmas presents. 'I've been wanting to thank you. Mr Henton was brilliant. And I know I'd never have got anyone as good as him if it hadn't been for you. I'd . . . I'd do anything for you, Ms Maguire.'

'Oh, call me Trish, do,' she said, thinking, could this happy, grateful, apparently ingenuous woman have done any of the things George suggested? Could she have seen Charlotte abused and murdered, and plotted with the killer to dispose of her body?

It seemed impossible.

'Would you really do something for me, Nicky?'

'Of course,' she said passionately. 'Anything.'

'Then tell me, is it true that you and Robert have been having an affair?'

Nicky's face turned poppy-coloured, but she didn't look away.

'I know I shouldn't ever have done it,' she said with difficulty, 'but I was so unhappy and he was so kind to me – and to Lottie. You won't tell Antonia, will you? Please, please don't tell.'

'Are you sure she doesn't already know?'

'Oh yes,' said Nicky, sounding much more adult than usual. 'She uses everything she can to criticise me, bullying me about what I look like and how I sound and what I do with Lottie and everything. If she knew about me and Robert, she'd have sacked me straight off.'

'I see,' said Trish, adding more brutally, 'What are you planning to do now, the pair of you?'

Nicky's eyes filled with tears and Trish felt almost ashamed of herself.

'We can't decide anything till we know about Lottie,' the girl said with surprising dignity. 'If she's . . . you know, if she gets back safe then I'll stay with her. If Antonia lets me.'

'Even though she's so critical of you?'

Nicky nodded. 'If Lottie comes back she'll need me, me and Robert. We're the only ones who care about her and play with her and all that sort of thing. She'll need us. We couldn't leave her.'

'And if she's not found?' said Trish harshly.

Nicky just shook her head as the tears flooded her cheeks. She sniffed.

'She must be,' she said after a while. 'She *must* be.'

'Nicky,' said Trish suddenly, 'will you tell me about the magazines that were found under your floor?'

'What about them? They were disgusting.'

'Why were they there?'

'I don't know. Honestly, Trish, I don't know. The police wouldn't believe me, but you must. If you'd seen them, you'd know I couldn't have ever had anything to do with them. They were . . . it was awful just looking at them.'

Trish did not comment.

'You must believe me. Someone put them there. I knew people had been going into my room whenever I left the house. And I knew they'd had some of the floorboards up because one of the edges was all splintery where it had been smooth before, but I thought they were just searching. I never thought they were putting things there.'

'Who was it?'

'I don't know,' she said, looking mulish. 'There's no point asking because I don't know.'

'Could it have been Robert?'

'No.' The fact that she hadn't qualified the denial in any way impressed Trish. More passion would definitely have suggested less certainty. But did her certainty come from knowledge or hope?

'If it's anyone in this house, it's Antonia.'

'Nicky, you cannot say that sort of thing just because she's been rough on you. Why on earth would someone like Antonia have anything to do with that sort of filth?'

'Because she doesn't like me.'

'Oh, don't be ridiculous, Nicky. Look, I've got to go in a minute. I only really came to talk to Antonia. Can I trust you to tell her I came and that I want her to ring me if she needs anything.'

'Yes,' she said, her face closing in. 'Ms Maguire, Trish, do *you* think there's any hope for Lottie?'

Could anyone sound so desperate if they knew the answer to that question?

'I don't know, Nicky. I wish I thought there could be.'

Nicky nodded and turned away.

'Don't go for a minute,' said Trish suddenly. Nicky looked back. 'Charlotte talked to you about her bad dreams, didn't she?'

The misery in Nicky's face was diluted with affection and even amusement.

'Yeah. Poor little thing. It was so sad. You know she loved gardening?'

'No. I didn't.'

'Well, she did. She liked digging and planting seeds and picking flowers, but of course Antonia wouldn't let her do it here. Her precious garden's much too important for a messy child to be allowed to play in it. But one of Lottie's friends is allowed to have her own patch in her parents' garden and when we went for tea Lottie always did some digging.'

'She must have enjoyed it,' said Trish, seeing almost pure pleasure in Nicky's memories.

'She did until the day she found the worms. She was happy as anything one afternoon, digging away with Mattie, but then we heard these awful screams. They'd turned up a kind of clump of the biggest worms you've ever seen. Great fat pinky-bluey things they were, all wound round each other and lifting up round the prongs of the fork. Lottie was terrified. And she had nightmares about them ever after. Every night I had to make a kind of checklist of all the places where she thought they might be and prove they weren't.'

'So did I once,' said Trish.

'Yes. She told me. She liked you, Trish. Is there anything else? Otherwise I'd better go. Robert's hungry, you see.'

'No. There's nothing else, Nicky. Thank you. I'm glad she had you to look after her.'

Trish let herself out of the house, trying to work out what she felt. Nicky's story was utterly plausible, much more so really than any of the other explanations for the wiggly worms. But if Nicky and Robert had really both been as good to Charlotte as Nicky's artless explanations suggested, there was nothing to explain what had happened.

Driving south again, Trish vaguely noticed that the trees lining the pavements and poking up from behind the houses looked unexpectedly full and green in the glow of the street-lights, but all she could think about was Charlotte. She felt that there must have been something she'd heard or should have guessed that would give her a clue. But she had failed. The fact that the police had failed too, in spite of their much greater resources, didn't help. There was an answer out there, somewhere. There had to be.

As she reached the Embankment and sat waiting for the lights to change, she started to think about her only other suspect. Ben had been just as plausible as Nicky, but he was older and cleverer and perhaps better at disguising his feelings. If Antonia had been meeting him, then she must have some suspicions, too. There was nothing else Trish could think of that would have made her cousin approach him. If Robert was right and they were together, then Bella would probably be on her own at the house. It could be a good moment to try to get her to talk.

Although it was after ten, Trish turned away from her route home and drove west along the Embankment to cross the river at Chelsea Bridge.

There was a delectable smell leaking out of the front door of the house in Clapham when she got there. She sniffed appreciatively and realised that she was hungry. She rang the bell. The door was opened by Bella, wearing an enormous blue-and-white striped butcher's apron and wielding a wooden spoon.

'Haven't you gotten your key?' she asked before she had seen who was on the step. 'Oh, it's you.'

'Ben not in?'

'No. If you want him, I can have him call you when he gets back.' Bella was not exactly blocking the way into the house, but she was defensive enough to show that she was not offering any kind of welcome.

'It's a bit more urgent than that. Could I come in and wait? I'd like to talk to him face to face,' said Trish with a placatory smile. 'That is, if it's not too inconvenient.'

Bella shrugged. 'I'm working in the kitchen. Do you mind?'

'No, of course not.' Trish followed her and the delicious smell down the dark passage to the kitchen, which was looking as colourful and chaotic as ever. A huge heap of sliced onion was being slowly sweated in a wide frying pan on the cooker and two covered pans were seething gently on the back rings. Four newly baked wholemeal loaves were cooling on a rack on the cluttered worktop, amid baskets of lemons, pots of growing basil and coriander, and piles of books. There were four children's paintings stuck up on the wall above the fridge.

'Those're great,' Trish said as Bella gave her pans a vigorous stir. 'Are they by Ben's pupils?'

Bella looked at Trish and then in the direction of her pointing finger.

'No. They're by his godson, Alex, and his brother. They were here at the weekend. D'you know them, the Wallingfords?'

'No, I don't think so. They must be since my time.'

'They're great little artists, aren't they?' Bella's face seemed to be showing genuine enthusiasm, which gave Trish the lead she wanted.

'Yes. You must love children to enjoy them so much.'

'I'd hardly work with them if I didn't,' said Bella, looking at her with a certain amount of derision.

Since she seemed to be deliberately trying to provoke a reaction, Trish merely smiled and pointed out that the smell of caramel suggested that the onions were burning. Bella hurriedly turned back to the pan and stirred the browning heap. When she turned back, she said in a less unpleasant tone, 'Ben's told me a lot about you, you know.'

'That must have been dull for you,' said Trish with enough conviction to make Bella smile.

'It was hard when I first moved in,' she said with

more direct honesty than Trish had expected. 'He was always saying, "You'll love Trish; let me ask her round". "You'd be so interested in Trish's work; why don't you call her? She might send you clients". And then he always added at the end: "Trish is wonderful; you'll really like her".'

'God, Bella, I'm sorry,' said Trish. 'I had no idea it was as bad as that. No wonder you looked ready to kill me when I first came. How could Ben have been so insensitive? He's usually well aware of what people are feeling.'

'Maybe you were just too important to him. He couldn't see why I didn't want you in my home.'

'Well, I can. But could we make peace now? Whatever there was between me and Ben – and it was almost nothing, I promise you – it's years ago now. I've moved on and so has he, long since. Couldn't you and I be friends at least?'

Bella didn't answer, only reaching for a small green bottle and saying, 'Can I get you some ginger cordial?'

'Actually,' said Trish, hoping she was not jeopardising her chances of building some kind of trust in Bella, 'I don't much like ginger. Could I just have water? I'm quite thirsty.'

'Sure. Fizzy or regular?'

'Fizzy, please. Thanks.'

Bella filled two tall tumblers with ice and poured their drinks, saying over her shoulder, 'Do you eat smoked oysters? I have a tin here.'

'Oh dear,' said Trish, wishing that she could lie but knowing that swallowing smoked oysters would be even more difficult for her than eating rare chicken livers, which were her worst culinary nightmare.

'You don't? No. We don't share many tastes, do we?

Except Ben.' Then Bella laughed and Trish thought it was going to be all right.

'Not many,' she agreed.

'Here.' Bella pushed forward one of the glasses.

'Thank you. The bread smells wonderful. I'm really impressed that you do your own baking when you're so busy at work.'

Bella looked at her, the newly friendly smile disappearing. 'I cook when I'm worried. It's the only kind of therapy that works for me. But it does mean Daisy has to be exiled to the garden. She goes wild when she smells the food and I can't cope. She's only just stopped barking.'

'Why are you worried now?' asked Trish, ignoring Daisy's plight.

'Charlotte, of course. Aren't you?'

'Yes.' Trish felt the frown tightening her forehead. 'But then I know her. You don't.'

'I'd worry about any child in this situation. But the worst is that it's hurting Ben. He was doing so well until she was taken.'

Trish frowned.

'He'd gotten over most of the damage Antonia had done and he'd gotten over you, Trish, and now this, bringing you both back into his life, calling into question everything he'd come to believe about himself, and then the child . . .'

Trish felt the coldness of her glass between her palms. She looked down at the bubbles rising jauntily to the surface and bursting as they met the air. She did not know what to say. Eventually she raised her head.

'Did you know that he'd been watching Charlotte in the park?'

'Not at first.' Bella's face had the look of someone in the middle of an attack of neuralgia. 'But after those calls of yours I made him tell me. It . . . it hurt some that he'd hidden it, but I can understand it. If he and I can't have our own kids, then it matters to him that Charlotte could be his. I can understand that.'

The frown deepened as Trish had to face the fact of Bella's generosity.

'And has he told you that he's been seeing Antonia?'

'Oh, sure. He tells me everything – in the end. She called him one evening to say that she was afraid of what her new man might've been doing to Charlotte. She was hysterical. Ben told her to tell the police and then when he heard her crying down the phone he asked if she'd like to meet.'

'Why, after everything she'd done to him? Didn't it make you . . . ? Bella, haven't you ever wondered whether Ben might have had some kind of brainstorm and taken Charlotte?'

'No. Oh, OK, yes of course I wondered. But I know he didn't. The man I know couldn't have. And if he had, he'd have told me by now. He always tells me in the end. He went to Antonia because he can't *not* help when someone is in need. You know what a generous guy he is.'

'Yes. At least, I thought I did.'

'And how the only thing that's given him any self-esteem in the past has been his ability to help people?'

'That too. I didn't realise at the time, but I've seen it since. He wants to heal the world.'

'That's because he was never allowed to feel that he was worth being healed himself,' said Bella with enough sadness to make Trish ashamed of her old childish dislike. 'I should have seen it coming, realised that if Antonia ever asked him for anything he'd drop everything to give it to her. You're not drinking. Is there something wrong with the water?'

'No. Goodness, it's delicious,' said Trish, hurriedly drinking about half the glassful, bumping her nose on the floating ice cubes. 'Bella, you understand so much, have you come to any conclusions about what drives Antonia?'

There was a short silence while Bella transferred her cooked onions to a wide plate to cool. Then she said: 'In what way?'

'Don't get me wrong, but Ben's not the strongest of characters,' Trish said carefully, still trying to share Bella's faith in him. 'And Robert Hithe is positively weak and, I'd have said, devious, too. What is it in Antonia that drives her to try to love weak men?'

'I'd say her fear of being controlled, wouldn't you?'

'Maybe,' said Trish, thinking over the past. 'She certainly can't bear anything she sees as a challenge to her power.'

'That's right.' Bella turned away to the cooker. 'Everything I've heard suggests she's borderline psychotic. Which is why if she hadn't been in the States when it happened, I'd be worried about what *she* might have done to Charlotte.'

'Oh Bella, don't be ridiculous. You don't know her. Take it from me; she's not psychotic. And Charlotte wouldn't ever present that kind of challenge to her power.'

'No? Sure of that, Trish? Ben's heard quite a lot about the child from the police now and from Antonia herself, and it's clear she's no pushover. If she'd stood up to Antonia – maybe had a temper tantrum – at a moment when she felt her control over other people beginning to slip, she could have—'

'But she *was* away,' said Trish quickly, even as she remembered all the things Nicky had said about Antonia's treatment of Charlotte.

'Yes. Luckily. You're her cousin, Trish, you must know about her childhood. What were her parents like?'

'I know very little. You see, our families have never had much to do with each other. It was our grand-mothers who were sisters, and mine married an Irish-man. Hers disapproved and they never saw each other again. Antonia and I hadn't even met until we'd left university. And she hardly ever talks about her parents. They're both dead, you know. Her mother died when she was about seventeen, I think, and her father a couple of years ago.'

'Pity.'

'Bella, you said something about the police talking to Ben about Charlotte, telling him about her?'

'Yes. So what?'

'That sounds as though they've seen quite a lot of him.'

'Sure. They never leave us alone. They've been to the school twice; they've been to my consulting rooms. They come here. They've talked to the neighbours.'

'Have they talked to Ben about me?'

Bella looked up from her cooking in surprise. 'I don't know, Trish. Why should they?'

'Someone has told them a lot about my past, things that have nothing to do with Charlotte but that they've turned into reasons why they can suspect me of . . .' Trish faltered '. . . of hurting her. I wondered if some of that information had come from Ben.'

Bella thought about it for a while and then shook her blonde curls.

'I doubt it. He's never said anything to me that suggests they've wanted information on you and, con-sidering how he feels, I can't think he'd give them anything damaging. Now, you want to eat something while you wait for him?'

Bella made sandwiches, laden with piles of thinly sliced ham and salad and mayonnaise, and they ate them at the kitchen worktop. Then, since there was really nothing more to say and no sign of Ben, Trish left and Bella went to rescue Daisy.

Back in the flat, she rang Antonia's number, late though it was, determined to try once more.

'Yes?' came her voice, full of suspicion.

'Hi, it's me. Trish,' she said quickly. 'Did you get my message?'

'I've got all of them. Since there was very little for us to say to one another, I didn't think I'd waste my time returning them.'

'Antonia, please,' said Trish, hating her cousin's hostility. 'Please, if our relationship has ever meant anything to you, tell me it wasn't you who gave the police all that stuff about my damaging children I was looking after.'

'I don't know what you're talking about. What children? Trish, what have you been doing?'

'I haven't been doing anything. That's the point. But someone's been telling the police that I have.'

'And you thought it was me? Trish, how could you?' The outrage seemed almost convincing. 'I haven't said a word to them except that first day to explain that you were coming round and that you were my cousin.'

'Haven't they asked you anything about me and Charlotte? About the evening when I took her up to bed?'

'Oh, that,' said Antonia, sounding surprised. 'Yes, of course. And I told them everything I knew, which wasn't much. That you volunteered to take her back to bed and that you were up there with her for twenty minutes.'

'Did they ask what I was doing?'

'Of course they did. And of course I told them

you hadn't been doing any of the things they were suggesting. Trish, how can you? In the middle of all this. Haven't I got enough to put up with?'

'Antonia, I'm sorry. I didn't mean it like that. I just wanted to make sure that you didn't think I could have . . . could have hurt Charlotte.'

'Will you shut up?' she shouted. 'I can't bear it. You keep on at me all the time, all of you, telling me you haven't hurt her. We all know that someone has. I can't trust any of you. And I can't bear it. I don't want to talk any more.'

'Antonia! Antonia!' Trish heard the buzzing on the line that meant the other receiver had been replaced. Most of her own anger had gone, but none of the hurt. The thought that Antonia, who had known her so long, could possibly believe her capable of damaging Charlotte – or any child – was awful. And yet the picture of her in such distress with no one but the adulterous Robert and Nicky to help was dreadful, too. If Trish had not been absolutely certain that Antonia would hate it, she would have got straight back into her car and driven to Kensington at once.

CHAPTER TWENTY-FOUR

The following morning, Trish was once again woken by the postman. He looked disappointed by the sight of her long, crumpled T-shirt, which merely had a picture of a woman atop a mountain under the slogan *Woman with Altitude*. He handed her another heavy package from her hopeful publisher.

'Thanks,' said Trish, still blinking the sleep out of her eyes.

She had had a better night, perhaps because of the peace she had made with Bella, or perhaps simply because the body takes the sleep it needs in the end. It had left her groggy and very thirsty.

Two large mugs of tea and a long, hot shower later, she was beginning to wake up properly. As soon as she had dressed, she opened Chris's package to find yet more deeply upsetting evidence of cruelty visited on children by adults they had trusted. Unable to confront it just then, Trish added it to the other heaps of paper on her long, untidy desk, and began to admit some of the anxieties she had been suppressing for so long.

After a while she dialled Emma's number, half-hoping

that she would get the machine, but for once Emma herself answered.

'Oh, I'm not so bad,' she said in answer to Trish's first question. 'We've had an offer for the flat that will leave me enough for a deposit on a place of my own. And sometimes I'm even quite pleased to be alone again.'

'Good for you.'

'But then I wobble. What can I do for you, Trish?'

'Emma, do you remember the day you went to Antonia's to administer the polygraph test?'

'Of course.'

'When you came here afterwards, you said something rather odd, something about it's being Antonia I ought to be worrying about, not Nicky. What did you mean?'

'I don't know. Did I say that?'

'Yes.'

There was a short silence before Emma said carefully, 'I didn't like her, I'm afraid. And I thought the way she attacked Nicky was unkind and rather silly, but then I reminded myself that she doesn't know anything about lie-detection and couldn't have known how counter-productive she was being. I think that's all. I found her a very unpleasant woman.'

'Ah. So you didn't mean you thought she could have done something to Charlotte?'

'God, no! Trish, of course not. She's Charlotte's mother. And anyway, wasn't she abroad?'

'Yes. I'm losing my marbles, Emma. Pay no attention.'

'I should think the anxiety's getting to you, Trish. I'm not surprised. It must be awful.'

'Yeah. Thank you, Emma. Look, I'd better go.'

'OK. Let me know if you need anything.'

'I will. Bye.'

Trish put down the receiver, knowing that she couldn't

leave it there. She had to talk to Antonia. She'd take her some flowers and pretend to be apologising for the late-night telephone call. That would be a way to start, and then she'd just have to force Antonia to talk. Somehow.

There were no good florists anywhere near the flat and so Trish stopped the car halfway to Kensington at a favourite shop, where she had a selection of bright red and royal-blue flowers made up into a tight, round bunch, tied with raffia. With the flowers surrounded by hard clear cellophane and carefully laid on the front passenger seat, she drove through exasperatingly clogged streets to Antonia's house, parked at a meter and rang the bell.

The sound of Hoovering from inside was so loud that she had to ring a second time and then knock before she was heard. Eventually the roar of the cleaner stopped abruptly; there was the sound of a muttering in Spanish and then some heavy footseps. A small gap appeared between the door and its frame.

'Yes?' said Maria, peering through the slit, her dark eyes glittering. As she recognised Trish, she shut the door again so that she could unclip the chain and then fling it wide open.

'Miss Antonia not in. You wait?'

'Yes. Thank you, Maria. Could you put these in water for her?'

'OK.'

'Is Nicky here?'

'Out. And Mr Antonia. No one in house.'

'OK. I'll wait in the drawing room, shall I?' said Trish, leading the way in spite of Maria's inarticulate protest.

The meaning of that was clear as soon as Trish reached the room. Maria's tools were all over it –

dusters, feather dusters, polish, cloths and the Hoover itself.

'Is upstairs clean,' said Maria severely.

'OK,' said Trish, amazed by the opportunity. 'I'll wait up there, shall I?'

Maria nodded vigorously and gestured with both hands and the expensive flowers as though she would have liked to push Trish physically out of the room. Obediently she went up the perfectly dusted staircase and wondered where to start.

The desk in Antonia's study was a shaming contrast to her own. The computer was neatly shrouded and the few papers on the desk were arranged in mahogany trays. A matching desk tidy held paperclips and an assortment of pencils and felt-tipped pens. Apart from the unmarked blotter, there was only a large photograph of Charlotte at about two, smiling up at the camera with wide damp lips and a gloriously mischievous glint in her dark eyes.

How could anyone have hurt a child like that? Trish went on up to Charlotte's bedroom and stood looking at all the places where she had searched for the menacing worms. Only the doll's pram was missing, which she had had to search with particular thoroughness. The yellow-and-white toy box still stood at the left of the fireplace and the huge teddy bear that her banking godfather had given her sat in stately splendour in a wicker chair opposite the window. He was enormous, far too big for a child to hold.

The clouds moved, letting bright sun flood in, glinting on the bear's ginger fur and shining back at Trish out of his glass eyes. They looked different from each other.

A second later Trish was on her knees in front of the bear, peering into the eyes, seeing in the left-hand one something that looked remarkably like a camera lens.

It had always surprised her that Antonia could have
seen the bruises on Charlotte's arms and suspected
Nicky of causing them – to the extent of leaving the
office during the day to come back and check up on her
– and yet not set up any kind of video surveillance. Here
was the unmistakable evidence that she had. Trish went
on to search the nursery bathroom and found another
camera attached to the side of the wall-heater. A third
nestled in the ornately carved frame of an ugly mirror
on the wall of Nicky's bedroom with a perfect view of
her narrow bed.

What had Antonia seen on the films? Trish asked
herself as she pulled the mirror away from the wall
to find out how the camera was attached.

'Hello, Trish. Just what exactly d'you think you're
doing?'

Trish let the mirror swing gently back against the wall
and turned. Antonia's face was contorted with fury and
what looked disturbingly like hatred.

'You saw them, didn't you?' Trish said. 'Nicky and
Robert cavorting on her bed in the middle of the
afternoon when he should've been at work and she
should've been with Charlotte. No wonder you've been
so angry with them both.'

'I don't know what you're talking about.'

'Oh yes, you do. I was surprised when you talked
about having to come home to check up on Nicky when
there's been all that stuff in the press about cameras
like these. I thought if you'd really been worried you'd
have had some put in here. But it never occurred to
me that you might have had some installed and said
nothing to the police about them. Why, Antonia? What
did you see that you didn't want the police to know
about?'

'Don't be ridiculous.'

313

'Why wouldn't you want them knowing about Nicky and Robert? That's what I can't understand.'

Antonia turned. 'I don't have to listen to any of this crap. Maria said you were here and I thought I'd better find out what you were up to. Now I have, and I want you out of my house.'

'I'm not leaving until you tell me exactly what's been going on, Antonia.'

'What the fuck do you mean, you're not going? You'll do as you're bloody well told. I don't want you in my house, Trish. Is that clear? You've caused enough trouble already. All the time you were pretending to be on my side, you were plotting with Nicky. You sided with her from the beginning, didn't you, and then when I'd persuaded the police to look seriously at her, you got her the best solicitor in London to stop her answering their questions. How could you be so wicked?'

'Antonia, I'm sorry you feel like that. My only thought all along has been to find out what really happened to Charlotte and – if possible – to get . . .'

Something in Antonia's eyes, something that looked almost like pleasure, silenced Trish. Her mind started working like a calculator, adding, subtracting, multiplying and producing an answer.

'But you didn't want anyone to find out what happened, did you?'

'You're mad,' said Antonia, just as the telephone began to ring downstairs. 'And sick.'

'Because you set the whole thing up to punish Nicky and Robert for their affair, didn't you? You wanted them suspected of harming Charlotte, but you didn't want it to look as though that's what you were doing: all those artistic protests you made that they must be innocent were just so much window-dressing, weren't they? After all, you made it entirely clear to me – and

314

presumably the police as well – that you were hellishly suspicious of them both. What have you done with Charlotte? You haven't hurt her, I'm sure of that. Even you couldn't—'

'Miss Antonia,' Maria shouted up from downstairs. 'Miss Antonia, phone. Is police.'

'Wait,' said Antonia as she ran down to her bedroom. But Trish disobeyed and followed her, hovering just outside the door as she picked up her call.

'You have?' Antonia was saying in a completely different voice. 'Oh, how . . . how fantastic! How is she? Is she all right? What's happened? How did she get there? What? Yes, I see. Of course I'm coming. I'll be as quick as I can. Tell her I'm coming.'

'So now you've arranged her miraculous return, have you?' said Trish, as Antonia came running out of the room.

'I think you've gone completely mad, Trish, but I know you're fond enough of Charlotte to be glad she's been found. I'm going to the police station now. She's in a terrible state, apparently, and they've got to examine her for . . . for all sorts of things. I've got to go.'

'Can I come with you?' asked Trish urgently. 'Please, Antonia. I . . . *Please.*'

Antonia looked at her suspiciously and then laughed. 'I don't care about anything any more, not now I know she's alive. Yes, if you want, come on. But hurry.'

Trish's certainty wavered, but not her determination to stick with Antonia and see for herself that Charlotte really was safe.

They left the house at a run, pursued by the journalists, scenting a story, and reached the police station breathless. The press were kept at the front desk while Trish and Antonia were taken straight to the rape suite, which was the softest-looking and most comfortable room in the station. Charlotte was there with Sergeant Lacie and Constable Derring and two other young women in plain clothes. There were no male officers anywhere to be seen.

Charlotte's face was stained with dirt and tears, and she was crying and clutching a large stuffed green fish. When she saw Antonia she dropped the toy and ran full-tilt at her, to press her messy face into Antonia's short, red skirt, sobbing, 'Mummy, Mummy, Mummy, Mummy. I was lost. In the park. I was lost.'

Antonia could not quite prevent the triumphant smile that flashed across her face. Trish saw it for an instant before it changed into a mask of sympathy as Antonia swung her daughter up in her arms until their faces were on a level.

'But you've been found,' said Antonia, sounding completely genuine. Constable Derring had to get out her handkerchief to wipe her eyes.

'You've been found now, Charlotte. And you're safe. Really, really safe. For ever.'

Charlotte laid her face against Antonia's neck and sobbed her heart out. Trish was so angry that she would not have dared to speak. She was as certain as she could be that Antonia had orchestrated Charlotte's disappearance.

She could have forgiven it if she had thought Antonia had done it to get Charlotte away from danger while she investigated the source of the threat. But if that had been her motive, she would never have tried to deny what the camera in Nicky's bedroom had shown her. The whole operation must have been driven by spite.

What Robert and Nicky had done would have made anyone in Antonia's position angry, but the idea that she had even considered using Charlotte as a weapon against them filled Trish with disgust.

Just as Bella had suggested, confronted with a challenge from someone she had thought was too weak to harm her, Antonia had lost her temper and all sense of proportion. Although Nicky and Robert had suffered – and a lot of other people too – it was clearly Charlotte who had come to most harm.

One of the women said something Trish could not hear to Sergeant Lacie, who answered quietly, 'Not yet. There's time for that. She needs her mother now.'

As though picking up the cue, Antonia said over Charlotte's shoulder, 'May I take her home? She needs to be at home with me just now.'

'Ms Weblock,' said the woman who had spoken to Lacie, 'I'm a doctor, a paediatrician. I have been asked to examine Charlotte.'

The little girl's arms tightened round Antonia's neck and her sobs turned to howls.

'I think she ought to come home now. Can't you do it in a day or two, when she feels more certain of her safety?'

'I'll have a word with the superintendent,' said Kath Lacie. 'I'm sure we can arrange something.'

Trish heard a familiar singing in her ears.

'Sergeant Lacie, could I have a word outside?'

'Of course, Ms Maguire. Come along.'

'Trish,' said Antonia over Charlotte's head. Trish waited. 'Charlotte needs me.'

Looking at the child pressed against her mother, Trish realised that for once Antonia had told the truth. She remembered Nicky's despairing outbursts about how much Charlotte loved her mother. Whatever happened later, at that moment, Charlotte probably did need to be with Antonia.

'Ms Maguire?'

'I'm sorry, Sergeant. It's all right. I . . . There isn't

anything that needs saying now. Do you want me for anything, Antonia?'

'Nothing at all, Trish,' she said, a hint of the triumphant smile flashing in her eyes again. 'I'll ring you in a day or two when Charlotte and I've had some time together.'

'Goodbye, Charlotte,' said Trish, gently touching the child's head. She let enough of her face slide away from Antonia's shoulder to look at Trish out of one eye. She almost smiled.

'Can I come and see you soon?' asked Trish, fairly sure that Antonia would never let her in the house again. Charlotte nodded her head up and down against Antonia's once-pristine silk shirt. Her thumb slid into her mouth. Antonia staggered slightly and Lacie quickly brought a chair for her. The other women clustered round.

CHAPTER TWENTY-FIVE

'Well, that's that,' said the superintendent, slapping the file down on his desk three weeks later. 'Nothing from the child except talk of swimming and ice cream and hamburgers and a nice time with nice people called Sue and Sammy and lots of songs and games. No sign of any physical harm done to her. No evidence whatsoever as to who Sue and Sammy are. Nothing on the couple who found Charlotte lost and howling in the park and brought her to us. Plenty of assurances from Charlotte that they weren't Sue and Sammy. No idea where the house was where she was held, except that it was in a field. Who's been making monkeys of us, John?'

There was a pause. Blake, furious himself at the wasted time, money, manpower – and anguish – of the five days of Charlotte's absence, did not want to add to the superintendent's rage by any unconsidered accusations.

'Come on, come on. You must have some idea, John. You've been talking to all these people for weeks now. And you're not stupid.'

'I think . . . What I think is that Antonia Weblock paid a ransom,' Blake said reluctantly.

'Without any of us getting any idea she was negotiating all that time? We had a phone tap from day one, before she even got back from the States. How could we not have known what was going on?'

'I don't know how they communicated,' said Blake unhappily. He was so angry with Antonia that he could not trust himself to admit it. Kath had told him a bit about what it felt like to be pregnant and lose the child, and he had enough imagination to translate that into what the mother of a living child might feel in Antonia's position. But she should have told him what she was doing. He'd gone through hell for her. One day he might be able to forgive her. But he was damned if he was going to let the Super know how he felt.

'We don't know how many mobiles she's had access to, sir. Or how she put the ransom together or got it into their hands. I've asked her over and over again, but she's sticking to her story that she didn't pay anyone anything and that the child's return was an inexplicable miracle. That's what she always calls it. But there's no other explanation that fits. She must have paid a ransom. After all, she's better placed than most to shuffle money inconspicuously about the world – and lay her hands on big amounts. It's the only thing that makes sense.'

'What about Maguire? It's not so long since you were telling me you were sure there was something fishy about her. You think she could have had a hand in keeping communication going between Weblock and the kidnappers?'

'I don't think so. And . . .' Blake hesitated, once again wanting to keep his feelings to himself. This case had stirred him up good and proper, and it was going to take him a long time to get himself back in order. Thank

God for Kath. At least the thought of her would keep him sane, unlike the pompous heartless fart in front of him.

'Come on. Spit it out, John. Don't forget I've got to answer for all this higher up – and to the media.'

'Forget the media, sir. They've had their fun with all those terrific pictures and stories about Charlotte's return. So long as there's no scandal they'll forget the mystery pretty soon. I'm surprised they're still running the story at all, but it's been off the front pages for more than a week now and it can't last much longer. All I was going to say is that I don't think Maguire would have gone behind our backs to help pay a ransom. She's too straight; too devoted to the law.'

'You've changed your tune. What happened?'

'A bit more research into her background,' Blake said slowly. It had shocked him to discover how much respect Trish Maguire aroused in people he knew he could trust. 'I've been talking to some of the blokes who've worked with her – some of our people, too – and they don't share any of Antonia's views about her character, her sexuality or her interests.'

'D'you think Antonia's views were genuine?'

Blake had to admit the man wasn't quite as stupid as he sometimes seemed, even if he was a pain in the arse.

'Probably not. I suspect we were round at her house too much and getting too close so that she had to shove us off onto another track before we found out she was negotiating with the kidnappers. I think she decided to sacrifice Maguire. I'm not sure that in her position I wouldn't have done the same. Can we really blame her for doing everything in her power to save her child?'

'I can. Maybe we should do her for wasting police

time,' said the Super, banging his papers irritably into line.

'D'you think the CPS would wear that, sir – with the child safe? I'd have thought there'd be a hell of a lot of sympathy for a mother with the means to ransom her child doing so as discreetly as possible. Even if the CPS went for it, I can't see any jury convicting. Can you?'

'Maybe not. But it sticks in the craw, John.'

'I know. But I can't help admiring her – in a way.'

'I can,' said the Super again, even more sharply. 'We'll have to see if we can't do her for money-laundering in a month or two. If she's really been shovelling cash off-shore to buy her kid back, there's probably something there. I'll look into it.'

Blake hesitated.

'What is it now?'

'Nothing, sir.'

'OK. Oh yes, by the way – I'm having Lacie transferred. Eye off the ball, John, and all that. Get on with it.'

Blake wondered how many other people had felt like strangling the superintendent. He went in search of Kath.

At least, he thought, if we're not working in the same nick we won't have to be quite so scrupulous about what we say to each other. Say and maybe even do. Every cloud and all that. Onward and upward.

CHAPTER TWENTY-SIX

'Why can't you tell me?' asked Stephen. 'Are you afraid whoever he is may not be able to keep you in the style I have all this time? Or put up with your peccadilloes? Is that it?'

'No, it isn't,' said Mike through his teeth.

'No new admirer at all? Really? I find that hard to believe.'

'I hate it when you're sarcastic. I've told you. Why won't you believe me?'

'Because I know how easily you lie. And how much you like having new admirers, the ones who don't know as much about you as I do. New admirers and nice new things. Nice new cashmere sweaters. And nice new expensive shoes. Come on, Mike, you might as well tell me. You know I'll find out who he is in the end.'

'There isn't anyone. Oh, why won't you believe me? You know I love you.'

'You've never said that before. Isn't that interesting? Withheld and withheld, until I no longer have the slightest feeling for you. An admirer I might have forgiven in the end, but not the alternative.'

'What d'you mean?' asked Mike drearily, hardly even able to hear the words, let alone work out what they meant.

'You've got too much money. There's no getting away from that. If it's not a rich new admirer – and I suppose I can just about believe that – then you've been dealing again down at your wretched gym. That's it, isn't it? Didn't the police crawling all over this place and the club and the gym frighten you out of that sort of idiocy for ever? Don't you remember enough of Feltham to save you from that?'

'Stop it. *Stop it!* I told you I'm not dealing and I'm not even using. The police arrested all the ones who were. They cleared me. I said I wouldn't and I haven't.'

'I don't believe you. You've got too much money,' Stephen repeated, almost shouting. 'I've told you a hundred times and more what would happen if you got back into drugs. Look – you'd better go and pack. I do not want to have anything more to do with you. Go on. Get out.'

Stephen sat at the perfectly set dinner table, smelling the food Mike had been cooking as the scent turned gradually from savoury fragrance to harsh burning. He let it burn, filling the flat with acrid charcoal smoke and no doubt ruining the expensive Cuisinox pan. As he waited, he heard the sounds of Mike scuffling in the wardrobes and drawers in their bedroom next door.

He knew that his father's watch and his own cufflinks were probably at risk, as well as the reserve cash he always kept at the back of the top left-hand drawer. But he did not care. All his emotions were gelid. One day they might thaw, but then again, perhaps they would not. Perhaps he would always be as he was at that moment, frozen by hurt and disillusion into uncaring.

He had loved Mike, and for a time he had thought it

might be possible to arouse genuine, un-selfregarding love in the boy. But he couldn't have been more wrong. When would he learn? Well, one thing was for certain. He was not going to make that mistake again.

Half an hour after he had sent Mike to pack, the burning smell had changed. Stephen was still sitting at the table, his hands clasped together and numb on the antique Wedgwood plate in front of him.

'I really loved you, you know.' Mike's voice was full of petulant and childish spite. 'And you'll never find anyone else like me again.'

Stephen looked up and saw his erstwhile lover standing in the doorway with the two Gucci grips at his feet. His face was as perfectly beautiful as ever.

'I would have done anything for you, Steve. I gave up drugs for you. I gave up all my friends for you. But you're a cold, hard-hearted, cruel, cruel man. And you wouldn't understand love if it stood up and bit your prick. I'm sorry for you. Very sorry. And I hope the flat burns down.'

He picked up the overstuffed and heavy-looking grips as though they were full of nothing but feathers and left the flat.

Stephen took his tinglingly sore hands off the plate and got up to deal with the burnt saucepans.

CHAPTER TWENTY-SEVEN

'Still no answers in Charlotte Weblock mystery,' read Renie Brooks as she straightened up with the *Daily Mercury* in her right hand. The left one was clasped over her hip, where the pain was getting worse every day. Soon she was going to have to see the doctor about it, but she didn't like him and was putting it off for as long as she could. The aspirin helped sometimes and a hot water bottle did, too. She'd be able to cope a bit longer.

'What's that?' Harold said from the passage outside.

'It's the child. The one Nicolette's been looking after that was lost. They still don't know what happened to her. Five days it was.'

'Rubbish!'

'That's what it says in the paper,' she said, giving it to him so that she did not have to argue with him. She went to the cooker to start the bacon while he read it.

'It's fishy, if you ask me,' he said when he got to the end of the article. 'Fishy. That's what it is. Anyway she's been sacked now, and she won't be getting another smart job like that one in a hurry, that's for sure.'

'Oh, don't sound so pleased about it!' shouted Renie, banging the pan on the cooker and making hot fat splutter into the flames. She'd been more upset than she liked to think about not having had an answer from Nicolette. It seemed cruel and unlike the child she remembered. It was making her think she might not have known her as well as she thought. It made her worry about the other child, too, the one Nicolette had been looking after, little Charlotte Weblock.

After all, she'd had that nice letter from Charlotte's mother so the letters must've got there. She'd said she was trying to keep believing her little Charlotte would come back to her, and how it helped when people like Renie, who understood what it was like being a mother, sent their sympathy. She'd actually thanked Renie for bothering to write to her.

So it wasn't as though the letters hadn't ever got to her house. Nicolette must've had hers too but, unlike the unknown but obviously kind Mrs Weblock, she hadn't even bothered to answer.

'Nicolette's had a terrible time and she must be feeling miserable,' she said, trying to believe it, 'and you're pleased she's not going to get another job. You're horrible.'

'What's got into you?' Harold said, looking at her in astonishment.

'Nothing,' she said dully, turning back to the bacon. 'I've got a headache.'

'Have you been in touch with her?' he asked, sounding almost dangerous.

'I wrote,' said Renie, who had been needing to share the information with someone for weeks, 'but she's never answered me.'

'There you are then. It's what I always said: selfish, ungrateful little brat. She always was.'

'No, she wasn't,' said Renie, sliding the crisp rashers onto the two warmed plates. She carefully turned down the gas, and when the fat had cooled sufficiently, broke the eggs into it. 'Not then. She was a sweet girl and the brightest we ever had and the kindest. I've missed her ever since they took her away. I miss her now, and I'll always miss her. If anyone's selfish, it's you. You scared the living daylights out of her.'

'Rubbish! I teased her like I always teased them. Did them all good.'

'Not Nicolette. Like I said, it scared her. There's your breakfast. Eat it while it's hot.' She put her foot on the pedal of the bin to raise the lid and scraped the other plateful into it.

'Aren't you having any?' Harold asked, sounding completely at sea.

'No. I'm going out.'

'Renie. Renie! What's the matter? What's got into you this morning, woman? You've gone mad. Renie, come back here!'

She closed the door on his voice and set off towards the station. She'd find Nicolette, somehow she'd find her, and then she'd get the truth out of her.

CHAPTER TWENTY-EIGHT

Trish stood in front of the mirror and settled the wig on her head, making sure that a few spikes of her own black hair showed in front of the yellowing horsehair curls. The sleeves of her black gown hung like wings from her arms as she adjusted the wig, and the bands at her throat had the crisp whiteness of the inside of a fresh radish. Her brief lay at her side, neatly tied in its narrow pink tape. She knew it backwards and, believing in its absolute legitimacy, could hardly wait to get into court.

'Hey, Trish. Great to see you back! How are you?' asked one of the friendliest of the silks as her reflection darted up behind Trish in the mirror. Trish swung round to confirm the reality of the image.

'I'm fine, Gina. Thanks.'

'I've been hearing great things of this book of yours. When's it due out?'

'Not till next spring.'

'Oh, ages. What a pity.'

'I know. And it's been on the gruelling side, but it's finished now, and I can get on with my life.'

'Good for you. What're you on today?'

'A case of George Henton's in Court Five.'

'Oh, I know. Going to win?'

'Of course.' Trish was still smiling. She could not help it. Even now, after five months of slowly growing confidence in her feelings for George, being able to say his name aloud to other people made her insides swim with pleasure.

'I'd better get on,' said Gina. 'Good luck.'

'Thanks. And to you. See you in the mess later?'

'Yes.'

The young QC left. Trish shut her black tin wig box with a satisfactory snap, straightened her shoulders, took a last look at her reflection and then bent to pick up her papers. She followed Gina out of the robing room, pleasantly aware of the swish of her gown and the click of her heels. Her whole body felt good to her and her mind was operating with a blessed independence of her feelings. George was doing his damnedest to feed her up, but she was resisting and was not yet weighed down by an ounce of spare fat.

She had a moment's anxiety as she left the safety of the robing room to make her first appearance in court for months. But it would be all right. It was her work and she could do it. Loosening her knees, she ran down the wide stairs to the long passage outside the courts, where the lawyers and their clients and witnesses for both sides gathered in a resentful crowd.

'Trish,' said a familiar, commanding voice.

Her muscles seized up at the sound and she had to think how to breathe. It was a shock to realise how close she still was to the line between freedom and the webtrap of anger and disgust that had held her down for so long. She looked at her watch. There were still fifteen minutes before she had to be in court. She turned slowly, smiling.

'Antonia. Good morning. What are you doing here?'

'Don't pretend you don't know. You must think I'm a complete fool, all of you. Plotting behind my back to get Charlotte away from me.'

'I've never thought you a fool, but I hadn't expected to see you here, that's all.'

'As you very well know, I'm here because you've manipulated Ben into trying to get involved in Charlotte's life. Aren't you representing him?'

Trish shook her head, glad of the wig and gown that distanced her a little from Antonia. 'No. I knew what he was trying to do and I've done everything I could to help. But I'm not acting for him and I didn't realise it was on this morning.'

'You know what'll happen if he succeeds, don't you?'

Yes, thought Trish, there will be someone around to keep Charlotte safe from any more of your devious games. I wish I'd been able to find out how you managed it, who 'Sue and Sammy' were and how you persuaded them to keep quiet about your plot. But you can't really have thought we'd have left a little child permanently with a woman who could do that to her own daughter.

'If you all get your way,' said Antonia with a hiss in her voice, 'she'll be brought up by that idiotic American, who can't have her own children and so has to steal someone else's.'

'She's not so bad,' said Trish, whose respect for Bella had been increasing each time they met and was beginning to turn into affection. 'And she has a lot of sympathy for you. You might find dealing with her over Charlotte helps.'

The dislike in Antonia's eyes grew colder as her jaw

hardened and the powerful little muscles at either side of her mouth pulled it down into a clown's grimace.

'She has no right to have anything to do with Charlotte – and the idea that she has the impertinence to feel sympathy for me makes me sick to my stomach.'

As Antonia swung away, Trish put out a hand to stop her.

'Wait. Don't go.'

For a moment Antonia was very still under her hand. Then she shrugged it off and turned back.

'What is it now, Trish?'

'You're not really going to fight Ben's action, are you?'

'Of course. Why not? I don't want my child involved with him and that American bitch. You're not going to try to stop me, are you, Trish? That'll be fun.'

'No, it won't. Antonia, if you force me, I'll—'

'You'll what? Start trying to get the judge to believe that ludicrous fantasy you invented on the day Charlotte was found? Oh, Trish. You'll ruin yourself, you know.'

'No,' said Trish steadily. 'We've all agreed that it would do Charlotte far too much damage if that story ever came out. It's for her sake that we've all held our tongues and let the police believe the fantasy *you* devised about secretly paying a ransom to get her back.'

There was not even a flicker in Antonia's granite-coloured eyes.

'You did a brilliant job convincing them that you'd concealed the payment of some vast sum,' Trish went on. 'They wouldn't listen to any alternative theories then, and they won't now. You've got away with it – unfortunately. But you're not a fit mother, and Charlotte has to see something of Ben, now that DNA test has proved he is her father.'

Trish thought of the meetings that had been taking place in Ben's tatty but floriferous garden over the past few months. The three of them, often joined by Emma and sometimes by Willow, had talked round and round what they were sure had happened and how they ought to deal with it. They hadn't involved Tom because of his official position, but they were holding him in reserve in case the judge refused to allow Ben contact with Charlotte.

They had agreed that the best way of presenting Ben's case would be to concentrate on his ability to spend much more of his time with Charlotte than Antonia ever could, and to give her a proper family life. Now that Robert had gone, Antonia and Charlotte had been living a bleak existence with a starchily uniformed nanny who never left the child alone for a moment. If the judge proved sticky, the fallback plan was to point out that Antonia's lifestyle and career had led her in the past to hire a nanny irresponsible enough to allow Charlotte to be kidnapped, but they all hoped it wouldn't come to that. And if that, too, failed then they were going to go to Tom, tell him everything they knew and guessed.

'So why aren't you convinced about the ransom, Trish? What makes you think you're so much cleverer than the police?' Antonia was smiling again, but this time there was real amusement in her face.

'Because I've seen you angry before. I didn't understand at the beginning. I was too involved, too terrified, and so – unforgiveably – I failed Charlotte and all the other people you tore apart. God knows how many of them there are.'

'You always were melodramatic where Charlotte was concerned. Frustrated mother complex, that's what it is, Trish. You ought to have some of your own. That might sort you out.'

'I can understand why you wanted to punish Nicky and Robert for what they did, but to use Charlotte like that. How could you?'

'Fantasy, Trish. Pure fantasy. Sick, too.'

'I know you arranged for her to be taken away for the week and I'm sure you took care that she wasn't ill-treated, but it's not good enough, Antonia.'

'And what did I do then in this little fairy-tale of yours?'

'You got rid of Robert after he brought you back from the airport and then set the stage. You planted the nude photographs and porno mags under Nicky's floorboards and you did a bit of digging in the flower beds to make it look as though someone had been trying to bury something there. I don't know if you put the polythene under the soil or if that was just a lucky coincidence that distracted the police for a few hours. You definitely put the soil into the doll's pram and I'm perfectly certain that you put the blood and hair in it too, even though I don't know how.'

'Hair? Blood? I don't know what you're talking about.' Antonia looked at her Rolex and brushed a minute piece of fluff from the cuff of her Jil Sander suit.

'I must go or I'll be late,' she drawled, 'and I don't want to make a bad impression on the judge. After all, I am fighting for my child's health and sanity here.'

Trish opened her mouth, but her protest was over-ridden before she could make it.

'I have to win, Trish. And I shall. I learned very early on that if I didn't take control of everything myself, nothing would ever be properly done and I would never be safe.' Antonia smiled. 'But I make sure it is, you see. And so I always get what I want. You ought to know that by now. I'll keep Charlotte, you'll see.'

Over my dead body, thought Trish.

EPILOGUE

She let herself into the house, hating the gloating voices that hummed all round her.

'How d'you feel about your ex-husband getting access to Charlotte after everything you did to get her back last spring?'

'Are you going to appeal?'

'What did Charlotte say when you had to leave her with him? Was she crying?'

'What are you going to do now?'

'Is there a new man in your life?'

'How d'you feel?'

'How d'you feel?'

'How d'you feel?'

Antonia slammed the door on them all and leaned against it with her palms smacked against the panels and her teeth clamped together. She could still hear them shouting at her through the thick wood. Vultures, all of them.

Her arms started aching as they always did when she was upset. She slipped her hands inside her shirt and stroked the skin of her shoulders. It didn't help.

Pulling herself away from the door with almost as much difficulty as the police had had getting Charlotte away from her on the day she was found in the park, Antonia took off her coat, shook it to get the creases out and hung it up. Then she went into the kitchen, which Maria had left as immaculate as ever, and took a bottle of white burgundy from the fridge. She screwed the cork out and poured herself a glass to take upstairs to her bedroom.

She'd lie on her bed, well away from the journalists, and work out how to get Ben out of Charlotte's life.

I am a winner, she thought. Trish is wrong. They're all wrong. They'll see. I will beat them all. That wimp Ben and his American bitch will have to give up in the end.

She drank, tilting her head back against the pillow so that the fragrant wine trickled smoothly over the back of her tongue.

In a way she had won the first skirmish of the war. There was some satisfaction to be had in that. She'd split Nicky and Robert up and made sure both of them would be looked at askance wherever they went for the rest of their lives.

All in all she'd managed pretty well, in spite of this latest hitch. There'd been some quite hairy moments, though, like the day when bloody Trish had brought her lie-detecting bimbo in to prove that Nicky's story about the playground was true. That had been a real pain, and typical of bloody Trish's inability to let anyone else get on with their lives without telling them how to do it better.

And then the police had found out about Mike's past and raided his gym for drugs and started cross-questioning him. Luckily he'd told her the truth when he swore he was clean, and he hadn't betrayed her when they interviewed him, but it had given her a sweaty few days.

He'd always been going to be the weak link, but even he had held. She'd chosen well with him, too. Luckily.

Antonia laughed and took a bigger mouthful of wine. God! It was good. A particularly luscious year. She was already feeling better.

As it happened, Mike had been an unnecessary elaboration. If she'd realised how easily that treacherous little slut Nicky Bagshot could be distracted from her job, there wouldn't have been any need to risk using Mike. Luckily he wasn't bright enough to realise what had been going on under his nose. When she'd paid him off he still seemed convinced that all she'd wanted him to do was drive home to Nicky that she was being watched all the time and that she must behave herself.

It hadn't been all that hard to persuade Mike to keep his mouth shut, when he said he thought he ought to tell the police he'd been there in the playground in case there was anything he could tell them that might help them find Charlotte. Antonia had only had to point out that with his record and his sexual proclivities, the last thing he ought to risk was being known to be in the area where a child had been kidnapped. Antonia laughed again as she remembered kindly promising not to tell anyone of Mike's presence. He'd been pathetically grateful and even offered to give her back the money she'd paid him.

'Sue and Sammy' – God, that sounded like a pair of performing seals at the circus – had been something of a risk, too, but it had been a calculated one and it, too, had paid off. They had done everything they'd promised and Charlotte had been happy enough with them. They swore she'd made no protest when they told her that her mother was waiting for her on the other side of the park and she'd gone with them as cheerfully as anyone could have wished. She had cried, they said, when she discovered that there was no sign of Antonia, but it hadn't taken her too long to cheer up and they had taken her straight to the cottage Antonia'd already checked and approved, and they'd given her a marvellous holiday.

There were no real worries about that. Charlotte *had* had a good time. It had been easy to see that the police were puzzled by everything she'd told their tactful interviewers about the videos she had been allowed to see and the toys she'd played with and all the burgers and chips she'd been allowed to eat. But there'd been no real danger. 'Sue and Sammy' were far too professional to risk betraying themselves.

And they were definitely safe. No risk of blackmail there. They had too much to lose and they knew she'd left no evidence that would implicate her if they did try to tell their story. They'd been well paid, too, and gone back to the States for good. That was that.

In fact, the only aspect of the whole thing that did cause Antonia a slight pang was the twenty minutes Charlotte had spent 'lost' in the park on her way back. Antonia had thought round and round the problem of getting her safely back without it, but there hadn't been an alternative. And it had been only twenty minutes. It couldn't have done her that much harm. Not twenty minutes.

In any case, it was her tears and terror when they found her, more than almost anything else, that had stopped the police from developing any dangerous suspicions. They were convinced that Antonia had paid a ransom for Charlotte, just as she'd meant them to be.

Shuffling the money around off-shore accounts had been child's play in comparison with making sure

Charlotte was all right, and there'd been a nice trail
for the police to follow as far as the Caymans, before it
had petered out. 'Sue and Sammy' had been paid their
whack out of it, and the rest was in trust for Charlotte
when she left university. It would be a nice little nest
egg for her then.

No, taken all in all, the operation had gone off
reasonably well. She would get Charlotte to herself
in the end. Ben and his American bitch would learn
that they had no right to interfere, just as Robert had
had to learn, and Nicky.

It was extraordinary what devotion that little slut had
managed to arouse in so many people. Quite apart from
Robert, there was Trish, who should've known better, and
the unknown Renie Brooks. Antonia could still remember
the two letters she'd written, showing far more trust and
affection than Nicky deserved. It was that affection, not
the cruelty of the anonymous filth, that had made Antonia
tell everyone she was burning the letters without reading
them. She couldn't risk Nicky somehow getting to know
of the one Renie Brooks had written to her. She didn't
deserve it. And she wasn't going to have it.

Dear Mrs Weblock, [Renie had written]
*I'm ever so sorry about your daughter. I wish I could help
you. I'm sure it's not Nicolette who's done it. I fostered
her, you know, for quite a while. She was always a good
child and kind with it. I'm sure she's not done what they
say in the papers. I don't have your proper address, but
I hope the post office will find a way to get this to you.
And I hope your little Charlotte will be safe. I'm praying
for that. I'm sure it's not Nicolette that's done anything.
She was a good child. I always loved her.
Yours faithfully,
Renie Brooks.*

It seemed the bitterest irony that a lazy, conniving little slut like Nicky should've had such care and devotion when Antonia's experience had been so different.

There were still times when she could feel echoes of the old terror, even after all these years. She could hear that terrible voice even now and feel the pain. She put down her glass so that she could stroke the ache away.

The marks round her arms had always been hidden by the sleeves of her dresses and she hadn't dared tell anyone about them or how they'd got there. Her mother would have seen them and stopped it happening, but she'd gone away to be ill. She'd gone away to hospital. And that woman had come to turn Antonia's life into hell.

'Do as you're told. You know what'll happen if you don't do as I say.'

She had known. And she had suffered. But it had stopped in the end.

Antonia could see herself, a thin little fair-haired child with bright eyes and a face that felt as hard and cold as glass, on the day that woman had left the house for the last time.

It wasn't relief she'd felt then, or even happiness: it was triumph. She'd known from that moment on that she'd always be able to win if she could just be strong enough and hang on long enough. She'd stood there in the cold wind with her hands balled into fists and her teeth clenched, swearing in her mind that no one else would hurt her and not be punished. No one. Ever.